SLEEPING DRAGONS

SLEEPING DRAGONS

Cat Collins

Five Star • Waterville, Maine

First Edition
First Printing: November 2005

Published in 2005 in conjunction with Tekno Books.

Set in 11 pt. Plantin by Ramona Watson.

Printed in the United States on permanent paper.

Library of Congress Cataloging-in-Publication Data

Collins, Cat.
    Sleeping dragons / by Cat Collins.—1st ed.
      p. cm.
    ISBN 1-59414-419-2 (hc : alk. paper)
    1. Intensive care nursing—Fiction.   2. Supernatural—
Fiction.   3. Nurses—Fiction.   I. Title.
PR9639.4.C65S57 2005
    823′.92—dc22   2005019066

Dedication

This is for my husband, Marty, who possesses many of the qualities of a Camarrhan hero, and for my dear friend Lynne, who always believed in me.

CAMARRHAN

ALTH RANGES
SANZ
KYANOR
KERSÁL
TWIN LAKES
CENTRAL FLATLANDS
TUAN·R
OURRAN
ILLITH
PYSAUR SEA
ché KEVATH
ISLAND OF THE HAND

Chapter One

Camarrhan

On a sudden, wicked impulse, Cael pressed booted heels to his horse's flanks and with a flick of the reins, leaned forward in his saddle. The big gelding needed no urging. Its muscled shoulders bunched and lengthened beneath the burnished coat as the animal stretched its legs in a joyous release of energy. Cael grinned as he and the bay thundered past the other riders. Unfair advantage, to be sure, but he knew they would take up his challenge. His shirt billowed behind him, and the wind snatched his hair back from his eyes, leaving his face bare to the sun.

He scanned the surrounding territory even as he revelled in the speed of his passage. Althar renegades had been sighted in the hills beyond Twin Lakes, eleven miles to the west, and evidence of their recent presence had turned up closer to home. The whereabouts of the renegades' base remained a mystery to the men charged with the defense of Kereál township, but it had to be close, given the areas in which the raids occurred. Small bands of riders rode a circuit around the outlying areas of Kereál daily, each band patrolling part of the perimeter and relaying information to the town's Leaders. They had yet found nothing.

As one of the town Leaders, Cael was not required to ride patrol, but he enjoyed the release from Council duties. The telepathy that formed part of his gifting as an Empath also gave his band of riders a communication advantage, and he felt the risk of danger to himself to be minimal. Or so he reasoned whenever Verra challenged him on the matter. Besides, he always required the same service of himself as he expected of others; he preferred to lead by example, not direction.

A fierce whoop behind him soared over the dull tattoo of pursuing hooves, and he turned his head to see who was closest. Telsen. His big black ate up the distance between them slowly, and Cael knew he would soon be caught. >*First to the pines!*< he sent, flashing a grin over his shoulder. Chad and Sorren trailed Telsen, each of the twins urging his horse to greater speed. The stand of pines loomed larger as he drew near, lofty spires of evergreen sentinels guarding the entrance to the valley that nestled beyond them.

Telsen and the twins rode patrol with him regularly. Twice over the past month they had cause to draw swords in a brush with Althar. Twice they had pursued a fleeing renegade, and twice had lost sight of him. It was a frustrating business. Althar had a talent for remaining unseen.

The black gained on him, its nose now visible at Cael's side. The animal's nostrils flared in great, air-sucking shafts, a hint of red revealed in their depths, and ragged pennants of foam flew from the corners of its open mouth as it gained another fraction. He heard Telsen urging the animal on and chuckled at his bondbrother's competitiveness, knowing that if not for his own unfair start the black would have outdistanced him by now. Reining in when the grass gave way to a sere carpet of pine needles, the riders sat tall in their saddles as the horses slowed, hooves sliding on the smooth surface.

"Not very sporting of you, brother." Smiling wryly, Telsen let the reins fall over the pommel of his saddle as he rubbed the black's sweaty neck. All four horses panted and blew, head tossing and stamping as they regained their breath, raising their rider's thighs on heaving ribs.

"Truth. It was not sporting at all, Tel." Cael looped his reins over one arm and rested his forearms on the saddle, trying to look contrite but not succeeding. He inclined his head to Telsen with mock chagrin. "I stand most humbly penitent before you."

Telsen grinned. "A good run, though. A little more warning next time, perhaps?"

"Perhaps . . ." Cael's tone and wicked expression suggested otherwise. The gelding danced, high-stepping, as Cael pushed hair back from his eyes and again took up the reins. He scanned the shadowed depth of the pines. "Chad. You and Sorren go ahead. Your turn to lead." Chad kneed his horse forward beside Sorren's. Cael followed the blond twins into the forested valley, his horse still blowing, still twitching and excited from its run. Beneath the trees, the air was cool and heavy with resinous pine and the must of old wood. He cast wary glances around them as they wove through the trees, ducking beneath low branches that swept their shoulders as they passed. Within half an hour, they exited the pines without incident. Cael and Telsen again took the lead as they rode in bright sunlight and open terrain.

A stretch of grassland beckoned. Cael resisted the temptation to begin another bid for equine supremacy, aware that the high jumbles of exposed rock that peppered the plain may shelter Althar renegades as easily as wildcats or stray sheep. Turning his attention back to duty, he sighed and kicked the gelding to a sedate trot.

Perhaps because he was looking only for signs of Althar trying as usual to evade them, or perhaps because he never suspected Althar might attack a band of armed men, he rode straight into the ambush.

Too late. Oh Gods, way too late! Cael cursed, seeing movement all around them. The bay gelding shied, snorted at the tight rein he held, rolled its eyes, trembled beneath him. Gods! At least forty Althar. He tugged the short-sword loose from his saddle-sheath, tightened his thighs on the gelding's ribs and pulsed soothing calm into the animal's brain.

Silent figures circled them. Cloaked and cowled, they closed in, black eyes narrow and hard. The four riders tightened their horses into a defensive position, rumps pressed together, facing the enemy like the spokes of a wheel. Cael hunted for an opportunity to break clear. He glimpsed the big black rear as Telsen drew his own blade with a defiant roar, ready as always to defend his back. Cael shot him a fierce smile, grateful for his loyalty and the bond of brotherhood that had drawn them so close.

>Hold!< Cael sent his silent message to all three of his companions. >Engage and we are dead!< Scanning the closing black circle, he assessed a likely weak spot. Their only hope was to use the horses to break through in one place before the Althar could overpower them. He realised with belated horror that he may be the target this time and cursed his sudden vulnerability. A Leader should be more careful with his personal safety. The Althar massed around them and began to press in. Narrowing his eyes in quick decision, he formed a clear and precise image of his intentions and pulsed it to the other three men.

As one, they dug heels into their mounts' sides and wheeled fiercely to the left, each horse responding to Cael's silent message to push hard and fast. Sorren's panicked grey hit them first. His short-sword cut at the Althar that

10

crowded to his right. Chad's mare lunged through beside him, her rider fending to his left, and then the two of them were through. Cael came after them, Telsen at his side, fending off Althar as the twins had done.

They were almost clear when a rank of Althar lunged for Cael. Several grasping hands found purchase in his clothing, tearing the fabric as he twisted desperately away from their grip. He dropped his reins, tossed the hilt of the blade to his right hand and flicked a knife into his left, unable to use his sword to full effect in such close quarters. Frenzied, the gelding surged forward, dark figures falling beneath its hooves and clinging to its flanks as Cael cut at the restraining hands that snagged him like briars. As he freed himself from the last grasp with a flash of his knife, he felt a solid blow to his shoulder and a sharp, tearing pain. His sword fell to the ground, his arm no longer obeying him, but hanging limp and heavy at his side. Telsen had broken through their attackers, turned his horse and now hesitated, waiting. The black danced its impatience, muscle-bunched and wild-eyed.

"Go!" Cael roared at Telsen, booted heels urging his horse to speed. Telsen's gaze slid to the bright bloom of blood on Cael's torn sleeve, the arm hanging slack at his side. The black's unleashed fear-prance propelled it close to the bay gelding, matching stride for stride as the riders followed the twins ahead of them, putting threat and danger behind. Cael saw Telsen's eyes on him, felt his consternation and knew his own expression was less than reassuring.

"Verra is going to have your hide!" Telsen shouted over the turf-eating thunder. "What is left of it, anyway!"

Oh Gods! Verra. Cael felt her vexation already. She warned them that morning of likely Althar presence in the area and wanted his word that he would not go far without her. As always when he felt restricted, he resisted her, riding out on today's patrol without his "nursemaid," although the Wayfinder was far more than that to him. He knew he needed her now. A bit more distance between him and the Althar and he would stop, call her, gladly accept her help. The Keystone he wore would bring her straight to him, a pigeon to the roost.

Both riders failed to notice the dark cloaked figure when it appeared, as if from the very air, concealed in the shadows of a stand of tall conifers. Cael thundered past, oblivious, Telsen's sweating black beside him.

The dark figure shifted and sighed, shaking his hooded head regretfully. "Oh no, son of Jarin, escape is never that easy." He raised a bow from his side and fitted a red-fletched arrow to the string. Drawing and releasing in one practised movement, he sent the death-shaft flying straight and true on its mission.

He scowled as he reflected on the failure of his Althar allies to capture the Empath. He had planned to extend and enjoy the young man's death. Seldom did he find one so fine and fair on his list for termination. Most of the Leaders he had eliminated so far were leathery old warriors, providing little outlet for his perverse pleasures. No matter. Die the Empath must, and die he would. The tiny surprise in the arrow's tip would see to that. The agonies to be endured before death came were easy enough to imagine and savour. He would have to content himself with that.

The small shaft buried deep into Cael's side. He grunted in shock at the impact, caught his breath in a sharp gasp and lurched sideways in the saddle, barely avoiding a fall. He clung to the pommel, steadying himself, and looked back for the source of the arrow. Nothing. The bright, spreading stain on his sleeve continued to grow, a red parody of a child's painted love-heart. The last Althar had used a blade on him, laying his left arm open, rendering it useless. *Since when did Althar carry weapons?* Looking down with disbelief at the shaft in his side, he saw his blood dark and thick on his thigh, flecking the bay's flank. His horse raced beside Telsen's black without needing his guidance, and pain-flares lit deep in his side with each stride. His head drooped. The horse's dark mane flicked, coarse-haired, over the knuckles of his hand clenched on the saddle. He would put some more distance between them and the archer before risking a stop, he resolved, but he knew he would need assistance soon.

After several more minutes of hard riding, they drew level with Chad and Sorren who reined in at Telsen's urgent shout. Telsen curbed the black's mad dash and with a hand on the bay's reins, slowed Cael's horse to the same pace.

Cael felt time slowing. The motion of the horse and the movement of the landscape past him became dreamlike; his breathing echoed harsh and hollow inside his head; daylight turned to grey at the edges of his vision. He did not remember beginning to fall, but he felt himself land heavily. The cantering bay clipped the side of his head with a rear hoof as he fell. His knee twisted under him as he struck the ground; hot pain seared through him as he rolled and the shaft of the arrow broke. Moments before the blackness took him, he sent a silent distress call to Verra.

From a far distance, Cael heard someone calling his name, insistent, dragging him back from darkness and peace. It was a voice he knew and trusted, and he struggled to respond. Water splashed into his face and jolted him back to awareness.

And pain. Gods, everything hurt.

He opened his eyes, focussing with difficulty on the face before him. Telsen knelt beside him on one knee. A waterskin hung dripping from one hand, and he scrubbed the other hand through close-cropped black hair as he searched Cael's face, his brown eyes dark with concern.

Cael drew his brows together against the pain that enveloped him. "I hurt, Tel," he said dully. Thick grass cushioned him where he lay in the shade of a smooth-barked pin oak, and his eyes followed wisps of cloud vapour drifting across the vivid summer sky above him. He flinched as Chad bound his damaged arm in tight pulls with cloth he had torn from his own shirt. Gods—his flesh was open from shoulder to elbow. Cael pulsed his thanks at him, biting back a gasp of pain.

His face tense, Sorren held the reins of all four horses and scanned the way they had come. The gently rolling foothills of northern Camarrhan where they met the Alth ranges evidenced nothing but serene stands of lofty evergreens behind the lighter hues of summer-leaved trees.

Telsen raised him and held the waterskin to his mouth. "Drink, brother. You have lost much blood." Cael drank a little. He was tired and his head hurt. His eyes closed, and Telsen shook him alert again, talking in a constant stream of words, keeping him from drifting off. He coughed and swallowed convulsively as more water trickled into his mouth and ran down his chin to mingle with the blood in his shirt.

>*I called. She is coming,*< Cael sent, and Telsen sighed in relief. As if on cue, he heard the familiar ring of singing crystal that announced the arrival of the Wayfinder. Cael

14

turned his head to see Verra emerge from the shimmering curtain that hung in the air before them. The outward portal of the Way appeared to be composed of the colours and textures of their immediate surroundings, mingled into a shifting, undulating pattern of lightlike oil colours on water. The shimmer faded behind her and was gone.

The Wayfinder shouldered past Telsen, cursing uncharacteristically at the scene. Her fierce expression spoke reprimand, and fire smouldered in her green eyes when she knelt beside Cael. She reached out and took hold of the fine, braided cord around his neck, running cool fingers around it until she located his Keystone. In silence, she looked deep into the stone. Cael felt her awareness reach into its depths, seek his pattern, re-arrange, re-align and strengthen the small flickering motes within.

"I can do nothing more here." Her voice was tight as a bowstring. She tucked a long dark curl back behind her ear and regarded them, her eyes cooling. "I have strengthened his pattern but he needs the Healer." Her gaze locked on his and softened as she shook her head at him. "What were you thinking?" she berated him gently.

He pulsed his regret and penitence. Shifting his position, he discovered the arrow stub and groaned aloud. >*Secret to share,*< he sent to her alone. She tilted her head at him, eyeing Telsen where he sat in silent worry on his haunches, shadowed by the twins. >*There is an arrow in my side.*< Verra sucked in her breath and reached to turn him. >*No! Do not,*< he sent in quick response. He closed his eyes. >*Try for a Way,*< he sent, >*but please, Tel has not seen the arrow and I would not have him know. It is of the Althar.*<

"Oh no . . . Oh dear Gods, Cael, no," she whispered. He winced as she slipped her fingers beneath him and found the rough stub of splintered wood. He pulsed her the image

15

of the red fletching and met her eyes. Both of them knew he carried a death sentence.

Verra's vision kaleidoscoped with tears. Battle sickness. So the affliction had been called since its first appearance in Camarrhan. The same dark soul who had a hold over the Althar had discovered a lethal weapon—a type of poison as yet unidentified—a minute amount of which was loaded into hollow arrow tips designed to penetrate deep into flesh and deliver death within three days. The victims lapsed quickly into coma, all bodily functions slowed to a point where life was only barely sustained. Convulsions in the early stages were typical.

No remedy had been found. All had died.

She met Telsen's questioning brown gaze but dropped her eyes before his intensity. "The wound is a bad one. I will take him to Karessa at the Guild," she lied. The old Healer had tended the Empath before. Pushing a tangle of wet gold hair from Cael's brow, she met his dazed amber eyes with bemused affection. "Can you stand, *chiaran?*"

"Long enough," he answered audibly for the benefit of the others.

Verra looked at Telsen with command in her eyes. "You and the others go home to Illiahn and inform her of this." He began to protest, but soon gave in to her compelling urgency. Cael's twin had twice cared for him as he recovered from injury, and Verra knew that Illiahn suffered agonies of worry for him.

She stood with eyes closed, holding Cael's pattern in her mind, stabilising the shifting, weaving fabric of thought and focussing his Need to a sharp point. She crossed her wrists and raised them above her head. Silver set into leather wristbands reflected the sunlight as she linked the disc bearing the Needs rune on her left band to the Activator on her right. She hoped the three she left behind would forgive her deception. Karessa could not help him this time.

If there was help anywhere to be had for him, the Way would find it. For a moment there was nothing, and she inwardly despaired. All of a glorious sudden, ringing crystal sounded, and from the wristbands fell the shimmering curtain of the Way, like a colourful haze of distant heat. A Way had opened—there was to be an answer. This time, at least.

Telsen and Chad hauled Cael to his feet. Silently thanking the Gods, Verra supported his bloodied and sagging body against her own, and dragged him with ungentle haste through the haze.

Chapter Two

Auckland, New Zealand: 2000

The music swelled around Jenna; thumping bass vibrated through her rib cage and filled her awareness. The instructor had chosen an older tape tonight. She loved this song—*You're My World*. A re-make, but a good one, and romantic to the max. A solid, driving beat always made the workout go faster.

"Dead lift—down for two—not past the knees." The instructor's voice was strident with challenge. "Power up—clean and press. Go!"

Sweat channelled between her shoulder blades and tickled the small of her back as it ran in thin rivulets down her spine. Four tracks into the Pump class and she was flying. She had loaded up the weights tonight; lots of frustrations and energy to work off and out. The lycra-clad instructor on the stage whooped, postured and exhorted. Jenna rolled her eyes. She could take or leave the hype. Her shoulders were tight with effort and the muscles of her back burned with each repetition. The music wound down, slowed and stopped. As she released and stretched her muscles, she sucked hard at her water bottle. Adjusting the weights on her bar for the triceps track, she flicked her long braid back over her shoulder and wiped sweat from her face with a towel.

"Kia ora, Jenna!"

She acknowledged her classmate, fanning her face and

grimacing. "Kia ora—hello to you too, Tem. Hot tonight or what?"

"Whoa man, due for a meltdown!" Tem grinned back, mopping his own face, white teeth strong behind his wide smile. He bent to adjust his own weights, and spread his towel on the top of the step bench at his feet.

Simon Lawton eyed Jenna's tall figure. His gaze swept the slim length of her legs, admiring the way her heavy, dark braid hung almost to her buttocks, a lustrous cable of rich chocolate brown and bronze so unusual among the short, sporty cuts of most women in the gym. Slim-hipped and small waisted, she worked out with great intensity, never sparing herself at all, and the evidence showed in her muscle definition. Despite that, she was full-breasted, this fact accentuated by the ribbed singlet she wore as it spread to accommodate its contents. He turned to the dark man beside him.

"I see you got a word or two out of the Ice Queen."

Tem smiled. "Jenna's okay man, she's just choosy. That's why she talks to me, eh? Great taste!" He gave the thumbs up sign and chuckled.

A lot of conversation included reference to "Lara Croft," as Jenna had become nicknamed among the gym fraternity. Her resemblance to the luscious Playstation heroine was uncanny. Her penchant for tight singlets and hip-belted jeans or cargo pants only served to increase the likeness.

Jenna was not oblivious to the effect she had on Simon, but had no desire to encourage his interest. She cultivated her reputation for aloofness, and the cool appraisal in her eyes restrained most men from approaching her with anything other than casual conversation. She smiled tightly. Simon was no exception.

The music for the triceps workout began. Jenna lay back on her bench, seeing only the cracked plaster ceiling of the aerobics studio. She focussed her attention on working the current muscle group. Great way not to think. The gym had become her haven, a venue of both release and striving.

As the class wound down, Jenna made a quick departure, gathering towel and water bottle in one motion and heading for the showers. She had become skilled at returning her equipment to the storage areas before the cool-down started, anxious as always to avoid the general social intercourse that followed. She had nothing to say to these people, wishing only to exercise and retreat before politeness demanded that she relate to them.

Catching only the flick of her braid as she disappeared from sight, Simon had to admire her skill at avoidance. God, she was good. He always stood only two positions removed from her in the Pump classes. A little to the left and one row back. Best view, he'd found. He was ambitious, single but looking, and had decided Jenna Wade fit the bill for future partner. One day soon he would get over her attitude and take her out. Kissing her full, curving mouth was a thought often on his mind, and she would be a prize worth displaying in his social circle, for sure and certain.

He was used to getting what he wanted, one way or another.

The blue Celica hummed down Victoria Street, past the market, and under the motorway. Jenna adjusted the fader to deliver more Moby to the rear speakers, and turned up the bass. Turning left into Franklin Road, she reflected on her plans for the remainder of the evening.

Her apartment was her private haven. She would spend the next hour or so preparing her dinner, catching up on correspondence she had neglected and taking in the news. That left enough time to check out Sky Movies' offering for the evening before she needed to leave for the hospital. Tonight was the last of a stretch of night shifts. Two weeks out of every six, she worked the graveyard shift at the ICU. She looked forward to slowly returning to normality over the next few weeks, joining the rest of the regular workforce in the traffic streaming into and around Auckland city in the mornings.

Nosing the car into her driveway, she braked, allowing the low-slung car to avoid grounding on the concrete incline. She parked and swung long legs from the car, grimacing as her tired thighs protested at the rise from the low seat. The heat of the evening enfolded her, stifling after the air-conditioned car, and she hurried for the relative coolness of the apartment building. She punched in her access code and entered. The corridor always smelled pleasant, but was airless and still, lit with a wash of white light from brass-rimmed down lights in the ceiling. Turning her key in the door bearing a brass number two, she was home.

As the door swung closed behind her, she tossed her keys onto the table beneath a wood-framed mirror in the hall. She kicked off her Reeboks and peeled off ankle socks, tossing them into the open doorway of her bedroom. Padding down the hall on thick cream carpet, she turned into the kitchen and filled the kettle for tea, noting no messages on the answerphone, and flipping it off. A small tabby cat lay sprawled in the late sun on the dining table, normally forbidden to her.

"You wicked little rat . . ." With a smile, Jenna scooped up the creature who opened sleepy, dark-rimmed yellow eyes and yawned, whiskers curling forward, revealing standard feline equipment of sharp white teeth and raspy pink tongue. Jenna unlocked and opened the multi-fold glass doors that formed the entire front wall of her living area, depositing Possum on the warm terra cotta paving of the courtyard and paused to caress the swirling patterns of the cat's soft coat.

The scent of honeysuckle hung heavy in the still air, and long tendrils of the creeping plant trailed from the beams of the open pergola that overhung the courtyard. Beyond the paving, a small but colourful garden flourished. The jasmine was long finished, but deep red climbing roses and purple wisteria dripped like icing on a child's birthday cake from the trellis set against the buttery concrete walls of her boundary. She inhaled deeply, and walked back through the living room into the kitchen.

Death by cream. The land agent had coined the phrase when showing Jenna through the apartment, and it had been an apt description. Carefully neutral, the decor consisted of cream walls, trims, and carpet, relieved only by brass fittings and wooden doors and benches the colour of dark honey. She had added colour. Vibrant splashes of colour. Two deep and seductively squashy couches accented the lounge with electric blue and vivid nasturtium orange. The spears of a tall potted yucca stood at spiky attention between the two at their intersecting angle. A thick rug combining the colours of both couches occluded most of the cream carpet in the living area.

A stack of audio-visual equipment gleamed from an equally reflective metal and glass wall unit, and Jenna picked up a remote from a pocket in the blue couch, selecting a disc at random from the CD changer. Queen. A bit of a shift in mood from Moby, but okay. She loved music. Pretty much any music. She loved the way it made her feel: alive, empowered and uplifted.

Turning her attention toward dinner, she rummaged in her deep freeze for a chicken curry, Thai style. Just what she felt like. She popped the Gladware container into the microwave to thaw, made herbal tea, and sat at the dining table to open her mail.

Investment news; advice of maturing investments; financial statements. Sighing, she pushed the pile aside to discuss with her accountant. She trusted Martin Lawrence and Co. with the tedious business of managing her affairs. The truth was that if she did not work, she would still live well. Her eyes rested on the framed photograph beside her telephone. The familiar twinge of resentment and loss stirred in her gut. *Thanks, Mum.*

Thanks for the small fortune. Thanks for leaving me alone. Not for the first time, she wished her mother had been a stronger woman, had managed to cope with the emotional minefield her life had become when Dad had left them. Jenna snorted in disgust. Michael Wade. Philandering, faithless jerk. But her mother had loved him.

She saw the fragility in the haunted indigo eyes that were so like her own. *You never really fitted in anywhere in this world, did you, Mum?* An unusually sensitive woman, her mother Lliahna had been her lifeline, her anchor and stability in her own fragile world. Always a loner, Jenna had never connected with her peers at school, seeing only their inconsistencies and shallowness, the competition between the sexes and the hurts that lay in wait for a girl who trusted. She had built her walls early in life. The day Jenna had returned from her last semester at nursing school, Lliahna had taken her own life. Jenna had stood, suitcase in hand, and watched as the St John's ambulance had taken her mother away. The memory faded, but the pain and loneliness remained. She swallowed against rising emotion and blinked away tears. *You were my best friend.* She sniffled and swiped at her nose, angry at her descent into maudlin girlishness.

She sighed and rested her chin in her hands, recalling the fantasy she had entertained in her girlhood. It had begun when her mother had explained what she knew of her background—almost nothing. Her own mother, Chiahn, had arrived in post-war Auckland with nothing but the clothes on her back, a fortune in precious gems, and a belly swollen in pregnancy. Of her husband, she would not speak, except to say he had died in the land of her origin, a land she would not name and would not be drawn further on.

Perhaps her mother, so different, so beautiful, was the long-lost daughter of some exotic prince, who would one day appear to claim his beloved family. She shook off the old daydream. Now she was grown, she understood mundane reality. *There was no rescue for you, Mum, was there?*

None for me, either, she reflected ruefully. Besides her father's example, her own experience of men and relationships was disastrous. Testosterone could make a fool of the nicest-seeming man. No. Men were a breed apart and best left alone. This was one Venusian with no further desire to visit Mars. Unless it was to scratch the odd itch, of course . . . She smiled and shook her head. Twenty-six-years old, and already so cynical.

Five high-pitched beeps from the microwave brought her mind back to the present as the smell of spices and lemongrass reminded her of dinner.

The last haunting notes of the movie's theme music accompanied the rolling credits. Wiping her eyes and blowing her nose for the third time, Jenna flipped off the television, took a deep breath and sighed, laughing at herself and her addiction to romantic fantasy.

Gladiator. She had enjoyed it just as much as the first time she had seen it, and loved the epic story. Maximus. What a man. Leaning back into electric blue softness, she reflected on the character as she automatically began to braid her hair, long since dry after her shower. She flipped the length of it over the back of the couch, combining three strands in a thick weave as a French braid took elegant shape beneath her practised fingers.

What a shame. A true Maximus was as unlikely to have existed then as he was today. The testosterone-prone were unworthy of trust and devoid of conscience, and it was foolish indulgence to think otherwise, despite the abundance of romantic portrayals to the contrary. She fastened the end of the braid with an elastic hair tie, and tossed it back over her shoulder, feeling the familiar weight on her neck.

Time? A quarter to eleven. Shit.

The last graveyard shift beckoned. She unfolded herself from the close embrace of the couch, smoothed her uniform over her hips and wriggled her feet into soft flat shoes, pressing the answerphone on and hearing its hollow announcement as she hurried down the hall. She flipped off the lights, retrieved her keys and nametag from the hall table and left her quiet cream sanctuary in the care of the cat.

Chapter Three

Collision Course

The Way was canny. Never did it open in a position where the travellers may be immediately noticed, or in any danger. Always, Verra emerged somehow concealed and away from attention. She never thought to question this phenomenon, as she never doubted its function or trustworthiness. It simply was.

As always, the Way opened undetected. The pair stumbled from the oily shimmer as Verra lost her battle to hold Cael upright. He fell forward onto hands and knees. His head hung low, and his arms trembled under his own weight. She knelt beside him, one hand on his uninjured shoulder as she closed the Way behind them and looked around.

"We are off-world," she murmured. She knew from the smell of disinfectants and other chemicals that they were in a healing establishment of a technological world. The Way had taken her to similar places with previous charges. They were out of sight around a turn in a wide corridor. Hearing sounds of industry around the corner to their right, she ventured a cautious peek.

Some distance down the corridor, a worker clad in pale green manoeuvered a large, wheeled bed through wide open doors to the left. Chairs lined the corridor to each side of the doors, and several of these were occupied. They were in luck. This was a parallel world to their own, inhabited by humans like themselves. From the signs on the walls and the float of conversation from the corridors, she knew the language here was similar to their own.

"Hold on, *chiaran*," she breathed, but Cael folded slowly to one side and gave up his loose grip on consciousness. Verra locked her forearms under his armpits and dragged his inert weight around the bend of the corridor directly into the view of the green-clad worker as he emerged again from the double doors. Those few seated in the corridor craned to see Verra and her burden, anxious, in the way of those who wait, for anything unusual to relieve the boredom. The orderly called through the doors for assistance and, as he hurried toward her, Verra ceased struggling and simply waited for him to reach them, her calm face belying the anxiety that roiled beneath the surface.

This part was never easy, she reflected. Her appearance always raised questions. She had found the best way was to vanish in as inconspicuous a manner as she could. Before the emergency was over and attention could be paid to the odd circumstances of their arrival.

"He is Cael," she informed the orderly, "and he is in need of your help most urgently. He does not speak your tongue," she added, a ruse she used often that allowed her charge to escape questioning. The orderly's eyes widened. Verra knew that her archaic speech and lilting inflection often produced such a reaction, but Cael convulsed at her feet and drew the man's attention. She swallowed. *It begins, then. Oh Gods, do not let him die.* The orderly crouched beside Cael, holding his shoulders in gentle restraint as his body heaved and shook in violent spasms.

Assistance arrived quickly. After a brief assessment, two green-clad men lifted Cael onto a narrow gurney and trundled him with some urgency through the double doors, a woman in white holding a hissing mask to his face.

Verra made her escape and opened the Way home in the same spot where they had arrived. No, not home, she thought ruefully—too many questions there, too. She would visit at the Guild for a while. It pained her to leave Cael, but she could locate him again via his Keystone. He need only call using his own empathic gifting and she would hear, and come. The Way had never failed. His answers would lie here, and her presence or absence would not change that. Ignoring the ache in her heart, she activated the Landmark rune, opened the Way and stepped through.

Inside his cocoon of soft darkness, Cael fought an unusual battle. Unaware of most external stimuli, he felt another presence begin to establish itself within his mind, a frightening event for one who had been taught the strictest controls over this most personal of arenas. Ironic that one who was conditioned to shun the thought of controlling another's thought-world should find himself so invaded and controlled.

The presence murmured into his mind. *Be still, be still. Calm. Still. Movement is pain . . . calm, still . . .* The murmur was constant, hypnotic, and backed by an occasional agony of intense pain that seemed to encompass every nerve ending in his body. He understood that this pain would be the penalty for movement, or even forming the intention to move. These episodes of punishment inflicted by the symbiot were causing his body to convulse, although he had only a vague awareness of the physical dimension. The alien presence began to add obscure images; feelings of nurture and pleasure; visual flashes of tiny transparent capsules each containing a pulsing entity with no apparent form, floating through his own arteries in ever-increasing numbers.

Trying to understand, he began to formulate a question. Desperately fighting the fuzziness of his thoughts, he attempted to disrupt the continuous crooning long enough to be heard. More pain, an intense agony this time that threatened to tear him asunder, was the only response.

Calm . . . still . . . all will be well, be still. Movement is pain . . . Again the visual flashes. He began to understand. This was no poison. A sentient being invaded his mind and body.

He was a host. His bloodstream was providing the environment necessary for reproduction, and apparently providing it well. Gods, this was what had killed the others inside three days. Why the stillness? Why so much pain? He lay motionless within his mind, trying to fathom a way to help himself with this new information, knowing all the others must have known the truth before they died. And none of them had been able to preserve themselves.

Jenna turned from signing in for her shift at the ICU desk and took the clipboard from the night staff pigeonhole. She flicked through the log, identifying new admissions, noting with sadness the passing of an elderly patient she had nursed for the past week. "Go well, Jean," she murmured. "No more pain for you."

Newbies. Two female cardiacs and one young male trauma victim. She sighed. *Let me hazard a guess.* The cynical thought came unbidden. A drunken fight? A car accident, probably also involving alcohol? What was it about testosterone that caused young men to strive to be the loudest, strongest, fastest or cleverest? She shrugged, filing her attitude away and putting on her professional face as she turned into the first room.

The trauma victim was on the right of the dimly lit, two bedded room. The eerie green glow of the monitor illuminated the dark blond head on the pillow. She unhooked the board from the end of the bed. Admission notes and treatment record for "Cael—Unknown." No personal details available. Taking one tanned wrist in her fingers and watching the small timepiece pinned to the front of her uniform, she noted his low pulse rate and frowned.

Someone had touched him. His skin did not register the touch, but he felt a shiver of recognition in his mind. The symbiot, as he now knew it to be, stirred into alertness. Pain impulses warned him to stillness. He complied. There was something familiar about that touch, something he needed to recall, something important. The memory forced itself back through the fuzziness in a rush.

A Linker. Oh Gods, that was what he had felt. The touch ceased and he desperately wanted it back, needed it back. Ignoring the spasming pain visited on him by the symbiot, he gathered all the strength of his gifting that was left to him and breached the barrier that separated his awareness from his body.

The symbiot punished his breach most severely.

Jenna was replacing the board on the bed end when the patient began to convulse. It was over quickly, and she checked the thin tube attached to the I.V. needle in the back of his wrist to be sure it had not pulled loose. As she replaced the adhesive tape holding the needle in place, his hand turned slowly; his fingers brushed hers and curled around them. Touched by the mute appeal, she held his hand and sat with him for a moment, waiting to see if he would regain consciousness. She reached for the dimmer switch above the bed and raised the light level a little, watching his face for signs of returning awareness.

He was very beautiful. Impulsively, she brushed damp hair back from his forehead, seeing for the first time the ugly, swollen contusion under the hair behind the left temple. His skin wore a light tan, although his face and arms were a little darker than what she could see of the rest of him. His features were strong, his mouth firm and well shaped in a very masculine way. His left pectoral bore a curious tattoo. Leaning closer, she identified a small green dragon, curled like a sleeping kitten, wings and tail wrapped tightly around its body to form a perfect oval.

His body was well muscled, the chest, biceps and shoulder muscles nicely defined under the skin. She found herself rather interested in the rest of him, and let her eyes wander the length of the long body under the plain hospital coverings. He was lean, well built, and obviously very fit. In idle speculation, she wondered how it would feel to hold and be held by such magnificent male flesh—and caught herself in quick irritation. Her isolation and long aloneness had left her vulnerable to such sojourns into fantasy, and she had found of late that passions tended to rise more and more unbidden.

Recognising the inappropriateness of her thoughts, she began to rise. His fingers tightened on hers. She glanced down and saw a faint glow of light around their joined hands. Blinking to dispel the illusion, she again dimmed the light over the bed.

The glow remained, brighter in the semi-darkness. A definite rose-gold aura lingered around her skin and his where they touched. She let go of his hand quickly, her heart beating faster as adrenalin answered her fear response. The aura faded and was gone.

He felt her disengage her hand, and the warm flow of strength from her ceased. He felt a little stronger, the fear of death held at bay for a while longer. He was comforted to have found someone capable of a link and was sustained by her life force so freely given.

The crooning continued; the pain remained, a constant agony now that he had transgressed so badly. Visual images flashed through his awareness, the symbiot showing him with pride its developing offspring within their microscopic capsules, a myriad of them, drifting in his slowed blood stream. It promised peace, promised well being; all would be well, all well.

>*Verra!*< His call was a silent scream, but there was only empty quiet. The barrier was back.

Jenna stood at the foot of the bed, staring unseeing at the records for "Cael—Unknown," trying to make sense of what had happened—if anything had happened. She knew the tricks that tiredness could play on perception after a week of night shifts, but reminded herself she could not afford such lapses while on duty in ICU of all places.

Where had the glow come from? Had she only imagined the light? No answers, but she was certain the patient had taken comfort from the contact. His pulse and breathing were stronger, and she felt a certain satisfaction that she had been able to reassure him with her presence.

"Jenna? You in there?"

"Hmm? Oh, yeah. Daydreaming though. I'm a little tired, that's all. What do you know about this . . . Cael?"

"Gorgeous, isn't he? Want to draw straws for bath duty?"

Jenna laughed, relaxing, feeling normality returning.

Tessa. The one person she had allowed to come as close as she dared let anyone. A friend who respected her distance and silences, didn't fully understand her but didn't seem to care, enjoying the friendship on the basis it was offered. Irreverent, irrepressible Tessa, as popular, warm and open as she herself was cool, aloof and withdrawn.

"Certainly a looker, but in bad shape, Tess. What happened?"

"No one knows for certain. He had no I.D., and the woman who brought him in gave one name only and disappeared. P'raps it was a passionate bondage and discipline session that got out of hand?" Tessa waggled her eyebrows with a lewd chortle. "Actually, the word is that it was most likely a Dungeons and Dragons event that turned a bit serious. The Uni has a fantasy sect that plays realistic games—James used to belong, but it got a bit weird for him so he quit."

Jenna privately could not imagine anything proving too weird for Tessa's brother, but kept her opinion to herself.

Tessa continued, enjoying the speculation. "I heard from Ben in ER that he was dressed in some out-there gear. I mean, you know, like leathers and boots, knives, the works!" She wrinkled her nose and poked out the tip of her tongue. "He was also very bloody and very sweaty. Obviously took the whole thing far too seriously. I wonder how the other guy came off? Strange there aren't two of them here . . ." She let the thought trail off. "Pretty foolish, however gorgeous," she sighed. "They just don't make a perfect one, do they Jen?"

Jenna's brows angled into a frown. He didn't look the foolish type—even unconscious as he was, there was a strange dignity about him. She felt it. Getting weird again, she warned herself. "I can't imagine a game would go that far," she said quietly. "What about the woman who brought him in?"

"As I said Jen, she disappeared. No one saw her go— they were all too busy trying to stop this one from dying. He was in a serious state apparently—took them half an hour to stabilise him. He's lucky to be alive."

"Hmm. So no one has suggested assault? No police involvement?"

"Well, yeah. Robert called them in. You know he has to if there's any evidence of assault. Or skullduggery, or the dark, criminal actions of a sick and depraved mind . . ." Her voice dropped theatrically, and she leered and limped her way out of the room. "Igor will go now, master . . . see you tomorrow, Jen, and save some of that for me." She nodded toward Cael's still form and disappeared down the corridor, grinning in a most unprofessional manner.

Jenna shook her head at Tessa's apparent indifference, knowing it covered a vastly tender and compassionate heart. *We each have our ways of coping,* she thought, and smiled to herself.

She focussed again on his notes, her frown returning at his recorded injuries. The head injury was obvious, but there was also a deep gash, presumed to be a knife wound, from left shoulder to elbow; a puncture wound, possibly an arrow—*arrow?*—to some depth in the left side; sprained right knee; extensive bruising and abrasions. She shook her head again, wondering what on earth a man could be involved in to damage himself to that extent.

Yawning, she checked the other patient in the room, an elderly cardiac, resting well and improving all the time. She noted the time, took his pulse and made her records on the chart. With a last reflective glance in the young man's direction, she moved on to the next rooms to check her female patients.

Over the next few hours, Cael's monitor sounded often. Each time Jenna hurried to his side, apprehensive of what she might find—and each time discovered him pale, his pulse dangerously low, his breathing shallow. The first time, she buzzed for the duty doctor, but as she waited beside him, holding the oxygen mask to his face, his hand again in hers, he had improved. Pulse strengthened, colour returned, breathing deepened. And she felt an inexplicable weariness.

He knew he was draining her strength, but he needed her desperately. He was afraid now, very afraid. He felt a cold darkness draw close around him, creep into his bones, hold him fast in a shadowy limbo from which he feared he could not return. In panic, he shaped a fragile but urgent sending: >*Verra! I need you . . .*< and cast it from him with the last of his borrowed strength. And the symbiot punished him.

Verra caught the faint echo of his call. So faint she may have imagined it, but she knew at once from whom it had come. She was so familiar with the pattern and essence of the caller she had no need for a name.

She had been reading in the extensive and beautiful gardens of the Wayfinders' keep at the Guild, on the Island of the Hand. After sharing time with her old tutors, feeling tensions dissipate as they always did in this timeless place, she returned with a jolt to the reality of her situation and her responsibilities.

She stood immediately and beckoned a nearby novice to take the book that had fallen from her lap as she arose. "Give my regards to Karessa at the Healers' keep," she requested. "I am called. Please inform her that I will return when I have more news of Cael." As the novice turned to obey, Verra raised her wrists, crossmatching the Keystone runes above her head, and stepped quickly into the shimmering curtain that awaited her passage.

35

With the canniness of the Way, she emerged behind the drawn curtain of Cael's cubicle as his monitor again sounded. With a brief glance at his face, she drew herself into the curtain, losing herself in the shadows as footsteps hurried into the room. Her brow creased in concern. His face was sheened with sweat and deathly pale.

Oh Gods, Cael, hold on!

Jenna silenced the monitor, held the silicone mask of the oxygen unit to his face and grasped his hand in hers. "Cael. Cael!" She called his name in an urgent voice. "Breathe. Come on, breathe!" He drew several deeper breaths, and she let out a relieved sigh. "That's it. That's better." Holding the mask in place, she sank to the chair she had placed beside the bed, seeing again the now familiar glow surround their hands. She shook her head, too weary to wonder anymore, and rested her forehead on the edge of the bed, feeling as if this night would never end. She heard a slight rustle of movement from the shadows. Her eyes opened; she turned her head slightly. A woman stepped from the concealment of the curtain and approached her.

"Please—do not call out," the woman began, and raised a cautioning finger to her lips as Jenna's head jerked up from the bed in alarm.

"What are you doing in here?" Jenna hissed. "This is intensive care—no visitors!" She scanned the woman's strange appearance, quickly taking in the soft, tan leather pants, tunic and boots, the strangely adorned leather wristbands and the shadow of care on an otherwise beautiful face.

"Do not be afraid. I am here for Cael. He needs my help. If I do not give it I fear he will die—you have seen his distress . . ."

"How did you get in here?" Jenna whispered, "and what do you think you can do for him?"

The woman hesitated, then appeared to reach a decision. "I am Verra," she said, moving swiftly to Cael's side. "I am Wayfinder to Cael, son of Jarin; his safety is my responsibility. We are not of this world—I brought him here through the Way, seeking the answer to his Need." Her wide green eyes seemed to assess Jenna's face for reaction to her words.

Jenna stared in disbelief as Verra reached for the cord around Cael's neck and took the small silver-caged stone he wore in her hand. Verra frowned into the stone and was silent for several moments. When she spoke again, her tone conveyed concern. "I cannot heal him. I can only lend order to his life force to sustain him until I can find the next Way."

Way? Jenna thought, what on earth was she talking about? As she watched, she weighed up all she had experienced so far. Another Dungeons and Dragons player? The strange woman, Verra as she had named herself, had an all too real intensity about her, an urgency of need that impelled her actions. Not of this world? Jenna contemplated calling Security, letting them sort it out, but she heard Cael sigh a little, felt him relax his light grasp on her hand. Whatever Verra had done had helped him. She stood, flexed her back, and regarded Verra with no few questions in her eyes. "I'm Jenna," was all she said.

Verra held Jenna's gaze for several heartbeats, and nodded. "Well met, Jenna. I know you have much to ask me, and I will give you understanding as you need it, but for now, I must seek a new Way."

Jenna smoothed back a few strands of hair that had escaped her braid and shrugged. "Of course. Go right ahead.

Don't mind me, I'll catch up later."

The Wayfinder did not react to the sarcasm. "I will take him wherever the answer to his need is. Only the Way knows where."

"You can't take him anywhere! He needs to be right here." She stared in astonishment at the strange woman, wondering if she was in her right mind or lost in a fantasy game.

Verra brought her face level with Jenna's, and Jenna found herself looking into intense, ocean-green eyes. "Be still and listen. I have his pattern in my mind, taken from the Keystone he wears. Within that pattern lies his. The Way will open only if there is an answer somewhere—any-where." Closing her eyes, she crossed her wristbands, touching two of the inset silver discs together as she did so, and murmuring what sounded like a brief prayer.

Crystal sang, and a shimmering haze dropped from the leather at her wrists. "Thank the Gods, we are not done yet!" She stepped one foot through the strange visual dis-turbance. Jenna gasped, seeing the Wayfinder disappear and just as quickly reappear. She glanced at the other patient in the room, but he slept, peacefully oblivious to the drama going on around him.

"It is a dwelling," Verra said in disappointment, "with no one there. That means there will be waiting, and we do not have the luxury of much time. I can widen the Way if you will help me take him through?"

Dazed by what she had just seen, Jenna pulled her thoughts together with an effort. "We can push him through on the bed—it's wheeled—transfer him and push it back through. The hospital may believe he simply recov-ered and left without being seen—no questions asked that way, and less trouble for me." She spared a thought for the security cameras that monitored the corridors outside the rooms. There would be no record of him leaving. Her thoughts in turmoil, she turned off the monitor and began to disconnect Cael from the paraphernalia that linked him to the machine. *I must be as crazy as Verra is.* She shook her head, aghast at what her hands were doing but unwilling to stop. Somehow, this strange man and even stranger woman had her behaving most out of character. As if they were in control here, and not herself. As if she were part of their game.

Verra smiled then, her face brightening. She widened the Way entrance, and together they manouevred the hospital bed through the haze. Jenna flinched as she stepped through, knowing she had just committed herself to something very big that she did not in the least understand. A tingle teased at her skin and blurred colour flashed at the edges of her vision. Sounds whispered past her ears, not stopping to be identified, and for the briefest moment, the scent of something almost-but-not-quite-musk hung in the cool air of the Way.

Whoa. World shift. She looked around in utter amazement. They were in her own apartment, her own bedroom, just as she had left it on her way to work. She stared in confusion at the scattered socks and Reeboks on the floor where she had tossed them. The answer was here? Verra laid a gentle hand on her arm with reassurance in her green eyes.

"Verra, this is my place! I live here." Panic edged her voice. "Oh, no. Don't rely on me. Shit, what can I do?"

Verra spoke with calm reason. "The Way has never lied, never failed. His answer obviously lies somehow with you, Jenna."

Reality check. Jenna gathered her wits again, aware that

she must be back in the ward before she or the bed was noted as missing. Praying no other patient would need her for a minute or two, she indicated her bed. "Over here," she said, pulling back the cover. She lowered the hospital bed to match the height of her own, and loosened the precisely tucked coverings. "We'll use the sheet to move him. Just do as I do." Together, they pulled on the draw sheet beneath the limp figure, dragging him across onto Jenna's bed. They covered him with her lime-and-white-daisy duvet, retrieved the hospital bedding and pushed the bed back through the Way.

Jenna peered cautiously from the curtained cubicle. All clear. They steered the empty bed back into its place, and Jenna, reckoning she would now be nursing a private patient around the clock, began to collect the items she knew she would need. Verra held the stack in her arms as Jenna loaded her up and lay what remained of Cael's clothing on the top. She had half an hour of her shift left to work. Pushing Verra toward the Way, she offered what she knew.

"I'll be home in an hour or so. If he becomes distressed, it seems to help if you hold his hand."

Verra gave her a puzzled smile. "I cannot help him that way. That is your gift, Jenna, not mine."

My gift? Oh Lord. This just gets weirder, she thought.

She showed Verra the operation of the oxygen unit, told her when and how to use it. Verra grasped her hand, thumb to thumb, backed through the haze and was gone. Jenna stood staring as the shimmer disappeared, her perception of reality fractured. She strove to pull the fragments together but, as quicksilver, they eluded her.

The real world flooded back then—but the bed remained empty.

The last half-hour was an eternity. Jenna worried about

the shift change and the discovery of the missing patient, but noted on Cael's chart a last check-in time of fifteen minutes prior to the end of her shift. She could easily dissemble about that last fifteen minutes. She was dealing with her other patients, checking, making comfortable; there were plenty of reasons she may not have seen him leave. She hoped that would be the conclusion reached, at least.

And then it was time. Her replacement, Claire, greeted her cheerily, and she handed over the ward log. "No problems now, but it was a bit of a rough night," Jenna mumbled, stretching and yawning.

Claire regarded her tired face with sympathy. "Go home and sleep well, Jenna." She smiled.

Jenna hurried from the ward, wanting to be clear away before Claire made her first round. She could face no questions today.

Dawn light was breaking as she drove out of the staff car park. The bright butter-yellow of the new day streaked long, sharp fingers between the shadows of tall buildings onto the streets as she pulled into the carport area behind her apartment complex. A lone tui sang from the tall banksia tree beside the driveway; she normally took the time to appreciate the bird, but this morning it did not even register in her tired mind.

She punched her code into the panel of the security lock and pushed her way into the corridor, wondering again at the wisdom of her actions that night. She'd had no choice! It would mean her job if she was found out. Who could blame her for an empty bed?

Why had she cared anyway? So much for the Ice Queen image she had cultivated with so much care. She snorted in confused disgust. Hadn't she sworn never to be taken in by another male? And yet, here she was risking her job, her future, on a stranger. Worse than that, a male stranger. Her key turned in the lock, and her door swung open. Throwing her keys on the hall table, she dropped her bag at its feet and went in to address the situation.

Verra slept in an armchair beside the bed, the oxygen unit at her feet and Possum curled in comfortable repose on her lap. Jenna quietly replaced the depleted plasma bag hanging from the bed-head with another from their purloined supplies. She checked the flow rate and the I.V., and felt her patient's pulse. Slow but steady. She noted dark pinpricks of blood seeping through the thin sleeve of bandaging on his arm and mechanically set about changing the dressing. A nasty wound. When she had finished, she dropped a blanket over Verra. Taking another blanket from the closet, she lay down, fully clothed but too tired to care, next to the man they hoped to save.

Cael knew he was alive. The pain left him in no doubt of that. The fear remained, but the cold darkness was in abeyance. The crooning continued, the reassurance that if he remained still, calm, there would be no punishment, all would be well, all would be well. He remained still.

The catflap in the lounge door squeaked and swung to and fro. Possum trotted down the hall and jumped onto the bed, treading dainty paw prints in the duvet, punctuating the daisies. She investigated the foreign presence with a delicate sniff, then continued stepping her way to Jenna. As she settled, purring loudly, against Jenna's chest, a loud sneeze launched her into a nervous feline leap. Jenna reached for a Kleenex, cursing her sensitivity to cat hair, cursing the fact she loved the animal so much.

Such a dichotomy. The story of her life.

Oh God.

Awareness flooded in and she turned to confirm her memory of the night's events.

Oh yes. It had really happened. Damn and double bloody damn. How could she have been such an idiot? Should have let security work it all out, it was none of her affair. Why on earth had she let the strange pair affect her judgement?

Shit.

Too late for regrets, she realised. What's done is done. She tumbled herself off the side of the bed and looked at the clock. Midday. The armchair was empty. Verra had gone, the blanket folded in a neat square on the seat.

She turned her attention to her patient, who had neither moved nor changed condition. He appeared comatose, breathing lightly through dry lips. She moistened her fingers with water from a glass on the bedside table and drew them across his mouth, following this with an application of her own lip balm. *Why did she care?* The answer came unbidden—he was hurt, vulnerable and alone. It was not in her nature to ignore such need. She smoothed damp gold hair back from his brow and cooled his face with a wet cloth. She was also undeniably drawn to him.

Possum settled herself against the visitor's thigh, purring her feline seal of approval on the matter. Jenna smiled. "So it's all right with you then?" she asked the cat. She checked his temperature and pulse, but found no change. His condition appeared to be more stable than it had been in the hospital. Curious. Satisfied he was as comfortable as possible, Jenna headed for the shower in her ensuite, dropping her uniform and underwear on the way. She pinned up her braid and stepped under the steaming spray of water, letting the warmth soak into her tired muscles. She soaped and rinsed, washing her face under a cooler spray before stepping out and toweling herself dry.

Wrapped in a towel she, and a cloud of steam issued forth from the ensuite, feeling somewhat restored. Cael had not moved. Shrugging, she dropped her towel, opened her lingerie drawer and pulled on a lilac satin chemise. She made herbal tea in the kitchen, absently ate a banana and some yoghurt, then took her steaming cup to the phone. Guilt turned her stomach and lent heat to her cheeks as she phoned the hospital, claiming an ailing relative as her need to be absent for a week or so. She hoped that would be long enough. The time-off she had been saving for a visit to Thailand would have to be sacrificed.

She drank her tea and performed the routine nursing tasks she could do in her sleep. Shooing Possum from her nest, she drew the duvet down to check the puncture wound in his side. She lifted the dressing. The flesh was bruised and swollen, but healthy enough. No bleeding at all. A good sign, she hoped.

She hesitated before drawing the duvet up again, seeing for the second time the smooth gold of his skin, the hard, flat lines of muscle across his belly, the swell of his chest. He was very beautifully made, and she was most certainly not immune to masculine beauty for all her distance and coolness. Of course, the odds were that as soon as he opened his eyes and then his mouth, he would prove to be just like all the other males of his generation—vain, arrogant and demanding. The lookers always were. That, or gay.

Yawning, she acknowledged her need for further sleep. She padded out to the living room, activated the answerphone then posted Possum out of the cat door and locked it. Returning to her bedroom, she debated very briefly with herself about propriety. It was a big bed, and the *only* bed. If she slept on the couch in her lounge, she wouldn't know if he needed her in the night. Too tired to argue the rights or wrongs of it, she slid in under the duvet beside her patient and was asleep within seconds.

The symbiot spoke to him openly now. Perhaps it was his gifting, or perhaps the previous victims had also experienced this. Cael shuddered at the thought. The alien presence was confident. Gods, he had seen how close it was to its goal—the domination of his nervous system. The symbiot crooned to him of shared strength, new ability and a future of mutual benefit. Althar and the symbiot had coexisted in perfect harmony for countless generations, he learned. The symbiot showed him how its microscopic offspring would attach to nerve endings throughout his body, feeding from his electrical impulses of energy, contributing a new dimension of physical strength and speed of reflex. He also knew now the reasons for the enforced physical stillness. The embryonic capsules were fragile, and any movement of his bloodstream past the slow pace it was restrained to would break them open, leaving them defenceless against the tiny protectors that roamed his blood. Never had he understood so much about his own body's functions; never had he thought to be privy to the minuscule workings of his own insides.

The embryo would hatch tomorrow. There was no reversal of the process once they were mature enough to freely inhabit his body. The barrier remained firmly in place. He was unable to feel any part of his physical body besides pain; confined within his own mind with a seductive, destructive presence. If he *could* move, he would—

would thrash like a madman if it would destroy the embryo and save him—but the symbiot now had complete control over his nervous system.

He knew without a doubt that the symbiot did not comprehend the fact that he was not Althar, his system incompatible with its program of domination and enhancement. The many deaths of his own kind had proved it. His hope faded into despair.

Chapter Four

The Bonding

Late January sun squeezed around the edges of the closed vertical blinds of Jenna's bedroom, and the aroma of a neighbour's barbecue teased her awake. She awoke ravenous, but ignored her growling stomach long enough to check Cael's condition. The same. She sighed. He breathed, his heart beat; and he was as unresponsive as he had been that morning. She touched his face. At least he was cooler.

Slipping from the bed, she made straight for the kitchen and raided her pantry to take the edge off her hunger. Chewing a piece of raisin bread, she opened the kitchen window, frowning at the heat haze that still shimmered from the roof of the carports. Sprinklers watered the professionally maintained back gardens as the afternoon passed into an evening that promised to linger long and hot.

It was well past time for her usual Pump class. Oh well. She was undecided whether she had the energy anyway, feeling as jaded and lethargic as she was.

Where was Verra? Cael's condition was unchanged, and she began to wonder if she possessed the necessary knowledge to help him any further. She changed his dressings, replaced the empty plasma bag with one of fluid therapy and noted a slight increase in blood pressure.

The bedroom was still and warm, and as it was on the cooler side of the apartment, she opened the windows, hoping the early evening breeze would clear the afternoon's heat from the room. Pulling the duvet from her patient's hot body, she flipped open a cool cotton sheet to cover him with. As before, she could not help looking at him with appreciation. Young he might be, at least several years her junior, but he was delicious to look at. His legs were long and athletic, his hips narrow. She traced the indented line of his thigh muscle with a light finger, wondering at her own temerity. Never before had she viewed a patient with anything but professional interest. In a curious way, his vulnerability intrigued her as much as his undeniable physical appeal. Feeling a little ashamed of her voyeurism, she covered his nakedness with the sheet, pausing just long enough for a final, lingering look.

The evening passed uneventfully, and again she wondered at Verra's absence. Surely the woman cared about her "charge?" She had only stayed long enough to stabilise his condition, whatever she had done with the stone around his neck. Jenna recognised it as an opal. The stones were uncommon and expensive, but not rare. She had inherited a necklace of nine opals from her grandmother, handed down to her by her own mother. Hers were set in gold though, not wrapped haphazardly in fine silver wire as Cael's was. But his stone seemed somehow functional, while hers were merely ornamental.

She did a little laundry, cleaned up her few dishes and answered some e-mail. By eleven that night she was again yawning, needing sleep. Not like her to feel so low. Making final checks on her patient, she readied herself for bed and again slid in under the sheet next to his still body, leaving the soft glow of the touch-light on should he awake in the night.

She awoke in the small hours, sweating in the still heat, pulse racing and disturbed by a recurring sexual dream. As always, it had left her aroused and considering whether to resolve her desire herself or try to bury it again. Cael had featured rather prominently in the nocturnal encounter, and the memory of his body heat and firm touch sent a delicious but guilty shiver over her skin. Her thigh came into contact with Cael's. His sharp male scent heightened her awareness of him; his presence was warm, solid and real. At some stage of the night she had shed her chemise, and the unaccustomed fleshy contact was both reassuring and exciting. Whenever she touched him, a strange feeling of connection, of affinity, filled her. It was as if she somehow knew him, as if they had once been lovers. Perhaps something to do with the odd light that surrounded their skin wherever they touched. Whatever it was, she was definitely drawn to him. A moth to a bright flame.

She ran a light hand over his belly, up over his chest and down his uninjured arm, feeling the contour of his muscles, the smooth heat of his skin under her fingers. Her cheek lay hot on his chest now, obscuring the tattooed dragon, and her breath came faster as she pressed against his thigh. Careful of his wounded arm, she raised herself on her elbow and regarded him closely. He was out of it. No response, no one home.

The desire to use his body was strong in her. Men were users anyway, so where would be the harm? Besides, she reasoned, he would never know. He was beautiful, he was here, and there was a kind of magic in it.

Abandoning ethics, she stroked his torso, ran her palms down the length of his thighs, allowing her arousal to intensify, feeling the familiar pulses of anticipation begin in her groin and shoot upward through her belly. Focussing on his mouth, she took his full lower lip between her own, tasting him with her tongue, her fingers stroking his cheek and slipping behind his neck to lock in the thick tangle of dark gold hair. His heat and scent filled her hungry senses, and the surrounding glow of rosy light seemed to lend a certain rightness to the deed.

Only just aware enough to be careful of his injuries, she lifted her thigh over his hips and lowered herself lightly onto his body. The contact was exquisite. His pelvis was in firm contact with her sex, and she moved herself wantonly against him. As her excitement mounted, she became aware that he was responding. She felt him firm beneath her, and reached to touch him. With a gasp of pleased surprise, she realised the full size of him. She moved along him. Lost in need, she drew him into her body, feeling him fill her. He groaned, the first sound she had heard him utter, but he did not stir. She moved faster, her heart pounding, and abandoned herself to the delicious sensation of lust fully embraced. Pressing hard against him with each movement, she raced toward the fulfillment of her need. It came quickly then, but not as usual, not as she had expected.

Her orgasm was powerful and intense. As she cried out and her body pulsed with release, she felt the man beneath her respond in kind. His hips arched, his hand came to her buttocks, holding her to him, his wild heartbeat pulsing visibly at his throat. Instead of diminishing, her own pleasure spiralled upward, her response somehow combined with his, was one with his. It did not end then but continued to intensify, lifting her further and higher than she had ever experienced as he shuddered beneath her. After several moments of immobilising pleasure, she folded over his body in a boneless heap. She lay against him, her breath descending from ragged gasp to slow heave, and turned her face to his. Confused, unfocussed amber eyes met hers moments before he slid back into unconsciousness.

★ ★ ★ ★ ★

Behind the barrier, he was again aware of the Linker's touch. This time the touch was not sustaining, but somehow demanding. As removed from experiencing his physical self as he was, he could only interpret the impressions received by his mind as intent. Her intent was very different this time. He was obediently still, unwilling to further risk the visceral, tearing pain inflicted by the symbiot that left him so diminished and unmanned.

He was aware of the symbiot's agitation. Then concern; vague flashes of discomfort accompanied visual images of microscopic capsules spinning, turning, disrupted from their slow, elegant dance through his blood. They pulsed and whirled, collided with each other, careened off his artery walls.

He felt the symbiot's panic within his mind and prepared for punishment.

It came.

White hot and intense, tearing muscle from bone and clawing at his entrails. He could not stop it this time with compliance. He was innocent of all movement and powerless to defend himself. How had he displeased the symbiot to this extent?

The intensity of the torture lessened. Recovering his wits slightly, he again caught the symbiot's panic. More visual flashes; capsules sped through his blood, colliding and bursting, fragile contents spilled out like the viscid liquid from a broken egg and dispersed in vivid crimson swirls to be lost from sight in the red tide of his blood.

The pain pulsed off and then on again, flickered off and disappeared altogether. The voice was gone from his mind. Reeling from the vicious assault, he reached a tendril of awareness toward the barrier, hoping the thin strand would escape the symbiot's notice.

Nothing followed. No tearing, no spasming, no torture. The barrier stretched against his gentle probe with the elasticity of melted cheese, and as he pushed further, allowed him contact with his body.

The sudden rush of physical sensation into the vacuum hit him with the intensity of an electrical storm. A violent mix of pleasure and pain assaulted his senses as he found his body responding with abandon in intimate physical union with another, his breath coming fast and his heart hammering at his ribs. His hips arched as his climax took him, the sensation powerful and enduring, overwhelming the pain messages from other parts of his suddenly re-connected self.

Something flickered at the corners of his memory, a thought his bruised and overloaded mind could not focus on, and yet he was certain he had forgotten something of great import. Before he could grasp it, it had slipped away again.

With great effort, he opened his eyes, but could not make them focus at all. Still breathing hard, he allowed himself to drift back into the comfortable peace that had been returned to him. The hypnotic crooning that had formed his mental wallpaper had ceased all together, leaving him exhausted and confused, but free of punishment and the fear of death.

For the first time in forty hours, he slept.

What the hell had she done? Jenna swallowed hard and stared at the white ceiling of her bedroom, showing grey in the darkness, seeing again the confusion in his amber eyes as he had almost found consciousness. If he should recall the events of the night, she would have a lot of explaining to do. A sudden surge of shame turned her stomach and sent a flush of heat through her face and neck. What magnetic force had caused her to ignore normal social taboos? Something outside her own desire had taken over—surely the rose-gold glow alone was evidence of something paranormal. The thought did nothing to dilute her guilt.

She slid from the bed, the darkness turning her pale nakedness into a figure of curving shadow, softly highlighted and contoured. Feeling for the switch, she flipped on the ensuite light, closed the door behind her and turned the shower on, pulling the curtain to contain the spray. Her face in the mirror was pale, the dark eyes shadowed, almost haunted. She met those eyes steadily until the steam misted the mirror over and she could see the guilt in them no more. Adding more cold water, she stood under the spray scrubbing at her body with a soapy loofah as if hoping to remove all evidence of the last half-hour.

She felt sick. There were no excuses, despite the strange circumstances. Violation. That was what she had done—violated a vulnerable other. One she was supposed to be assisting, caring for. She was appalled at how easy it had been to justify herself at the time. Her desire had been a runaway train, and she had proved herself to be no better than any of the men she had experienced and despised. Worse, in fact.

Anger powered her wrist as she wrenched the shower mixer hard right. Gasping in the steady stream of cold water, she realised she would not find a quick absolution. She towelled dry and slipped on the white cotton robe that always hung behind the door. She wiped the mirror and stood in front of it, uncoiling her hair from where she had pinned it away from the water. The small, stylised dragon embroidered on the left breast of the robe came into a sudden sharp focus, and with a quiet curse, she leaned against the cool tiled wall and buried her face in her towel.

There was no further sleep that night. She had the "guilts," as Tessa would say, good and proper. The faint lightening of the darkness found her in her lounge, bare feet tucked beneath her on the squashy blue couch she favoured. She leaned her head back with a heavy sigh, fondling Possum's ears as the sounds of traffic began on the streets outside. The local early risers beat the birds most mornings, providing a constant automotive version of the avian morning chorus that followed soon after. As the dawn reached in through the cream blinds, she stirred herself. Stretching her legs out experimentally, she felt the blood return to her feet and calves in a fuzzy tingling, like sherbert on the tongue.

Possum gave a wide yawn and stretched her legs one by one, paws flexed wide and claws extended, displaying the dark fur between her toes and prickling Jenna's thigh beneath the white robe. The small animal arched in a delicate leap from the couch and stretched again before making an exit through her catflap in the glass of the lounge doors.

Testing her legs, Jenna crossed the room and opened the blinds, fully retracting them to let in the pale wash of light that heralded the sunrise.

Thirst. Extreme thirst, and violent headache.

Neither of them hers.

A burst of pain then, enough to make her sit back down on the couch she was passing. She pressed trembling fingers to her temples, her eyes wide with fright, not comprehending the strange rush of sensation she was experiencing.

He was awake.

She knew it as surely as she knew her own state of consciousness. Standing again, her heart beating in a wild stress response to the strangeness, she gathered her courage and rolled it up into a hard little ball. So armed, she returned with reluctant steps to her bedroom. She pretended calm as she entered, and he watched her approach, his amber-gold eyes wary under drawn brows.

"Welcome back!" Her smile was as much to allay her own fears as his. He continued to survey her warily, and again she felt his thirst. *His* thirst. Panic rose in her throat, and she fought to control it before her face betrayed her. "Here." She poured water from the jug on the nightstand into a glass, and helped him raise himself to drink. Propping several pillows behind him, she would have held the glass to his mouth, but he raised his eyes to hers and took it himself. His arm shook as he drained the water in long swallows. She steadied him with a hand under his elbow, then poured more and offered it. He drank again before subsiding onto the pillows, every movement causing him pain. Pain she felt as a sharp-edged echo of sound, like the ring of a bounced ball in an empty gymnasium. His eyes closed and he covered them with one tanned hand, rolling dry lips into his mouth to moisten them with his tongue. He raked the hand back from his brow through the golden tousle of his hair, opened his eyes and fixed her with a penetrating gaze.

It was not so much a question as an accusation. She flushed and lowered her eyes, avoiding the issue she saw there. "I'm sure Verra will be here soon," she offered, trying to give him one familiar reference point amongst the strange environment he had woken to, hoping also to change the direction this encounter threatened to take.

"You have met Verra?" His voice was husky with disuse, and held the same soft lilt as the Wayfinder's. Finding common ground, she answered him with no small relief, her gaze still not meeting his. "Only briefly. She left you here. She said the . . . 'Way' . . . had brought you to me." She noted his confused expression. "I know your name is Cael; that you are 'not of this world,' whatever that means. I have seen her disappear. Actually, I've seen many things this last day or so that I don't understand, and I'm not sure I want to. But she cares for you very much, and I promised I would help her." With this last pronouncement, she raised her eyes to his face. She saw a curious mix of consternation, understanding, and pain that was not physical. "I'm Jenna," she added with a self-conscious smile.

He recalled the strength given in his hours of distressed torment as the symbiot had sought to discipline him to stillness, the comfort he had drawn from her link with him. He knew in a flash of memory and insight what it was that had disturbed him. The thing he knew he should remember had eluded him like a dream that fades on waking. It had been her body hot on his, giving and yet demanding.

Oh Gods. They had Bonded.

Chapter Five

Keystone Communion

Bonded.

After twenty-three years of careful preservation of his virginity, he realised he was no longer in control, no longer had anything to preserve. *May the Gods forgive me.*

His old tutor's words rang in his memory. *Keep a tight rein on yourself, boy, and do not be tempted into dalliance by any maiden who offers. An Empath cannot afford such a colossal mistake.* All his early training at the Guild had ensured he control his social interactions, reserving his innermost self for the privacy of family and close friends. The social taboos that constrained him so closely had been for his own protection. Once the bond was given, it was given for life. No second thoughts, no second chances, no repentance or regrets would change it. That was why the exhortation to "be sure" had been instilled into him from childhood. *Wait. Wait for a woman with whom you share the three,* he had been instructed. The three: love, trust and passion. Gods, they were inscribed on his heart.

The passion had not been difficult for a young man to find, but never had he found a woman who held his heart with all of the three. He once hoped Verra might be the one. While they shared a closeness akin to love and he trusted her with his life, he felt no great passion for her beyond an acknowledgment of her obvious beauty. Much to his chagrin and her confusion.

He looked into the deep indigo eyes of his bonded mate. Probing, he felt her fear, apprehension and shame. He could not, would not invade her mind to seek further than he could already read in her present emotional state. The conditioning against such things was so strong that he would consider it no better than rape. He laughed silently at the irony.

The bond would mean a "knowing" of her, a gradual revelation of soul and spirit, an understanding that each of them would have of the other: the essence of the person beneath the flesh. Day-to-day thoughts and emotions could be shielded from the other, but physical sensation, not being of the mind, could not. From this day on, they would share each other's pleasure and pain, ensuring a tight-knit unit of mutual nurture and protection, each caring for the other's needs, each responsible for the physical well-being of the other. This was the way of the bond, given only in first-time intimate union. He sighed, shifting his position and regretting the movement as pain lanced through his injured arm. What would this unfortunate incident imply for his future? The sexual initiation of an Empath had long been known as "waking the dragon," an apt description of the creature of fire and passion he would become when aroused. Bonding would normally mean the end of his celibacy. Bonding would *normally* have been *his* choice and his bond given, along with his virginity, to his chosen.

And it had been stolen from him. He swallowed, considering. With the dragon awake, self-control would be more arduous than ever. His jaw tightened. Then so be it. He would not surrender control of his life to a whim of Fate.

Jenna flushed. His silence spoke with more eloquence than anything he may have said at that moment. The ring of singing crystal provided a welcome diversion.

Verra stepped into the room from the hazy curtain of the Way, the fresh scent of the ocean clinging to her garments and spicing the air. A wide grin split her beautiful face as she hurried the few steps to the bed, taking Cael in a long embrace that threatened to crush the breath from him.

"Gods, *chiaran*, I had not thought to see you alive," she murmured into his hair. As she turned from him, he grimaced with the pain her enthusiastic embrace had cost him. Jenna had caught the echo of it, and it was still etched on her face as Verra caught her up in a similar wild hug.

"Jenna!" The Wayfinder's tears spilled over. "Whatever happened here, I owe you his life." Verra brushed at her face, wiping away tears of relief as she sank down to sit on the bed at his side. As the Wayfinder and the Empath communicated, Jenna retreated to the kitchen. "Whatever happened here." Such a loaded statement.

She filled the kettle and took a ceramic teapot from a shelf. Deciding that chamomile was what they all needed, she dropped in several tea bags, adding two of St John's wort as an afterthought.

Possum rubbed at her ankles, and she poured a little milk into a saucer and set it on the floor. She loaded a tray with cups, the teapot and a small pot of honey and returned to the bedroom, depositing the tray on the dresser just inside the door.

As she poured, she listened as Cael related his battle with the sentient symbiot. He described its reproduction, its promise of enhancement, the disciplined lack of movement, and the pain visited on him in punishment. Verra listened, her green eyes wide.

Jenna set two steaming cups on the bedside table and offered honey. Settling on the wicker chair, she sipped her tea, and listened. Again, she found her perception of reality turned upside down and inside out.

>*I have to tell her, Jenna.*<

She jumped in alarm as his low voice spoke inside her head, and tea slopped over her hand. Sucking the heat of the spilt tea from her fingers, her eyes darted to his face as the slow flush again crept over her own.

He glanced at her briefly. >*It is done. I know you feel shame. Perhaps you should. But it would be ungracious of me not to thank you for my life.*<

Her eyes were huge with puzzlement, both at his meaning and his mode of communication.

He met Jenna's questioning look as Verra stirred honey into her tea. >*When you . . . that is, when we . . .*<

She bit her lip and gave a slight nod.

>*The symbiot and its offspring were destroyed—its hold broken and removed by the increased flow of my blood. I will show you, if you are not afraid . . .*<

Again she nodded, and a thought-picture flashed into her mind, its meaning and content clearer than a thousand words could have made it. She understood. She recalled her own pulse racing as their sexual excitement had reached its peak.

Sex had saved his life? Well. This situation just got stranger and stranger.

"Verra, the hearing of this will be difficult." He took the Wayfinder's fingers in his hand. >*Do not stay if you do not wish to,*< he sent to Jenna. She needed no further encouragement to escape the room, grateful he did not require her to sit and listen as he expounded her shame. For such a young man, he was displaying remarkable composure and mature consideration for the feelings of all concerned.

She flopped onto the blue couch and waited, feeling like

a witness outside a courtroom. Her stomach growled and she thought of breakfast, but dismissed it. Reaching for the stereo remote, she started one of her relaxation discs, hoping the sounds of birdsong and falling rain would ease her mood.

>*It is well.*< she heard a short time later. She inhaled and let out a long sigh. Still she sat, having no desire to face Verra's censure, but heard the other woman's approach over the gentle sounds of a waterfall.

Verra had been crying. Her face was pale but composed. "May I sit?"

Wordlessly, Jenna made room for her. They sat, cross-legged bookends, facing each other from the ends of the wide couch. Jenna pulled the white robe around her legs, feeling self-conscious and vulnerable, still naked beneath the soft towelling.

Verra gave an unsteady sigh, her green eyes luminous and sad. "You do not know what you have done, do you?" came the quiet question.

The truth floored her.

Her already stretched mind tried to compute all the implications of what she heard—tried and failed. What the hell to do now? What sort of a dimension was it where a simple sexual encounter had such exacting consequences?

She and Cael were . . . bonded. She knew it for truth. It was borne out in her new awareness of him. She felt the pain of his injuries, his weakness and nausea, the headache he had woken with. She felt it all, not as pain in her own body, but rather as an echo is heard, as a whisper does not carry the impact of a shout.

Verra did not berate her, nor blame or censure her, nor cause her to feel more shame than she already did. In a matter-of-fact way she outlined the effects of the bond, although Jenna was aware of the pain it cost her.

"You love him, don't you?" Jenna asked at one stage. Verra's smile was wistful, her reply truthful, driving a knife-edge of remorse through Jenna to reside with the guilt.

They ate a quiet breakfast together. Cael refused food, but took the nourishing liquid concoction she made. Verra would not transport him through the Way until he was well enough to stand, and Jenna reckoned on his presence for another day or two at least. She had to clear the air between them.

"I need to . . . talk to Cael," she said. Verra raised a brow, her green eyes suddenly cool. "If I may have a little private time with him, that is?"

Verra's lips thinned a fraction. "Of course. You do not need my permission, Jenna. I will leave you alone."

Heat rose in Jenna's cheeks as she returned to the bedroom. Opening his eyes from a doze, Cael blinked at her sleepily. She shut the door and leaned against it. "I . . . want you to know how sorry I am." She swallowed and took a deep breath. "It was inexcusable of me. I . . . don't know what came over me, but I . . . oh, shit." She pressed her hands over her hot cheeks. "I'm embarrassed and ashamed. There's not much else I can say except sorry."

"You are *sorry?*" He stared at her, his eyes hard points of topaz. "I appreciate the sentiment, Jenna."

"I couldn't have known what would happen, Cael! This is—no, *you are*—completely outside my experience." Her heart thumped against her ribs. She shook her head in frustration. "I'm a normal person. This is a normal world. Things like this just don't happen here!"

He held up a hand. "Stop. There is no need for you to justify yourself. It will change nothing." The hardness in his eyes remained. "You acted in ignorance, I understand that, but I find it difficult to reconcile such a transgression." He rubbed a hand over his eyes and dragged it back through his hair, leaving finger-furrows among the gold. "It is a deeply ingrained protocol, Jenna. An Empath is conditioned against casual coupling, for obvious reasons. The sleeping dragon would have warned a Camarrhan woman from me, but you did not know its significance. We each have to deal with the consequences now."

Jenna folded her arms over her chest and averted her eyes. "Some consequences," she muttered.

"As you say," he assented wearily. "You do not yet understand the complexities of it." A line appeared between his brows. He closed his eyes. "There is nothing more to be said."

Feeling dismissed, Jenna picked up the empty breakfast cup from the bedside table. She felt his weariness, his constant pain. What he could feel from her, she hated to think, hoping he was unaware of the lustful feelings he inspired in her. While embarrassing to remember, their encounter had also been a sensual feast, brief as it was. One she would very much like to repeat. Flushing again, she left the room.

She tended him in silence for the most part after that, not knowing what to say, fearing to make things worse by saying the wrong thing. Verra hovered in the doorway while Jenna changed the dressing on his side. He watched her quietly. *Time to break the silence again.* "How *did* you come by this?" she asked.

"I was shot."

She waited, but he was not forthcoming. "So it *was* an arrow?" He nodded briefly. She peered closer at the wound, pressing with gentle fingers at the raised, red edges, looking for signs of infection but finding none. He flinched, sucking in his breath. The tattooed dragon twitched in its sleep as the muscle beneath contracted momentarily. "Sorry," she apologised, laying a hand on his shoulder and darting a glance at his face.

"No matter. I have had worse." His jaw muscle jumped.

As always, renegade strands of golden hair hung over his brow. She resisted the temptation to brush them back from his amber eyes, now so intent on her hands as she re-dressed the wound. The thought of him leaving was not one she entertained gladly. She began to realise she was en-joying his presence, despite his cool manner. Shit. Who was she kidding? A mild infatuation had begun, no matter her careful barriers.

He pulsed polite thanks to her as she finished. His silent communications intrigued her. The pulses of feeling, the images and words spoken into her mind did not take her by surprise quite as much as they had in the beginning. Strangeness seemed to be becoming the norm.

His headache had become steadily worse. She rubbed at her own temples, bothered by the echo of discomfort, and touched gentle fingers to the swelling beneath his hair. No change. Looking into his eyes, she noted a vagueness that had not been there before, and feeling uneasy, moved her hand slowly across his line of vision once or twice.

>*I cannot focus properly.*< he sent.

Jenna frowned. "Since when?"

>*Since I awoke. It has worsened.*<

"What is it?" Verra had watched her working, but had not been privy to the silent communications.

"I don't know." Jenna searched her memory. These were symptoms of concussion, but it was a little late after the in-jury for that to be so. "What else can you tell me?" she asked, running through likely diagnoses in her mind.

He spoke audibly. "Nothing to tell."

"Show me then," she requested, with a light touch on his hand. He pulsed an image at her. Drowsiness being fought off, the pain of the headache intensified by the attempt to focus, a slight darkness around the edges of his vision, frustration at his weakness and slow recovery. She smiled at this last, but her concern grew.

Haematoma.

"Head injuries sometimes bleed slowly into the brain." She wrinkled her forehead in thought. "It creates pressure, resulting in symptoms such as these. Without treatment, it can lead to confusion, or coma at the worst." It was apparent they were not out of the woods yet. She sighed. They would have to return to the hospital, with all the difficulties that would entail.

If she was right, he required surgery.

They spoke in low, urgent voices, arguing together over their options. Verra stood, arms folded against her chest, hips cocked to one side, her green eyes adamant. "It did not open, Jenna. I cannot *make* a Way; I can only focus the need and search for one."

Jenna set her brows at a dangerous angle. "Then take us to the hospital through the Way," she pleaded. "You said you could go back to a place you had been before . . ."

"Jenna, you are not listening to me. If your hospital could help him, the *Way would have opened there!* Do you understand now? If you take him there by another means, he will likely die," she added as Jenna headed for the hall and her car keys.

Jenna pressed her fingers to her aching temples, not believing this could happen after they had come so far. Cael's condition had deteriorated. He drifted in and out of consciousness, barely able to supply a coherent answer to the simplest question. He did not seem to know where he was or what had happened. Although frantic to help him, she was completely without resource. She wanted to weep with the powerlessness she felt, but had denied herself weeping for years. Verra had "sustained" him, using the Keystone, but it would not do for long.

The link. She had almost forgotten. The strengthening power of what Verra had identified as the link was worth trying. She spun and left the perplexed Wayfinder to follow her down the hall to the bedroom.

Rose-gold light surrounded their hands as before.

"What is it you do with the Keystone?" Jenna inquired.

"Not something that is easy to explain." Verra settled herself next to them and eyed their linked hands. "You should control the flow of strength you deliver. The aura only happens when you are using a full-needs link—it will leave you exhausted. Try to believe he does not need your help as much as you want to give it."

Jenna tried, her forehead wrinkling with concentration. The glow remained.

Verra leaned forward and tapped Jenna's wrist. "Concentrate. Try relaxing your concern for him and pull back the emotional energy."

That was asking a lot. Jenna closed her eyes and swallowed hard. She was already entertaining feelings for him that had not stirred for years, and the prospect of losing him so soon was unfair. Trying another tactic, she recalled every hurtful thing about men that she could bring to mind. The glow began to recede, and gradually disappeared over the next several minutes.

"Good. Now you can sustain him while maintaining

your own reserves." Verra reached for the Keystone. "The stone attunes to the pattern of the wearer," she began, turning the caged stone in her fingers. "When you know someone well, their pattern becomes familiar to you. Look into the stone and see what you may."

Jenna leaned over the steady rise and fall of the muscular chest and studied the stone. In its depth was a small, gilded galaxy of dancing light. Gold, orange and red abounded in that depth, and as she looked, the points of light seemed to move, to circle and form waves of pulsing energy. Again the light tap on her wrist.

"You must use more than your eyes, Jenna. The secret is in the knowing. Try to find what you know of him in the pattern."

Jenna rolled her eyes at the cryptic advice but concentrated harder, redirecting her attention to the pulsing arrays of light in the stone. The room receded in her awareness as she focussed deeply.

Oh! A wave of gold and orange motes combined in a synchronised pulse. Strength and physical beauty. *Yes.* A single row of gold pulses: courage. And then, chivalry, a row of red behind the gold. Integrity pulsed as white gold, a triple wave this time. Loyalty, alternating orange and red, intertwined with the pulsing gold and red of self-discipline. Finally, a deep red bank of intense glowing motes pulsed passion at her, causing a physical reaction she hoped Verra was unaware of. *Oh yes.* If that was "knowing," it was a rare pleasure.

She lingered, finding small discrepancies, small breaks in the energy waves. Her awareness was now fully in the stone. The essence that was Cael surrounded her, and she felt embraced and protected, safe and cherished. In the distance of the pattern, an intense knot of pulsing white heat drew her attention. Curious, her thought-self drifted through the pattern, feeling heat and a shiver of desire as she crossed the deep red bank. The hand she extended toward the knot was indistinct and ephemeral, the arm merely a shadowy tendril. She touched the aberration.

White light exploded in her mind as she felt herself flung with great force out of the stone.

Gasping, her eyes watering, she found herself back beside the bed, still linked to him. Verra watched her, concern evident on her face. Ignoring her, Jenna threw her awareness back into the stone, back through the pattern, and confronted the arrogant white heat with an attitude all of her own. She surrounded the pulsing amorphous mass with her shadowy tendril arms, not touching it but confining the light, drawing it into herself. Each pulsation vibrated through her arms, manifesting as pain before passing through her thought-self and disappearing from sight and sense. For some time she remained, confining and restraining the knot, pulsing it away through herself. Gradually, the intensity of the heat and light lessened. The glow faded to dull red, dimmed, and made a final disappearance.

With a sense of triumph and invigoration, she moved to the next aberration, less intense but just as painful to process. She found four more after that first fierce challenge, and pulsed them all away. After each one disappeared, she felt renewed exhilaration, empowered enough to continue forever.

She knew she had helped him. More than helped. She was happy to drift among the essence of his pattern, feeling more alive than she had for a long time. Alive and oh-so-valuable.

Cael stirred, flexed the fingers of the hand that still held Jenna's, and opened his eyes. Her forehead lay warm on his arm, and he could only see the back of her head where her complex braid began high on the crown, the intertwining strands of chocolate and bronze running like a thick cable down the middle of her back.

He raised his eyebrows at his Wayfinder. >*She is well?*<

Verra's worried expression spoke volumes. "She has not returned, *chiaran*. I fear she is lost in the stone."

His eyes narrowed, now fully focussed and alert. "How did she come by this knowledge?"

Verra dropped her gaze and answered him, her tone miserable. "There was no Way, Cael. You were at risk. She was using the link to try to help you . . ."

"You instructed her?"

"I did."

"But neglected to complete the instruction, it seems." His voice was grim.

Verra bowed her head. "I did not think she would be able to access the stone. She was merely curious." Her forehead creased into a frown. "I should have warned her. Experiencing the essence of another is always seductive, and yours is uncommonly strong. She does not know how to break free. Forgive me, *chiaran*, I meant her no harm."

Cael reached with gentle precision into Jenna's mind. He called her name, heard no response. He withdrew his arm with care from beneath her, and held the back of her neck under the thick braid, massaging slowly with his thumb to provide a physical focus, and continued to call her name in the empty corners of her mind.

Eventually he heard a far cry, and moved toward the direction from which it had come. >*Come back, Jenna.*<

I can't, she wailed in his mind, *I can't find you . . .*

>*I am here. I will not leave. Call, and I will find you.*< His sending was reassuring, but he knew the dangers of ex-

ploring another's mind—too deep and it would be difficult to return. Still calling, he ventured further. Soon, he sensed she was close, so near he could hear her thought-self sobbing like a child in frightened despair, and he cast himself toward the sound into the outer edges of unfamiliar territory.

Contact.

Ephemeral and gossamer thin, but he had her.

Casting about in directionless dark, he held her, calming, soothing, drawing her along with him as he sought to connect again with his physical self. He found the anchor he had put in place, and focussed on the sensation of his hand moving on her neck, drawing her back with him, back through the stillness, back to herself. Withdrawing from her, he let his hand rest on the soft warmth of her neck. She gave a violent shudder, raised both hands to her head and began to shake with distressed sobbing. Verra's arms went about her, holding her close as she murmured soothing words and stroked her hair. Her eyes met Cael's over the top of Jenna's head as he pulsed reassurance and calm to them both.

They comforted her then. Jenna lay between the two of them, cocooned in body heat and closeness of spirit, feeling as fulfilled and content as she used to feel held close in her mother's embrace. They surrounded and protected her with their bodies and their concern, all agendas and differences suspended in the face of her need.

Surfacing at last, she reflected on the momentous events of the past few days. She recalled her experiences of the pattern within the stone, and raised her fingers to Cael's temple, feeling for the swelling she knew would no longer be there.

It was not.

She sat up and looked closely, seeing only the faint yellow-ochre of old bruising beneath the tawny hair. Verra sat also, arms around her knees as she watched Jenna investigate her patient's body. Cael's steady gaze rested on Verra as he submitted to Jenna's touch.

Jenna removed the dressing from his wounded side, touching new pink skin against the gold where the arrow puncture had been. Like a child on Christmas morning, she unwrapped his arm, again revealing healthy new scar tissue, a fine line from shoulder to elbow. Verra's eyes widened until the whites were visible all the way around the ocean-green of her irises.

"My knee is likewise restored," he added to the gift pile, "and I feel no bruising at all."

Jenna squealed with delight and took his face between her hands, planting a firm kiss on his cheek before turning to Verra and doing the same. She sobered quickly, recalling their situation, and drew her arms around herself, exultant and relieved that she had saved him, but unsure of how she had done it, or what that might mean.

Verra's eyes were still wide. She divided her gaze between Jenna and Cael, then examined her runed wristbands as if searching for a flaw in the leather. "Only a holder of the nine can do that." The flat statement lay still where it was delivered.

>*Truth.*<

"But there *are* none besides Galaen!"

>*Hmm?*<

"There are none . . ." Verra's words died as she turned to Jenna, her expression as startled as a rabbit caught in headlights.

"A holder of the what?" Jenna tucked stray bronze strands back into her braid.

"A Healer from the old days," Verra responded. "There is only one on our world now. She is the last, and one of the Hand, inaccessible to common folk."

"The 'nine' refers to the stones a Healer carried," Cael said, "passed from mother to daughter as was the gene. It is a female inheritance only. Men do not heal."

Men don't heal? Tell me something I don't know, boyfriend, Jenna thought. Suddenly recalling his rescue of her thought-self from the stone, she was ashamed of her cynicism. She slid off the end of the bed and crossed to her dressing table. Opening a drawer, she extracted a small blue velvet case and returned with it. Sitting on the end of the bed, she opened the case, displaying the contents to the Empath and the Wayfinder.

"Did they look like this?" she asked, her eyes anxious with the question.

As it turned out, no they did not.

Set into fine gold, her necklace of nine perfectly matched opals did not resemble that of a holder of the nine. A holder kept her stones like Cael's, caged individually in fine silver wire and attached to a braided cord worn around her neck. Easily detachable, each stone was available to be attuned to a patient needing advanced aid. The kind of aid she had given to Cael.

As a Wayfinder, Verra owned five of the stones, one of which Cael wore permanently. Two sets of eyes viewed Jenna with speculation.

"Who was your mother?" Verra asked.

Jenna shrugged. "Lliahna. She was an ordinary type of person. Not outstanding in any way, but a good mother to me. My father destroyed her with his affairs and his drinking. I think she gave up on life fairly early. These stones were my grandmother's. I never knew her. Her name was kind of Asian. Chiahn." Jenna owed her height, her generous fall of hair and unusual eyes to her mother.

"You must return to Camarrhan with us . . ." Verra broke off at Cael's warning gaze. "*Chiaran,* she *must!* Look what she has done here—the evidence is before you!"

Cael gave her a dark scowl of disagreement. "We will continue as we were," he pronounced. "We have knowledge now. We can fight battle sickness—it is one less weapon the Althar can hold against us."

"She is a *holder of the nine,*" Verra persisted stubbornly. "Camarrhan needs her; we need her. *You* will need her, if you will but admit it."

Jenna sat examining her hands, fresh misery lancing through her. He did not want her. Well, that's no more than she deserved. She had made herself no better than an inconvenience, a problem with no immediate solution. A holder of the nine and a person of value? Not here. Here she was only Jenna Wade: nurse, gym junkie and isolated Ice Queen.

"Take me with you," she asked, unable to keep the plea from her tone. "There is nothing here for me to stay for. I have no family. I had no . . . magic . . . until you arrived into my life. I don't understand what is happening to me, but I want to find out. If you leave me, I will never know. *Please.* Let me come with you."

There. She had said it. Leaving them to make what they would of it, she escaped to the kitchen.

Verra faced him with a look that should have denied argument. She knew the reason for his reluctance, and spoke to the Leader in him, the man she knew held the welfare of Camarrhan in his heart.

73

"The Guild will want her, Cael. How many have been lost for the want of a Healer?" The systematic elimination of those Leaders with magic had been slow, but she knew many could have been saved.

"She will be a danger to herself . . ." His expression was fierce.

"Then we will protect her."

"Our world is too different to this—she would never adapt."

"Her mind was strong enough to accommodate the shocks it has had since we arrived. There is no reason to believe her reaction to Camarrhan will be any different."

"This world is full of comfort and convenience. How will she re-learn the living of a *day,* let alone weeks or months?"

"Gradually, *chiaran!* She is strong. And she greatly desires to come."

"And I greatly desire her to remain. Gods, Verra! It will be difficult for me. How am I to explain a bonded mate with whom I choose not to share my life?"

Verra had waited for the real issue to surface. "Your honour is therefore more important to you?" His honour was beyond question, she knew, and it hurt her to speak to him this way. "Or is it your future discomfort that you seek to avoid? I would urge you to reconsider. You need not make the bond known. There will be difficulty, yes, but you are no stranger to that."

"Difficulty? Gods! Whenever the woman looks at me, I feel her desire. Whenever she recalls . . . our encounter, her body responds and I know it." He growled in frustration. "I will not be manipulated into a relationship not of my choosing, not after so long. It is still my life to live as I determine. Alone, if I have to!"

Verra sighed. She knew his newly awakened sexuality

74

would be enough of a . . . *difficulty* for him without having to constantly experience Jenna's tensions as well. Exactly where that left his future prospects she did not know. She did, however, understand that his needs were secondary. His life was Camarrhan.

Chapter Six

Return to Kereál

Jenna looked in on Cael. She smiled, sensing his impatience, knowing the frustration he felt at his infirmity. The healing had left him as weak as an infant, just as Verra had predicted it would. For the first day, he had been unable even to sit up unaided. Apparently a side effect of the . . . magic.

Magic. She stifled a manic chuckle. I will *not* laugh. I am *not* crazy. Cramming the last of her carefully chosen belongings into her hiking pack, she let her gaze roam the apartment. This had been her life for a number of years, and she had no idea when she would return. A shiver of anticipation ran the length of her spine. She wondered about the world she would soon find herself in. Verra had told her some of what to expect and how to deport herself, and she was grateful for that. Tugging the straps closed, she sighed and smoothed back several stray wisps of hair.

Thank God for Tessa. She would move in tomorrow, only too glad to abandon her own digs to play caretaker to Jenna's luxurious accommodations. The longer, the better. Possum and the apartment would be in safe hands until she returned. She had said her goodbyes to the cat with a few tears. Suffocated by the attention, Possum had wriggled free of her embrace and now sat on the garden wall, back turned and tail twitching, ignoring her completely.

Jenna propped the envelope containing last minute explanations and instructions beside the telephone—the one place she could guarantee Tessa would see it. Her letter of resignation to the hospital had been harder to write. Never comfortable with lies, Jenna's hand had trembled when she penned the falsehood of an elderly, sick and frail aunt who had no one left but Jenna to care for her. She squared her shoulders and shook off her misgivings. Her life had changed radically, for better or for worse, and she may as well just get on with it. There was no undoing things.

On Verra's advice, she had dressed simply. Old Levi's belted at the hips in her usual fashion, brown leather walking boots and her usual body-hugging singlet disguised by a loose white linen shirt. She removed her watch and had not packed any item that could be considered "technology."

Verra had explained the sanctions on her as a Wayfinder. She must never bring a foreign technology through the Way to Camarrhan. The land's ruling body, the Hand, intended to maintain the balance of life at its optimum. Their experience of other worlds had led them to the opinion that nothing but pollution, decay and destruction came from "technology." It was a thing to be abhorred and avoided.

Jenna sat back on her heels and sighed as Verra pronounced them ready. Tying her thick curls back with a leather thong, Verra turned questioning green eyes on Jenna.

"Are you sure?"

"I'm afraid, Verra, but never surer about anything." Her face tightened. She lifted her chin in determination. She wouldn't show just how apprehensive she was. Together they entered her bedroom where Cael waited, dressed in leather breeches still stained with his blood despite all their scrubbing.

The Wayfinder closed her eyes briefly, then raised her

wrists and cross-matched two of the runes on her wrist-bands. Singing crystal preceded the shimmer, and Verra widened the Way to allow them all passage. Throwing Jenna's pack through the haze, she turned to the bed, and the two of them assisted Cael to his feet.

He swayed and leaned heavily on them, an arm draped around each of their shoulders. "Go quickly," he cautioned, his face whitening. "I will not be upright for long." She exchanged a quick glance with Verra, and the three of them lurched into the shimmer of the Way.

"Mama, Mama, Verra's coming!" Mi'Cael ran up the steps to the front door, banging it open and hurtling, in the way of small boys, through the house in search of his mother. She ran to meet him and he took her hand in a grubby grip, tugging her toward the door. She followed him outside, almost stumbling over a pack on the bottom step.

Three figures emerged from the shimmering curtain that hung at the Waypoint, several yards from the front steps. Illiahn smiled in greeting at her brother and his Wayfinder, but her smile soon faded into concern. Cael blinked and shook his head as if trying to clear his vision. He managed a crooked grin before his knees gave way beneath him. His eyes rolled up. The two women staggered as they took the full weight of him.

Verra smiled ruefully as she and the strange woman disentangled themselves from his limp embrace and lowered him to the ground. "He is all right, Illiahn, just very weak—nothing is suffering but his dignity," Verra reassured as she closed the Way behind them. Illiahn sank down beside her brother in dismay. *Oh, brother of mine, what have you done now?* Cradling his head in her lap and brushing dust from his gold-stubbled cheek, she looked a question at Verra and her companion.

"Illiahn, meet Jenna Wade. Is Brenn here? Or Telsen? We could use some help to get him inside."

"Well met, Jenna-wade." Illiahn blinked at Jenna's unusual clothing. Where had the woman come from?

"Well met to you too, Illiahn," Jenna-wade answered. Telsen's tall figure erupted from the doorway of the barn across the yard and loped toward them with Mi'Cael in his wake.

"Tel!" Verra greeted him with a quick hug. "I see Mi'Cael is as resourceful as ever. Hello, sprout . . ." She squeezed the boy's shoulder, and he grinned at her and wriggled away to stand by Illiahn.

"Mama? Is Uncle sleeping?"

Illiahn smiled up at her son with a shake of her head. She turned to Telsen. "Will you take him inside, Tel?"

With a curious glance in Jenna's direction, Telsen knelt beside Cael and raised one limp arm, lifting him from Illiahn's knees. He dropped a broad shoulder into Cael's belly, grasped the back of his breeches and stood, staggering a little under the weight of him. The small procession trailed him up the steps and into the house. Illiahn swept ahead of him in the wide hallway, and Telsen followed her skirts into the large room at the back of the house that was at once the kitchen and living area. He deposited Cael on a low couch where she indicated and hovered as she made him comfortable. He turned then, his dark eyes finding Verra.

"He will live?" He asked the question lightly, but anguish lurked in the words. Verra turned a gentle smile on him.

"This time, Tel. This time."

He exhaled in a rush and sat down.

★ ★ ★ ★ ★

Jenna flicked a glance at Verra as Illiahn searched her twin for injury. Verra frowned. Laying a reassuring hand on Illiahn's shoulder, she spoke in a soothing tone. "There is nothing for you to do, *chiara*. He is healed—rest and sleep are all he needs now. Come and sit with us, there is much to tell." Verra seated herself on a long bench at the heavy wooden table and motioned Jenna to sit. "By rights, he should be dead," she began. "I did not tell you he took an Althar death-shaft before we left." Telsen and Illiahn turned twin expressions of horror on her. Jenna frowned. *Death-shaft? Ah, the arrow.*

Verra continued. "I *could* not, knowing what that means. But I found a Way, and it took us to Jenna." Verra looked sideways at Jenna. Heat rose in Jenna's face, and she shifted her gaze to the wooden rafters above her.

"She healed him of battle sickness; she healed him of three major wounds; she linked and sustained him with her life-force when he was close to death. And she is a holder of the nine." Silence greeted her pronouncements. Two pairs of startled eyes, dark brown and amber, fastened on the discomfited Jenna.

"We owe you much, Jenna-wade," Illiahn said, "but how can this be? None have ever recovered from battle sickness, and forgive me, but you do not appear to be of this world. Even here, healings such as this have been unknown for many years."

At Verra's gesture, Jenna drew the necklace of opals from her shirt pocket. "This was my grandmother's. She died before I was born. My mother passed it to me before *she* died. As to the healing, I don't know how it happened. I think I could do it again; I remember the . . . feel of it, but I can't explain what I did." *Shit, I don't know what I did.*

Illiahn rose, frowning, and took a cloth from a drawer. Water splashed from a stoneware pitcher as she wet the cloth in a basin of dull metal set into the vast bench. She returned to the couch where Cael still lay senseless and wiped his face gently, leaving the cloth across his forehead. Mi'Cael sat on the other side of the couch, his small face a perfect miniature of his uncle's, only softer and rounder with the tenderness of the very young.

He raised serious amber eyes to his mother. "Uncle's waking up soon," he stated.

"I hope so, my darling," she responded, raising her eyes to the child's grubby countenance. "Go and wash your dirty face so he can see a nice clean you when he does." The child slid from his seat, paused to give his mother a fierce hug, and went out the kitchen door. Jenna heard a metallic squeak followed by the splash of water. Illiahn returned to the kitchen and sat beside Verra. "Who are you, Jenna-wade? How is it you can use this world's magic?"

"I don't know." Jenna shrugged, suddenly reminded of her difference to everyone she had known in Auckland. The years of voluntary isolation wrapped in work, exercise and her own company seemed like someone else's life. "I don't have a sense of belonging anywhere, really. I don't know much about my family—I'm sorry, Illiahn, I have no answers for you, but you don't need to be suspicious of me. I mean no harm, and Verra says I may be able to help you defend yourselves against the Althar."

"She can." Cael's voice was unsteady as he raised himself on the supporting cushions. His sister ran to him and he held her close, smiling as Mi'Cael joined the fond welcome, wriggling under their arms to press his small cheek against his uncle's face.

"Gods, it is good to see you," he breathed. "I thought I

81

would not be coming home this time."

Illiahn shushed him affectionately. "We have missed you, *chiaran*. Brenn will want to talk long with you when you are well."

"I am well," he growled, but he pulled on her hand to sit himself upright and supported himself on both arms as he swung his legs to the floor. The corners of Jenna's mouth twitched as she suppressed a smile. She knew he resented his weakness, and she said nothing, leaving him to decide for himself how well he really was.

He raised a fist in salute to Telsen, who acknowledged him in kind, relief and pleasure mingled on his face. Cael leaned his back against the wall, his cool gaze resting on Jenna. "I see you have all met. Where *is* Brenn? I must speak to him on several matters."

"In the village with the girls. They will return before supper." Illiahn filled the large kettle for tea. The kitchen smelled most deliciously of baking bread, and the atmosphere was heavy with the heat from the wood stove, although the window shutters were thrown wide open to the morning air.

>*I do not want them to know.*<

Jenna grimaced as she caught his sending. *I expected that.* She gave him an almost imperceptible nod, shifting her gaze to the open windows. Lightly forested hills rolled behind the house, and in the distance beyond, the peaks of a mountain range thrust themselves in ragged splendour against the paintbox-blue of the sky, stretching as far as her limited view could see. Nothing she had seen so far seemed in the least bit alien. In fact, she could almost believe she was in a rustic country village somewhere in her own world, as if she had stepped back in time. She had certainly seen similar places portrayed in many movies.

"Jenna?"

She came back to herself with a start. Telsen was watching her with a curious expression. He held out a steaming cup, and she took it, smiling her thanks. The brew proved to be an herbal tea, not familiar, but pleasant and light scented.

She sipped in silence and listened as the others caught up on general news and the state of the Althar situation. She studied the faces around her. Verra, face half obscured by a curtain of tight-curled dark hair as she regaled Illiahn with details of their travels off-world. The blonde woman listened with a slight frown, golden eyes intent on the tale. She was so much like Cael. Dark gold hair highlighted with honey streaks and tied back with a leather thong; a smooth brow over deep amber eyes as clear as Steinlager; a straight nose and a full mouth that smiled readily.

A charcoal portrait on the wall behind her depicted a family: a serene Illiahn next to a tall, rugged and smiling man Jenna took to be Brenn; Mi'Cael, eyes bright and laughing; and two small girls, wide-eyed and serious, one in each of their parents' arms. The artist must have known the family well to capture such soul and feeling in the subjects. Quite a talent. Her attention shifted to the men.

Cael remained on the couch, but had conceded to his condition and stopped trying to stay upright. He lay back on cushions against the wall, one long leg stretched out in front of him, the other bent and flopped comfortably sideways on the dark green fabric of the seat. He was pale and his eyes dark-shadowed, but his face was animated as he talked to Telsen about their new understanding of battle sickness and the symbiot that was its cause. The dark-eyed man leaned his elbows on his knees and listened, interjecting questions, his jaw tightening as he understood the implications. Telsen's eyes closed occasionally, and she realised Cael shared a little of his experience in mind pictures to aid his friend's understanding of the symbiot.

She never grew tired of looking at him. Such a beautiful male. Her eyes strayed over the length of his body. The familiar heat rose within her.

>*Stop!*< His sudden sending startled her. He raked her with such an intense look that Telsen turned in surprise to spot the unlucky recipient. She coloured and looked away, and then heard in a more gentle tone.

>*Please. Remember the bond. Whatever you feel affects me too.*<

Telsen rubbed a large hand through his hair, raised dark brows and looked questioningly at the Empath, who only shook his head and continued the conversation, leaving him to wonder at the transgression.

Also unaware of the silent exchange, Verra caught her eye and smiled. "I will take you to the Guild," she began. "Not now, of course, but soon, when you have become acclimatised to Camarrhan. I believe you may find the answers to some of your questions there. At the least, they can assess your abilities; at best, your stones may be recognised."

Illiahn reached over and took her hand. "Thank the Gods you were able to help my brother, however you did it. A true holder of the nine has not occurred in many years. Please forgive me for expressing doubt—you are welcome in my house, Jenna-wade, for as long as you wish to stay." Her clear eyes conveyed her sincerity, and Jenna was grateful for her words.

She smiled. "I'm just Jenna. The 'Wade' bit's not important."

Afternoon passed into evening. Brenn had long since arrived home, bearing his two small daughters before and behind him on his horse. Jenna liked the large blond man as soon as she met him. He had an easy manner, a kind, broad face and very blue eyes. The twin girls were almost three years old, Illiahn said. They were white-blonde moppets with large blue eyes like their father, fine featured and fair-skinned. Myst and Raen, they were named, and had been put to bed in the upstairs nursery with a protesting Mi'Cael shortly after supper. She smiled, remembering his indignant protests. "But Mama! I am *five* now!"

Brenn and Cael were deep in conversation in the living area of the large room. The soft light from oil lamps in wall sconces played over their features and reflected in their eyes. Jenna sat with Illiahn in the kitchen area, answering Twenty Questions about life in Auckland. Illiahn's last question was most direct. "Are you wed?" Jenna didn't miss Illiahn's appraising glance at her brother.

Telsen went in search of the absent Verra and found her outside, sitting on a long bench beneath the shuttered kitchen window, gazing at the night sky. He sat beside her, nursing a mug of herbal brew. "Why so quiet, Wayfinder?"

Verra turned pensive green eyes on him. "Just thinking, Tel." The crease in her brow deepened, and a hint of moisture in her eyes glistened, reflecting the starlight. "Sometimes life just does not happen the way you think it should." She dropped her head, her fall of dark hair obscuring her face.

He waited. The scent of crushed herbs rose in the still night air, mingled with traces of smoke from the kitchen chimney. A nightbird called into the stillness. She raised her face, pulled her hair back from her shoulders and gathered it behind her neck. She looked at him then, with a tight smile.

"I thank you for caring, my friend. There is nothing I can tell you—only that things are not quite as they were, and not quite as they seem."

Telsen chuckled. "I thank *you,* my friend, for the riddle! I have not heard anything quite so cryptic for a long time." He took her chin in his hand and turned her face to him. "Verra, you do not need to tell me any more than you wish to about anything. Any time you choose, I will listen. And if you choose not, that is also well, but your pain disturbs me and I would help you if I can."

"Ah, but Tel, you have already. You are a balm for a tender spirit." She stroked his cheek with a light finger and stood.

He struggled against the desire to say more, to touch her, embrace her, but only followed her slim form with his eyes as she glowed for a brief moment in the pool of light from the open doorway, and returned inside.

He had loved the Wayfinder for two years. And she wanted his closest friend. Verra was right. Sometimes life was like that. Spirited, keen-witted and as beautiful as a spring morning, Verra had captivated him from the first time he saw her. She had returned Cael from the Guild, newly assigned to him as Wayfinder when he had become a Leader. The dark spiral curls of her hair hung below her shoulders and bounced with every step, and her eyes of luminous green were like calm oceans he longed to fall into. Over the ensuing months, he had watched her become fond of Cael. And then, one day, she had confided in him. "My dearest friend," she had called him, and it had cut his heart deeply to hear of her feelings for Cael.

Verra yet hoped for Cael, although the bonding unnerved her. As for Cael, Telsen knew he was undecided. And so he continued to love her from a distance, hoping for the day she might turn her attentions to him. His loyalty to his bondbrother allowed for nothing else.

Chapter Seven

Confusion and the Dragon

In the following days, Jenna familiarised herself as best as she could with the time warp in which she found herself. The land and property Brenn had inherited was substantial, and set in a landscape spectacular enough to feature on a travel poster urging tourists to a place like Switzerland. Like his father and grandfather before him, he bred and trained horses, having an eye for good breeding and a love and understanding of the beasts.

Brenn gave Jenna a bay mare to ride, and ride she did, revelling in the freedom and speed of the animal's stride, the fresh scent of clean earth, and the warm summer sun. She revived her childhood riding skills, again practising saddling up, taking care of tack and grooming the gentle mare given into her care. The complicated turn her life had taken could almost be forgotten as she explored the ranch and its surrounds.

After a brief but detailed geography lesson from Verra, she knew that the town of Kereál lay in the foothills on the shore of Lake Tuan between the source of the Tuan River to the east, and the underground waterway of the Ré Shan Torrent further away to the west. Brenn's ranch was around two kilometres from the village, Jenna reckoned. Set back from the lake's shore by about half a kilometre, the property was bordered on the eastern side by the upper Tuan River where it fed into the lake. The sound of water flowing over the large rocks and channels in its course formed a constant murmuring backdrop of noise, both calming and reassuring. Jenna spent hours walking its banks, exploring upstream and following the river to the flurry of its entrance into the lake.

Again she was struck by the similarity of this world to her own. Ducks and other water birds were unremarkably the same, as were the horses and cattle she had seen so far. The horses were larger and more powerful beasts than those of home, but that could be a product of Brenn's careful breeding, as were the small ponies he raised for children.

Even the vegetation appeared to be the same. Flowing willows wept over the water, trailing bright fingers in the dark surface. Spear-like poplars stood in single-file along green meadows, and what she recognised as daisies and buttercups grew in sunny profusion amongst the grasses. If she examined any one thing she found minute deviations: a dissimilarity in leaf shape, colour shade, scent or tactile appeal, but she had to look closely, like the children's picture book activity of "spot the difference."

She often entertained the children, allowing Illiahn to don breeches and shirt to ride out with her husband. The twin girls were content with her company, but Mi'Cael preferred to be wherever Cael was. Myst and Raen were a delight, and she did not begrudge the time spent with them. Sharing songs and stories of her own childhood with her small charges brought her mother to mind. Watching Myst's face light into a beaming smile when she mastered playing pat-a-cake, Jenna saw her young self through her mother's eyes, and experienced a new understanding of the nurture she had given. It wasn't as sacrificial as she had thought. It was simply love.

Cael had recovered quickly, and split his time between

Council duties and rebuilding his strength in blade practise with Telsen. He avoided her, and it hurt to be reminded that he had not wanted her to come at all. An odd ache nagged inside her whenever she thought of him, but she ignored it, interpreting it as a symptom of her guilt. Whenever she could, she enjoyed the sight of him. Sometimes, she watched their swordplay from the house, admiring their strength, skill and economy of movement as muscles bunched and flexed under sweat-bright skin with each lift of the sword or turn of the body. She laughed when one would attempt to mislead the other with a feint, aiming to sweep his legs out from under him to tumble in the dust, or smack the flat of his blade harmlessly across shoulders or backside in passing, grinning his victory at the other.

Testosterone. Some things were *not* so different, she reflected wryly, although what she knew of Cael set him apart from the judgements she made on the men of her own world. Besides, she knew the practise was more than just play. There were real threats to be defended against. She shivered. Her own world, with its police forces and armies, seemed sanitised and, well, *civilised*. To have to defend one's territory in such a manner was almost medieval.

Although enjoying the leisurely pace of life in Kereál, Jenna missed her exercise classes. She maintained her fitness by walking, riding, and solo kickboxing routines to keep her skills fresh. Today, clad in shorts and singlet, she exercised behind the barn, releasing pent up energies in the execution of many combinations of kicks, turns, dips and punches. Her long braid flew and whipped around her for an hour, until fatigue stopped her. Panting and running with sweat, she stretched her body before retrieving her towel from the fence railing and heading for the river.

★ ★ ★ ★ ★

Watching her go, Cael felt her satiation and fatigue. Each new aspect of her intrigued him. Her intensity and speed had impressed him as he watched unseen from the barn, drinking from a wooden dipper and still wet from his own exertions. A jingle sounded behind him. He turned to see Brenn hang a harness on the wall.

"The *chekuán* amuses you after all?" Brenn asked with a quizzical smile.

Cael snorted at the word. A horseman's term describing a spirited, somewhat wayward, but very beautiful purebred filly. The old language could always do that, he thought: cram so much meaning into one word. "The *chekuán* has much to offer us, brother," he evaded.

The larger man clapped a strong hand on his shoulder and turned away. "It is *you* she wants to offer it to, brother." He stopped before reaching the open double doors and faced Cael again with a grin. "Do you not consider yourself up to the task? I warrant *that* one will not take to the bridle easily . . ." He chuckled and sidestepped to miss the dipper of water Cael fired at him. "But when a *chekuán* is gentled, brother, ah then, then you have a rare treasure." Brenn's blue eyes held his gaze for a moment, then he continued on his way out of the barn.

Gods! It was becoming impossible not to think of her. If others could read him so easily, he was not as in control as he had thought. He felt her now at the swimming hole, the caress of slow water cooling her heated body, and closing his eyes, he slipped beneath the surface with her as she unbraided her hair. He felt the current pull dark ribbons of hair like weed strands around her face and body as she sank to the river bottom before pushing off and rising again. He broke the surface of the water with her, gasping from the cold. She swam to the bank with quick strokes and hauled herself out. Runnels of water from her hair divided around her hips to run down the length of her legs to the ground. He allowed himself to feel the rub of the coarse towel on her body as she dried herself, the late afternoon sun warm on her shoulders, and the cling of tall grasses on her wet calves.

A mistake. Cursing himself for an indulgent fool, he drove the heel of his hand hard against the rough wood of the doorframe, taking savage satisfaction in the splinter that pierced his palm. Pushing sweat-damp hair back from his face, he strode to the pump outside the barn, stripped off his shirt and held head and shoulders under the cold stream as he worked the handle.

The blighted bond had strengthened.

He found his sister and Jolie, a village girl, pulling vegetables in the kitchen garden. Myst and Raen played in the doorway of his den, waggling dry grass heads enticingly before the last of the summer's crop of kittens. "It is time Jenna went to the Guild," he announced.

Illiahn tilted her head to see his face from under the wide-brimmed hat she wore. "I'm surprised you have put it off so many days, *chiaran*. Jenna is as keen to go as you are to be rid of her."

He blinked at that, still hoping his private hell was not evident to any but himself. He propped himself in the doorway, shrugged and continued. "I thought it best to give her time to become familiar with our ways. I think she now has a good understanding of the situation here." If Illiahn read more into that statement than he had meant, she did not say, but he knew her well enough to read her ambivalence.

Jolie studied him from beneath the brim of her own hat, but he ignored her scrutiny, long familiar with this behaviour in women, especially when he was shirtless. It was not only his looks that drew them but also a fascination with the reputation of the dragon. They all seemed to feel it was their personal challenge and destiny to be the one to awaken it. If they only knew the discipline it had taken to keep it slumbering, he thought wryly.

The tattoo he had carried since puberty warned prospective lovers of his gifting as an Empath. Its sleeping posture signified his status as not yet bonded and therefore available. By long tradition, an Empath who had taken a bondmate would extend the tattoo, the small oval becoming the body of a full dragon rampant. A proclamation he did not care to make.

"Why do you avoid Jenna so openly?" his sister asked in her usual blunt fashion. "It would be obvious to a blind man that she hungers for you, yet she runs like a startled rabbit when you come near. And *you*, brother, for all your protestations to the opposite, have a way of looking at her that tells me that you hunger also."

Jolie flushed and dropped her eyes at the straightforward conversation.

"I have spent my life dealing with one hunger or another, Illiahn." He left the doorway, stepping over tumbling kittens, and crouched beside her, his face intense. "You know better than most how it has been." Jolie fled inside to the kitchen, leaving them alone with the twins. "Why do you question me now with this particular woman? I owe Verra as much as I do Jenna. And Verra, at least, I can trust . . ." He broke off in agitation, not wanting to reveal more than he feared he had already.

"Had you decided to offer your bond to Verra?" she inquired. He was silent. "No, I did not think so. *Chiaran,* you have no *passion* for her . . ."

"Ours is a long relationship, built on trust and respect. I owe her much . . ." He stopped again, hearing himself clearly for the first time and alarmed at his own words.

"Cael," she sighed, "you owe her nothing. She loves you, I know, and she has saved your life several times—both out of that love and because it is her duty. This does not bind you to her, and she knows it. She is not blind to the situation, and is already accepting comfort from Tel. She will grieve awhile but ultimately, *chiaran,* she is wise and strong, and *will* be able to live without you." She said this last with a fey smile, poking his ribs with a gloved forefinger. "You are so busy wrestling with yourself that you miss what is happening around you. Tel has a very strong affection for Verra."

Gods! He knew Telsen held Verra in very high regard, but had not considered the implications of it. So Tel had spent quite some time forswearing his own interest out of loyalty? Distracted by the thought, he dug sun-browned fingers into the loose earth, crumbling the soil and disturbing small creatures that wriggled or scuttled away from his hand. He was silent for long moments. Illiahn loaded her basket with earthy vegetables, their green tops already wilting in the heat of the sun.

"I am sorry to have hurt her," he said. "You are right, as usual. You know me better than I know myself, it seems." He straightened, picking up her basket to keep her a few moments more. "I cannot trust Jenna Wade." The flat statement hung between them. "She has already . . . compromised me once. I have dealt with *hunger* before; I will do so again, and there is an end to it." He held her eyes a moment longer, then turned and strode toward the kitchen with the laden basket.

★ ★ ★ ★ ★

Illiahn blew a gusty sigh, removed her gloves and held her hands out to the twins. *Oh, brother of mine.* She replayed her last evening conversation with Jenna. Distraught, hurt and confused, Jenna had taken advantage of their growing friendship to unburden herself. Through floods of tears and pleas for understanding, Jenna had told her everything, unable to live with her burden of guilt any longer.

Illiahn sat stunned before the off-worlder that had bonded with her brother. "You . . . you did *what?*" Unable to conceal her expression of horror, she did manage to offer a large handkerchief. Jenna took it and buried her face into the linen, sobbing with unrestrained shame and sorrow.

"I didn't know, Illiahn, I didn't know what would happen." She gasped and wiped her face, but still the tears came. "I'm sorry, so sorry, and I know Cael can't forgive me, but I . . . I . . ." She dissolved into weeping again. Illiahn bit her lip and waited, already understanding Cael's strange behaviour in the light of this new information. *Oh, Cael. What a mess.* She sighed, considering the implications of the unfortunate bonding. The bond was given. Well, taken, at least. Either way, it was not recoverable, and he would have to come to terms with it in his own time. Jenna hiccupped and caught her breath, trying to control her weeping. "I don't know what you must think of me," she said, not meeting Illiahn's eyes. She swiped at her nose and sobbed once.

"Does it matter what *I* think, Jenna?" Illiahn said softly. "It seems you are doing enough condemning for both of us. It is done, and cannot be *un*done. I do not know how the two of you will live with this, but it remains that you must." She sighed again and stood, meaning to put the kettle on the stove for tea. Jenna's shoulders shook. Illiahn's heart ached for her brother, but this woman's grief touched her maternal soul. She sank down to the bench beside Jenna and laid an arm around her shoulders, giving her a comforting squeeze. "I have no advice for you, but I will listen whenever you need to talk. I will not betray your confidence, either. Cael need not know you have told me, although it hurts that he has not confided in me himself." And it did, but she could understand his reticence on the matter.

"He didn't want anyone to know," Jenna murmured, wiping her eyes on the sodden handkerchief. "He's embarrassed by the whole situation." She raised reddened eyes to meet Illiahn's. "The problem for me is that I . . . have fallen for him." She looked away again, her brows angling in chagrin. "I love him. There. I've said it. I've fallen stupidly and helplessly in love with a man who can't bear to have me around."

Illiahn patted Jenna's shoulder. "You are not the first, nor will you be the last." She stood and went to fill the kettle. "You should be honest with him, Jenna. Do not let him believe you care nothing for his . . . affections." She set the kettle on the stove and looked directly at her brother's new bondmate. "He is more likely to be considerate of your feelings if he knows they are involved."

"I should tell him?" A troubled frown creased Jenna's forehead. "I'm not sure I want to. I feel stupid enough as it is—I'm behaving like a silly teenager."

"You are behaving like a woman who is confused by her own feelings, and unsure how to proceed in a difficult situation." Illiahn smiled gently. "If your mother were here, she would offer you comfort and understanding, not censure. I will do no less." She set two cups on the table. "Tell him how you feel. It will temper his reaction to you, I promise."

Jenna sniffed and gave a watery smile. "You seem very sure."

"Cael is a man of honour. Engage his protective nature. Show him you are vulnerable, and not always as strong as you appear." Illiahn filled the pot with hot water and set it beside the cups.

Jenna was silent for a moment, and then nodded decisively. "You know him better than I do. If that's what you think will help, then I'll do it." She grimaced. "I'll have to pick the right moment, that's all."

"I can help to . . . arrange that," Illiahn said. "A little encouragement is all he needs."

Dragging her thoughts back to the present, Illiahn sighed and shook her head. What he hoped to accomplish by trying to fight the bonding, she did not know, but she knew it would ultimately defeat him, no matter how much distance he sought to put between them. It was an inexorable process.

She understood his feelings of betrayal over the loss of something so carefully guarded. After so many years of self-discipline, the bond preserved for the woman he would choose as his life-mate was lost, taken from him in an instant of vulnerability.

The twins skipped and chirruped to each other like spring sparrows as Illiahn wandered back to the house, a small girl's hand tugging at each of her own. As alarming as she had found Jenna's revelation, she understood her intuitively, having heard something of the woman's past life.

Add to that Cael's undeniable charisma. A rueful smile tugged at her cheeks. She had noted the common female response to him since she was old enough to notice, even before *he* did. As he matured, the interest had become sexual, the advances often intense and difficult for him to avoid without causing unpleasantness and hurt. She and Telsen had taken to providing their company as chaperones, helping him to avoid moments of vulnerability in this cruel game. And always, she had been grateful that her gender had spared her the Empath's gene. As he passed into manhood, he developed an easy manner and a confidence to deal with the problem himself, while hoping daily to find the one who would put an end to the waiting.

If Jenna Wade had thrown herself at him, it was understandable. But Illiahn did not doubt that he would continue to hold the woman accountable.

Cael was absent from supper again that night. Telsen found him later at the river. He lay near a small fire, reclining on one elbow in the grass, watching the flames and deep in thought. As Telsen drew near behind him, Cael raised his fist in salute, firelight reflecting from the silver band on his wrist, the runed twin to Telsen's own.

"I warn you I am not good company tonight, Tel."

"And have not been since your return." Telsen settled himself beside the fire. "What is it that eats you from the inside?"

Cael glanced at his bondbrother, taken aback by his unaccustomed directness. "I do not wish to discuss private matters," he said tightly.

"That would make it the first time, brother. When has there been a matter so private you could not discuss it with me? I am not completely ignorant—I would have to be blind not to see the three of you circling each other like wary cats. The Wayfinder will not meet your eyes, Jenna Wade keeps her distance from you, although I note not *too* far, while you hide in your silences. Why will you not make your choice between them clear? Either of them would have you."

"Because I have not found the three with either of them," Cael spat, pulsing frustration and irritation, needing to talk but fearing to admit his dishonour.

"Gods, man! You never will if you drive them away from you." Telsen shook his head and stood, looking out over the dark ribbon of river.

"So you also would advise me as to how to handle my affliction?" Cael's voice was quiet, his tone dangerous.

"No, brother." Telsen swivelled back to him, his hands raised in appeal. "Your options. And I would not advise you, but by the Gods, you cannot continue this way. You do not eat or sleep, you are distracted from every other matter by your refusal to resolve this one." He subsided to a crouch, resting on his heels by the fire, and Cael heard the frustration in his deep sigh.

Cael regarded Telsen, eyes watering from a brief sting of smoke, knowing he spoke only the truth out of concern for him. And he was right. Nausea roiled his stomach everyday, his head ached from the constant effort of avoiding the double issue of Jenna and Verra. He was sick of the tensions and his own confusion, sick of feeling responsible for Verra's pain, sick also of feeling Jenna's desire—no, *lust*—for him.

And certainly losing the battle for control over himself. He was no closer to finding the truth in this matter, for all his sleepless nights. Running fingers through his hair, he stared moodily into the flames. A long silence followed. The fire burnt lower.

"You need to bed her." Telsen averted his face. "Gods, man, by all the signs you want her. Whatever may have been between you and Verra was never like this . . ."

Cael uncoiled with a curse, unable to contain his miserable conflict any longer. "You do not understand, man!

Gods, is it not obvious to any who have eyes to see? She *has* bedded me. I had no choice—could not say yes, no, or even maybe. She stole the bond from me, Tel. While I was insensible, in her world, in her bed. Gods!" He took a deep calming breath. "It was hard enough denying the wanting *before* this, knowing there was always the consequence. All my life I have known the consequence. *Be sure* was instilled in me along with letters, numbers and conscience. This . . . cursed dragon I wear reminded me every day to *be sure*. And now, even now, the choice is not mine, and I am *on fire* with the wanting!"

He sighed then, a short distressed sound, closed his eyes and rubbed them tiredly. Sinking back to the ground, he stretched out full length on his back, feeling the damp coolness of the earth beneath the grass, and opened his consciousness to the night, seeking peace in the small sounds of animal and insect, earth and weather.

Telsen let the silence deepen. He very much wanted to offer his support and comfort in the aftermath of the turbulent confession, but he was familiar with Cael's need for distance at times like this. His input would not be welcomed. With a compassionate glance at his troubled friend, he withdrew from the fire and began the walk back to the house. His thoughts were confused. This was not what he had expected, and he was suddenly quite without counsel. The situation was now very clear.

He heard the echo of Verra's words. "Things are not quite as they were, not quite as they seem." The tensions, silences and strange demeanour of all three were now fathomable. Gods, what a mess. And yet, he had found his own personal hope in this private exchange. There *was* no real choice, as Cael had pointed out. The power of the bond would draw Jenna and Cael into an inevitable relationship of one kind or another. Only time would tell if it would contain more than the lust of a woken dragon.

"Be sure" was wise counsel indeed. For those with a choice.

The night eventually passed, although Cael wondered at times what delayed the dawn. He had returned to the house when all had retired for the night and taken a solitary meal of bread and cold meat before sleeping in short snatches for the rest of the dark hours. Rising early, he saddled his gelding and rode hard, blowing the fog from his brain and preparing himself to meet the day.

Illiahn cornered him as he rubbed the animal down outside the stables. "Jolie has kept breakfast for you." She fixed him with her no-nonsense look.

He groaned inwardly. "Illiahn," he began, but broke off as she folded her arms. A vertical line appeared between her brows. He sighed. "I will eat, I promise." The gelding snorted and butted his thigh, prompting him to resume his sweeping strokes over the glossy bay hide.

"I want you to talk to Jenna."

Cael scowled and brushed harder. The gelding stamped in protest. He ran a soothing hand over its neck. "Am I a child at your knee, sister? I am Mi'Cael, that you may bid me so freely."

She snorted. "No. Not Mi'Cael. He is far too sensible. Your behaviour does not become your years, *chiaran*. The . . . situation must be eased. Will you not at least break your silence and speak to her?"

"To what end, Illiahn? I do not wish to encourage her . . . interest." He tightened his jaw and leaned on the gelding's shoulder while tapping its foreleg. It raised its hoof obediently. He checked the hoof for stones and began to inspect the others.

"Have a care for the rest of us, Cael. The tension at table is so thick I can almost see it. The children are confused at your silence, and Jenna herself is embarrassed to be the cause of it." She thrust out her bottom lip and grimaced. "You need not . . . encourage her interest as you put it, but for the sake of peace, *chiaran*, will you at least be civil to the woman?"

Cael released the horse's last hoof and straightened. He brushed his hands together and met her eyes. That his behaviour had affected the children shamed him. A familiar resentment at her adept management of him stirred, but he buried it beneath a chagrined smile. He slipped the halter from the gelding and gave its rump an affectionate slap. It would head straight for the home paddock behind the kitchen garden. "Forgive me, sister. I was unaware that any suffered beside my churlish self." He kept his tone light.

Illiahn's golden brows rose a fraction. "The *Empath* was unaware? I find that difficult to believe. I think perhaps the Empath is having difficulty deciding his best course of action, is he not?" She placed her hands on her hips and tilted her head to one side.

Cael hung the halter carefully on the hook set into the barn's lintel. He coiled the attached rope in slow circles and dropped it over a hook beneath the halter. How much had she guessed? She spoke as if hinting that she knew. He shook off the unlikely thought. Facing her squarely, he resisted the urge to push his hands deep in his pockets like a recalcitrant child. He pulsed her a wave of affection followed by apology, and laid his hands on her shoulders. "I will mend my ways," he promised. Surely he could keep the contact minimal and still appear civil?

Appearing to anticipate his compromise, she shook her head. A small smile curled the corners of her mouth. "A word or two will not suffice. She is only here a short while. Before she leaves for the Guild, please try to establish at least a polite acquaintance. Ease the tension, *chiaran*. Please? I will make sure you two are undisturbed for the rest of the morning."

Resigned, he nodded slowly. His flesh echoed Jenna's physical exertion and told him where he would find her. Turning away from Illiahn, he hesitated. >*Must it be now?*< He glanced back at her in appeal.

"No time like the present." She grinned.

He swallowed and rubbed his jaw.

"Go on . . ." Illiahn flashed an encouraging glance at him as she pushed him in Jenna's direction, her hand in the small of his back. "She will not bite you, Cael. Do it for *me*."

He moved with reluctance toward Jenna's usual spot behind the barn. Gods! What was he to say? He could not compromise keeping his distance from her. His now rampant libido was barely containable. If she could not control her carnal desires, then he would continue in avoidance. Either that, or he would have to concede defeat to the dragon and tumble her into bed at the earliest opportunity, a concession his social conditioning rendered him incapable of making. He cursed under his breath.

He rounded the corner of the barn and stopped. Folding his arms over his chest, he leaned against the weathered planking, waiting for her to finish her routine. He had already decided on an approach to ease the awkwardness between them.

When she saw him, her face registered surprise. She reached hastily for her towel, wiping away the perspiration that beaded her face and darkened the singlet she wore.

"Will you . . . teach me this?" he asked.

She considered him warily, head cocked on one side as she regained her breath. She wiped her face again and nodded. "Why not? I could use a worthy opponent." Throwing the towel back over the fence, she ran an appraising look over him. "Basics first. Stance and balance. Move from here," she instructed, placing her hands on her hips. "Balance your weight evenly on both feet, and keep your knees bent, always. Watch where I plant my foot before I turn or kick."

He watched and followed as she executed a simple combination of block, step, kick and punch.

"Now you."

He repeated the movement as she watched.

"Good. Move your body weight to balance your kick. Lean. Like this . . ." She pressed his shoulders lower and raised his leg above hip height, her hand firm and warm beneath his thigh. He glanced at her, assessing her intentions. She had refrained from touching him since he had made his boundaries clear.

"It's a contact sport, Cael." There was amusement in her voice, and her mouth twitched at the corners. The heat of her fingers ignited a small fire in him, but he inclined his head briefly, and she continued.

"It's all a question of balance and counter balance. Lose that balance and your opponent has the advantage. Follow me."

For the rest of the afternoon she taught him. His eyes followed her every move, fascinated with the rhythm and flow of the routines. His awareness of her through the bond allowed him to feel her point of balance, her angle of flexion, how she stabilised her position and loaded her kicks and punches to fully utilise body-weight shifts. As he became familiar with the combinations, his speed increased until he was able to perform several basic routines matching her intensity.

"You learn so quickly!" Her chest heaved with exertion as she drew breath and wiped her face. "It took me months to get that far." Sweat stuck dark wisps of hair to her cheeks and brow and glistened on her chest.

"I have an advantage, *chekuán*. I can *feel* how you move." Turning to the pump, he filled a wooden bucket and handed her a dipper of cold water.

She drank thirstily and splashed her face with more. He averted his eyes as water ran between her breasts. Upending the bucket, he doused himself and wiped his face and neck with the coarse towel she offered. They both subsided to sit on the edge of the water trough. An awkward pause followed. Cicadas clicked and buzzed in the trees around the homestead, swooping from tree to tree in occasional mad flight through the heat. A light breeze floated down from the ranges, bringing the scent of pine as it cooled him.

They drank again, and Jenna broke the silence. "I can't change how I feel, Cael. I try to keep a lid on it for your sake, but it won't go away." She sighed and lowered her head. "There's no easy way to say this. I . . . I'm . . . I think I'm in love with you."

Oh Gods. Cael closed his eyes and swallowed hard. Not again. The "I love you" speech was never easy, no matter who it came from.

Jenna continued quietly. "If it's your friendship only, if that's how it has to be, I'd rather have that than nothing at all. But please, don't shut me out of your life anymore." She twined the end of her braid around one finger.

Cael lowered his shielding and let the wash of her emotion drift over his mind as he reflected on her words with some surprise. Her appeal touched him, although she was far from the first to make a declaration of love to him. He had not considered she felt anything more than lust, and was startled to discover otherwise. Her feelings ran very deep. He felt her aloneness, the bleak emptiness of spirit that caused her to think of home and familiar surroundings. With great care, he exercised his gift, easing her emotional distress, contributing peace and strength from his own reserves.

"Jenna, I did not know. Forgive me if I have been harsh." He rubbed a hand through his hair and gave her a troubled look. He had no idea what to say next, and that was unfamiliar to him.

She shrugged and looked away, hugging her arms around herself. "I didn't realise it myself for a while. You make me feel things I have never felt before."

Cael cursed inwardly in frustration. Gods, she confused him. It would be hard to maintain his cool distance from her without the fuel of his disapproval—which was evapourating like a puddle in sunshine. A single tear ran down her cheek. She brushed it away angrily and swore.

He turned brooding eyes on her and offered her the comfort of his arms. >*I regret to have caused you pain,*< he sent, pulsing his chagrin to her as she leaned against his chest and accepted his embrace. >*I have been unaware, and have behaved badly.*< The tears returned. She swiped at her eyes and looked away. He took her chin in his hand and turned her face back to him. Her candour made him want to reciprocate.

"You must know I desire you greatly, so much that the thought of you consumes me." He dropped his hand and looked away. "But that is the nature of the dragon, and I

105

am less than a man if I allow it to rule me." He tightened his jaw. The frown returned.

"I don't understand! How can you feel like that, and yet insist on containing it—is it only your pride that's keeping you from me?"

"Gods, Jenna, no!" He shook his head with vehemence, his hair falling into his eyes with the movement.

"Then help me understand, Cael, because I sure as hell don't know where you are coming from!" Her eyes flashed with angry hurt, and again he sent reassurance to her, soothing her confusion and blunting her pain.

He stood abruptly, at war with himself and his conflicting emotions. Taking a deep calming breath, he pulsed an image at her.

How it should be between bondmates.

She gasped at the intensity of the image, the depth of intimacy he had shown her, and he knew she understood. She had never heard of the three, but in a heartbeat he communicated all she needed to know.

"Do we not have *any* choices, Cael?" He did not meet her eyes. "As we're bonded anyway, and you want me like you say, what difference will it make if we . . . share a bed every now and again?"

He sighed. "The difference is between us, Jenna. I cannot take the subject of physical sharing as . . . as lightly as you do. All my life I have been conditioned not to. I do not censure you for being a product of your culture, but what you did transgressed every boundary I hold. I have difficulty with that."

He felt her search desperately for solution, not wishing to let this new honesty pass.

"You can enter my mind, can't you? I want you to do that."

"You do not know what you are asking."

"I want you to know me, to understand me. You show me so much with your mind, and I understand. I want to do the same."

"It is not that simple, Jenna. It will be uncomfortable for both of us."

"Is there a danger?"

He shook his head.

"Then please . . ." His eyes assessed her resolve, and he touched her cheek lightly with his fingers as he considered. Standing, he held his hand out to her and she took it. He drew her across the yard into the shade of the house, where they sat on the front steps like children.

Her eyes were wide, and he saw the pulse race at her throat. "Relax, *chekuán*. I am told that I do this well." He smiled at her for the first time. "Show me what you wish." He closed his eyes and reached into her mind.

Jenna felt a pressure within her mind, like the persistent push of a mild headache. She closed her own eyes and waited. A sudden flooding warmth filled her. Her eyes flew open, but he had not moved.

>*I am here, chekuán.*< It was more intimate than his normal sendings, his tone low and warm.

She began to show him herself. Selected memories, long hidden parts of her life that defined and described her. She dusted them off and offered them to him. Desires and repressions; accomplishments and dreams; hopes and disappointments. Jenna the child and then the woman. When she was done, she opened the last door to him: the simple truth of her feeling for him, her hurt over his rejection of her. His surprise and discomfort shivered in her mind.

He withdrew from her. As she became aware of her surroundings again, she found her head resting on his shoulder. Reluctant for him to do so first, she straightened and broke the contact. He regarded her with a thoughtful gaze, his brows drawn. His sending startled her.

>*You are a very strong woman, Jenna Wade. What would you have me do?*<

"Love me back." She laughed wryly. "But failing that, just believe in me." She paused a moment to collect her thoughts, wanting to feel his arms around her again. "I'll do whatever it takes to gain your trust."

"Give me time, Jenna." His eyes were full of bewilderment. "I am what I have been made, and this situation was never foreseen by those that taught me. It appears I am a prisoner of my own culture. I will seek counsel on this, but you must allow me time. And distance."

His expression softened. "It is well you go to the Guild soon. It has been difficult for me to think clearly while you adorn the homestead with your presence." He glanced sideways at her, the corners of his mouth quirking into a smile that lent warmth to his eyes. Her spirit lifted in response as she felt the echo of his desire.

As he left her and crossed the yard, she closed her eyes and sighed. The change to his face when he had smiled at her was like sunlight on water after a storm. She shivered, recalling his arms strong about her, his chest firm and warm beneath her cheek, the scent of male that clung to his skin.

She laughed at herself somewhat shakily, and shook her head. Shit, I'm living in a Mills and Boon novel. The man had melted the Ice Queen into marshmallow. Tessa would find the change hysterical.

Chapter Eight

The Guild

Jenna smoothed the fabric of the deep blue skirt around her hips with a dubious frown. Not her usual style, but "appropriate," Verra had insisted. She wore a short-sleeved white blouse under a sleeveless bodice that laced at the front and tied at the waist, matching the blue of the skirt. It intensified the colour of her eyes in a most satisfying manner. The long skirt was a light weave, fitting at the waist to drape over hips and flow around the ankles. It was cool and comfortable, but she feared tripping over the hem or snagging it with the buckles of the new leather sandals she wore.

She had spent two days in Kereál township, fitting skirts, shirts and breeches in preparation for her introduction to the Guild. While she favoured the new soft leather pants, she had accepted Verra's recommendation of her present attire. Verra piled the last of their parcels into the tray of the small market cart, motioning for Jenna to climb up.

Verra also wore skirts, and gathered them around her knees as she stepped up onto the cart and settled herself on the seat, taking up the knotted reins and clucking to the sturdy grey mare. The harness creaked as the cart began to move through the wide street. Verra kept the mare at a walk until they left the main trading area, then increased the pace to a trot. The small grey's hooves thudded softly on the packed earth of the street.

Kereál had captivated Jenna. The trading area had been

alive with people, and had reminded her of school history texts. She had explored the many small businesses that thrived along the wide streets of the village centre, supplying Kereál's population of several thousand with both life's necessities and luxuries. Ranchers and farmers from the land around the village came into town to trade, and travelling merchants brought more exotic goods up the Tuan River from the coastal town of Illith, Camarrhan's main port. Precious gems and metal ores from the Althar mines were transported down-river to Illith and traded at various towns along the southern coast. Of late, the activity of rogue bands of Althar against Camarrhan's Leaders had led to tensions and a reluctance to trade with Alth.

Street merchants added colour to the town centre with their canopied stands of luscious summer fruits. The heavy scents of peach and citrus mingled with the savoury smells of roasting meats and the fresh, yeasty waft of breads. Jenna sniffed in hungry appreciation, observing a group of children gathered at the window of a confectionary shop. Clutching coins in grubby hands, they contemplated the treats they would soon enjoy, laughing and wriggling with the joyously unaffected body language of the very young. She smiled, remembering toffee-milks, jelly babies, fizzy sweets and the fifty-cent mixtures that always surprised as eager fingers explored the rustling white paper bag.

The population seemed affluent. There was no sign of poverty or hardship anywhere, although she had looked for it, disbelieving the uniform prosperity she saw. The atmosphere in the village was one of calm enjoyment of life. Folk treated each other with courtesy and respect; harsh words were rarely spoken. Women carried themselves with dignity and pride, and the men walked tall, supremely confident in their manhood without the need to prove it.

Jenna sighed, reflecting on the contrast to her own world. The conflict between the sexes, the constant competition to remain one up on the other. Her cynicism on the subject had led her to judge Cael when she had first encountered him at the hospital. How wrong could she have been? She had badly misjudged him. The feeling of belonging here was strong, as if she had come home. She was certainly at home with the courteous deference the young men gave her. Their interest was obvious, yet they refrained from suggestive comment or glance, their decorum offset by the humour of their conversation as Verra introduced her to various friends of hers or Cael's.

She enjoyed the company of Chad and Sorren. The brothers escorted her around the village, filling her in on local information and personalities while Verra made the rounds of fabric vendors, dressmakers and cobblers. Identical twins, the two young men had grown up in Kereál, sharing their boyhood with Cael and Telsen who, although unrelated, chose the brotherhood bond when they reached manhood at sixteen.

Gazing up at Chad as he explained his country's trade routes, Jenna realised the men of Kereál were all quite imposing. Few were less than six feet, and she began to see that Cael's six feet and four inches of height were not so unusual here.

Remarking on the high incidence of twins she saw, she discovered that multiple birth was a commonplace event. Twins were as usual as single births, and a set of triplets occurred every once in a while, being the cause of great celebration. Camarrhan considered its children a precious treasure. Many families were large, but birth accidents abounded, leaving babies un-twinned, parents bereft, and many mothers incapable of bearing more children.

The lack of medical knowledge saddened her. Although generally robust and healthy, Camarrhan's people were vulnerable. She knew full well that Cael would have died from his injuries in this environment if not for her healing ability, and she saw much evidence of poorly mended injury. It was her nature to heal, and she keenly anticipated the training she would receive at the Guild to enable her to perform healing on folk other than her bonded mate.

She sighed. Bonded mate. As much as she liked the sound of the term, she had her doubts. Would there ever be anything between them other than the one way street of her own deep affection and desire?

Cael had been easier in his manner with her since she had declared her feelings, no longer seeing her as lusting after him, merely helplessly in love. And he *had* admitted his desire for her, even if his ethics would not allow him to pursue it.

She realised with a start that they were back at the ranch. Turning to Verra in embarrassment, she apologised for her reverie.

"No matter. Reflection is good for the soul." Verra smiled as she slipped from the cart and grasped the mare's bridle. "Much good comes of long thought. So. Have you set the world to rights?"

"I wish." Jenna appreciated Verra's sympathetic friendship. Verra knew exactly how things stood between them all, being part of the triangle herself, and her presence was a constant source of strength and support. Surprising. Jenna had, after all, effectively crushed Verra's hopes for a future with Cael.

Verra's attention was turning more and more to Telsen, as he offered her the same resource of support. They made a good pair, Jenna thought. Telsen's devotion to Verra was obvious now that he need not hide it, and the Wayfinder had begun to respond to the tall, darkly handsome man. Get over it and get on with it seemed to be the principle most Camarrhan folk adhered to.

Mi'Cael ran out to meet them, his fine blond hair flying, his amber eyes excited as he viewed their parcels.

"Sprout!" Verra fished in her pocket for the confectioner's packet hidden there for him. He grinned up at her and laughed as she pretended to find nothing, unable to contain a small jump of enthusiasm. Verra stopped teasing and handed him the paper parcel.

"Thank you, Verra," he said very properly, before wrapping his small self around her in an impromptu hug.

"Ah well, sprout, a girl would do anything for a hug from such a fine young man!" Verra laughed, returning the hug. She tousled his hair as he opened the packet and peeked inside.

Jenna smiled at the child's easy manner, and transferred packages from the cart to the wooden verandah of the house. A stable boy led the horse and cart away to the barn as Illiahn appeared at the doorway, her face flushed with kitchen heat.

"Jenna! You look wonderful." She beamed in approval. "Skirts become you well."

Jenna grimaced, preferring her jeans, but managed to be gracious in her thanks. Verra would transport her to the Guild that afternoon. There had been no new instances of battle sickness in Kereál or its surrounds, but they had already waited a dangerously long time to share their new knowledge. It had been ten days since her arrival in Camarrhan, and they did not know what had transpired in the rest of the land.

Cael was absent. He represented Kereál at the quarterly

113

Council in Illith, and Brenn accompanied him in his role as deputy. They would bring news with their return. Jenna missed his presence terribly, but she knew he would have an easier time without her. Since his confession of desire, she had been aware of the dogged self-denial that caused his constant tension, aware also that her presence only intensified matters.

As well they would be apart for a while.

It was time. Jenna hugged Illiahn and the twins, and shook Mi'Cael's small hand. He frowned up at her.

"Uncle is not here to say goodbye."

"He is at Council, sweeting. He will be home soon." Illiahn gave her son a puzzled look.

"He will be sad." The boy pushed out his lower lip and frowned.

"I think he'll be very happy to have one less person to worry about, Mi'Cael," Jenna replied, wondering at his meaning. He was a perceptive child, and she had come to trust his solemn pronouncements.

Mi'Cael shook his head, rippling silken blond hair and biting his lip. "He will be sad," he reiterated.

Jenna raised her eyebrows at him as she shouldered the pack containing the rest of her new "period clothes" as she thought of them. Telsen had come to see her off, being temporarily charged with the care of the family and ranch in the absence of Cael and Brenn. She hugged him with genuine fondness, and as he kissed her cheek, he murmured to her.

"Do not give up, Jenna. He does not know his own mind on this matter. Be sure to return."

The warmth in his dark eyes touched her, and she flashed him a startled look. "I hadn't thought not to."

"Unless you make it clear you are a bondmate, the Guild

114

may assign you where they wish," Verra explained.

"Cael doesn't want me to make it clear to anyone." Jenna lifted her chin. Heat crept into her cheeks.

"Be that as it may, if you wish to secure your return here, you must tell them you are bonded. Simply do not name him. Illith would be their first choice for a trained Healer." Illiahn's calm tone belied the concern in her eyes.

Goodbyes done, Verra opened the Way. As she stepped into the shimmering curtain, Jenna turned to see the people she was beginning to think of as family and marvelled again at the acceptance she had found here.

I *will* come back. Just try to stop me.

As the crystal ring of the Way faded, Jenna blinked at the strong sunlight reflecting from the white stone face of the Island of the Hand. They stood on lush turf at the bottom of wide, hewn-stone steps that drew the eye, sun-blinded, toward the imposing establishment of learning that was the Guild. Gulls wheeled and cried overhead, some dropping small shellfish to break open on the rocks below and descending to squabble over the shattered morsels. A sharp ocean tang imbued the fresh breeze with childhood memories of tide-wrack and sand castles from Christmas holidays spent at the beaches of the Coromandel coast. Jenna inhaled the scent of nostalgia and smiled.

Verra had given her another brief geography lesson before they left. The island lay a mile from the coast of Camarrhan between the main ports of Illith and Durran, where the Tuan River and the River Cam, respectively, emptied into the Pysaur Sea. The seaward side of the island rose in high white cliffs from the ocean, and bore the brunt of the surf, heard as a constant low boom. Only when the swell came in from any southerly direction, Verra promised.

The Guild was housed in the stone of these cliffs, carved into the rock from the landward side of the island. The initial appearance was forbidding. Approaching the formal step-and-column entranceway, Jenna noted several youngsters clad in simple clothing of various solid colours, engaged in a vigorous game of what appeared to be kiss-catch.

Verra smiled at the game. "The blue tunics are Wayfinder novices, the green are Linkers, the white, Healers. There are no Wielders present, but the gold tunic you see over there," she indicated a boy in his early teens trying to remain invisible behind a neatly trimmed hedge, "is an Empath, and doubtless the real target of this particular band."

Jenna turned to observe the chasers for a moment as they ran through the extensive gardens. The swathe of flowered green sloped downward at a gentle gradient, dividing the hewn stone of the Guild from the white sweep of beach, where the lazy roll of wavelets hissed over the sand. "Wielders?" she inquired. "What is a Wielder?"

"One who is gifted with the rarest of the land's magics—and probably the most aggressive. A Wielder can call up fire, use it for light, heat or as a weapon. He may also wield a Hand—amplify the magic of four other users—but that is a complexity you do not need to understand just yet."

Lifting her skirts above her ankles, Jenna followed Verra up the wide stone steps toward the grand, arched entranceway. It was cool inside, and as Jenna's eyes adjusted to the lower light level, she marvelled at the skin-smoothness of the pale stone, and wondered at the hands that had fashioned this place. Rune-carved panels ran along the walls at chest height, and single runes appeared on the heavy, iron-hinged doors that lined the hall. Corridors ran off the back of the hall in every direction, lit by oil lamps in the walls wherever the light from cunningly directed sun-vents did not reach. Twin staircases spiraled upward to the left and right of the hall, wide enough to accommodate several people side by side. Verra headed for the left staircase, and they began to climb.

Several minutes later, breathless and a little dizzy from the constant turning, Jenna found herself once more in bright sunlight, standing on a white stone terrace facing the shore of Camarrhan. A woman stood at the waist-high balcony wall, silhouetted against the light. She turned to face them as they approached.

"Karessa!" Verra greeted the woman with warmth.

"Well met again, so soon, Verra," came the older woman's reply as they embraced. "How fares Kereál?"

"Kereál fares well. Well enough to bring you a great surprise." Verra slipped an arm around Jenna's waist. "Karessa tu Bellayna, mentor of the Healer's Keep, may I present Jenna tu Lliahna, who carries both the Linker's and Healer's gene, and who we believe to be a holder of the nine."

Silence met Verra's pronouncement. The old Healer's faded blue eyes bored into Jenna's, her face guardedly neutral beneath its tracery of fine lines.

"Show me your stones, child," came the gentle prompt.

With a worried glance at Verra, Jenna opened the neck of her shirt and unfastened the clasp of her necklace. She drew the stones from her neck and offered them for Karessa's scrutiny.

The Healer held the stones in her palm and allowed the sunlight to play across them. Jenna saw flashes of opal fire reflect in their depths as they responded to the light in a way they had never done at home. Karessa clasped her fingers over the necklace and her old eyes closed for a moment. When she again looked at them, there was joy on her face and moisture in her eyes.

"The Keys have returned! Thank the Gods, the magic is not lost!" She sank to the stone bench at the foot of the terrace wall, gazing again at the stones in her hands, shaking her head, her expression one of awed disbelief. "We must convene all mentors and approach the Hand." Karessa rose in swift decision, her silver-trimmed white skirts swirling around her ankles as she paced the terrace. She handed Jenna the stones with obvious reluctance.

"What of your mother, child?" Karessa's voice was gentle.

"She died some years ago, Healer."

"Grandmother?"

"Also dead, Healer. I never met her."

"Chiahn . . ." Karessa breathed the name, her eyes fixed expectantly on Jenna's face.

Jenna's eyes widened. Her mouth dropped open in astonishment.

Karessa smiled. "Close your mouth child. You are the image of your grandmother. Blessed Gods! I never thought to see this day."

Verra's impatience got the better of her. "This is not fair, Karessa. Tell what you know."

"Ah, Wayfinder, I cannot. It involves a prophecy of the Hand. What I *can* tell you is that since these stones left the world, true Healers' magic has been absent. They belonged to Galaen."

"Gods! The Keys to Healers' magic have been off-world for two generations?" It was Verra's turn for astonishment. "Why were they not pursued?"

"The Wayfinder who transported Chiahn was slain by the man from whom she sought to escape. The stones themselves were never keyed to any other Wayfinder. She went without a trace."

"What of the needs focus?" Verra demanded. "Could the Way truly not find her?"

"Truly. All attempts to find Chiahn and the Keys failed. We can only assume the Gods somehow intervened in destiny, sending the prophecy to reassure us all that the Keys would one day return."

Jenna's thoughts spun in confusion, question after question arose in her mind. Chiahn pursued by a man who would kill a Wayfinder? And possessing the "Keys" to a magic? Way too much information to process at once. Looking Karessa in the eye, she asked her most burning question.

"Who am I, Healer?"

Later that day, five solemn faces regarded her around the table. Jenna sat between Verra and Karessa, attired in white, which she would apparently wear for the duration of her stay. Such a practical colour for a Healer, she thought with a wry smile. The discussion chamber was cool and well lit by three sun vents to the outside, focussed with clever precision to provide optimum light.

They heard her testimony. She talked for close to an hour, telling her history and answering their brief interjections. Gowan, the gold-robed Empaths' mentor, asked permission to view her mind, but she refused him, feeling enough invasion without this further indignity. He accepted her refusal with good grace. Indeed, she had been treated with great courtesy, for all their questioning.

The fact of her bonding soon came to light, as they investigated the healing she had wrought through a Keystone. She did not name Cael and they did not press her, although she realised it would be a matter of simple deduction. She knew there were eleven Empaths in Kereál, and only three of those were single and of marriageable age.

"Are we agreed?" Quan, the red-robed Wielders' mentor laid his hand, palm up, on the table. When she saw the fourth palm laid, Karessa added her own.

"Jenna tu Lliahna tu Chiahn, holder of the nine, you are granted audience with the Hand."

"The Hand?" Jenna cast a suspicious glance at the mentors around her.

"The five keepers of magic, Jenna. There are five magics in Camarrhan, and the secrets of each are held by the keepers on Ché Kevath: the sacred island, the centre of the land's magic. Only two or three may leave the island at one time, so you will not meet them all tomorrow."

"And will *they* tell me who I am?" she asked, unable to contain her impatience.

Karessa and Gowan exchanged glances. "You are a daughter of Camarrhan, child. Granddaughter of Chiahn, Healer of the Guild; great-niece of Galaen, keeper of Healers' magic—Healer of the Hand. Chiahn was Galaen's twin. The rest must wait. Galaen will tell you what she wishes." Karessa's tone was sympathetic but final, and the five mentors stood to dismiss Jenna.

"Health and strength, Healer." They all saluted her as she left the chamber, touching the fingertips of their right hands to their hearts. The mentors carried the device of their office on the breasts of their robes. Karessa's was a white dove bearing a runed gold leaf in its tiny beak. Gowan wore the dragon rampant, and Quan, a fist of fire. Blue-robed Chereth wore the Wayfinder's open door, and Sheytan, in green, two linked hands against rose-gold. Looking down at the green-edged hem of her white skirts,

Jenna supposed she might be seeing something of Sheytan, although she had some rudimentary knowledge of the Linking magic. She had so much to learn.

Verra left that evening. The audience scheduled for the next morning did not require her presence, and she departed for Illith. Cael and Brenn awaited her at the conclusion of the Council. Jenna's heart twisted as she saw Cael's face in her mind, wearing the warm smile he had graced her with so recently. The familiar ache inside set in, and she wondered if she would ever find ease for it. She used to laugh at such nonsensical behaviour in others. It had always pleased her that she had never mooned about like a lovesick girl, had never had the need. Rolling her eyes at the irony of it all, she drew a deep breath and squashed the longing for him back down.

Karessa had introduced her to the novices at the Healers' keep, and shown her to her room: a small but adequate chamber, vented to the outside and containing a wide bed, a desk and stool, and a comfortable easy chair before an empty fire recess. Oil lamps on the desk and the small table beside the bed glowed with soft blue incandescence, providing light for reading or writing. This evening she would do neither, preferring to walk the beach beyond the gardens.

Quite a day. Jenna reflected on the changes she had assimilated over the last two weeks as she stood at the ocean's edge, white skirts gathered around her knees. The slow ripples of clear water came and went, swirling around her ankles and stealing the sand from beneath her feet, tickling her soles and causing an odd sinking sensation. The coolness of the evening and steady swish of the water was refreshing, and as always she enjoyed the chance to be alone.

The prospect of the morning's audience was a little daunting, but excitement at the thought of meeting her grandmother's twin countered her nervousness. Her only living relative—when she thought she had none. With a last look at the distant lights of Illith, and lingering thoughts of Cael, she turned from the sea to retrace her steps through the gardens and back to her chamber.

Tomorrow beckoned. She knew sleep would evade her this night.

Chapter Nine

Prophecy and a Summons

Clouds had gathered in the night, and the day dawned grey and wet. Heavy cumulus rolled in from the south, and the wet smack of rain on the rock face of the Guild softened the distant thunder of surf at the island's back. A slow rolling swell gathered itself from the horizon in murky green undulations and threw arms of white spray around the island as the swells broke on its seaward cliffs.

Jenna woke early as reflected lightning flared in the sun vent, filling the bedchamber with sudden white light and the tang of ozone. Morning ablutions complete, she breakfasted with the novices in the common dining hall, feeling self-conscious of her seniority among such youth. Despite the age difference, the youngsters were courteous, respectful and interested in this new arrival and what she could do.

The girls wearing the white tunics were in awe of her healing ability, knowing this particular magic had been absent for years. Fourteen-year-old Trista attached herself to Jenna, gazing at her with open admiration, and now followed her to the balcony of the Healers' keep where she was to meet Karessa.

As they waited, sheltered from the rain beneath the overhanging stone, Jenna noted how cleverly the stone had been worked to catch and channel the rainwater. The Guild was self sufficient for water, each period of rain refilling rock cisterns deep within the island as the channels collected the water from every surface and funnelled it down. The cisterns were accessed by pumps and wells, providing a constant supply of cool water, faintly flavoured with minerals.

The rustle of Karessa's skirts preceded her. "Good morning, Jenna. I trust you slept well?" Karessa's eyes were kind, her smile warm.

"Well enough, thank you." In truth she had slept little, rehearsing in her mind the information she knew Galaen would seek. She would not speak Cael's name, but knew she could not hope to keep their secret for long. Karessa knew him well, Verra told her, and it would only be a matter of time before she made the connection.

Karessa fixed the young novice with a quizzical stare. "Why are you not at your studies, child?" Trista coloured, murmured apologies to her mentor and fled back down the spiral stairway.

The old Healer smiled again at Jenna. "It seems you have an admirer. Indeed from this day, the novices have cause for great celebration. With the return of the Keys, true healing will once again be possible, and all the young ones will learn mysteries deeper than the herbal lore they have been limited to." She beckoned Jenna to follow her as she turned with brisk steps into the passage from which she had appeared. "My own skills have been limited to pain relief and herbals, but always, I knew how it used to be, and longed for the magic that was lost. Jenna, you have brought us a priceless gift." Karessa shot her a smile of understanding. "I know it must pain you to be separated from your bondmate. We will endeavour to begin your training with all haste and return you to him."

A shadow fell across Jenna's face as she followed Karessa into the discussion chamber. Karessa did not press her to reveal to whom she was bonded, and for that she was grateful. Or perhaps she had already made the deduction.

They entered the austere chamber, lit today by oil lamps, the sun vents closed against the driving rain. Set deep within the Guild, the chamber had no windows, its stone walls relieved only by richly worked tapestries depicting various forms of the land's magics. Quan, Gowan and Sheytan sat waiting around the extensive wooden table, and Karessa greeted them all formally, as etiquette required, before joining them. She had briefed Jenna on the niceties of meeting in a discussion venue. Chereth, the Wayfinders' mentor, was absent, but before Jenna could wonder at it, there came the familiar sound of a Way opening in the chamber. A tall, slender figure robed in white emerged from the shimmer, followed by Chereth, who closed the Way behind him. All present stood. Touching fingertips to their chests above the heart, the mentors greeted the newcomer with deference.

Jenna closed her mouth, which had fallen open at the sight of the woman, and swallowed. She could be looking at herself in a few years time. Thick hair the colour of chocolate dusted with glossy bronze cascaded to her waist, although a hint of grey teased her temples. Dark brows arched elegantly over large, almost navy-blue eyes, and the skin of her high cheekbones appeared smooth and youthful.

"That is Galaen," Karessa whispered. "Wait for her to address you."

Galaen appeared to be in her late thirties, Jenna guessed. Indigo eyes rested on Jenna as Galaen smiled in greeting, her full mouth curving open to display even white teeth.

"Jenna tu Lliahna tu Chiahn. You could be no other with such a countenance." Her voice was soft and musical. "Greetings, great-niece. This is indeed a very great day."

125

She crossed to Jenna and took her in a warm embrace, pressing her cheek to Jenna's before holding her at arm's length, her hands on Jenna's shoulders. "I have heard in brief from Gowan of the nature of your return, Jenna. You are indeed a surprise and somewhat of an enigma, but Camarrhan rejoices today that a lost magic has been restored to us. As has a precious child of this land. Welcome home, daughter." Galaen seated herself in the high-backed chair at the head of the table as the others took their seats. Jenna sat down stiffly. Hugging complete strangers had never been her thing. "You may speak, child," Galaen invited.

"I don't understand. If you are my grandmother's twin—how can you be so young?"

Galaen's smile was gentle. "That is a mystery of the magic, child. I have eighty-two summers, fifty of them spent on the island of Ché Kevath. It is the centre of the land's magic, and sustains all five of us who form the Hand. There is much you need to know, Jenna," she added kindly, "and it will not all be told today. The most urgent matter before us pertains to prophecy, and a second issue of equal importance is the stones you wear."

Jenna fingered the necklace, then unclasped it and handed it across Karessa to Galaen, who was unfastening a cord from her own neck. Taking the gold necklace, Galaen examined the stones and their setting, her beautiful face assuming an expression of sadness.

"Dear sister, I could not save you." She sighed, slipping the necklace into a pocket of her robe. She picked up the finely braided cord necklet she had removed and passed it to Jenna. The necklet bore nine opals attached in the same way as Cael's Keystone, each wrapped in fine silver wire and hooked into the braid. "This was Chiahn's. It is a very long story, that I shall tell you on another day. We exchanged stones to confuse an evil man who pursued her. It was a very grave mistake. It cost Camarrhan one of its magics, and Chiahn, her heritage. The Wayfinder who aided her escape was slain, and Chiahn was left with no way home." Galaen paused, weighing her next words.

"We believe Lliahna to be a child of Chiahn's marriage, but there will always be some doubt. Jabeel, the man who pursued her, also forced himself on her. When her husband sought vengeance, the vile one killed him. Such a one has disturbed the balance in Camarrhan. They were deeds of great evil, the consequences far reaching."

Jenna tapped her fingers on the arm of her chair. Galaen was raising more questions than she was answering. "Lliahna—how did you know the child was a girl? My mother was born in New Zealand."

"A holder of the nine learns to be as aware of her own body as she is of those she heals, Jenna," came the patient reply. "Chiahn knew and named her daughter before she left us."

A sudden sympathy for the grandmother she never knew filled Jenna's heart. A woman abandoned in a world so different to her own, where evil was commonplace and integrity scarce, almost the complete antithesis to the land of her birth; bereft of husband and twin, alone and a mother. A strong woman, to have borne so much.

"We must address other issues now, child." Galaen's tone was businesslike. "We have awaited this return. It is foretold by prophecy. Some details are obscure, but it is often the nature of prophecy to be unfathomable until all players involved are revealed. Hear it, ponder it, tell me if you hear meaning in it."

Jenna nodded, toying with the caged stones of her new

necklet. This is *your* world, lady. *I'm* supposed to ponder it?

Galaen spoke as if reciting something long committed to memory. "On the return of the nine, the nine and the three have become one and together will avert the threat to the five. Four in union will travail and prevail if the hearts of the one are true." Jenna and Galaen shared a quizzical look, fine brows describing the same angle above their dark eyes.

Galaen spoke again. "The numbers are mostly known to us, but as for the combinations, we cannot be sure. You, Jenna, are the nine. We, the Hand, are the five. We understand you are a bondmate?"

"I am," Jenna acknowledged, avoiding Galaen's eyes.

"Then we assume your mate is the three. He is that to you?"

"He is." She swallowed, remembering Cael's mind picture of how it should be between bondmates. The three essentials for lasting intimacy. Love, trust and passion. He was certainly the ideal of all those things to her.

"Then why are you so secretive, child?" Galaen asked gently. "Who is he?"

Heat crept into Jenna's cheeks as she lowered her head in embarrassment. She desperately did not want to betray Cael further, but it was being requested of her. Still, she did not speak.

"I believe I know, Galaen. He is of Kereál." Karessa shot Jenna a questioning look. "I do not understand Jenna's reluctance, but I am sure she has her reasons. He is Cael; son of Jarin, son of Merad. He is a Leader of Kereál, and their Council seat."

It was Gowan's turn to be surprised. "When did this occur?" he asked, eyebrows leaping into an expression of astonishment.

Jenna wanted to sink through the stone floor and disappear. She managed to answer with a calm dignity she did not feel. "Fourteen days ago. It's still new between us. Is that such a terrible thing, Gowan?"

The Empath leaned back in his chair, clearly perplexed at this new information. He shook his head and spread his hands. "Your pardon," he apologised. "I meant no offence. It comes as a surprise to me. I am even more surprised he consented to be parted from you so soon after the bonding. You are a beautiful woman, Jenna, and the dragon is a demanding master."

"Cael is master of himself," she flashed back, "not a slave to the dragon!"

Gowan eyed her as an appraising smile spread across his face. >*Well said. I see he has chosen well,*< he sent, adding aloud "I apologise for any offence, Jenna. It is usual for me to be notified, but by no means compulsory. I am happy for you both, and hope to share my congratulations with Cael soon."

Just great. She knew how much Cael would appreciate that. *Shit.*

"If we may return to the current matter?" Galaen had followed the exchange with mild interest, but Jenna could see that the prophecy was a pressing issue on her agenda. "We further assume your hearts are true. As the 'one,' that would be a prerequisite. The 'four' puzzles us. Do you have any insight here?"

Hearts of the one are true? Jenna groaned inwardly. One they might be, but the complexity of their non-relationship denied *that* particular piece of the prophecy. With a sudden flash of insight, she saw Verra and Telsen's blossoming relationship in a new light. "It could involve Verra—the Wayfinder who is responsible to Cael."

Galaen nodded encouragement.

"She is very close to Cael, and is becoming fond of Telsen, his bondbrother. We are all bound together in one way or another. If Cael and I are the 'one,' then together we may all be the 'four.' "

"Well spoken!" Galaen's indigo eyes lit with interest as she considered this new input.

"What is the threat to the five?" Jenna asked, curious to know what it was they were to avert.

"Another prophecy speaks of this," Galaen answered, her smooth brow wrinkling into a frown. "The essence of it seems to mean that when the magic leads the land no more, the balance will be destroyed, and the way to the five will be open. As we speak, this process is taking place. It is not by natural means that our Leaders with magic are declining, and therefore we assume that someone is attempting to force Fate's hand by making it his or her destiny to fulfill the prophecy.

"This person has influenced many young Althar, turning them into a threat where there has been none before. The balance in the land is severely threatened: if the way to the five is opened, we are indeed vulnerable. At yesterday's Council conclusion, news was received of another death. A Leader of Twin Lakes is no more." Galaen shot a sympathetic glance at Gowan. Most town Leaders were Empaths, their natural skill with people suiting them to the role.

Gowan muttered a curse. "Alth should take more responsibility for the situation. Camarrhan's borders have always been open to all, but times change."

"Enough to warrant a state of hostility?" Galaen folded her hands in her lap. "Although the threat to our Leaders is very real, we must remember that it is only a renegade band of Althar youth who prey upon them, and not a hostile act by the nation itself."

"Only? With respect, my Lady, that renegade band you speak of so dismissively has so far eliminated seven good men, all Empaths of my Keep. The time has come to take a stand. Mere patrols accomplish nothing, as this latest death proves."

Galaen lowered her eyes and nodded patiently. "That is why it is imperative to utilise our new knowledge of battle sickness to avoid further fatalities. Without that weapon, the Althar will be unable to cause death in such an invisible and deadly fashion."

"Be certain, Galaen. Have the Hand close the borders to Alth."

"No." She looked Gowan in the eye. "The Land will remain in peace. We are confident that we can resolve this issue without conflict. The prophecy tells us that 'the four' will achieve resolution. Believe it, Gowan."

The silver-haired Empath subsided, rubbing a hand over his jaw and pulsing his disquiet to all present.

"Besides," Galaen went on more gently. "When we are able to identify the wretch who buys the Althar youth to accomplish his purposes, we can dispose of the problem at its source. That one has much to answer for. It is only a matter of time before he is discovered. Should that one prove to be Althar, then you are mitigated, but my feeling is otherwise. I believe it is one of our own who leads them; one who is no stranger to causing misery and destruction to achieve his aims."

Gowan shifted morosely in his chair. "It makes no sense. How does it profit any of us to seek the destruction of magic?"

"It is a quest for power. If Ché Kevath is breached, the Hand will cease to be." Galaen rose. "Enough. I must return. Gowan, you will summon the son of Jarin, son of

131

Merad and instruct him to attend us with all haste, along with the other pair named by Jenna. I would meet this . . . *four*."

"Health and strength, my Lady." Gowan acknowledged her request as he stood, touching fingertips to his heart.

Galaen smiled at Jenna. "We will meet again soon, child."

All stood, and Chereth opened the Way. As Galaen departed, Karessa glanced sideways at Jenna with a look of bafflement, then met Gowan's eyes and shrugged. Jenna sighed, grateful the whole truth had not come to light. Let them believe what they would.

Illiahn held the halter as Brenn inspected the young mare, due to foal within days. Like an anxious father, he had confined the mare to a small paddock attached to the back of the stables, awaiting the outcome of a special breeding. Satisfied with the animal, he stroked the glossy chestnut neck with a firm hand, patting the mare's rounded rump as Illiahn released her. Brenn looked up at the sound of horses approaching.

Five riders cantered toward the ranch, raising no dust after the night of rain. He recognised Cael's bay and Telsen's black at the head of the group and relaxed. Since Cael's recent brush with death, these small security patrols had been of real concern. They were necessary to remain alert should renegade Althar threaten outlying farms and holdings, and partly what the men were trained to do, but were not without risk, despite the extra precautions they now took. Master metalworkers in Illith had fashioned a fine chain mail for Cael, which covered him from shoulders to knees when on horseback. The mail was imbued with Wielder's magic, allowing no penetration. Althar death-shafts would not find his flesh again.

The riders slowed as they drew near, raising hands in greeting as they passed. Cael left the group and approached Brenn. His big gelding snorted and stamped in displeasure at the delay, chewing at the bit, eager to be unsaddled and free to roll. Brenn saw from Cael's thunderous expression that something had vastly displeased him. He glanced at Illiahn, anticipating the coming storm, twitching a tiny smile to her along with a conspiratorial wink, and turned to his brother-in-law. "Problems, brother?" he inquired, knowing Cael caught their brief exchange. Not much escaped the notice of an Empath.

"Only for me," Cael said with a dark scowl. He leaned forward and rested his forearms on the saddle as he spoke, the horse shifting restively beneath him in echo of his mood. "I am summoned to the Guild. Tel and Verra also."

"They know, then." Illiahn gave her brother a sympathetic look. "Why Tel, I wonder?"

"The Hand are also involved. It seems there is a prophecy coming to fulfillment that concerns the three of us and Jenna." Cael steadied his horse as it threw its head up and down, pulling at the reins impatiently and sidling toward the open pastures. "I will leave Chad and Sorren with you, brother. We saw no Althar, but there are signs of recent passage from Twin Lakes. I will send when I know more. We are instructed to make all haste." With a wry smile, he allowed the gelding to turn toward the yard.

"This will be awkward for him." Brenn watched Cael dismount at the barn where the other riders unsaddled their horses.

Illiahn smoothed back a tendril of golden hair, her eyes also on her brother. "So much has happened so fast. No sooner does he begin to wrestle with one issue, another appears." They began to walk back to the yard. Illiahn draped an arm around Brenn's hips. "I wish only to see him at peace, as he was before all this began, but I fear that is a long way off. There is much to be resolved."

Brenn drew her close and kissed her brow. "A man's destiny is just that, *chiara*," he said as he released her. "Those possessing the magic have a larger part to play in this life than us . . . lesser mortals. Fate toys with them, and they respond as their character allows. He is in conflict now, but imagine how great his peace when all is done."

Illiahn leaned into him. "I hope he has kind words for Jenna. The Guild did not find the truth from her, I know." Brenn smiled at her certainty, and they parted at the house with another affectionate kiss.

A door slammed shut as Cael strode from the den, tucking the tail of a clean linen shirt into his breeches, and shrugging on a tan leather vest, the Empath's dragon device visible on the breast of the shirt beneath. He had received Gowan's summons as the riders had completed their patrol, and after making it known to the others, had maintained a tense and angry silence until they arrived back at the ranch.

Verra and Telsen waited for him in the yard, also dressed for reception at the Guild. Verra had changed into skirts, and wore the Wayfinder's emblem on the left of her figure-hugging blue bodice, although her distinctive wristbands were evidence enough of her station. She had gathered her wayward hair into a long plait, but small wisps escaped here and there, haloing her face with tiny dark curls. Telsen raised wary eyes to Cael as he approached. Cael pulled his fingers through wet hair to lend some semblance of order to his appearance. He knew he radiated exasperation, but hoped he looked less dangerous than he had appeared on their return ride. Verra's eyes were a mirror at times like these, and her reactions to him always tempered his mood.

>*Forgive me. I am behaving badly,* < he sent to them both, not trusting his voice lest it further betray his anger. He had no wish to provoke Verra's disfavour.

Telsen raised his hands in protest. "Not necessary, brother. Much confronts you. I am pleased not to be in your boots for this day's issue, at least."

Verra rose and hugged him, adding her reassurance to Telsen's. "You are only mortal, *chiaran,* and not yet a God." She grinned at him. "If you did not behave badly at times, how would we know you are somewhat less than perfect?"

Cael managed a tight smile. Verra always knew how to disarm him with her words, stopping him from taking himself too seriously. He pulsed an image to her that spoke of gratitude and warm regard. It seemed as good a moment as any to ease the awkwardness that haunted the three of them. "I wish you luck with that tongue, brother!" His eyes flashed humour at Telsen, taking the edge off his words.

Verra coloured and lowered her eyes.

>*It is well,* < Cael reassured her, feeling her discomfort. >*He is a good man. Treat him well—he adores you.* < He caught Telsen's cautious reaction to his words and felt his apprehension. >*It is well, brother,* < he sent. >*I have no claim to her. You would do well to make one.* <

Filling an uncomfortable pause, Verra placed her pouched belt around her waist and laced and tied it in front, her pink face betraying her relief that the issue had been addressed at last. She looked a question at Cael, and he signalled his readiness.

The Wayfinder opened the Way to the Guild, and within seconds the yard was once again empty, a faint ringing tone hanging in the still air.

★ ★ ★ ★ ★

The mentors were gathered again in the discussion chamber awaiting the summoned trio. Jenna toyed with the stones of her necklet, anxious to see Cael. She hoped the summons hadn't annoyed him too much. Agitation always made him more distant from her.

>*Peace, Jenna.*<

Her heart thumped when she heard his familiar low tone.

>*There is no blame. I know this is not your doing.*<

She relaxed, encouraged by the warmth of his sending. Her pulse had quickened even at his voice, and she hoped it would not further betray her when she saw him. The man affected her more than was comfortable.

>*It will help me if we can give the appearance of bondmates. Gowan will want a full account of me if he perceives the truth. I will greet you accordingly.*< His mind picture followed. And her pulse betrayed her.

The door to the chamber stood open, and Verra entered first. "Health and strength, mentors of the Guild." Her greeting received the appropriate response. "I bring Cael, son of Jarin son of Merad, and Telsen, son of Corr." She indicated her tall companions as she spoke.

"Welcome, and be seated." Gowan watched Cael keenly as Verra and Telsen joined the mentors around the vast table.

Cael held out his hands to Jenna. She rose from her place, went to him and laid her hands in his. His fingers twined around hers and their eyes locked as he drew her full length against his body. Their clasped hands met behind his hips. He pressed his lips once to her forehead, and she raised her mouth for his kiss. Enjoying the moment, she leaned into him and pulled him closer, breathing the soap-clean scent of him. His body tensed in resistance.

>*You take unfair advantage,*< he sent as their lips parted. His eyes flashed in brief admonishment, but he lowered his head to her, and she kissed his brow beneath the damp golden tousle, squeezing his fingers as he released her hands.

The mentors all smiled their approval, even Gowan appeared satisfied with the greeting. As the couple took seats at the table, Karessa clasped Jenna's hand and patted Cael on the shoulder.

"I always thought that one would have trouble finding a worthy mate," she whispered as conversation began around them, "but I believe you are well matched. Has it been . . . difficult?"

Jenna coloured as she caught Karessa's meaning. "As I told Gowan, Cael is master of himself," she answered in a taut whisper. "But no. I can't imagine the physical side of our relationship ever being difficult. He's all I ever wanted. In *every* way."

"Then you are luckier than most, my dear!" The old Healer's eyes sparkled, pleasure-bright, as she turned her attention to the meeting.

Galaen arrived late, transported by the Hand's Wayfinder, Luath, and accompanied by their Empath, Grinore. The prophecy was repeated, its meaning discussed. Verra and Telsen's relationship was questioned and clarified, as was that of each of the supposed "four."

"It would certainly appear you are 'four in union,' " Grinore remarked. "Let us hope you will indeed 'travail and prevail.' "

"Against what and against whom?" Cael asked.

"Against the threat to the Hand, and hence the land's magic. Should Ché Kevath be breached, all magic will fail," Galaen answered. "As to whom, our suspicions rest on

Jabeel son of Kren, son of Labicheth. Jabeel was responsible for my sister's misfortune and the loss of the Healers' Keys. He seeks not only power but revenge. The Hand neutralised him for his crimes."

Jenna nudged Karessa. "Neutralised?"

"They removed his access to magic, Jenna. He was a very powerful Wielder."

"They should have removed his testicles while they were at it," Jenna muttered. "Rape is unforgivable." She bit her tongue.

Cael turned toward her and lifted his brows. >*Really?*<

She raised her eyes to the stone ceiling, feeling the blood race to her cheeks. *Shit. What a faux pas.* Pressing her hands to her hot face, she leaned back in her chair and sighed. Suddenly piqued, she whispered in his ear. "You know, boyfriend, in my world, a man who found himself in your position that night would have been in seventh heaven."

>*Perhaps so. But what would he have to lose?*<

"You're impossible!"

>*I will not spar with you, Jenna. Gowan already doubts us. Do not add to his suspicions.*<

"Fine." She laid a deliberate hand on his knee and ran it seductively up his thigh, out of sight under the table. "Then let's aim to convince him."

He swallowed, blinked, and laid his hand on hers, holding it firmly still. >*Please, do not! I may appear as rock, but I am only flesh. I asked you for time, chekuán, and time I still require.*<

She let her hand remain under his. "What about Gowan's opinion?" she murmured, knowing how she affected him and shamelessly enjoying his reaction.

>*I will know later, no doubt,*< he sent, his tone resigned. >*Gowan knows me too well.*<

A voice penetrated their communion. "Son of Jarin?" Jenna felt Cael's startled reaction.

"Your pardon Gowan, I am distracted." Cael inclined his head toward Jenna, and Gowan nodded his understanding.

"The question on the floor is whether Jenna tu Lliahna can successfully treat battle sickness wherever it appears."

Jenna suppressed the urge to laugh aloud at Cael's mortified expression. She squeezed his thigh and answered for him. "There is a drug, a medicine, in my world that can raise the pulse rate high enough to destroy the symbiot," she began. "The delivery of the drug is through the lungs. Your prohibition of technology may make the administration difficult."

Galaen raised her eyebrows at Grinore. "Are we willing to make a concession here?" she queried. "We can confine the technology to private use at the Healers' keep."

"Your permission to share?" Cael asked Galaen.

"Granted. We are curious to know the nature of this." Galaen rested an inquiring gaze on Jenna.

>*As am I, chekuán! Show me first!*<

She opened her mind to him and, as she felt the heat of his presence, showed him the inhalers used by asthma sufferers.

Ventolin.

As a child, she had foolishly played with a young playmate's inhaler, the result being an unusually elevated heart rate that had sent her mother into a panic and on a mission to the hospital emergency room. Investigation had revealed a sensitivity to Ventolin, the drug she had inhaled.

After long discussion with Karessa, she now recognised other sensitivities, such as caffeine and cat hair that she had long believed to be allergies, for what they were. Basic incompatibilities of her Camarrhan physiology with the world of her birth.

Cael's brows rose as he viewed the information, and he relayed it to all present. >*I am relieved you will not have to deal with all who suffer from battle sickness as you did me, chekuán,*< he sent. She choked back an indignant protest and glowered at him. His hand tightened on hers, and she felt him struggle to maintain his composure. >*Please remove your hand. If I am required to stand, I will only embarrass us both.*< Jenna flushed and complied reluctantly, as permission was given by Galaen to import the inhalers to Camarrhan.

"Your first priority, Jenna, is to bring a sufficient supply of this drug to treat any battle sickness victim and to instruct its use to the Healers at the keep. This gains us time to confirm that it is indeed Jabeel we seek, and locate him in order to bring him to justice."

"What of her training, Galaen?" Karessa inquired.

"She is already advanced, Healer. She may have a week of initial instruction after her ability has been assessed, but then she must return to her world to collect this . . ."

"Ventolin," Jenna offered.

"As you say. Verra tu Kerran, you will transport her." Verra nodded in acquiescence.

"Son of Jarin, you are required to escort her, as is the son of Corr. As well to keep the four together."

"My Lady." Cael inclined his head deferentially.

"We will reconvene when this has been accomplished." Galaen, Luath and Grinore prepared to depart, and all stood, making formal farewell.

Gowan eyed Cael as he stood. "I would see you. My study. Alone."

★ ★ ★ ★ ★

Cael's temper was barely under control. He drew stormy brows over eyes that brewed thunderclaps to match the weather. Gowan had been relentless in his pursuit of the truth, having perceived the couple's unease from the beginning. Cael had tried to protect Jenna, but ultimately the truth had to be known. Gowan was taken aback by the unusual circumstances of the bonding, and concerned for the outcome of the prophecy.

"Why do you resist her?" Gowan demanded. "This is not a matter over which you can continue to exercise control. There are irresistible forces at work here."

Cael stood at the arched window, frowning out at the heaving sea, his arms crossed over his chest. The moist breeze cooled his face and stirred his hair. "I resist her because I can. I desire her, of course. How could I not, now that the dragon no longer sleeps? But I *did not choose this!*" His voice rose in frustration, and he pulsed indignation at his mentor. "This resistance you speak of is the last control left to me, and I *will not* be manipulated by Fate, prophecy, or anyone!

"Should I let the dragon rule me? What of the three? And what of the ethics and controls you taught me yourself?" He faced Gowan accusingly, his eyes bright with anger. "And what of myself? Am I not a man, able to take my own decisions? Or must I concede defeat on *your* advice, as a boy at your knee?"

Gowan sighed and sent him a pulse of calm, soothing his affronted dignity before he spoke. "You speak of ethics, control, defeat and concession. I see this has become a matter of honour for you. That is unfortunate." He smoothed his thick silver hair with a gesture Cael remembered from his time at the Guild.

141

Something unpleasant was coming.

Gowan fixed him with a piercing look. "You think you can avoid this situation, but you cannot. You think you will beat it, but you will not. Do not fight it, Cael. Sometimes Fate does the choosing. She *is* the one."

Cael returned the older Empath's hard gaze for a moment before growling dismissively. "I thought at least *you* would understand, Gowan. I see I was mistaken." He strode from the study with a last dark look at his mentor.

Gowan fielded the angry glance, regret etched on his face. "That is where you are wrong, my young friend," he called. "I understand only too well."

>*Return if you have need of counsel,*< came his final sending. Cael projected a short burst of ironic laughter as his only reply.

Cael sought Jenna after his angry words with Gowan, and together they walked the beach. Telsen and Verra strolled a short distance ahead of them, each couple affording the other distance and privacy.

"Verra will return you to Kereál at the end of your week. You can instruct us more fully in the ways of your world then. We will not blend in easily, I think. I do not know what assistance we may give—you would do better at this task alone." In truth, he was uneasy at the prospect of spending time in her world but did not want to admit it.

"Galaen seems certain she must keep us all together." Jenna frowned and glanced sideways at him. "I'm glad you are coming with me but I don't see her reasoning in this. I can get enough Ventolin by visiting only a few pharmacies. We should be back here within a day if all goes well."

"Tel is the only one truly wanting to go." Cael's gaze rested on his bondbrother. "Or is he?" he inquired, turning to face her. He pulsed a query of homesickness to her.

She tilted her head at him, deep indigo eyes catching the late sun in a flash of azure. "I miss hot showers, my entertainment system and my cat," she teased, "but were I to stay there, I would miss *you* more than any comforts I could name." Her fingers traced the gold-embroidered dragon on his shirt and lingered for a brief instant. "Besides, I'm needed here. That's a good feeling, Cael."

Her earnest expression touched him. She had a way of angling her fine brows and tilting her head that gave her face an elusive, almost ethereal quality that he was beginning to find captivating. He pushed his hands deep into the pockets of his breeches and surveyed the horizon.

"All your life you have been special," she continued. "Your family and friends all know and acknowledge that. I know your gifting has brought its own particular burden, but have you ever felt insignificant?"

"I had never considered it that way," he answered truthfully. Again, she surprised him.

"I have found *myself* here. Despite certain . . . complications." She poked his ribs for emphasis. "And I don't want to return to a life of insignificance. I thought I was happy, but I was living a compromise."

Beautiful eyes, he thought. So expressive: long-lashed and tilted, at once both innocent and knowing, able to arouse him with their slightest sultry glance. Oh Gods! He had almost leaned in to kiss her. If he allowed his own body to betray him, he would be lost indeed. Distance was required, and quickly.

He brought his physical responses back under tight control and stooped to pick up a large round stone. Drawing his arm back, he sent the stone arcing out over the water with a snap of his wrist. He followed the stone's trajectory with his eyes, and it flew a satisfying distance before landing with a silent splash. "Then you will remain here for reasons other than me? I would not give you false hope." And yet my own control slips daily. Gowan's words sounded in his memory—*Do not fight it. She is the one.* He tightened his jaw and turned back to her, awaiting her answer, his frown masking his thoughts.

Jenna's face was calm. "I'll stay for my own reasons, Cael. Even if you should . . . choose another, I'll stay."

He felt the sharp stab of pain she experienced as she spoke. Gods! Did she not know how impossible that would be? He stepped close to her, his face very near hers. Her eyes widened at the invasion of her social space. "There will be no other choosing for either of us, Jenna." His voice was low. "Can you not imagine why?" Her questioning look said she could not. He held her gaze with intensity and pulsed her an image. She paled and backed away, shaking her head.

That was not as deft as he had intended, and far from gentle. He had allowed his agitation to colour the image. *>Forgive me, chekuán, but you needed to be aware of this,<* he sent as he soothed her with pulses of calm.

The bond.

Should he ever lie with another, Jenna would share the physical experience with him, feeling each touch, every sensation in her own body. As would he, should Jenna ever be in that situation. Jenna's eyes spilled tears as she absorbed this new implication.

"I am so, so sorry," she murmured, her voice thick. "If I could undo all this, I would." She subsided to sit in a miserable heap on the dry sand. Cael knelt before her on one knee, resting his forearm on the other as he thumbed away the tears that channelled over her cheeks.

She dropped her head into her hands and wept. He felt each emotion as it surfaced. She wept for him and what she had taken from him; she wept for herself and what she could not have. She wept until he sat beside her and held her in his arms in concern, drew her against his chest and soothed her distress in constant, calming pulses. Her hair lay fragrant and silken beneath his chin, and he stroked stray strands from her wet face as she struggled to control her crying.

At last, the weeping subsided, and he released her. She looked ruefully at the front of his shirt, wet from her tears, as she wiped her face on the hem of her skirt. "Please don't look at me. It can't be a pretty sight. And don't be kind to me—it only makes me cry." She sighed as he offered her emotional strength, closed her eyes and accepted gratefully.

Cael stood and held his hand out to her. He pulled her to her feet and held both her hands in his. >*It seems I have a talent for upsetting you.*< His sending held apology.

Her smile was watery and thin. "How else can I get you to hold me?"

His brows shot up. He laughed quietly, raising an answering laugh in her, part sob, part relief at the passing of tension.

"Jenna tu Lliahna tu Chiahn, you are an intriguing woman." His smile was genuine, surprising himself as much as it did her. He released her fingers, and they walked toward Telsen and Verra who stood waiting for them, ready to depart but not wanting to intrude.

Verra eyed Jenna's tear-damp face, but wisely abstained from comment. "We must go, *chiara*." Jenna smiled at the term. "I will be back for you after a week."

Telsen gave her his usual bear hug and kissed her cheek in farewell. Verra opened the Way home to Kereál and motioned Telsen through first, waiting as Cael took his leave of Jenna.

>*Friends?*<

"At least."

>*It is appropriate for friends to embrace.*<

"It is?"

She moved into his arms and he held her, conscious of her softness and woman-scent. His eyes met Verra's over Jenna's thick, chocolate-brown braid. >*Gods, Verra, this is an impossible situation,*< he sent, pulsing his confusion and exasperation. He released Jenna, and she stroked his face before stepping away from him.

"My love to Illiahn. And you . . . you take care." She tilted her head at him, a wry smile lighting her farewell.

One week. Time for serious reflection, he thought, conscious for the first time that he did not want to leave her. He turned resolutely and stepped through the Way, all the while doubting his ability to make a rational decision on the matter.

The bond was making itself felt. She was getting under his skin.

Chapter Ten

Lakra

The week began uneventfully enough. Cael's band rode patrol on alternate days, their circuit taking them from the ranch around the lakeside outskirts of Kereál village to the mouth of the Ré Shan Torrent, a north turn, then back around the northern borders of the village. They were half an hour into the patrol, about to follow their northern course for two miles before turning south once more.

A sudden flight of birds flashing white wing tips against the distant blue of a clear sky had Cael riding alert and wary. Verra rode beside him, her chestnut mare stepping quickly to keep up with his long-legged gelding. As they neared the vicinity, he noted with approval how each rider scanned the surrounding landscape, looking for possible places of concealment. He knew the Althar talent for remaining unseen, and the thought made his spine crawl with great unease.

They approached a stony outcrop, a tall tumble of flat rocks and rounded boulders that had weathered free of the small hillock from which it protruded. Meagre scrub grew around the base of the boulders, and straggling green growth clung to crevices in the rock, roots reaching deep for nutrients and a hold on life.

>*Ward left!*< Cael sent to Telsen, who rode to flank him, sword at the ready. Riding up the gentle incline toward the outcrop, they split. Cael, Verra and Telsen rode around the

tumble to the right, while Chad trailed Sorren to the left. They crossed behind the rocks, and met back where they had begun.

Nothing.

The unease remained. Below the rock, the low rumble of the Ré Shan Torrent could be heard, its dark waters curving and curling like an invisible titan water slide around the tortuous channels of the waterway far beneath them. Beginning high in the ranges northwest of Kereál, the torrent emptied into lake Tuan, its course so steeply angled at its source that the pressured water literally burst into the lake at its mouth.

Cael stood in his stirrups, stretching his legs and surveying the loose rock structure. He focussed deeply and opened his senses, seeking any discrepancy in the usual feel of things. >*Something is in there. Sentient, but not an animal.*< He suppressed an involuntary shudder as an echo of pain brushed his mind: not his own, not that of any of his riders.

Verra reined her mare closer to him, and spoke in a whisper. "Send Chad. Sorren will cover him." Cael raised his brows at her.

"You are the one most at risk, *chiaran*," she hissed. He indicated his light mail covering with an exaggerated gesture and grinned at her, dismounting. Rolling her eyes, she also dismounted, and took the big gelding's reins as he drew his blade from the saddle sheath. She shook her head, not bothering to hide her exasperation, and Sorren winked at him in a private aside.

Chad leaned from his saddle and tweaked her plait. "Want me to cover his back, Wayfinder?"

"It is his front I am more concerned with at this moment," she remarked drily. "Your Leader seems to be intent on risking himself at every turn."

"Truth. You will not go alone, brother." Telsen slid from his saddle and handed his reins to Sorren. Cael shrugged and loped up the incline, hearing his bondbrother's steps close behind him.

On reaching the outcrop, they exchanged a glance, seeing the recently crushed greenery at the foot of an apparent opening in the rock pile. Cael placed a hand on Telsen's chest and pressed him back. >*I will do this, brother. There is only room for one to enter.*< Telsen stood back, courteously indicating with a mock flourish of his hand how welcome he was to proceed. Cael grinned. Holding his sword in front of him, he brushed aside fern fronds and stepped cautiously into the gloomy passage, ducking low to pass beneath a large boulder wedged between several flat slabs that supported it.

The sound of harsh breathing reached his ears as he found himself in a small space, dry and musty smelling. Although doubled over, his tall frame filled the height of the space, and the cling of cobwebs caught at his hair. Tiny fingers of wafer-thin light reached through eroded chinks in the piled rocks, and in the dimness, Cael caught a slight movement. Keeping the sword between himself and the dark shape, he waited for his eyes to adjust to the gloom. The shape began to resolve itself into a human-like figure. A few moments more, and he could distinguish an Althar female. Apparently in the later stages of labour. She lay curled on her side, arms protectively around her belly, her dark eyes wide and her face betraying her fear.

Oh Gods! He laid down his sword. "Tel! No danger—but I think our assistance is needed." He pulsed the image of the scene to Telsen, who waited in the passage behind him. And heard his startled exclamation as the image was received. >*Verra—please bring a waterskin. We have a problem.*<

Within minutes, Verra replaced Telsen in the narrow passage. She tugged at his shoulder, and he moved slightly to allow her to see the situation.

"What do you know of birth?" He knew little, and his harried tone conveyed that.

"Gods, Cael, I know nothing! The process, yes, but not how to assist it. Should we even try to help one of them?"

He pulsed indignation. "It is *life,* Verra!"

"They have tried to take yours often enough," she replied in a voice that would etch rock. Cael turned, surprised at her tone, and caught her glare of disapproval at the female.

A spasm rocked the lithe body beneath the travel robe the Althar had covered herself with. Her dark eyes closed, and the harsh breathing began again as she twisted the heavy fabric of the robe between slender fingers.

Cael ran his hand through his hair in indecision, ducking his head to do so. He took the waterskin from Verra and offered it to the female. She shrank back, radiating suspicion. Like all Althar, her eyes were uniformly black. No iris, no white, the pupil invisible, making it impossible to gauge any response from them.

"He will not harm you," Verra shot at the woman, "but *I* might. Better for you to keep him between us." He turned horrified eyes to her, and she shrugged. "She is not likely to harm you *now,* is she?"

"Only if she understood you, Wayfinder, and I am unsure that *I* do. If you will not help, Verra, wait outside." Her attitude shocked him, and he could not keep it from his face.

"I will be within earshot, Cael. Do not trust her." Verra leaned past him. "Harm him, and I will kill you myself," she warned, her eyes dark with menace.

"Ki te'ah Lakra. Ki te'ah A'Thek. Alakem toh meina kara t'akailem koh." The woman spoke between gasps, and it seemed the birth might be imminent.

Cael had spent some time with Althar when his father had been a gem trader, and had learned some of their tongue. Enough to understand her name, her status, and that she was no threat to them. Her name was Lakra, and she was A'Thek: fertile female of high status, possessed of sex magic, trained to pleasure only Althar males of status who had been selected to breed, contributing superior intellect or physical ability to the gene pool. Many Althar women were infertile, relying on the A'Thek and the lesser, non magic-gifted Thek to produce children for them. It was most unusual for one of such high status and value to be alone so far from home.

"You understand our tongue?" Cael asked.

Lakra nodded. "And speak, little." Spasms overcame her again, and he waited for it to pass.

"Should I leave you alone?"

"No . . . !" she panted, "stay . . . please . . . time is soon." She accepted the water he offered, but drank only a little, splashing some over her sweating face. The water trickled beneath her head to puddle in the dust of the earth floor, and he pulled off his mail and then his shirt, rolling it into a makeshift pillow to keep her face from the mud that would form there. She studied him between spasms.

"Why help?" Her face showed gratitude for the extra comfort.

"Because you need it." He sweated in the confined space despite the cool of the sheltering rock, unsure of what help he could be, ultimately. "What can I do?"

"Stay." Her eyes closed as a groan escaped her. She reached slender fingers toward him and he held her hand, not knowing how to help her. Tightening her grip on him, she began to push. He knew enough to know the child was coming.

For the next twenty minutes, the spasms came closer, one upon another, and Lakra pushed and swore in the Althar tongue, gripping Cael's hand as if he was her lifeline, her only way back from the pain.

Finally the child came. She drew the small slippery body from between her thighs, a female infant, pale-skinned and capped with fine dark hair, and held the child against her breast beneath the coarse travelling robe. Threads pulled from the robe served to tie off the umbilical cord, and Lakra touched the small knife in the sheath at Cael's wrist.

He looked at her questioningly.

"You . . . cut?" She indicated the tied cord.

Oh Gods! "Where?"

She showed him and he complied, his nature helping overcome his squeamishness. She raised herself, unpillowed his shirt, wrapped the infant in it and handed the bundle to him. "Take. Wait. I finish."

He needed no urging. The child whimpered and squirmed, turned her birth-creased face to his chest. He held the warm scrap in one arm, the mail and his sword in the other, shielding her from the overhanging scrub and fern as he exited the confining rock into the fresh air and breathed deeply. His male companions grinned at him and clapped in melodramatic applause as he emerged, blinking, his eyes adjusting to daylight. Verra slouched against the rock, arms and ankles crossed, a picture of disapproval.

>*Peace, Verra,*< he sent, pulsing calm to her. >*As you can see, I am unharmed.*<

She shook her head in exasperation. "You are also exposed. Give me the child and put that back on," she commanded, indicating the chain mail over-shirt in his hand. He complied with a grin, and Verra held the infant while he did so, inspecting the tiny face with curiosity.

"Now what, O saviour of the Althar race?" She cocked her head at him as she returned the small bundle. He handed her the sword, and she slid it into the sheath at his saddle.

"We take them home, I would think. It would be generous of you to offer the Way, Verra."

"To Alth?" Verra's tone was incredulous. "Do you not *like* living?"

"Verra." Telsen spoke gently. "Cael is right. There is no threat from Alth. Alth's Council is as concerned as we are about the renegade action."

"Apart from threatening the peace, their actions are also affecting trade. Many towns have laid sanctions against trade with Alth," Cael put in. "Both councils are committed to halting the rebellion for the mutual good." The infant in his arms set up a protesting wail, the small mouth wide with newborn distress, and he rocked the child gently as he had seen Illiahn do countless times. Verra's suspicions appeared eased, but Cael knew her concern for his safety ran deep.

"I will offer the Way," she conceded, "but we will all go, and *you* will stop putting yourself at risk and remain between us."

"As my Lady wishes." He gave her the title and deferential salute normally reserved for one of Galaen's status, and she coloured a little, suddenly aware of her high-handed treatment of him. She muttered something inaudible and turned away, apparently impenitent.

The twins stared past Cael, and he knew Lakra was behind him. He turned and offered her his arm, and she took it, her face pale even for one of her race. She was wary of the others and careful to keep Cael between herself and Verra, not taking her eyes off the woman who had threatened her. The travel robe covered her to her ankles, and she drew the hood up to protect her fair skin from the sun. Her strange dark eyes gave her an alien appearance, although she was possessed of a delicate, angular beauty. Her hair was fine and dark, cut very short in a feathery fashion, only a few short spikes now visible beneath her hood. She had high cheekbones and a small nose and mouth above a slightly cleft chin. The only relief to her monochrome appearance was the pale rose of her lips.

"You are well?" Cael's expression was one of concern as he noted her pallor and slow walk.

"Well." She nodded once and held out her arms for the child. Her eyes slid to the tattoo visible beneath his chain mail. "You . . . speak, here?" Lakra reached up to touch his temple as she asked, and he gave her a nod of confirmation. Her dark brows arched, and he felt a gentle stroke on his mind.

His face registered surprise, but he said nothing of the brief contact that hinted at secrets. "My Lady over there will transport you to your home." Cael fixed Verra with an intense look.

"Travel magic?" Lakra cast an anxious glance at the Wayfinder.

"I need only a landmark near your home." Verra's tone was heavy with reluctance.

Lakra shook her head vigorously with an expression akin to panic, and backed away from them. Cael and Verra exchanged looks. "There is no danger, Lakra," Cael reassured, not understanding her reaction.

"Yes danger, big danger," she replied, patting her chest

and nodding rapidly. She could not explain further; they had reached the limits of the language barrier.

"Does she wish to return home or not?" Verra stared at the Althar woman with open dislike.

>Peace!< Cael pulsed his impatience with Verra's continuing hostility, turning forceful amber eyes on her. She shrugged, folded her arms and waited, diverting her gaze to the hills. The baby wailed, having picked up her mother's distress and Cael automatically pulsed soothing waves of calm as he had to Myst and Raen as babies. The wailing ceased abruptly.

>Tel, talk to her. She is frightening Lakra and causing delay.< Telsen's dark eyes acknowledged him as he took Verra's arm and murmured in her ear, leading her away from the confrontation. Chad and Sorren talked quietly, patient bookends, well used to situations such as this. The level of familiarity among the three often led to disagreement, but Cael's wisdom and acknowledged leadership always re-established the balance.

Cael turned to Lakra, searching her face. He attempted a sending, but as with all Althar, she was impenetrable to him. Yet she had touched him with her mind. He did not like puzzles. "Do you speak here also?" He frowned and touched her temple as she had done to him.

Her face was anxious, and she hesitated. Then: * Affirmative, but this is not for all to know. * Her mindspeak was a combination of concepts and words, at once unfamiliar but understandable, bridging the difference between their languages.

>Althar secret?<

* Affirmative. Few alakem know. *

>Alakem?<

* Flatlanders. White-eyes. *

155

Cael grinned his understanding. >*Why will you not travel? Where is the danger?*<

* To me—to my symbiot. Once fully matured, it is incompatible with alakem travel magic. If the symbiot is destroyed, I die. *

Oh Gods! It was going to be a long day. >*Why could I not reach your mind before?*<

She smiled apologetically. * My barrier was up. My symbiot allows me protection from alakem Empaths unless I desire otherwise. *

Cael had personal experience of the symbiot's barrier, and shuddered at the memory. >*How did you come to be here?*<

* I travelled after my brother. He is a young hothead and came to join the renegades. I hoped to persuade him of his foolishness and dishonour. He rejected me and I was returning home when the birthing took me. * She gazed at the sleeping infant. * She came early. The rocks were the only shelter I could reach. I owe you much, Empath. *

>*I did nothing, Lakra.*<

* Your protection from the angry one and your presence when I feared. Your help and your patience. These are something. I owe. * Her black gaze was direct and proud. * I am A'Thek. Whenever you have need, I will honour you in pleasure. *

What she offered him was indeed a great honour, and he felt a stirring in his groin despite himself and the strange circumstances. The reputation of A'Thek ability to give physical pleasure had gained legendary status. >*You honour me already, A'Thek, with your offer. I am unable to accept. I am bonded. The magic of the bond keeps my physical pleasures only to my mate. Besides, Alakem are loyal to their mates.*< Amongst other reasons, he thought.

* For that, I am sorry. It would have been my pleasure also. *

>*You honour me again.*<

She smiled knowingly, and he flushed, suddenly discerning her awareness of his arousal. *And you have doubled my debt and increased your own honour by your refusal. You show great restraint, Empath. *

Cael raked his hands through his hair, waiting for the heat raised by the exchange to ease. The others were watching curiously a little distance apart and he sent a brief message of explanation to them, leaving out the fact of Lakra's mindspeak, saying only that they had reached an understanding.

Lakra sat down and drew the child inside her robe. * Thank the angry one for her offer, but I cannot use her magic. *

>*Are you well enough to ride?*<

* Affirmative, but have never done so. * Althar rarely used horses, their mountainous territory being an unsuitable environment.

The riders received the news graciously enough. Verra resigned herself to the situation, and agreed to transport Chad to Kereál to bring back supplies for the two-day journey to the nearest Althar settlement of Kyanor. The horses were hobbled and grazing, the saddles and bridles resting on saddle blankets on dry ground. Lakra leaned against the rocks, the child still invisible inside her robe, her eyes slitted in watchful repose.

"She came a long way alone," Telsen remarked. "For an emotionless breed, she took a great risk for her brother."

"Althar are very private, brother. There is much we do not know of them. They are not unemotional, just reserved toward those they have not yet come to trust. Understandable, I think." Cael glanced over at Lakra, his face thoughtful. She had told him she would be fully recovered from the birth in a few hours, one of the benefits of the symbiot. Enhanced perception, agility and strength were among the other benefits. Althar had few enemies and disdained to use weapons, relying instead on their enhanced physical ability alone to settle any fighting. The young renegades however, had no regard for the social rules of their culture, and some had begun to carry blades, one of which was responsible for the fine scar running the length of Cael's upper left arm. He ran his fingertips down the scar in a now familiar gesture, thinking of Jenna.

Verra would not leave Cael, and sat beside the open Way waiting for Chad. He soon returned, his imminent arrival announced by several bedrolls that flew through the Way ahead of him. Waterskins and saddlebags of food supplies were loaded onto the horse he led through the shimmer. He threw a shirt to Cael and tossed a small pack to Lakra.

"Illiahn has sent a blanket and garments for the child," he explained as he pulled the saddle and the burdens from the horse's back.

They ate an evening meal of bread, meat and fruits, and settled close to the rock outcrop for the night, which passed dry and uneventful. The next day was cooler as they approached the mountains, their horses blowing hard at the constant, upward passage of the increasingly rocky terrain. On the second day of travel, the trail levelled off after they entered the pass that would take them to Kyanor.

They rode in single file. The track was plenty wide enough for two to ride safely abreast, but the horses were unused to the mountainous region, accustomed only to the foothills and plains; they shied from the edge if they came close enough to perceive the drop. A light, penetrating rain began to fall, misting the horses with beads of moisture and running in fine rivulets from the riders' oiled travel cloaks. The horses twitched their ears and blew invading droplets from their nostrils in steaming snorts, bridles jingling as heads tossed fitfully in the drizzle.

Cael led Lakra's horse as he had done for the entire journey. Its reins were looped over his arm, allowing her to attend to the infant, dry and warm beneath her robe. They had communicated periodically, and Cael had come to enjoy the Althar woman's intelligent wit and perception. She had sought to clarify his relationship status almost immediately.

* The angry one is not your bondmate? * she asked.

>*Verra? No. And she is not angry, just fearful.*<

* Fearful of me? *

He chuckled. >*No. Of threat to me from the renegades of your kind.*<

* She cares. *

>*It is her duty. She has been Wayfinder to me for more than two years. But yes, she cares.*<

* You are a leader then. Which town? *

>*Kereál. My hometown.*<

* And your mate is there? *

>*My mate is at the Guild, pursuing her own gifting. She is a Healer.*<

* She is beautiful? *

Cael's answering smile was carnal as he replied with a most categorical affirmative. This last impressed Lakra immensely, and she discontinued the questioning, clearly satisfied that her rescuer was well catered for.

The rain was beginning to find its way even into their clothing beneath the oiled cloaks, and the chill breeze grew steadily more insistent as they neared the end of the pass.

Lakra straightened in her saddle, suddenly alert, searching the rock face of the pass as it widened into a shallow basin between several low peaks. Cael saw nothing through the drizzle, but sensed the presence of others, and he was aware that Lakra was mindspeaking.

* They have been watching our approach. *

>They?<

* Watchers from Kyanor. *

>Friendly?<

* Affirmative. Suspicious, as are all Althar, but we have spoken. There is no harm here. *

Before long, several Althar pass-watchers seemingly materialised from the bowels of the mountain and strode to intercept the riders. Cael wondered if his eyes had deceived him, but could see no evidence of the watcher's passage where they had appeared. He tested the rock with a surreptitious shove. It was as solid as it looked, and he cast a puzzled glance at the watchers. They were all at least a head shorter than the Camarrhan men, but as lean and strong, bred to inhabit the mountains and traverse rock and snow, their hardiness enhanced by the symbiot each of them carried.

The watchers greeted the party formally, exchanging cordial though diplomatic words and handshakes, thanking them for their care of a valuable A'Thek and her child. They treated Lakra with great respect that she accepted as her due, and assured her of an escort to her own settlement whenever she wished it. She approached Cael, who waited apart from them, his face cowled in the hood of his cloak against the rain. He met her black gaze steadily.

>So.<

* Even so. * She regarded him from beneath her own dripping hood, her pale lips curving into a smile. She

stepped in close. * I would kiss you farewell, but you are alakem. *

>*Truth. I am unattractive?*<

* Negative, flatlander! Just tall. *

He returned her smile as she reached a hand behind his neck and allowed her to pull his head down toward her as she rose onto her toes. Her mouth was soft and warm, and he felt the flicker of her tongue on his lips for an instant.

* Should you reconsider my offer, Empath, the honour would be mine. My debt is large. So is my talent. * Raising her brows suggestively, she held his eyes for a moment before turning to acknowledge the others in thanks. And then she was gone, surrounded by the watchers in protective formation, heading for the shelter and relative comfort of Kyanor.

Looking around at the dripping, disconsolate group of riders, Cael rested his gaze on Verra. Contrite, ocean-green eyes slid from his regard. "Take us home, Wayfinder," he said gently, pulsing her a warm wave of forgiveness, understanding and a desire to be dry. He set his foot in the stirrup, hoisted a long leg over the bay gelding's rump and settled himself in the saddle. >*If you please, my Lady,*< he added with a crooked smile.

Chapter Eleven

Simon

Jenna spent long days in the Guild's infirmary. Wayfinders from all around the land brought in those too ill or wounded for their local Healers to tend, in the hope of gaining the help they required. A great variety of needs and a regular flow of patients resulted, placing demands on the limited number of trained Healers. Since the return of the healing magic, all Healers would have to learn how to use their gifting. Karessa was one of only five remaining Healers who had trained before the magic was lost. She was also the youngest of them.

Jenna worked hard, assimilating all the information Karessa imparted and what she could gain for herself through observation and practice. The "initial" training was so detailed that she wondered what she would encounter at the next level of instruction. She straightened her linen tunic over her dress and concentrated on her mentor's voice.

"Your thought-touch and perception must be finely honed before you attempt this, Jenna. It is an advanced technique, and the consequences of a careless touch are frightening. Follow me and observe." Karessa leaned over the newly arrived patient, a young girl wrapped in wet sheets as first aid for the extensive scalding she had sustained. The girl's mother sat in silence, wide-eyed with her daughter's pain, holding the child's hand and watching the

Healer's every move. The girl sobbed in frightened gasps, whimpering with pain and fear. Karessa took the Keystone in her hand and focussed on its depths. Jenna followed. She watched in awe as Karessa deftly turned off first the child's pain-centre, then the centre of consciousness. Surfacing from the stone, they found the girl relaxed and sleeping, her mother weeping quietly into her sleeve.

"Consequences, you said?" Jenna suppressed a shudder as she remembered her ignorance when she had first healed Cael's injuries, thankful she had caused him no damage.

Karessa gently unwound the sheeting from the girl's body, tutting at the extent of the scald. "Touch the pain-centre awry, and you risk paralysis. A careless touch in the consciousness-centre and coma may result. Of course, when it is done with skill, it is a blessed relief for a patient in pain, and an invaluable tool."

Jenna held soft towels ready as the old Healer assessed the damage and sluiced water over the burned skin to clear away any cloth particles that remained. "Why turn off both centres? Surely one or the other would be enough?"

"Turn off pain and you have a very frightening sensation: being awake but unable to feel your physical self. The pain-centre controls not just pain, but all sensory experience except sight and hearing. Adults will cope with that if they are warned, but not a child. Turn off consciousness, and the pain remains—but you may not respond to it. Neither situation is desirable, I think you would agree." Karessa began the healing.

Over the next half-hour, Jenna watched blisters and cracks meld and seal; twisted, red skin straighten and pale finally to healthy pink, as the healing concluded. "We will leave her to sleep. Come take a cup of tea with me," Karessa said to the girl's mother. "I wish to speak with you

163

regarding safety in your kitchen. Jenna, perhaps you would be so kind as to assist with Trista's group."

"Of course, Healer. Ah, how may I 'assist'?" Jenna turned to see the group of novices Karessa indicated.

Karessa leaned forward with a colluding smile. "Rescue her from pattern practice. She struggles, and could use some expert guidance," she whispered. "You have a re-markable ability to see the pattern within the stone. Impart some of that wisdom to Trista and I will be grateful. She has great potential, otherwise."

Jenna sighed as Karessa left with the penitent mother in tow. She didn't mind the assignment, was flattered really, but Trista had become her constant shadow whenever their differing schedules allowed. She found the girl's admiration both endearing and a little unnerving, especially when the subject of conversation was Cael. Trista had seen them to-gether on the beach as they had taken their leave of each other and, with teenage enthusiasm for romance and in-trigue, raised the subject often. She sighed over "Jenna's dragon" to the other novices who would sometimes gather to listen. Liaison with an Empath seemed to be an ambition they all cherished, although Jenna privately wondered if the young girls understood the nature of such a liaison.

According to the avid chatterers, a certain amount of clandestine "fooling around" went on. Jenna was amused at the girls' desire to experience some of these secret pleasures with various village boys who appealed to them. They were all in firm control of their fertility, at least. She was begin-ning to develop an intimate knowledge of her own body's rhythms, and would soon be able to control many of its functions, fertility included.

Unfortunately, not libido, she thought with a sigh. That was as pressing a need as ever. Sighing with desire as a young girl was one thing, but a woman ought to be able to scratch where it itches. Quite an untenable situation. She had begun to dream of Cael. Erotic, heated scenes. And knew with embarrassment that he felt the echoes of these dreams, distance being no barrier to the physical sharing of their bond. Twice she dreamed, and twice he responded. First with an involuntary physical reaction, and then with a sending: >*Gods Jenna! It is well that I am alone.*< His sending on the second occasion had been just as succinct: >*No shame. I thank you for sharing.*<

She heard the dry humour behind his words with disbelief. Was it possible he was relaxing his guard, or was he simply sparing her further embarrassment? This lack of censure was typical of Camarrhan culture. Adults felt no need to point out others' mistakes or engender guilt.

Thinking about it was not the smartest thing to do either, she gave herself a sharp reminder. Keep busy, get involved, don't think about it. Usual routine. So bolstered, she caught Trista's eye and beckoned her from the group. This would be her last afternoon at the Guild. Verra would arrive tomorrow to take her back to the homestead to prepare for their day trip to Auckland. Jenna hoped she could see Cael again without blushing too fiercely with the memory of the dreams between them.

Fortunately for them both, she could. He stood as she entered the kitchen, and they greeted each other with courtesy as had become their habit. His light embrace surprised her further. The thin fabric of his shirt transmitted his body heat, and her fingers lingered on the long muscles of his back.

"Welcome home, Healer," he said as they parted. Jenna eyed him curiously, not yet secure in this new easiness of manner.

"Jenna!" Mi'Cael flew through the doorway at her in a flurry of arms and legs, blond hair flying as he came. She caught the boy up in a hug, surprised at the intensity of his greeting and how much she had missed him. "It is good that you are here!" The child's tone was emphatic. Only Jenna caught the glance he threw at his uncle.

Myst gathered a fold of Jenna's skirt in both small hands and held it to her cheek as Raen smiled up at her past the thumb in her mouth. Jenna took them both into a gentle hug, dropping a resounding kiss on each plump cheek. The twins climbed into her lap as she sat and fished out tiny, pearlescent shells, sand dollars and other beach finds from her pockets. She held the small girls on her lap for an instant longer before they wriggled free to take their treasures for their mother's inspection. Jenna smiled as they went, straightening her skirts and longing for her Levi's.

Cael leaned easily against the solid wooden bench that lined the back wall of the kitchen, the morning sun through the window casting a fine aura of gold around his hair and shadowing his face. "The children are fond of you, *chekuán,*" he observed.

Jenna raised her eyes to find herself the subject of his amber gaze. "You never did tell me exactly what that word means, did you?"

He frowned and looked past her at Illiahn, who chuckled and shook her head. "You are in your own paddock with that particular bull, *chiaran.*" She laughed. Jenna's brows inclined further, and she widened her eyes at him in question.

He released a rueful sigh and pulsed her an image. *Oh. A horse.* Exquisitely formed and wild-spirited, but still, a horse. "That's not so bad, is it?" Jenna looked at Illiahn who still shook with laughter at her brother's discomfort.

"Actually I found the comparison rather flattering. I choose to take that as a compliment, knowing how much your horses mean to you all." With a mock curtsey to Cael, she prodded his chortling sister in the shoulder and made a dignified exit.

His sending halted her. *>Jenna? It was always meant as a compliment. Please forgive any offence.<*

She leaned her head back around the door and winked at him. "None taken," she answered, wishing again she could show him her own thoughts with such eloquent clarity. The image he had shown her had been beautiful.

Later that day, they were ready to leave, dressed in as inconspicuous a manner as possible. All wore breeches and shirts, besides Jenna, who wore her jeans. Verra had keyed her apartment as a landmark. The Way would take them straight there. The time zones seemed fairly parallel, but she could not know if they would encounter Tessa. A chance they had to take.

"Home later tonight, Illiahn. I want to show them how the other half lives!" Jenna said, indicating Verra, Telsen and Cael standing by the haze of the open Way. Verra stepped into the shimmering curtain and beckoned the others through. All clear then.

Blinking in the afternoon sun, Illiahn shaded her eyes and waved. With a ring of crystal, they were back in Jenna's apartment, a world away, separated only by the thin fabric of a different reality.

Possum arched and spat, retiring under the table in a flurry of feline indignation as the intruders entered her domain. Jenna laughed, cajoling the wide-eyed creature with small, familiar sounds of endearment. Eventually, Possum succumbed and allowed Jenna to draw her from her shelter, and wild purring ensued as their relationship reinstated itself. Jenna cradled the cat as she threw open the door to the courtyard, surveying the subdued, early autumnal garden.

>*You have missed this.*<

It was a statement, not a question. Jenna turned to meet his serious regard as Possum escaped her embrace and fled outside. "Of course. This was my home. My sanctuary, really." Sinking into the plush blue couch, she sighed and leaned back.

Cael felt the huge dose of comfort she experienced at the familiarity of her world. He exchanged a look with Telsen. >*This is her territory. I feel as if I am intruding on her.*<

"No more than you did before, brother," Telsen murmured in reply. "And it was here that she saved your life. Gods, man! There is more to her than you give her credit for."

>*No, Tel. You mistake me. Much happened here and much changed—both for Jenna and myself. Just being here unsettles me.*<

"We have the afternoon to collect a few inhalers." Jenna nestled deeper into the soft depths of the couch. "I want to take a class at the gym for old times' sake, and then my friends, I want to show you how we *eat* here!" Telsen's face lit with anticipation.

"We are dressed rather differently, Jenna," Cael observed, indicating their leather breeches and soft linen shirts. "Will we not raise eyebrows?"

Telsen chuckled. "That has never bothered you in the past."

"I have never sought to be different, Tel. It is best for us to avoid drawing attention to ourselves. Where will you tell them we are from, should you be asked?" Telsen subsided without answer.

"People here are tolerant of difference, Cael. Anyone wondering will probably see you as alternative lifestylers— neo-hippies—maybe even actors! We could invent anything. It really doesn't matter." Jenna smiled his concerns away. He wished he shared her confidence of her culture's acceptance.

A half-hour later, Jenna folded them into her Celica and drove into the city. She parked, and they began to wander through the streets of downtown Auckland in pursuit of their quest. Verra and Telsen walked hand in hand. Cael pushed his hands deep into the pockets of his breeches as they walked, and Jenna tucked her hand beneath his arm. Catching their reflection in a shop window, she tilted her chin defiantly. They certainly made an odd-looking group.

There were several pharmacies to visit within three streets. The procedure was quite simple. Jenna would approach the pharmacist. "I'm from out of town. I've left my inhaler at home."

The inhalers were expensive but easy enough to obtain without a doctor's prescription. She also purchased a spacer at each shop, the device that enabled children to use Ventolin by holding a small mask over nose and mouth to breathe the contents of the inhaler. She reasoned the device would be required for unconscious patients.

Within an hour, the task was complete. Her off-world companions were ill at ease in the city, overwhelmed by the soaring constructions of concrete, glass and metal; the noise and odours of traffic; the strange attire of the people of this world. Some stared openly at the tall, strangely dressed trio without bothering to hide their reactions. Both men were drawing their share of female attention. Cael remained outwardly composed, but Jenna noted his tension and felt his readiness to react to potential trouble. Taking his hand, she stopped and captured his gaze. "I know how different all this is to you." Her eyes swept the city streets. "But there is no danger here. Try to relax a little?"

His eyes betrayed his discomfort. "I want to go back, Jenna. We all do."

"Even Tel?"

"Even Tel."

A sudden siren wailed, eliciting a nervous jump from Telsen, and Jenna realised with sudden guilt how tense they all were. "Will you give me this one night? If this is too hard, Cael, you go home. I want to go to the gym, exercise, maybe eat. You needn't stay. I understand. Verra can come for me later." Her dark eyes were luminous with her plea, and he did not deny her.

"If you stay, *chekuán,* I will not leave you. Galaen would have my hide!" He smiled crookedly. "Your great-aunt can be very persuasive when she so desires."

Jenna took his face in her hands. "I want to show you," she said, demanding audience with his mind. He entered, and she showed him her intentions. The waterfront; wharves and anchorages; boats, yachts and ships, large and small, commercial, private and luxurious; the restaurants, bars and bistros that lined the area, the food, atmosphere, views and ambience.

He smiled at her enthusiasm to share this part of her world and relayed her images to Verra and Telsen.

"How can we say no?" Verra's green eyes glowed with affection. "We will walk the paths by the harbour where the ships lie. You go to your place of exercise and we will meet when you are finished."

Cael nodded in ambivalent agreement, pulsing reassurance and acceptance to Jenna, although his expression remained guarded. She knew he felt a burden of responsibility for her, for them all. He felt out of his depth in this unfamiliar world, unable to protect them.

Jenna chuckled as the two tall men again folded themselves into her Celica. With their knees almost level with their shoulders, they endured the ride home in uncomfortable silence.

"I have keyed several landmarks this afternoon. I think we will use the Way to transport us tonight," Verra said, failing to suppress a smile. Cael agreed immediately. The women's eyes met in the rearview mirror, sharing their amusement.

Simon Lawton's face darkened as the Celica turned out of sight. His fingers drummed irritably on the leather upholstery of his Mercedes.

So, she was back. And apparently attached.

He had spotted Jenna's car that afternoon quite by accident and waited in an unobtrusive spot until she returned to it. Three weeks of brooding over her disappearance had soured him. His obsessive nature would not allow him to let go his pursuit of her. And now, to add insult to injury, here she was fawning over some walking anachronism several years her junior.

A small hard knot of anger began to form in him, coalescing further with every thought of her with the boy. He could not accept that Jenna was out of his reach. Never had he let "no" be an answer, and he was not about to begin now.

He started his car and nosed it into the flow of traffic, pondering his next move. The boy must be dissuaded. Made to see how inadequate he was for a woman like Jenna. First things first. He would speak with her, make her see what a fool she was making of herself.

171

Simon was confident she would find his approaches agreeable. He was, after all, attractive, ambitious and already highly successful. His future was bright and secure. He had a lot to offer a woman.

She should be flattered.

Oh God! Jenna knew she would pay the price for this class tomorrow. As she stretched her protesting muscles, she felt Cael's presence nearby. A quick glance around showed her he was not as close as she thought. Maybe outside.

The cool-down music finished, and hoping to avoid stiff and aching muscles tomorrow, she stayed for a few further stretches before taking her bar and weights to the racks.

"Well, well, Lara. It's good to see you back!" Jenna coloured. She was aware of the nickname and understood his reference immediately.

Damn. In her distraction she had neglected to make her usual fast getaway. "I'm not staying, Simon. Just tying up a few loose ends. I'll be leaving again tonight."

"Oh? Business or pleasure?" He removed the weights from his bar.

"Neither. I'm just leaving." She offered nothing more as she loosened the keepers on her bar and slid the weights onto the stack.

"Surely not without letting me buy you a drink?" He flashed a practised smile at her. "I've been wanting to ask you for months, but you always seem to evapourate like mist after class."

She smiled politely. "Thanks Simon, but I'm in a relationship now."

"I'm inviting you for a drink, not asking you to marry me," he joked. "I'm harmless—promise!" His predatory

172

smile belied his words as he draped his towel around his neck and held an end in each hand.

"Maybe next time," she replied, knowing there may never be one. Her mild expression softened her words, but she could see he still chafed at them.

"There's something I'd like to discuss with you. Over a drink, preferably." His body language telegraphed that he was being as charming as he knew how, but his boyish expression seemed a little manufactured on one so urbane. "Please?"

Shit, Simon. Just go away.

Thinking quickly, she sucked water from her bottle. "I'm meeting my partner and some friends on the waterfront for an early dinner. Why don't you drop in for that drink? We can talk then, if you like." Check.

"That's not quite what I had in mind." His tone was abrupt. "Can you give me half an hour before you meet them?"

Shit. What could he possibly have to discuss? "I'm sorry, Simon, I can't. I'm meeting them very soon. They don't know Auckland—they're relying on me as tour guide." Checkmate.

She saw his exasperation at her neat avoidance of him. His eyes hardened. His charming smile slipped. The predator was back.

"I saw you in town today with your new . . . partner." He used the term as if it tasted bad on his tongue. "He's a *boy*, Jenna. You are making yourself look foolish." He looked around and lowered his voice. "I can't believe you see anything in him. What could he possibly offer you?"

Jenna shook her head in disbelief. She picked up her towel and turned her back on him, heading for the showers. He laid a restraining hand on her shoulder and she spun around, her braid flying across his chest and completing its arc behind her. She shook off his hand.

"You are a very poor judge of people, Simon!" Her indigo eyes flashed with pique. "That *boy* is more of a man than any I have met. Present company included," she spat. With a sudden desire to meet offence with offence, she added, "What can he offer me? Satisfaction and happiness, Simon. More than all your money could buy. What else do *you* have to offer?"

"Jenna, listen . . ."

"No, Simon. Save it." Her brows rose to a dangerous angle. "It was men like you that made me decide to leave the lot of you alone. I have nothing more to say to you." She injected as much disgust into her words as she could, and left him standing in impotent anger as she departed for the change rooms.

Simon showered and dressed. His anger at the exchange festered. Slamming the locker door with a satisfying crash, he frowned sullenly at his reflection in the mirror. If she thought she could insult him like that without consequence, she could think again. At least no one had heard. That would have been just too embarrassing.

He took the stairs two at a time as he exited the gym and stopped in shocked surprise as he turned into the street. The oddly dressed young man he had seen with Jenna was propped against the wall of the building, ankles crossed, his head turned away from Simon.

Perfect.

Simon smoothed his hair back from his face, pulling it into a spiky sweep across his forehead. He approached the fellow, confident of his own mature superiority.

The scruff turned his head, raising his brows in apparent query as he saw him.

"I'm Simon. You're waiting for Jenna Wade?" A single slow incline of the head was the only response. The boy appeared to be gauging him, measuring his worth. Good. Let him. "I think you should know that she and I have an understanding."

The golden brows rose further. "Really?"

"Yes, really. Nothing has been decided yet, but I have plans for our future and I'm advising you to back off." Simon's voice was terse, conveying his annoyance. He straightened as amused amber eyes swept him from his designer haircut to his Nike cross-trainers.

The corners of the boy's mouth quirked. "Jenna is free to make her own choices," he said mildly. "She has not spoken of you before."

Simon had not expected such a neutral response. "She has class. She wouldn't want to embarrass you. What can you offer a woman like that, *junior?* Look at yourself. You can't even dress like a man, let alone offer her a future!" Simon's sneer was designed to provoke.

"A man's worth is not defined by his years, Simon, nor his clothing. And my name is *Cael.*" The boy remained relaxed. His nonchalance irked Simon further. Who was in control here?

"Look, whoever you are, stay away from Jenna. That's your only warning." The hard knot of anger grew. He dropped his gym bag to the ground beside him.

"I am unable to do that." The golden eyes hardened. "And a small man, such as you are proving yourself to be, is in no position to make threats." He pushed himself from the wall and stood up straight. Simon became uncomfortably aware of his stature. He glared up in dislike at Cael, who sighed and shook his head. "There is no need for hostility. The choice is not ours to make; it is Jenna's.

175

You would do well to accept that."

Condescending bastard. "I don't need your advice, junior." Simon narrowed his eyes and stepped closer to the tall figure before him. He stabbed holes in the air with his forefinger as he spoke. "Just piss off to whatever backwater you came from and do us all a favour."

"No, little man. I think it is you who should . . . piss off." Cael planted his feet firmly and folded his arms.

The knot exploded.

Simon snarled and swung a heavy fist at him, expecting to connect with his jaw. A sidestep and a raised arm later, Simon found his wrist held firmly in Cael's hand.

"You swing like a girl," came the bored comment. "Care to take another shot?"

"You'll end up like Brer Rabbit on the tar baby if you do, Simon." Jenna spoke from behind him and moved to Cael's side to lay a restraining hand on his chest. Simon wrenched his arm free of Cael's grasp, glowering with dented pride.

"I see you've already met Cael." Her voice was cool. She turned her back on him and planted a deliberate, lingering kiss on Cael's mouth. Simon thought he detected a flicker of surprise in the boy's golden eyes. Or was it disapproval? Curious.

"You see how things are, Simon. Who is looking foolish now?" Jenna arched a brow at him.

Simon flushed at the ice in her eyes, her denial of him. "I can't believe you would waste yourself on this . . . this scruffy *boy!* It's obvious you don't have the sense I credited you with."

"Trouble, brother?" A tall man and a woman, both clad in similar fashion to Cael, approached behind him, arm-in-arm.

"Nothing a boy cannot handle." Cael's tone was light, his smile even, but the hardness remained in his eyes.

Simon backed away, retrieved his sports bag and slung it over his shoulder. Shaking his head in disgust, he turned his back on them and stalked away with as much dignity as he could salvage.

Putting the unpleasant scene behind them, they managed to enjoy dinner. Jenna chose one of the many bistros that lined the waterfront, offering spectacular views of luxury yachts and lights dancing on the dark water. They sampled a wide variety of foods, and Jenna's smile grew wider as she enjoyed their appreciation of such exotic fare. Knowing the taverns of Camarrhan served wines and ales, she had ordered accordingly. She sipped a Chardonnay, resting a fond gaze on Cael as he and Telsen compared the lagers they drank.

"We may have to visit again, brother!" Telsen's mood was expansive, his enjoyment evident.

Cael's demeanour was odd. He was quiet and withdrawn, although she was aware that he tried to cover it. Jenna smiled as he glanced up at her, feeling her regard. Are you okay? she mouthed at him.

>*It is not over, Jenna. You shamed him and he means you harm.*<

Simon? she mouthed again, and he nodded once. His concern touched her. She leaned toward him. "We'll be gone soon. What can he do before then?"

He shrugged, draining the last of his beer. >*Just a feeling,*< he sent, >*one I have learnt not to ignore.*<

Jenna ordered a selection of cheeses. As it arrived, she excused herself to the bathroom. When she returned, Cael was absent. Bathroom, probably, she thought. Verra exclaimed over the blue cheeses, which were outside her experience, and again Jenna felt the warmth of their growing friendship. Telsen straightened suddenly, his eyes alert.

"Tel?" Verra laid her hand on his arm. He pushed his chair back and stood, taking a wedge of soft cheese from the board.

"Stay here." His smile told them not to be concerned as he sauntered from the restaurant out into the night.

Cael stood in the shadows, neon-flicker from eating establishments painting puddles of coloured light on the warm asphalt of the wharf.

Three men stood around him. One of them he knew. Simon had been looking for them, had not seen them at the back of the bistro. Cael had seen *him* however, and quietly left the table without comment.

Simon had been drinking. A reasonable amount, by the look of him. His two companions also smelled of strong spirits, their courage bolstered with alcohol. One was tall and lean, the other well built and large-featured, his face dominated by a broad nose.

An evil smile spread across Simon's face. "Not so fucking clever *now,* are you?" he slurred.

Cael snorted in amusement at the irony. Satisfied they were no threat, he settled himself to play. >*Tel! Come watch this . . . and my back, if you would.*< He raised his hands to guard his face, balanced himself lightly, weight evenly distributed, one foot forward, waiting.

Simon launched himself at Cael, cursed, swung a wild blow at his face. Cael blocked the swing, stepped forward, pushed Simon's face hard, open-palmed. Simon stumbled, almost fell, cursed again. The big-nosed man circled behind Cael, the other came at him as Simon had done. Propelling himself backward, Cael slammed an elbow into the belly of the stocky man behind him. He stepped forward again, dropped his shoulders to avoid the coming fist, unloaded a roundhouse kick across the lean man's rear, sending him off balance into a stumbling roll. Simon swung at him again, closer this time. Cael blocked easily, pushing away the blow. Again Simon swung, face contorted with angry frustration. Cael stepped back, caught the fist. He pulled, sending Simon headlong to the ground, propelled by his own momentum.

A body slammed into Cael from behind. He let himself fall. Curling a shoulder, he rolled and regained his feet, noting the position of all three. And Telsen, leaning against a large shipping container in the shadows, grinning over folded arms. >*Good of you to attend, brother.*< Telsen inclined his head in gracious acknowledgment.

"Hold him!" Simon grated, wiping blood from the cheek grazed by his fall. His cohorts approached Cael, wary now, doubt plain on their faces.

Cael stood, calm, balanced, waiting. They came.

Both made a grab for his arms. He allowed one to connect. Using the man as a prop, he swung his legs hard into the other's belly. The lean one collapsed with a great whoosh of loosed breath, and Cael landed atop big-nose, both felled by the force of the move. He rolled, twisted, pushed himself clear with both feet, rolled again to avoid Simon's vicious kick.

"Fuck you, Cael!" Simon screamed at him, control lost in a frustrated rage. "I fucking *warned* you to stay away from her!"

Cael heard a whisper of steel behind him. A small sound but familiar, followed by a soft gasp. He did not move.

Telsen's voice came from behind, quiet and dangerous.

"My brother yet only plays with you. It would not be to your advantage to annoy him. Drop the knife." A blade clattered to the ground. "Much better. Now play nicely."

>*Very courteous, Tel.*< Cael's glance flicked thanks. His kick sent the knife skittering away into the darkness, and a soft splash told them where it landed.

Simon swore loudly, chest heaving, taking stock of his situation. His tall ally sat hunched over, still fighting for breath. Big-nose rubbed his wrist, approached Simon, whispered to him. Eyes narrowed.

Cael waited. >*Last round, Tel,*< he sent as the two moved.

They charged him together. He rolled his eyes, incredulous at their clumsy lack of skill. A boy half his age could fight better.

He sidestepped, rotated his torso and brought his left elbow up hard under the knife wielder's jaw. "*That* is for being dishonourable."

Big-nose collapsed bonelessly. Stepping forward, Cael cocked his hips and pivoted, releasing a sweeping kick against the back of Simon's knees. Simon's legs crumpled. He fell sideways and rolled onto his back. His eyes widened as Cael dropped a knee into his chest, pinning him down.

It was the glint of steel that held Simon's attention. A wicked throwing knife was sheathed in stout leather at each of Cael's wrists. The buttons at his cuffs had been torn off during the fight, and the sleeves hung open, the knives clearly visible. The lean man scurried off into the night. Simon swallowed, panting, and raised his eyes to meet Cael's hard gaze.

"You could have used those at any time," he said, his face showing incomprehension.

Cael maintained the pressure on Simon's chest. "I have

no desire to harm you, Simon. I would not draw steel unless my life was threatened."

"So you didn't feel threatened? Why the hell not? I tried hard enough." Simon barked a short, humourless laugh and raised his hands as if in surrender. "Now get the fuck off of me."

Cael shrugged, removing his knee. "You have been drinking. Never a good state to be in when you make a challenge."

Simon's face twisted into a dark grimace. He ignored Cael's offered hand and pushed himself unsteadily to his feet.

"We are not so different." Cael pulled his sleeves around the knives at his wrists. "We both care enough about someone to want to make a stand." They eyed each other a moment. "Sometimes a man's choices are not his own, Simon. There is no shame in that."

Simon dabbed at his bloody cheek with the back of his hand, a disdainful sneer curling his mouth. "That's where your whole philosophy is wrong, boy. A *man always* makes his own choices." He drew himself up with amusing dignity, turned his back on Cael and stalked off into the darkness with only a slight lurch. "Give my regards to the ice queen," came his parting shot. "She's not as hot as I thought."

"Where did you learn to fight like that, brother?" Telsen expressed his surprise as they walked back. "I have not seen that before."

Cael chuckled. "My lady Healer. She is as capable of inflicting injury as she is of healing it."

Jenna stood anxiously at the bistro door as they approached.

>*Peace, chekuán. It is well.*<

181

"Your shirt! What have you done?"

"He has 'tied up a loose end,' as I think you would say," Telsen answered for him.

"Simon?" she asked, frowning. "Did he hurt you?"

Cael raised his brows at her. "As if," his look said.

"Did you hurt *him?*" Her frown intensified.

"Would you care if I had?" He knew his eyes held challenge, but her disapproval agitated him, and he could not stop his reaction.

Jenna looked away. "I know you well enough to believe you would never dishonour yourself," she evaded.

Ah. So the lady *does* care. A reptilian writhing churned in the pit of his stomach, curled there, restive and cold. "Your friend is unhurt. His pride will recover—he is not entirely without good sense," he answered.

"He's not my friend, Cael, but I'd not like to see him hurt. I think we should go." They were attracting stares. Verra joined them outside. She glanced at Cael, then Jenna. Tension crackled between them. They ignored her.

"You were always free to stay, Jenna," he said softly, his eyes intent on hers. "Nothing has changed." He held her gaze for a moment, then turned his back on her with an impatient gesture to Verra.

The cold twisted again, settled, and stayed. What had he done? Gods, what had he been thinking? Discouraging Simon had not been his decision to make. He set his jaw and stepped grimly through the Way as soon as it opened. He did not look back.

Chapter Twelve

The Healer

The infirmary hummed with activity as Jenna entered, bearing a stack of freshly laundered towels. Novices came and went in small groups, shepherded by tutors, observing as those more experienced practised the craft of healing. She noted Trista's bright head as the girl frowned in concentration over the Keystone held by a dark-haired tutor. Pattern diagnosis. Jenna smiled, remembering her own introduction to the topic.

Three months had passed since her return from Auckland, and the second month of Camarrhan's winter had just begun. Maintained at a higher temperature than the rest of the stone chambers and corridors of the Guild, the infirmary felt pleasantly warm. Wielder's fire glowed blue in recesses along the walls, silent and smokeless, and kept constant by Quan's novices.

She walked the length of the long chamber that housed the male patients, reflecting on the difference between health care in her own world, and the system she had learned here. Such a welcome change to the uncertainty of life in the ICU of Auckland Hospital. Here, healing was performed in one of several private chambers. After the healing, workers moved the afflicted to the main infirmary and left him to sleep it off. The patients required no real nursing, only assistance to drink and eat while strength, depleted by the healing, gradually returned. Once a patient could stand, he could go home. Simple. Only the most traumatic of injuries could not be healed. Death still occurred, just less often.

Depositing the stack of fresh-scented towels into the shelving along the back wall, she took one to a basin set into a metal stand, poured water and washed her hands. She turned her attention to her next patient.

"Keo. How're you doing?" Taking his Keystone in her fingers, she focussed within its depth. Her awareness returned to the patient, whose deep blue eyes met hers in perfect trust. It was humbling, as always—there was no doubt in his mind that he was in safe hands. "You'll be home soon, maybe tomorrow if you continue to improve so quickly. Send to your wife. I know how she must miss you." Smiling at the recently healed Empath, she felt a pang of envy. And a healthy dose of self-pity. Bonded mates in every respect, Keo and his wife shared a closeness that transcended their individuality, rendered them inseparable.

>*I owe you a great debt, Healer,*< he sent, imbuing the message with respect and gratitude. >*I understand you are the one responsible for the cure for battle sickness?*<

Jenna flushed. This issue always arose. She could never tell the whole truth, either. Madame Curie she was not. "Hmm. That was a lucky accident." That much she could admit to.

>*You were born off world, I hear?*<

"You hear a lot for one so incapacitated," she teased, raising him on the pillows and helping him take some water.

>*Truth! There is little else to do here but listen.*< He subsided with a grimace, pulsing his frustration at the time his recovery was taking.

"You are alive, Keo!" she chided. "Sleep now. It will speed things up." She stood and drew the blanket around his chest and shoulders with the barest glance at his tattoo. The dragon rampant. She sighed, pressed her lips tightly together and moved to her next patient.

>*Healer?*<

She turned back to him.

>*Your bondmate. Why are you not together?*<

Shit. "You *do* hear a lot, don't you?"

He chuckled. >*No, Healer. I read your pain. It is strong in you.*< Keo's eyes closed.

"He is . . . somehow angry with me. I'm unfamiliar with many of the ways of this world. Misunderstandings happen," she said, surprised at her answer.

Keo pulsed his understanding and sympathy. >*It will be well?*<

"I hope so, Keo. Time will tell."

"What will time tell, Jenna? When we can eat, I hope—I am ravenous!" Trista said, her face disappearing momentarily as she pulled off the loose tunic that protected her clothing. Fine blonde hair haloed her head, static-mad. She smoothed it down, straightened her skirts and blew out an impatient pout of a sigh. "I am sure lunch gets later every day."

Jenna smiled fondly at the girl. "If you're finished what you've been given to do, there's no reason you shouldn't go persuade the kitchen to feed you early."

With a roguish smile, Trista tucked her tunic under her arm and headed for the door. "I hoped you might say that," she said. "See you soon?"

"Soon." Growing girl. Just turned fifteen and already considered a woman. Puberty had decided that. Jenna shook her head, amazed at the responsibilities assumed by one so young. Camarrhan culture was indeed interesting.

As Jenna tended her next patient, Karessa appeared at the foot of the bed.

"Come, Jenna. Lunch. This afternoon we have a lot to cover." She gave Jenna a close look. "Are you well, child?"

Jenna knew she did not look her best. The mirror that morning had shown her dark-shadowed eyes, large in her pale face. "I haven't been sleeping well," she admitted quietly. "I miss Cael, Karessa. I miss him but I think he is angry with me. I don't understand why he doesn't speak to me, and it hurts." She stood, removed her tunic, and they left the warmth of the infirmary.

The vast curving stone corridor was cooler, the recesses of blue fire spaced further apart, lighting their way with eerie incandescence. The sun vents were closed against the cold, and Jenna longed for the return of summer.

"He has not contacted you?" Karessa asked.

"No. Not since our return. He has withdrawn again."

Their voices echoed in a faint rustle along the stone walls. Karessa looked perplexed. Her faded blue eyes held sympathy as she frowned, creasing her brow into its usual, well-folded map of wrinkles. "It is not like him to withdraw in anger, Jenna. I have known him since his birth. I understand how he thinks, as much as any can understand an Empath."

They approached the dining hall and Jenna stopped, knowing Trista waited inside for her. "I don't know what to do. We were becoming easier with each other, but now I feel we're back to square one."

"Square one?"

Jenna smiled at Karessa's puzzlement. "Back to the beginning. Something changed between us as we left my world. Something I did . . . or said . . . I don't know. He *looked* angry, and he as much as told me that I needn't come back here with him. He shut me out; he stopped talking. Every day I feel he's further away." Her throat constricted. She looked away.

"Come. I will have lunch sent up to the study. You are in no state for Trista's chatter." Karessa sent a passing novice to the kitchen with her request, and Jenna followed her gratefully to the study.

As they sat, Karessa regarded her with a thoughtful stare. "Not many know that I was once a bondmate." She reached for a small, leather-coated flask, drew two tiny ceramic cups from her drawer. "I have been alone now for forty-five summers." She poured viscous golden liquid from the flask, and offered a cup to Jenna. "He was tall and strong. Not as beautiful as Cael, but we were well matched. And how we loved!" She sipped from the cup, her eyes far in the past.

Jenna took a tentative taste of the liquid. Spicy floral warmth crept over her tongue and glowed in her throat. "I suspected that. You seem to understand so much and question so little. Everyone else wants all the gory details, wants to know every little thing about the bond and the dragon." Sudden empathy for the older woman's aloneness filled her. "How did you lose your mate?"

"Raef died from a simple wound because the healing magic was lost. His blood became poisoned; there was nothing I could do to help him. He died slowly, in great pain, and when he went, I thought I would die also."

"Oh, God. I'm so sorry." Jenna saw the pain-remnant in the older woman's eyes and shivered with sick understanding. "There was no Way?"

"No. It was his time. No one understands the Way, not even the Wayfinders. We all have our opinions though, and most concur that the Way is attuned to Fate. A partnership, I suspect." She sipped again. "I tell you this not to wallow in my past, but so you may know that I understand. And that I know Empaths. Cael does not harbour anger, child. You must look deeper."

Jenna sipped more of the golden liqueur, leaning back into the deep leather chair. "Did Raef ever shut you out? Withdraw?"

"Only twice. In twenty years together, only twice. Both times it was to protect me."

"From what?"

A soft knock sounded at the door, and Karessa rose to admit a novice bearing lunch. The girl set the tray down on the carved wooden desk and left them.

"From himself, I think. He withdrew so my choice in a matter would be entirely my own, not directed by him through the bond, or through my loyalty to him."

"I'm not sure I understand." Jenna picked at dried fruits, poured herbal tea. Karessa wrapped a piece of cold meat in a slice of soft brown bread, took a bite and chewed thoughtfully. "If Cael believes on some level that your personal future would be better without him, he may withdraw. If he perceives that you desire a different path to his, he would certainly withdraw. By removing himself from the equation, a bondmate allows you your own choices."

"It sounds more like emotional blackmail to me," Jenna answered. "I want to be with him, no matter what the path."

"There is the matter of perception, Jenna. Any situation may be interpreted differently by all concerned, especially one of conflict. Think on that."

Oh great. And how do you interpret this particular situation, Miss Wade? Shit. Men really are from Mars . . . and Empaths possibly from as far out as Pluto.

Karessa's eyes flew wide. She stood quickly. "Another battle sickness case. We are called."

That made three in as many days. Sighing, Jenna pulled herself from the easy chair, tugged her tunic back on over her dress and followed Karessa into the corridor.

Sleeping Dragons

★ ★ ★ ★ ★

Illiahn watched from the kitchen as Cael split wood for the fires. Four hours had passed and he showed no signs of stopping. The afternoon was cool, the breeze holding the hint of snow from the ranges, but the occasional runnel of sweat still ran down his naked back to darken the leather of his breeches.

His intensity frightened her. He stacked the last batch of split wood in the lean-to beneath the kitchen windows, and began on the next pile. The pine split easily, but on occasion the axe struck a knot with the resistance of stone, provoking a loud curse as he wrestled the axe free from the wood.

"Come away, *chiara*. He is done when he is done." Brenn handed her a steaming mug and steered her to sit with him at the vast wooden table. They drank tea in silence, watching Myst draw chalk symbols on a slate, and "read" them to a solemn Raen, whose thumb was firmly in her mouth as always.

Illiahn offered slices of sweet apple to her daughters. The axe thunked in a continuous rhythm. "He is going to injure himself," she muttered.

"That is his choice, *chiara*." Brenn's gaze engaged hers. "You are not his mother, my wife, and he is not a boy. A man must do as he sees fit." She knew her eyes pleaded with him and knew he would respond. "If he still cuts within the hour, I will distract him. Peace, Illiahn."

She smiled, grateful for his concession.

The rhythm of the axe faltered. Cael wavered, drawing harsh breaths as he struggled to release the blade from the grip of a stubborn knot. The sharp tang of pine-scent clung to him, and black smears of resin streaked the skin of his

189

belly and chest. He rested but a moment, then again began his relentless swing. His back and shoulders were on fire. His wrists ached, and his head resounded with the repetitive thunk of iron connecting with wood.

Tonight he would sleep, he was sure of it.

Jenna held the rubber mask of the spacing device over the patient's nose and mouth. Depressing the aerosol spray of the attached inhaler several times, she deliberately overdosed him with Ventolin. His body convulsed. Trista held his head between firm hands, not allowing the movement to interfere with his ingestion of the drug.

Within minutes his pulse began to race. Jenna felt her usual relief spread in a prickle of warm release through her limbs. She still feared for each new victim, feared the treatment would not work for all. So far, all had proved to be as sensitive to the drug as she was.

The man relaxed. Trista released him. Over the next few minutes, they watched him slowly return to himself. As his eyes opened, Jenna saw the now familiar confusion. "It's all right. You're back. The symbiot is gone. Your mind is once again your own." Patting his shoulder in reassurance, she reflected on how easy it had become. Battle sickness was no longer a death sentence. She pulled the coverings around his shoulders as his eyes closed again. When she was sure he slept, she and Trista left the chamber, sending in another novice to watch over him.

Jenna started as a young Empath spoke into her mind. >*A visitor for you, Healer. She will wait for you at the keep.*< She recognised the voice. Trista was fond of this boy. Just turned sixteen, he was to receive his tattoo and final instruction next week. Jenna had no doubt there would be tears when he left. She sighed at the thought, and hurried to the keep, wondering who waited for her.

Verra looked up and smiled when Jenna entered the chamber. "I thought it about time I came to visit you again, *chiara*. The last two weeks have flown by." She held her hands to the small Wielder's fire in Karessa's study, her nose pink with cold from her brief wander in the bare and uninspiring winter gardens. "You have become quite a legend, Jenna! All Kereál speaks of you, proud to claim you as their own."

"All Kereál?" Jenna gave her a dubious glance.

"Almost. Many women have not yet forgiven you for taking Cael's attention, but I am sure they will recover from their disappointment." Verra grinned at her, unfastening her thick green cloak.

A shadow crossed Jenna's face. She refused it landing. Taking Verra's cloak, she hung it up behind the door and sat beside Verra in front of the fire. "How is Illiahn?" She forced a smile that quickly became genuine as she listened to reports from home. All was well. Illiahn was with child again; Mi'Cael had mastered the pony Brenn had given him; Myst still "instructed" Raen at every opportunity. Verra and Telsen were to handfast in the spring— Camarrhan's public declaration of commitment. Jenna hugged her friend in warm congratulation.

"About time! I thought babies would begin to arrive before you announced a wedding." Verra's light blush reminded Jenna of the difference in their cultures on these issues.

Shit. "I did it again, didn't I? Sorry, Verra, I was only teasing you." It still amused her that these highly passionate people were so private about matters of intimacy. All of a sudden, she missed Tessa. It had been so normal to talk to her about anything that came up. Even sex. Especially sex. Shit, change the subject.

191

"I'm truly glad for you and Tel. I . . . felt really bad about . . . well, you know." She dropped her head and studied her hands, afraid she would not find the absolution she sought.

Verra was quiet a moment. She leaned closer to the blue flames as her forehead furrowed briefly, then smoothed again. Her eyes were a calm sea. "Perhaps there is not so much to forgive. I think I always knew Cael would not choose me. In truth, I have always been a little afraid of him, of waking the dragon. I loved him, yes, and I still do, but as the very dear friend he has become." She shifted her gaze to the blue flames before them, and smiled. "I find that I am relieved to have found love with a less complicated man. Tel holds my heart gently, and I need never fear for him. Fate does not dog the footsteps of the non-gifted."

Jenna ventured a glance at her. "I know it hurt you at first, and for that, I'm sorry. You were always so accommodating, despite my . . . despite what happened. I never intended to be the cause of so much upset, and I'm grateful for your friendship. I'm not sure I could have been as forgiving, in the same circumstances."

"We are all responsible only for our own actions, not those of others. It rarely helps a person to sit in judgement on another—sometimes it only serves to prolong the hurt. We forgive; we get over it." She shrugged and smiled. "As I said, there was not so much to forgive as you think. Tel has always appealed to me."

"He *is* rather gorgeous," Jenna admitted, glad the awkward moment had passed. *I love your philosophy, my friend,* she thought with gratitude. Lifting her eyes from her lap, she looked at Verra directly. "You've been careful not to mention Cael in your news from home."

Sympathy filled Verra's expression. "He is well. He

works too hard, rides too far and continues to take risks he should not. Do you see these grey hairs of mine?" Verra shook her dense curls in mock exasperation.

"Does he mention me at all?" Jenna asked, affecting indifference.

Verra sighed and fell silent for a moment.

"No. But by his very omission it is clear that you are the devil that drives him, pardon the expression. What happened between you? We had thought you two were reaching an understanding."

Jenna shrugged. "So did I. Something has changed that. I don't know what."

"Jenna?" Verra laid her hand on Jenna's knee. "Do not pretend you do not care. I know your heart better than that, *chiara*. Will you not talk to me?"

"There's nothing to say. It's Cael you need to question. Ask him why he's so bloody pig-headed." She regretted the words as soon as they were spoken.

Verra moved to sit beside her and laid an arm around her shoulders. Three months of cold hardness cracked and tumbled from her like a broken clay mold. Her dam collapsed, and she wept in emotional release for the second time in years.

An ominous silence filled the stone chamber. Incense hung thick and heavy in the air, its smoke drifting in misty layers of sweetness. Oil lamps sputtered softly, sending shadows leaping and retreating across the pale faces of the gathered elders. Each forehead bore a rune, soot smudged onto the skin, describing the magic each elder brought to the small Circle.

An even smaller Circle, Arkell reflected, unless help was obtained for the elder who lay dying before them. Holder of

Althar warding magic, Kohen had languished comatose for days now, and the Circle feared both for his life and for the magic that would be lost to them forever. Arkell shook his head. As holder of the shaping magic, he was one of five elders of the Circle: holders of magic and the ruling body of Alth.

"We must seek assistance." Arkell broke the silence, drawing the attention of several pairs of narrow black eyes to himself. He bowed his head in acknowledgment of his breach of etiquette. The lamp cast spangles of light from the gilded cord that bound his black hair at the nape of his neck. "With respect, we travail without progress." His troubled face turned back to the prostrate figure before them.

"Alth has never sought alakem intervention," Kreahn rasped.

"Alth has never faced a loss such as this. We dare not let him pass, Kreahn. Do not hold so hard to tradition that you jeopardise the future!"

"Arkell speaks true." The grey-haired elder raised her lined face as she spoke. "It is clear that Kohen is beyond us." Akara's pale eyes roamed the room with the random pattern of the sightless. "Do we let our pride steal one of the magics that remain to us?" Her long fingers trembled as she extended her hand. Making contact with the dark-robed body that lay before her, she ran fingertips down the arm she touched, groping for the heavy gold ring on the still hand, tracing the rune inscribed deep in the metal. "Alth declines daily." Her voice rose in challenge. "Our youth rebel because we cling to old ways. Our hope for the future of our race lies with the young who leave us in increasing numbers. We must look to change. If we do not seek help from the alakem, full knowledge of the warding magic dies with Kohen."

"His son holds much of his knowledge . . ." Kreahn began.

"And his son runs with the rebels like a dog without honour," Isanko spat in disgust. She glowered at Kreahn, her fingers tightening on her runed staff. "If I had my way, he would be brought to heel and leashed."

"If you had your way, Isanko, our children would have no freedoms at all. Perhaps the disciplines of your magic have caused you to forget what it is to be young?"

Isanko bristled. "Why should A'Thek magic require more disciplines than your own, Kreahn? Does the Traverse now require no sacrifice?"

Arkell clapped his hands twice. "Elders. We are not children. Do not let the frustrations of the day cause us conflict." Isanko and Kreahn subsided.

Silence returned. Akara bowed her grey head. "I may be old and blind, but I see clearly. I will not allow Alth to decline further. We will send for an alakem Healer." She held up a hand to forestall objections, light reflecting softly from the gold band of office on her finger. Rubbing the sooty rune from her forehead, she stood. "You may yet have your way, Kreahn. Our youth have caused many alakem deaths. Their Council may decide to withhold assistance."

"Let us pray their decision will be favourable." Arkell rubbed the rune from his forehead. "It is, after all, one of their own who leads the rebels against them."

Three solemn faces acknowledged the truth of his words as the Circle withdrew from the chamber, leaving their comatose colleague once again to the care of his women.

Karessa settled herself into an easy chair as Galaen and Luath arrived in the discussion chamber. Quan filled the fire recesses with instant heat, Wielder's fire flowing in copious blue streams from his hands.

Gowan sighed, leaning himself closer to the heat. "Every winter seems colder," he complained.

"Every winter we are older, my dear," Karessa said, her face folding into the lines of her smile. "Where are Chereth and Sheytan?"

Gowan raised a hand and curled his fingers in counting mime. Three . . . two . . . one . . . the Way shimmered open, and the two mentors stepped into the chamber, seating themselves as the Way closed. Karessa chuckled at the old Empath's predictive ability.

"I speak for the Hand," Galaen said in formal opening. Five heads inclined in acceptance. "Camarrhan will offer assistance to Alth in this matter."

Gowan's brows drew in disapproval. He said nothing.

Galaen continued. "We know what it is to lose magic. As the Hand exists to guard Camarrhan's magic, so the Circle exists to guard that of Alth. We propose to send a Healer to the Circle. One you shall name, Karessa."

"Can Chereth not transport the one who ails through the Way?" Karessa asked.

"Althar may not safely use the Way. A Healer must go to them." Galaen's musical voice held understanding. "Safety has been guaranteed, Karessa. You need not fear for whoever you send."

Gowan cleared his throat. "It does not sit well with me. We have lost many Leaders to Althar death-shafts . . ."

"I understand your concern, Gowan, but we work toward peace. Alth is slow to correct the social structure that has led to such rebellion. Their Council is in session as we speak, and will not rise until a way to resolve these issues can be agreed upon." Galaen stood as Luath opened the

Way for them to return to Ché Kevath. "Send to me or Grinore with news of the outcome, Gowan." She acknowledged the other mentors as she left.

"It would greatly ease me if you would send an Empath with my Healer, Gowan. I do not wish to send her into the bosom of the Althar without means of communication." Karessa's face held unease. Her fingers tapped a staccato on the arm of the chair.

Gowan ran a hand through his thick silver hair, a wicked light appearing in his grey eyes. "How is Jenna's training progressing, Healer?"

"She is competent in most facets and excels at some. Why?"

"There is a certain situation that may be addressed if you consider her able to fulfil the task."

"I had not thought to send Jenna, but I believe she is capable, yes." Dawning comprehension lit her face. "And you will send . . ."

"Exactly. I see we understand each other."

Karessa patted his shoulder as she passed him. "You always were a devious old fox, Gowan."

The atmosphere in the den was tense. "Again we are to be thrown together!" Cael resented Gowan's manipulations, knowing this was no coincidence. His jaw tight, he pushed the last item into a leather rucksack and slumped into a low-backed chair.

"You have the most experience with Althar, *chiaran*. Who else would he send?" Verra moved behind him and began to massage his neck and shoulders, defusing his tension. So often these days it erupted into a frenzy of physical activity that ended only when exhaustion took over.

197

"You believe that?" He tipped his head back and looked at her upside-down.

"I do, Cael. You speak some of the language, you know the symbiot and how it functions, you remain unbiased against the race despite their actions. Of course he had to send you." She pushed his head forward again and continued to knead the tight muscles of his shoulders. "Besides, perhaps he is hoping you will share your A'Thek with him." Her tone was not quite innocent.

"I should not have told you." He loosened a little under her hands. "Lakra is a friend, nothing more."

"We could all see that she would *like* to be, *chiaran*. I fear her life-debt is one she greatly desires to repay, and I also have some idea of the currency."

Cael chuckled suddenly at the oblique comment. "Hmm. Flattering as that may be, it is not a possibility." Verra's dislike of Althar was overcoming her native caution on the mention of things physical.

"She is a *predator,* Cael, and it bothers me that she is so forward with you. The evil black-eyed witch should stick to her own kind." She huffed a short sigh.

Verra's thumbs rubbed warmth deep into his muscles, and he allowed himself to relax, ignoring her outburst. The last three months had proved difficult. Jenna had stayed away. He had not communicated with her. Verra had visited her periodically. Each time she returned without Jenna, he retreated a little further into his coldness. He did not press Verra for news of her. If Jenna no longer desired his company, he would certainly not intrude on her.

Frustration, both physical and emotional, ruled his life. He lay awake at night, aware of her as she slept, knowing when she did not. Even his dreams betrayed him. Rich brown hair against the smooth honey cream of her skin; the curve of her breast; teasing indigo eyes full of warmth and passion; the touch of her hands on him as she stole caresses against his will.

That she now also resisted the bond only proved to him that he had transgressed by driving Simon away. He had assumed he knew what she wanted. An arrogant mistake. Gods! She was better off without him getting in her way. She had to feel free enough to return to her world if she so desired.

Blessed Gods, when would life get easier? The dragon rose in him daily, and daily, he quelled it. He was still in control. Of himself, if nothing more.

"It is so difficult," Trista exclaimed in disgusted frustration as she pulled sections of her long hair from the braid she was attempting. "I will never be able to do it!"

Jenna plopped herself down on the bed beside the girl and began to weave the fine blonde hair into a French braid. "It just takes practice, Trista, lots of it." Jenna's braiding had become popular with the novices, but she was right—it took a lot of practice. As she fastened the end of the braid, she felt Cael's familiar presence.

He's here. Adrenalin dump.

She tidied her own thick braid and studied herself in the long mirror on her chamber wall. She had gained a little weight in these cold months without opportunity to exercise at her usual level. The fine wool dress clung to every curve, flowed around her ankles as she moved. White suited her complexion, but made her feel wide all of a sudden. She reached for her pack and her thick wool cloak. No way of knowing how Althar dwellings regulated the winter's cold.

"Are you going already? I thought you were to wait for

Cael." Trista flipped her braid experimentally, admiring the effect in the mirror.

"He's here. I can feel him." Jenna folded the cloak into its hood and tucked it into the top of the pack, her fingers trembling as she fumbled with the straps.

Calm down. Deep breaths. With a quick hug goodbye, she took her leave of Trista.

>Jenna? We are on the front steps.< His familiar mindspeak lacked the warmth she remembered. Her heart thumped harder as she approached the arched stone entrance of the Guild.

Verra stood in the pale winter sun, wearing leather breeches and a fine wool shirt and tunic under her dark cloak. Cael waited beside her, similarly clad. An oblique shaft of sunlight caught Cael's eyes as he turned, flashing gold for an instant, returning to amber as he acknowledged Jenna with quiet deference.

Such a beautiful male. Why does this have to be so difficult? He was leaner. Verra had said he was driving himself hard, and it showed. His eyes lingered on her, and she felt his involuntary physical response. Good. At least they still shared that much.

"You are wintering well, Healer." His tone was courteous, his expression politely neutral.

"I'm well insulated, you mean!" Jenna attempted to lighten the moment. "Have you kept well, Cael?" She tucked her hands behind her back, resisting the impulse to touch him.

"Well enough." He shouldered his pack as Verra prepared to open the Way to Alth. "We are to be met at Kyanor. It is the only settlement Verra has keyed. There we will be given the Waypoints for the settlement where the elders reside."

Jenna sighed, inspecting her boots. "Cael."

"Healer?"

"I'm still Jenna. And it's good to see you." Lifting her gaze, she looked at him directly. "So let's drop the formality, huh?"

The travel progressed smoothly, and after receiving Waypoints in Kyanor, they arrived at their destination. Set high in the Alth ranges, the settlement of Sartz was bitterly cold, making Jenna glad of her hooded cloak and woollen undershift.

Watchers awaited them when they emerged from the Way, breath streaming in misty whorls. "Welcome, alakem." A watcher inclined his head to Cael. "For a second time."

>*I know this one,*< Cael sent. >*He watched the pass as we returned Lakra.*<

Jenna had heard the story from Verra, laced with invective against the Althar and her exasperation with the man she had sworn to protect. His lack of prejudice, despite the rift in cultures and two attempts on his life, was another facet of him that intrigued her.

"Healer. Wayfinder." The watcher greeted the women with a curious hand gesture. Thumb and small finger extended, a flick of the wrist to each side. Jenna smothered a smile. This race could not know how closely their greeting resembled a surfer's "hang loose" salute. The three followed the watchers into the settlement, their boots squeaking on the packed powder of the trail.

Snow-coated stone structures squatted below the rock face that loomed, sentinel-like, over the settlement. Their escort ushered them into the largest of these. Snow slid from the angled slate roof as they entered, and they sidestepped to avoid its cold dusting.

The structures proved to be antechambers to the rock-hewn dwellings and meeting places of the settlement. Linked by a labyrinth of corridors, Althar resided deep within the heart of the mountain. As she observed her surroundings, Jenna knew that Althar hands had also worked the stone that housed the Guild. The rock face was worked smooth with great skill, and ornamented with designs both familiar and fantastic.

>*Althar magic,*< Cael sent as he ran his hand across a beautifully rendered burst of mountain flowers that turned their faces eternally to a clear sky. >*Shapers. Stone becomes as wet clay to those so gifted.*<

As they moved deeper into the settlement, the corridors became wider, meeting in broad sweeps of open space at each junction. Children played in these areas—wiry scraps of children, raucous as seagulls and as monochrome. Their dark hair and eyes contrasted with white skin, the scene relieved only by the bright colours of their clothing and the playthings scattered from dwelling doorways. The children were notably few, but as noisy and happy as children anywhere.

"Where does the light come from?" Jenna asked as they trailed after the watcher. She could see no light source, or heat for that matter, but the passages were pleasantly warm, causing them all to remove their cloaks.

"Althar magic again. The rock is imbued with light. It just releases it slowly." Cael glanced at Verra. "Wayfinder? You are looking unhappy."

"I do not like Alth or trust Althar, Cael. You know that." Her green eyes glittered in the luminescent glow of the passage, her voice low and hard. "I will not leave you, but I am far from happy to be here. If I had been made to be surrounded by rock, I would have been created a gemstone."

Jenna shot her a concerned look. Claustrophobia? Verra's tension and pallor seemed to confirm the observation. Shit. That could be awkward if they were here for any length of time. It did explain why Verra spent as little time actually inside the Guild as possible, though. She had always preferred to remain outside whenever she visited. Several minutes later, the watcher halted them. Jenna saw no reason why. There were no chambers, no doors. "The elder's chambers are concealed," their guide explained, taking a small cube of rock from a pouch in his robe. Pressing the cube to the wall of the corridor, he spoke two words. The cube morphed neatly into the rock. With a sound like the groan of thawing ice, the rock wavered and withdrew in a widening rectangle from the spot where the cube had been. Jenna gaped at the newly revealed passage and started as Verra caught her arm in a frantic grip.

"Gods! That is going to seal behind us." Verra's voice was tight. Cael appeared unfazed, following the guide without comment or a backward glance. Jenna took Verra's hand and pulled her through the opening after Cael. She broke the rules and touched him.

"Can you do anything to help Verra? She fears being trapped down here. If she panics, it will cause a problem."

Cael moved away from her touch. Her stomach lurched at his tacit rebuff. "That was childish and unnecessary," she muttered.

He lifted an eyebrow at Verra, who nodded, green eyes wide. >*I thank you Jenna. I was unaware. It will be well.*< Verra relaxed visibly, and Jenna knew he exercised his gifting to calm her. Crisis averted. Personal pain inflicted. Damn him.

Cael flicked her a cool glance. >*The warding of this place prevents access to the Way. Verra knows this. It scares her as much as the confinement.*<

The rock did indeed seal behind them. When they turned from the phenomenon, a figure stood before them.

"I am Arkell." His voice was clear, his hair black and long, bound behind his neck. Less than forty years showed on his face. "Alth thanks you for your assistance."

>*Diplomat. Ambassador. I have heard of Arkell.*<

"I would offer you refreshment, but our need is dire. Please come."

They followed his dark robe from the small chamber they had entered, across a narrow passageway of smooth stone and into a larger chamber, redolent with incense and lit with oil lamps. A still figure lay on a low, padded slab of stone against the rear wall. Two women were seated beside the figure and rose as the group entered, vanishing wraith-like behind a thick hanging that concealed a doorway.

Arkell moved toward the slab, his brow creasing into a frown. "Kohen is an elder of the Circle; he holds the last of our warding magic. His predecessor was an ancient, only recently passed, but Kohen is new to the Circle; his apprentices are not yet filled with his power. If he passes from this life, so does much of our magic."

Cael and Verra sat where Arkell indicated, on soft couches laden with cushions and furs. Jenna dropped her pack and cloak beside them and moved toward the slab. Unhooking a Keystone from her necklet, she drew a thin cord from her pocket.

"What happened to him?" she asked.

Arkell's alien eyes met hers. "We do not know, Healer. He was discovered thus, and all attempts to reach him with magic have failed. He is sustained by the warding of the chamber, but Alth does not possess healing magic."

"Linking?"

"No, Healer." Arkell's head bowed deferentially.

>*He pays you honour, Jenna. Elders need bow to no one. You should acknowledge.*<

"Elder, you bestow honour where none is deserved." Jenna glared sideways at Cael. "I am not a keeper of magic, only a Healer. I am here to serve."

Cael's eyes held wary approval. >*Well said.*<

Arkell raised his chin. "Even so, your presence honours us. Alakem Healers command much power."

Jenna approached Kohen. She loosened the robe, fed her cord around his neck, fastened it loosely and attached the Keystone. As she waited for the stone to attune to his pattern, she checked his vital signs. Slow, faint pulse. Breathing shallow, barely sustaining life. Comatose. "Has he convulsed at all, Arkell?" she asked, feeling something familiar.

"No, Healer. He has not moved at all."

She thumbed his eyelid open. The pupil was invisible against the black iris. Frowning, she turned to Cael. "Can you reach his mind?"

He shook his head. "Althar are impossible for me to reach. The symbiot blocks me."

Arkell's head turned in sharp surprise. "You are a mind-speaker? You know of the symbiot?"

Cael acknowledged Arkell with a tight smile. "Yes, and yes. I had the privilege of taking a death-shaft from Althar renegades. I survived only because of my lady Healer's . . . talents."

"You are a Leader?"

Cael gave a nod of affirmation.

"Camarrhan pays us great respect. This will not go unrepaid." Arkell's demeanour betrayed his surprise.

"I also know you mindspeak. Will you allow me to do so with you?"

Cat Collins

Dark brows raised over narrow black eyes. "You surprise me indeed, alakem—your pardon—Empath. Your knowledge of us is large."

Jenna focussed deeply on the Keystone. The pattern was unfamiliar, alien in its rhythms and appearance. Touching her fingers to her patient's temple, she sank her awareness into him. Her thought-self travelled his body, seeking areas of unease.

Perfect harmony. Nothing wrong.

Re-emerging, she considered quickly. "Elder, Cael. Please join me." As they approached, she took Kohen's hand and linked herself with him. "Elder, please try to reach his mind. Cael, follow, and share with me."

The three established a careful thread of rapport as Arkell lowered his barrier.

Wow. Three way calling. Without Telecom. Jenna suppressed the urge to smile.

Again she probed the Keystone. There! A brief flash of response. The men zoned in, pursuing the flicker they had all felt.

>*Gods! It is the symbiot!*< Cael's sending held warning, panic. He recoiled from them, breaking the link.

"There is nothing to fear, Empath. If Kohen dies, so does his symbiot. It seeks only to restore him." Arkell's tone held puzzlement.

Jenna laid a hand on Cael's shoulder without thinking, but he did not move away. "Peace, Cael." She deliberately used his own language structure, seeking to calm him. "There is no harm here, only sickness. Help me find it."

Dark gold hair fell across the abhorrence in his eyes as he tightened his jaw, bowed his head and returned to the link. And suddenly, she knew. Like a pinpoint on a map, the symbiot showed her where to go. She had no reference

206

points, no knowledge of this unusual being's pattern. His wiring was so different that she was lost without the symbiot's guidance, amplified and relayed to her by Arkell and Cael.

A simple blood clot moving toward the brain. The symbiot had slowed the Althar's bloodstream to avoid propelling the clot into the brain, producing the symptoms she recognised. Low pulse, barely breathing: so similar to battle sickness.

She pulsed the obstruction away and cleared other blood vessels to the brain, strengthening and cleaning against future damage. And withdrew. Kohen gave a great sigh and began to breathe normally.

Sweat beaded Cael's forehead, token of his loathing of the symbiot. His eyes further told of his stress. Jenna pushed his hair back as she had not done for months, wanting to hold him, comfort him. Her hand lingered on him, brushed his cheek.

>*Forgive me, Jenna.*< He looked away, embarrassed by his fear.

Arkell noted the change in Kohen's condition. "He sleeps, no longer beyond reach," he pronounced, relief and gratitude on his face as he turned to Jenna.

"He will be well, Arkell. *Alakem* require a day or two to recover strength from healing. I can't predict what Althar may need." She retrieved the Keystone, slid the cord into her pocket, and hooked the stone back onto her necklet.

Arkell laid a hand on Cael's shoulder. "It is well with you, Empath?" he inquired.

"Forgive me, elder. My experience of the symbiot was a painful one. The memory is strong in me." Cael shuddered.

"I am curious to know the nature of this." Arkell cocked his head to one side as he spoke, his alien eyes reflecting the oily-yellow lamp light.

"You desire a sharing?"

The elder shrugged. "My barrier is down, if you do not object . . ."

Jenna waited with Verra as the men communed in silence. "You all right?" She squeezed Verra's cold hand, nudged her with a gentle elbow.

Verra shuddered and closed her eyes briefly. "Fine. Just get me out of here!"

Cael watched as Jenna spoke quietly with Kohen, explaining what had happened and what she had done to heal him. The Althar's symbiot aided his recovery; he had awoken within a half-hour. Verra sat beside Cael, her head in her hands, as he restored her calm and pulsed away the tension she felt at their confinement. The incense no longer burned, but the sweet resinous scent lingered in the air. Arkell appeared in the doorway and beckoned to him. "There is one who would speak with you."

Cael unfolded himself from the low couch and followed the elder from the chamber. Verra made to follow him, but Arkell turned and politely forestalled her. "Alone, Wayfinder."

Verra subsided with a frown. Cael knew she was unhappy for him to be out of her sight, but neither of them had authority here to protest. >*Peace, Verra. There is no harm here.*< He pulsed reassurance to her as he left. Besides, without access to the Way, there was nothing she could do if any harm *did* eventuate.

Arkell ushered him into a small antechamber, curtained from the view of the corridor. The walls of the chamber bore a panoramic mountain landscape, the design showing the same detail as a painting. A long, low divan, upholstered in plush red velvet and scattered with cushions of the same, was the only furniture in the room. A thick woven textile curtained the entrance and fell closed as Arkell withdrew without a word. Obviously he was to wait. Impatient to leave Sartz, he paced the small room, noting another thick textile hanging at the rear.

A sudden shiver of sensual pleasure vibrated the full length of his body, causing him to catch his breath in a surprised gasp. "Gods . . . Lakra?"

* Affirmative. You recognise my touch, alakem? *

>*I recognise A'Thek mind caress . . . who could forget?*<

The red hanging drew aside, revealing Lakra as he had not seen her before. She smiled, pale rose lips parting against perfect teeth. * I heard you attended the elder, Kohen. I requested the right of reward. There is not much Arkell cares to deny me. * Her garment shimmered as she moved, seeming to possess its own light within the folds of dusky plum fabric that clung to her body, its sheerness revealing a suggestion of softly curving flesh beneath it. Her dark hair was cut close to her head in A'Thek style, feathered into her neck and softly spiked over her forehead.

>*My bondmate is here **also**,*< he sent with heavy emphasis. >*You take advantage of my vulnerability here, Lakra. That is beneath you.*< He felt the light flush of arousal creep into his face.

* Perhaps. * With an arch glance, she indicated the doorway through which she had appeared, her invitation clear.

He remained where he was.

* I see resistance has become a way of life for you. * She sounded amused. * A shame! * "Shanek! Tiana eminé," she called. * At least share a little wine with me. It is Illith's finest. * Taking his hand, she drew him toward the divan.

A girl appeared with a flask and thin silver goblets, poured wine of intense red and vanished again behind the hanging. Lakra reclined on the divan, her elbow disappearing into soft pillows as she sipped wine and watched him, a small smile curling her lips. * I have a strong inclination to bed you, flatlander. It is only the fact that I also like you that restrains me. You know I could defeat your resistance if I chose. *

>I know it. I am grateful for your forbearance, A'Thek.< Oh Gods! Sit up, woman. Her breasts pressed against her gown, dark nipples clearly visible beneath the filmy plum fabric. His flush deepened. She smiled in feline satisfaction over the rim of her goblet.

>You know I cannot do this,< he sent, as he removed himself from the divan.

* I offer invitation only, flatlander! No coercion. Not yet. *

Distance, quickly. >Your interest flatters me, Lakra. I regret I must leave before you tempt me beyond my control.< He moved toward the exit.

* I would certainly like to see that! But forgive me if I have teased you. *

"Teased?" He spun back to face her with a frustrated curse.

* You are angry with me? *

"Yes! . . . No." He growled aloud in irritated confusion, relaying to her his state of continual tension and the impossibility of resolving it. >It is not only you, Lakra. But you are not helping matters at all.<

* I see. And you choose to live with this? * She shook her head with mock sadness. * You Alakem are a very strange people. * Cael laughed, shaking his head in sudden amusement, and she smiled, recognising the irony of her words.

She rose from the divan, raised the goblet in salute. * So. *
>Even so.<

* We will meet again, flatlander. *

>*I think not.*<

* I am not a bad person . . . Cael. *

>*No.*< He turned to push the heavy curtain aside and stopped in surprise as months of accumulated sexual tension suddenly drained from his body. Blessed Gods! It was as if every muscle had suddenly turned to bread dough, without the actual physical release that should precede such a feeling. Staggering a little, he reached forward and steadied himself against the wall, unsure whether it was a pleasant sensation or not. He cast a glance over his shoulder at her, astonished at what she had just done.

* My gift to you. * Her smile was coy. * I would have preferred a more intimate method of delivery, but I cannot allow you to bear that particular burden any longer. *

He flashed her a relieved grin, returned to her and kissed her cheek. >*Not a **bad** person, Lakra, but definitely a little wicked.*<

He left her, retracing his steps to find the chamber where Jenna and Verra waited.

Jenna swallowed hard and pressed her fingers to her temples. Her pulse raced, nausea swam in her stomach, and she couldn't seem to draw enough breath. She fought down the urge to vomit.

"Jenna?"

She opened her eyes to find Verra staring hard at her. "Whatever is the matter? You are the colour of chalk."

"Nothing, it's nothing. I'm fine." She pressed both hands to her middle and slowed her breathing.

Verra's eyes flew to Jenna's hands. "You are not . . . are you?"

"What? Pregnant?" She gave a mirthless laugh. "You

have to *do* it first, Verra. No, I'm not. Just a bit dizzy. I . . . I could use some fresh air." Avoiding Verra's concerned eyes, she leaned back into the furs on the couch. *Shit, Cael. That really hurt.*

She turned her head away from the entrance as Cael returned with Arkell close behind him. Verra regarded her quizzically, but said nothing. "Can we go now, *chiaran?*" Verra asked in a hopeful voice, shifting her gaze to Cael.

"Will you not stay and share refreshment with me?" Arkell invited.

"I thank you, elder, but my Wayfinder does not cope well within the confinement of your settlement. I would be happier to ease her predicament and leave now," Cael said.

"As you wish, Empath. Healer?"

Jenna turned, avoiding Cael's eyes, to find Arkell holding out his hand to her. She went to him and took it. "We owe you a great debt. Should you ever have need of assistance, this elder would be pleased to provide it." He bowed slightly, and Jenna flushed, aware now of the honour he paid her.

>*You have made a very valuable friend, Jenna,*< Cael sent. She ignored him.

"Thank you, elder, you're most gracious. I'm pleased we could help you." She turned her back on Cael to gather her pack and cloak from the couch. Verra stood ready to leave, bouncing almost imperceptibly on her toes in her eagerness to be gone.

Arkell escorted them to the sealed entrance where they had arrived and opened the rock. A watcher stood in the passage and waited as they took their leave of the elder, then beckoned them after him. They followed him out the way they had come, and soon exited the warmth of the passages into the antechamber that preceded the gelid air outside. The watcher withdrew with another hand gesture and a smile. "Fare you well, alakem."

Verra drew huge gulps of fresh cold air as they emerged from the settlement into darkening twilight. A light snow fell, dusting their hooded cloaks, silently erasing all marks in the snow around them. "Now?" Verra seemed anxious to remove them as far from Sartz as she could.

"I think now would be excellent, Verra," Cael agreed, his breath steaming as he pulled his cloak close around himself. Jenna waited, quiet, her face lost in the deep cowl of her hood as Verra's wristbands flashed overhead with reflected moonlight.

"As well we did not need to stay longer. Your skill has grown, Jenna. You impressed the elder greatly." Cael stepped back, inviting Jenna to precede him into the Way as it opened. She lifted her chin and swept past him.

The cool night air of Kereál was a welcome contrast to the bite of Sartz's winter. Shuttered windows leaked gold-warm light, and smoke from the kitchen range and living room fires rose, ghost-like, from the chimneys at each end of the homestead. The tang of wood smoke mingled with the blend of pine and horse that always scented the air of the ranch. Stabled horses stirred, whickering in soft response to the travellers crossing the yard.

As they neared the front steps, Verra took her leave of them. "Cael can call me when you wish to return to the Guild, Jenna." She gave her a quick hug and was gone. The Way would take her straight to Telsen, drawn by the Keystone he now wore, token of their relationship.

Jenna laid a firm hand on Cael's arm as he turned toward the house. "I need to talk to you."

He removed her hand gently. "It is cold, Jenna, and I need food. You also need to eat. Come inside. We can talk later."

213

She tucked her hand back into her cloak. "This won't wait. I can't face your family with this . . . incident undealt with." She felt his hunger, and part of her regretted keeping him from comfort. Another part felt a curious satisfaction.

He pushed her hood back a little. "Incident?" His cool eyes searched her face, his breath misting and mingling with hers.

"When you left Kohen's chamber with Arkell, and Verra was not permitted to follow."

"Ah. Come, then." He turned back across the yard, and she followed him to the den. He lit oil lamps as she closed the door behind her, and held a flame to the kindling set ready in the fireplace. She looked around her, rubbing cold fingers and seeing part of his private world for the first time. A large easy chair squatted in the yellow glow of the growing fire. Large enough for two. As was the wide bed against the back wall.

A table occupied the left corner inside the doorway, bearing an open book surrounded by scattered charcoal sticks of varying thickness. Loose leaves of thick paper bearing rough sketches of human figures lay in a pile. The open book displayed a finished drawing of a fine-boned young horse, long-legged and wild of mane, caught in a frozen moment of motion that captured the animal's energy and passion on the page.

There was one word below the sketch.

Chekuán.

Cael straightened from the fire that now blazed. He motioned her to the easy chair, pulled up a stool and settled himself, leaning back against the wall beside the hearth. They were silent a moment.

Jenna loosened her cloak, shrugged it from her shoulders. "Who was she?" Her voice was tight. She stared into the flames.

"It was Lakra. Only Lakra."

"*Only* Lakra? That makes it all right? I felt it Cael, like you said I would. I never believed you would do something like that."

"You felt . . . Jenna, no! I did nothing!"

His shocked expression touched her. She wanted to believe him. Innocent until proven guilty, your Honour.

"Explain to me what I felt, Cael. You were in some sort of an . . . *anxious* state for a while there." She tilted her eyebrows at a dangerous angle, conveying exactly what she meant. "And then, suddenly, you *were quite all right!*"

He smothered a smile. Too late; she saw it. Righteous anger began to rise in her.

"Peace, Jenna. The only way to explain this is to show you. Will you let me? It is not quite what you think." The fire crackled as sap popped loudly from the split pine. Cael relayed the scene, and she watched behind closed eyes.

A hot, slow flush crept up her neck, stained her cheeks. She shared his relief as Lakra took his tension away. Her eyes flew open, alarmed at what she had accused him of.

>*Peace. I understand your judgement of what you felt. I had not thought to explain.*<

"She *knows* we're bonded, Cael! She played with you to test her own power over you!"

>*No. Maybe. She did not use her power. I would have been helpless. She is A'Thek!*<

"Is that Althar for whore?" she spat. Shit. His face showed no understanding. Back up a little. "What is A'Thek?"

He showed her. Every facet. She shook her head in disbelief, only now aware of the restraint he had exercised. "It's an Althar magic?"

"Hmm." He stretched long legs out and rested one ankle atop the other. "What is 'whore'?"

"Share." She showed him.

>*Similar, but different. Resistible.*< He added wood to the fire. >*Not always desirable.*<

She laughed. "No."

A silence followed. They both watched the fire. Jenna shifted her gaze to his face, needing to say more. Firelight threw jumping shadows across his cheekbones and reflected orange-gold in his eyes.

"I'm sorry. I was jealous. And hurt. I shouldn't have doubted you."

He gave her a long measuring look, opened his mouth to speak but appeared to change his mind and looked away.

Talk to me, Mars. What is it? "Do you remember last summer, when you learned to kick-box?" she asked. His eyes told her yes, of course. "I feel as shut out of your life as I did then. It hurts more than before, because I know you care for me, even if only as a friend."

"You have stayed away, Jenna. I assumed you wished to keep your distance." He folded his arms across his chest and watched the fire.

"Why? I stayed away because of *your* distance. Something changed. *You* changed."

"No, not changed." His voice was low and quiet. Glancing up at her from beneath lowered brows, he looked young and vulnerable. "I made a mistake. I assumed I knew what you wanted and took it upon myself to make it happen." He shrugged. "It was arrogant of me. I will not assume again."

"What are you talking about?" Her brow furrowed in confusion and she leaned forward in the chair, seeking to understand him. *Come in, Mars, I'm not receiving you.*

Again he showed a moment's indecision. Then: a kaleidoscopic image, a rainbow of response. The bistro; Simon's

216

face in the night; fighting; tension; Telsen's hand closing around a fist bearing a wicked knife. Simon again, on the ground; angry, resentful. Herself: brows drawn, waiting; accusing, evading a question.

Images flashed off. Pulse: surprise, confusion, withdrawal. She felt his reactions, felt the coldness settle inside him. *You were always free to stay, Jenna. Nothing has changed.* She remembered his words of that night, and understood.

With a relieved sigh, she leaned back in the chair. "You thought I disapproved of what you did to Simon? He gave you no option! He was a fight waiting to happen. I was concerned for him, yes, but only because I know how competent *you* are!" She left the chair and knelt in front of him. "Did you think I would still choose a life there over what I've found here?"

"Life would be simpler for you, Jenna. He was right in one thing. I have nothing to offer you and no right to expect anything from you."

"And the bond? Doesn't that give either of us any 'rights'?"

He was silent, staring morosely into the fire.

Again she saw his youth and wanted to hold him close but refrained, knowing his boundaries. She sighed, choosing her next words with care. "I have spent the last three months missing you desperately because I respected your request for time and distance. How could I have known what you thought? Cael, concentrate on your own options, not mine. I know what I want. Do you?"

His expression was unreadable, his flame-gold eyes intent on hers. *You hide your soul well, beautiful man.* He sat up and leaned toward her, resting his forearms on his knees.

"What is it you want, Jenna?"

217

"Only you." She tilted her head at him, waiting.

He reached toward her, ran a gentle finger over the curve of her cheek. "You are not disappointed in me?"

"Not at all. I'm your greatest admirer."

"You trust me again?" He tugged the end of her braid.

"Implicitly."

"You will forgive my mistakes?"

"Already forgiven. What else do you need?"

He leaned further forward and pressed his lips to her forehead. "My supper," he said, his mouth curling upward at the corners and devilment dancing in his eyes. Standing, he took her hand, gathered up her cloak and led her toward the door.

Chapter Thirteen

Capture

Small red-fletched death-shafts clattered against the rock wall of the chamber, propelled not by bowstrings but by a vicious blast of Wielder's fire. The quiver that had held them lay shattered and smoking in the corner.

"Useless! All of these weapons—useless! I cannot believe the woman has countered the symbiot!" Jabeel's face was pink with anger. He bared his teeth in a snarl and kicked the ruined quiver, sending it bouncing from the wall to narrowly miss him on its way back to the stone floor. His thin chest heaved, and he narrowed his eyes, leaning both hands on the desk of smooth stone before him.

Newly arrived from Illith, a young messenger lounged in a cushioned alcove illuminated by the soft glow of light magic emanating from the stone. He flicked several of the death-shafts from his lap and continued. "There is more. Your Empath friend from Kereál still lives." The youth eyed him with an expression of easy insolence, as if measuring the effect of his words.

"How so?" The leonine Empath's golden features roared into Jabeel's memory. He had only seen him from a distance, but oh, he was fair. And Jabeel's loins had stirred at the thought of hurting him.

"He was the first she healed. They are now bondmates."

It was not like Fate to offer second chances. This one he would not miss. And bonded! Some interesting situations

219

could be created out of this with a little thought. "The Wayfinder. She still shadows him?"

"Oh yes. But she shares the bondbrother's bed."

Interesting. "And the fair one sleeps alone." Jabeel's thin smile was calculating.

"It would appear so. The Healer remains at the Guild."

"You have done exceptionally well this time." Jabeel pulled a small pouch from his robe and flicked it to the young Althar. Hearing the soft chink of coin, the messenger pocketed the pouch with a satisfied smile.

"Alakem say much when promises of A'Thek are made . . ." The boy gave Jabeel a sly wink.

"You, my young friend, are an insolent rogue. It is a pleasure doing business with you. Send in Strick and Adrek. I have plans to make." He poured himself wine as he waited for his young Althar advisers, made a silent toast to Fate, and chuckled.

"Interesting measures for interesting times, gentlemen," Jabeel greeted the new arrivals. "Come, sit. I need your input on a matter." He poured wine for them. "The Healer has brought a drug from off-world which counters the symbiot. My need is to cut off access to this."

Lamplight flickered as Adrek closed the chamber door. "How many know which world it comes from?" he asked, reaching for a cup.

"Apparently only one that matters—the Wayfinder. The Healer, the Empath and his 'brother' have no way of returning there without her knowledge of its location." Jabeel stared into his wine. "I need the Wayfinder. I want the Empath for . . . personal reasons. The bondmate could prove interesting. The 'brother' does not matter to me."

Strick gestured impatiently. "It seems obvious. Take one, and the others will attempt a rescue. You alakem are all foolish in your emotional attachments. Bait a trap, Jabeel."

Adrek snorted in disgust. "And bring them all down on us? How can we 'bait a trap' without revealing our location to all Camarrhan?"

Jabeel looked at them both with delighted interest. "You are both right. I do so enjoy our chats." He began to pace the chamber. "Take one; the others will come. The Healer is beyond our taking if she remains at the Guild. We cannot reveal the location—but if we take the Empath, the Wayfinder will home in on his Keystone, and need not know where we are. And the Empath sleeps alone. Sometimes my friends, life is just too good to me!"

"You propose to take him from his *bed?*" Strick was incredulous. "How?"

"That, my dear Strick, is what I have you two for. Organise it. Use only the smartest and the strongest. No fools. This will pay extremely well. Tell Kavlek to be ready for an . . . interrogation. I am sure he can provide some entertainment for my Empath friend."

Adrek's black gaze slid to Strick. I wish they would not do that, Jabeel thought. Mindspeakers could be so rude.

Darkness lightened to grey as the pink of dawn approached. Telsen's arm lay heavy across Verra's waist, waking her when she turned. She rolled toward him, feeling his breath stir her hair. She yawned and stroked the muscles of his chest and arms. He roused and kissed her. Kissed her again.

Laughing, she pushed him away. "It is dawn, Tel. I would like to stay. You know I cannot, not today."

Growling with mock irritation, he pulled her toward him, rolling her onto his body. Her dark hair curtained his

221

face and fell, sleep-tousled, across his chest. "Hurry back, Wayfinder. I miss you already."

She dropped another kiss on his mouth, disentangled herself and rose from the bed. She dressed with haste. He watched with appreciation. "Will I see you tonight?" he asked, brows arched in question.

"Of course." Verra squeezed his knee as she passed, gathering her belongings. Pale light washed her face as she swept her unruly corkscrew curls behind her head and tied them with a satin cord. Council convened today. It was her job to transport Cael to Illith. "I will breakfast with Illiahn," she said, knowing Telsen's bachelor life-style did not cater for visitors. "Take care, lover." With a flash of runed silver, she was gone.

The Way shimmered open in the yard at the ranch. Long dawn shadows receded across the hard packed earth, and birds called, show-off-loud and musical, their best songs reserved for the first light of the new day. Verra crossed to the den and knocked. "Cael?" No answer.

Wood smoke curled in a lazy spiral from the chimney as she pushed open the gate of the kitchen garden, taking the path around the house to the back door. The village girl employed to assist Illiahn stood at the stove, feeding wood into the firebox. She straightened, seeing Verra.

"Illiahn is with the children," she said, jerking a thumb upward, indicating the nursery upstairs.

"Thank you, Jolie. Have you seen Cael this morning?"

"Not yet, Wayfinder. He may be riding."

Of course. She had not checked the home paddock for the bay gelding. Lifting the copper kettle from the stovetop, she filled it with water from the jug and pulled out a crock of herbal blend for tea. Mi'Cael wandered into the rapidly warming kitchen. Jolie handed him a mug of milk, and honey-smeared bread warmed on the stovetop.

"Thank you, Jolie." He drank the milk, a white film remaining on his lip as he took a bite of bread. Verra reached over and thumbed the moustache away.

"What exciting things will you do today, sprout?"

"Hmm, riding I think. I want Father to show me how Uncle can jump onto his horse as it passes him." Verra killed a smile. Brenn was as able a horseman as Cael, and the boy adored his father, but Cael remained his hero.

"Verra! Telsen still does not do breakfast?" Illiahn's trademark smile gentled her words.

"Some changes still remain to be made," Verra answered, returning the smile. "Will Brenn attend Council today?"

Removing the boiling kettle from the stove, Illiahn poured water onto the herbal concoction Verra had placed in the pot. "Not this time. His mares are in need of his presence, and Mi'Cael bothers him for more riding skills. Where is Cael?"

"Either riding or sleeping." Verra reached for a wedge of bread and dribbled honey over it with the slotted wooden dipper.

"Riding without you?" Illiahn raised her brows.

"The chain mail has made him more confident than he should be. I do not like what he does, but you know how he deports himself. He has always loved the dawn." Verra sipped hot tea, reflecting on how difficult it was to keep tabs on this particular man. Cael always did whatever he would, no matter what she had to say about it. Part of his charm, she supposed.

"Mi'Cael, my darling. Go and see if Uncle yet sleeps." Illiahn stroked her son's silken blond hair.

He finished his milk and slipped from the bench as Brenn appeared, wearing a daughter on each hip. "Good morning, Wayfinder." He smiled at Verra in greeting. Depositing the twins on a bench at the table, he took warm bread from the stove for them as Illiahn poured milk. Jolie opened one shuttered window to the morning, and pale sun drenched the kitchen. She turned, startled.

"Mi'Cael comes running, Illiahn!"

Verra turned to the window, feeling a shadow cross the morning's promise. He did indeed run. He burst into the kitchen, eyes wide, blond hair flying.

"Mama! Uncle is gone—everything is in a big mess, Mama, and he is gone!" He caught his breath in a sob. Brenn swept the distraught child into his arms and strode out of the house, his broad face a picture of dismay.

The door to the den stood open, as Mi'Cael had left it. All around were signs of struggle. The bed had not been slept in, the coverings still drawn over the pillows. The easy chair by the fire was overturned, and the table inside the door stood at a crazy angle, sheaves of paper and charcoal sticks scattered on the floor beneath the broken stool. The door at the rear of the den hung open, swinging on its hinges with an insistent squeak in the light wind. Brenn set Mi'Cael down and moved to the door, his anxious blue eyes scanning the area outside.

Verra felt the blood leave her cheeks. "I should have been here. Gods, I should have been here." Her heart beat hard in a frantic fear response as she surveyed the scene. *Oh, Cael. Forgive me.* She stooped to retrieve the scattered drawings, rustling them into a pile to relieve her feeling of helplessness.

Mi'Cael stood by the bed and reached for the sheet of coarse paper that lay on the pillow. He handed it to his mother. Illiahn read it aloud.

"It is addressed to Jenna. 'Healer, I have your lover. Only the Wayfinder can reach him. He will need your skill soon, but you will feel that. Do what you must.' "

"He has not called me." Verra considered the implications with growing horror. *Oh Gods, no, surely not.* "I must go to Jenna. She will know if he . . . suffers. I will bring her home." She ran from the den and was on her way to the Guild within moments.

Cael opened his eyes slowly, wincing at the pounding in his head. Althar body-blocker. That was what had felled him. He had given a good account of himself until the precisely placed pinch was administered at the base of his neck. As inexorable as anaesthesia, he had felt it take effect almost immediately and knew he was in trouble. Until the pinch, he was sure he could overcome them and had not bothered to call for assistance. A big mistake.

Leaving the house late in the evening, he had gone straight to the den, expecting only peace. The dark shadows had come alive, catching him by surprise. His last conscious memory was of the coarse rug against his cheek and the weight of several bodies on his back as he was bound. He had no idea where he was now, or how they had transported him.

Oh Gods! Is it morning? >*Verra! I am taken. Unharmed so far, but bound and confined. I am in a stone chamber, the Gods only know where.*< There was nothing more he could tell her. He sat up cautiously, groaning at the stiffness in his muscles. He had lain on the stone floor with nothing beneath him for he did not know how long. Lifting his bound hands, he saw the cord that restrained him running through an iron ring embedded in the wall. He scanned the chamber. It was small, cut from rock, and lit with residual

225

light magic. An Althar settlement, then. The only exit was a panelled wooden door. He did not like the look of the iron hooks that protruded from the rough ceiling, or the rusting fetters attached to a length of chain in the opposite corner. A narrow ventilation shaft brought the scent of snow on cool air, but there was no telling how deep in the rock he was.

Jenna. She would be sharing his discomfort through the bond. He cursed and sent quickly to reassure her. >*Jenna! I am unharmed.*<

>*Cael? Where are you?*< Gowan's sending came almost immediately. >*Jenna is with me. The Wayfinder has reported what occurred. Who holds you?*<

>*I have seen no one,*< Cael replied. >*I was taken by several Althar. I assume they are with the rebels. I have a bad feeling about this, Gowan. Keep the women away.*<

>*The Wayfinder has tried to reach you already. Wherever you are, it is warded. The Way is blocked.*<

Gods! Cael sat down heavily. Never before had he been beyond Verra's help. This was going to be bad.

Gowan continued. >*There was a note left in your room. It invites Jenna to reach you with the Wayfinder.*<

>*But the warding! Someone is playing with us!*<

>*So it seems. Verra blames herself for this.*< Gowan's sending held regret.

>*No! Verra—there was nothing you could have done. There is no blame. Jenna, do not let fear rule you. I will send when I know more.*< Cael rubbed at his temples, feeling Jenna's distress.

>*Send any detail that may help us locate you, Cael.*<

>*Gowan, take care of Jenna. If anything should happen to me . . . help her.*<

>*Of course. I understand.*<

Cael stood beneath the air vent, breathing fresh, cold air. He shivered, wearing only a thin wool shirt over his breeches, and moved away from the draft. Last evening he had worn no weapons and now felt naked without his knives. The bolt outside the door grated. With a complaining creak, the door opened just wide enough to admit a bowl of water, a wedge of dark bread and a bucket.

"Wait! Where am I?" There was no answer. His frantic mind probe revealed nothing.

The ominous silence returned. Cael ate the dense bread, drank water. Time passed, and he amused himself as best he could, sending sporadic messages to various individuals. To Gowan, who relayed messages from Verra and Jenna. To Telsen, commentary; observations, thoughts and insights.

>*Gods, Tel! Forgive me if I ramble. I am in a twilight place. It is cold, and I fear.*< Later he slept, curled in on himself on the bare stone.

He roused as the door again creaked open, iron hinges protesting the movement. His restraints allowed him just to reach what was placed inside. More bread, water. A slab of cold meat. A small woollen blanket. After wrapping the luxury of warming wool around himself, he ate hungrily, the food a welcome diversion as much as sustenance. Still no answer to his questions, no response to his probes.

>*Jenna? I miss you. Does that surprise you?*< He sat propped against hard stone, staying out of the draft of the air vent. >*I have a lot of time to think. I close my eyes and see all the good things in life. My family, Verra and Tel. And you. Chekuán, if I do not come back from this, I regret only that I have not told you of my great regard for you. You humble me, and I have not been worthy of you.*< He pulled the blanket tight around himself and drew his knees close to his chest

227

for warmth. Why was it so much easier to admit those feelings now that she was not present?

>*Cael?*< Gowan's voice spoke into his silence. >*Jenna is with me. She cries.*<

Ah no, Jenna. >*Chekuán, do not weep for me. I am fed and warm. Remember how friends may embrace?*< He pulsed a wave of concern, encouragement and enfolding warmth.

>*Nicely done.*< Gowan's tone held respect. >*She smiles, but still weeps.*<

>*Send her home, Gowan. She will be happier with Illiahn. Send an Empath with her.*<

>*Of course. Consider it done.*<

>*How much time has passed? Is it day or night?*<

>*It is morning. You have been held for two nights. Verra still has no access to you.*<

>*I wonder at the purpose of this.*< Cael yanked in frustration at the cord that held him like an animal, cursing at the restraint. The bolt slid back. He stood quickly as the door opened. >*Gowan. Someone comes. Share.*< He began to relay events to his mentor.

A lean, grey-haired man entered the chamber, clad in breeches, shirt and boots all of deepest black. "Good morning, fair one." Steel grey eyes swept over Cael and narrowed in appreciation. "You are even fairer at close quarters." An unusually large Althar male appeared behind the man and stood against the wall of the chamber, hands behind his back.

"What do you want with me?" Cael shifted uncomfortably under the man's strange scrutiny.

"That will become apparent very soon, my dear. Let me introduce myself. I am Jabeel. I command the Althar rebels. They assist me to achieve my aims; I provide them with the venue for their rebellious statement to the culture they reject. I also pay well for favours." Jabeel leaned against the door, pushing it closed.

"I have eyes and ears everywhere, son of Jarin. Your lady friends have become something of a nuisance to me, but they are most inaccessible. You, on the other hand, are rather careless with your personal safety." Jabeel extracted a small metal case from a pocket of his coat, flipped the lid open and ran a slender finger over the waxy contents. Clicking the lid closed again, he rubbed his finger across the gums inside his top lip. "Would you care to partake?" He waved the case at Cael.

Cael tightened his jaw and shook his head.

"The naj is very good this year." Jabeel returned the case to his pocket as his eyes brightened, the pupils shrinking hard and small. A faint flush of colour appeared on his pale skin. "A long dry season always gives a concentrated resin, my dear. Perhaps you will allow me to introduce you to the pleasures of naj later. It enhances the enjoyment of any . . . proceedings quite considerably."

"Why am I here? I assume it is not to be lectured on your personal indulgences?" Cael watched him warily. Gods, the man was oily. Jabeel—where had he heard the name? Gowan's sending provided the answer on cue.

>*Beware, Cael. It is Jabeel, son of Kren, son of Labicheth.*< With an imprecise clunk, the pieces dropped together in his mind, making a possible whole of the puzzle.

"Son of Kren," he breathed, watching the man's face. A barely discernible flicker of surprise in the stone-grey eyes was soon mastered. The dark head tilted, considering him. "Rapist; murderer; defiler of magic," Cael continued softly. "Balance-shifter."

>*Take care, Cael. He is unpredictable.*<

>*He is neutralised, is he not?*< Cael maintained his steady

stare. Jabeel attempted a grin, achieving only a grimace.

"I see my reputation precedes me. How much do you really know, Empath? Or has the witch told you what she wants you to hear?"

Cael blinked. "The witch?"

"Galaen, lad. Galaen." Jabeel paced impatiently. "Witch-twin to the teasing seductress who lost herself to escape my . . . displeasure."

Again Gowan's sending supplied background. >*Chiahn. Galaen's sister. Jenna's grandmother. Gods, but the man must be mad. Chiahn wanted no part of him—she feared him, and for good reason.*<

"Displeasure?" Incredulous, Cael shook his head and frowned. "I heard you raped her—killed her husband, and her Wayfinder, when her whereabouts were kept from you. That was . . . *displeasure?*"

Jabeel's expression darkened. The naj case reappeared and he rubbed a thick smear of resin over his gums. His lips spread in the parody of a smile that did not reach his eyes. "Actually, fair one, it was decidedly *pleasurable.*" He closed his eyes and drew a deep breath, emanating satisfaction and lurid memory.

Cael shuddered. >*Gods, Gowan. The man is depraved.*<

"Power is a most interesting concept, fair one." Jabeel's eyes opened into narrow slits. "To take a woman who resists and fights and spits insults only heightens the power of the conquest. The pleasure is considerable." Faint colour flushed his face. "The man she chose over me thought otherwise. He also overestimated his ability to . . . punish me for taking his wife." Jabeel barked a short laugh. The Althar behind him smirked. Gathering control of himself, Jabeel straightened his shirt, smoothing non-existent wrinkles from his immaculate sleeves. He folded his arms over his chest and tapped fingers on his thin biceps, regarding Cael with a speculative look. His voice lowered. "Death also, fair one, has its interesting side." He swept Cael from head to toe with blatant interest. Cael's uneasiness grew. A man should not inspect another in such a way. "Prolonging death heightens perception, did you know?"

Cael averted his eyes, suddenly very conscious of his situation. "Not a subject I have investigated." He swallowed. >*I do not like the way this is heading, Gowan.*<

>*Nor I. Do not press him further.*< Gowan pulsed restraint.

"And so, again. Why am I here?" Even as he asked, Cael knew the answer.

"A question of expediency, my dear." Jabeel laughed quietly. "And because you . . . attract me." He spread his hands wide and arched his brows. "Debauchery is *so* underrated."

"Expedient how?" Cael growled, sickened.

Jabeel smiled indulgently. "You have, on your very lovely person, a device by which your Wayfinder may reach you. I do not doubt you have been in constant contact, so you will be aware of the warding here. I am going to modify that warding soon. Your friends are free to attempt your rescue. Of course, there are some rules to this game. The warding will not be lifted completely. It will block any male who attempts the Way."

"Then I may not leave?" Cael asked.

"You do not listen, my dear. It is a one-way warding. Of course you may leave. Should your lady friends be brave enough to attempt to free you. They will be unable to bring men to help you, though." Jabeel paced the chamber, not taking his eyes off Cael. "Every good game has an element of risk, wouldn't you agree? This is no different. My friend

231

Kavlek here, and myself, will leave you alone for short periods of time. Of course, you will never know if we remain outside the door, or are gone for tea. That is a chance you must take."

Cael shook his head. "That is *no* chance. You are a fool if you think they will be taken in by a crude game of cat and mouse."

"I think that given the right encouragement, your ladies will prove you quite wrong, my dear. What they must decide is . . . are you worth the risk?" Jabeel gestured to Kavlek who approached Cael, a stout cord in each hand. "I warn you not to resist. You are deep in the rock, and there are many of us."

Kavlek reached for Cael's wrists. Cael brought his knee up into Kavlek's groin and hammered his bound fists under the heavy chin as the Althar doubled over.

"You really should not have done that." Jabeel's voice was soft. He raised a hand. Blue light flared in Cael's vision, slamming his body against the rock behind him. He slid to the floor where he lay stunned, unable to see, or hear past the constant whine in his ears. He felt a hand on his neck deliver the disabling pinch that had begun this nightmare.

Oh Gods! The man was *still* a Wielder.

Jenna sat in Gowan's study, her head in her hands and her sickened heart in her boots. She raised her head to Gowan and saw an expression of deep concern etched into his face. He had relayed Cael's sharing to her and Verra. It had ended in an abrupt burst of pain and blue light, leaving them all in shock and afraid for Cael, aware that consciousness had left him.

"The Hand was correct. Jabeel, son of Kren is behind all

this." Gowan ran a hand through his hair. "The man is a Wielder, one of great power. He was neutralised and exiled when he refused to abide by the code. How it can be that he still wields, I do not know."

Jenna sat quite still, overcome by Cael's encounter with Wielder's magic and hard stone. Echoes of his hurt had played through her body, causing her to catch her breath until the pain disappeared abruptly along with his awareness. She rubbed at her neck, wondering what had been done to cause the sudden vice-like pain she had shared with him. The bond was at once both a blessing and a curse. She stared at Verra, seeing her own fear mirrored in the green eyes. "So it's you and me, then?" she said softly. Jabeel's spelling out of the rules had made that clear.

Verra nodded, her face pale. "We wait. It would be foolish to do anything until he can again communicate."

"He wishes me to send you home, Jenna." Gowan said.

Jenna shook her head. "No. I can't face Illiahn without him."

"Nor I," Verra agreed.

Jenna plucked at her long white Healer's dress and rose to her feet. "I am not dressed for this. Lara Croft would not be in skirts. I'm going to change."

"Lara Croft?" Gowan queried.

"A . . . heroine from *my* world. Looks a lot like me." *And what I wouldn't give for her arsenal right now,* she thought grimly. She left the study, lifting her skirts and increasing her pace to a run as she headed for her chamber. Verra followed close behind.

Cael was again bound by his wrists, and stripped to the waist. Strong cords held him, each looped over an iron hook driven into the ceiling two yards or more above his head. The play of the rope held his arms at shoulder level, chafing his wrists painfully whenever he was knocked from his feet by a recovered Kavlek.

Kavlek used his fists with brutal force, and employed a heavy cudgel for variety. The chamber smelled of blood and sweat, and the faint, burnt odour of spent Wielder's magic.

"Call for her." Jabeel's face was close to his, narrowed eyes intent on him, his breath hot on Cael's cheek. "You know you need her. Call." Cael sagged against the restraints as Kavlek hit him a backhanded blow across the face.

"No! Not the face—do you remember nothing?" Jabeel stroked Cael's cheek, clucking in soft irritation. "Now that is too bad. This face should never be spoilt. You were made to be looked at and enjoyed, my friend."

Cael did not deign to communicate in any way with his torturers. Jabeel nodded to Kavlek, who slammed a fist into Cael's belly with impassive obedience. Cael coughed and retched, but previous torments that morning had left him quite empty.

"Call—her—now!"

Cael had no intention of making the call until he could formulate some sort of plan. He had no doubt they would both come. Jenna would be feeling his pain, but he knew Verra would wait for him to call. The Wayfinder's code forbade interference without invitation, unless her charge was incapacitated. Which he could be, very soon.

He had warned them off. *Do not come,* he had sent to Verra. *It is a trap. He means harm to us all.* And to Jenna; *If you love me, chekuán, you must stay away. As long as I am bait, I will live.* Until he tires of the game, Cael thought bleakly. The ultimate end that Jabeel had outlined filled him with abject horror.

Kavlek picked up the cudgel again and swung it hard against Cael's back, twice across the shoulders then into the kidneys. The next blows landed against his rib cage, driving the breath from him and dropping him to his knees, wrenching his shoulders painfully. Oh Gods; that last blow broke something. Hanging by his wrists for an instant, he fought for breath against the savage pain. He recovered his feet, panted air back into his lungs and glared fierce opposition at Jabeel.

"That must have hurt," Jabeel purred. "This is all so unnecessary, my dear. Call her." He circled behind Cael and drew a slow finger through the slick pain-sweat that ran in occasional runnels down the length of his bruised back.

Cael flinched away from the touch, sickened by the man's blatant pleasure. He confined his breathing to shallow gasps, trying to avoid the pain that blossomed with each breath.

"I *will* have them. You know it. I have no doubt you have warned them, but they will come. Foolish loyalty will draw them to you like moths to a flame." Jabeel spoke from behind him, uncomfortably close, his voice full of soft menace.

Cael considered Jabeel's words. The women were capable of doing just as he said.

"Save yourself considerable suffering and *call*, my dear. Bring them here and hasten the whole process." Cael jerked his head away from Jabeel's caressing hand. Jabeel sidestepped as Kavlek again drove a rock-like fist into his victim's belly.

Cael's body spasmed as broken ribs shifted and grated with the blow. He gasped and retched miserably but would not cry out. Fighting against the pain that threatened to claim his consciousness, he blinked back the encroaching grey mist from his vision. "I will resist you until I know they will be safe," he panted with stubborn resolve. "I will *not* call, knowing you wait to pounce like a cat. Do what you will."

Jabeel considered him with a thoughtful expression. "Such courage deserves reward, my dear. Very well. I will make it more interesting. You may have some time alone. A sporting chance, yes? Two minutes I give you. A gift! You must decide if you can effect an escape in that time."

Cael coughed and spat blood at Jabeel's feet. "So you may step in the moment you hear the Way? Try harder, old man."

"Ah now, where is your gratitude? My offer is an honest one. Two minutes, I give you my word. Take it or leave it, it is no matter to me." Jabeel slid closer to him and fingered the blood-flecked mouth. "You bleed inside, son of Jarin. How uncomfortable for you. Call her, and I will ease you." He licked the blood from his fingertips with suggestive slowness.

Cael did not respond. Jabeel took his chin in a firm hand and locked eyes with him. His steel-grey eyes were bright with excitement. "It is of no matter to me if you die eventually, Empath. In fact, that is the desired result. The slower, the better for me." He swallowed and rubbed his own groin once. He pressed his face closer. Cael could smell the sweet stench of naj on the man's breath. "The moment of death is said to be almost ecstatic, given the right stimulation." He lowered his voice to a conspiratorial murmur. "My friend here will leave us." Jabeel stroked Cael's mouth again, his breath coming faster. "And I will have you at the end, fair one: use you as you die. There will be no one to save you, to stop me." He shrugged. "Unless, of course, your ladies come through for you." Jabeel gave him a twisted smile and gestured to Kavlek, who again hefted the thick cudgel from hand to hand. "We will see if you are still open to persuasion."

Cael groaned and closed his eyes.

"Payback!" Kavlek grunted. The cudgel connected with Cael's groin in a sickening thud.

This time the cry was torn from him as an agony of pain exploded through his body, driving all conscious thought from his mind and filling his vision with fractured shards of rainbow light.

"One's manhood is both one's strength *and* weakness, my dear." Jabeel's synthetic chuckle sounded beside him.

Cael's legs shook as he hauled himself upright, his whole body trembling with shock from the low blow. He glared scorn at Kavlek, coughed and spat another mouthful of frothy blood. He was breathing with difficulty now, aware that his time was running short. "I will take the two minutes," he panted, feigning capitulation in a desperate bid to buy time. Gods, this was bad. He was battered and swollen, damaged inside and out, and blood ran from his wrists where his weight against the cords had opened the skin.

"So you are coming to your senses, fair one. Excellent!" Jabeel gestured again to Kavlek. "Bring him ease."

Kavlek crossed to the door and pulled it open. "Agrev emine!" he bellowed in the Althar tongue. A hooded female appeared, bearing a wooden bucket. "Kurek li alakem." Kavlek nodded toward Cael, and the woman held a cup of water to his lips. He drank, grateful for the reprieve. And felt a familiar brush on his mind. The woman sopped a coarse cloth in the bucket and met his eyes as she bathed his face and neck with cool water.

>*Lakra!*<

Her black-within-black eyes slid from his, but her face

held warning. * *Do not respond to me. They must not know.* *

>*How did you find me?*<

* I am . . . Arkell's. I hear much, being so close to the Circle. I could not betray my brother by giving this location away, despite his rebellion. I had to come myself. *

>*Can you help me?*<

* Affirmative. * As always, it was a positive concept, rather than a word. * You need me, flatlander, that is why I came. *

>*How many are here?*<

* Seven only, but many more within calling. *

>*Are you at risk?*<

* Negative. I am A'Thek! They do not know yet, but if they threaten me, they will know soon enough. If I can release you, I know how to get out. Try to avoid taking any more damage. You need to be able to move fast. *

>*Too late, Lakra. I am hurt beyond escape.*<

* Do not give up, flatlander! I am not finished with you yet. *

He flinched as she washed blood from his mouth, and she pulsed a gentle mind-caress.

"Laneketh li alakem, kethet stol!" Kavlek glowered at her as Jabeel folded his arms, fingers tapping on his thin biceps with impatience.

Lakra gathered cloth and bucket and rose hastily.

>*Stay open to me?*< Cael avoided eye contact, not wanting to betray their communication.

* Of course. I will be close. Tell me when they leave you again. If they have truly left, I will release you. * She left the room without a backward glance.

Thank the Gods, Fate seemed to be on his side. Cael made the call to Verra, sending details of the time restraint and his bonds. Two minutes. It seemed too easy. As twisted as Jabeel was, Cael had tested the truth of his words, and detected no lie. He would not interfere until two minutes were up. Besides, Lakra would warn of any deception.

Jabeel gave him an oily smile. "Well, my fair one. You shall have your short reprieve. Use it wisely." He turned to follow Kavlek from the chamber. "Oh, one more thing. The chamber is warded against weapons. Unfortunately your bonds have grown rather tight with your resistance, but your friends will be quite unable to transport a blade to cut them. It has been a pleasure spending time with you, my dear. If you remain, we can begin again. You have some idea of what to expect, do you not? Think on it. Fare you well."

The heavy door thudded closed, and the rasp of the bolt sliding home sounded ominously final. He waited, hearing their footsteps recede. >*Lakra? Do you see them?*<

* Negative. *

>*Do not put yourself at risk. The Wayfinder is coming for me. Stay where you are.*<

Cael sent the call Verra waited for. Gods! The time allowance now seemed desperately short. The bonds were indeed tight, too tight to be unknotted with ease.

Crystal sang as the Way opened before him. Verra peered with caution through the shimmer before hurrying toward him, exclaiming in dismay at his condition. Jenna followed, showing the effects of his hours of torture.

"The knife would not transport," Jenna began, then stopped, staring. Her eyes widened, dark with shared pain. "Oh, Cael . . . oh, shit."

"Raise me," he panted, eyeing the ceiling and flashing them an image of his intentions. He coughed more bloody froth.

Jenna swore again. "Don't try to talk. Save your breath."

239

She and Verra together held him around the hips, struggling to lift him high enough to work the loops of rope free of the hooks. His injured groin protested their tight embrace.

>*Not high enough.*< Grasping each cord as far up as he could, he strove to pull himself higher. His biceps and shoulder muscles knotted, cramping with the strain as he inched toward the ceiling. With a last determined heave, he lunged for a hook with one hand. His fingers made contact and curled around the iron. >*Gods—oh Gods!*< Agony erupted in his side as his damaged ribs expanded with his weight, and he clamped his lips against the stream of curses that threatened to escape him. Hanging from one hand, supported by Verra and Jenna, he worked the cord loose from one hook. He repeated the process on the other, and they lowered him, steadying him as he staggered and rubbed feeling back into his hands while the blood returned. Verra ran to the Way, motioned Jenna through first.

Jenna stopped dead.

"Quickly, we have only seconds," Verra urged.

"I can't—it's like a brick wall!" Fear reflected from Jenna's face.

Verra pressed a hand into the Way. "Gods! The warding is back. We cannot leave." Her eyes were huge, and horror filled her expression.

Jabeel had trapped them neatly. He had not lied. Just omitted a detail. *It is a one-way warding* . . . Cael heard Jabeel's words again with new understanding, cursing himself for a fool, cursing the weasel who had fooled him.

"Wait," he rasped, "there is another." >*Lakra! We are betrayed. Unbolt the door!*< His sending was an urgent appeal. The stone felt cool against his skin as he leaned on the wall, panting in short, painful breaths, listening in heart-pounding suspense for the sound of release. Gods, was she there? Would she indeed double-cross her own kind to liberate him? He stared in silent apprehension at the heavy door, willing her to respond.

The bolt slid with a metallic grating and the door swung open. Lakra stood back in silence as the three surged past her, and she bolted the door again behind them.

* Come. Jabeel is not here but coming soon. He does not hurry because he is confident he will find you all inside. We must move fast. *

Cael no longer had breath to spare for speech. Jenna and Verra supported him on each side as they followed Lakra into another chamber adjoining the main corridor. Throwing back crumbling tapestries, she motioned them through into a small passage, urging them to as much speed as Cael could manage. The passage was dim, the light magic waning with age. A coughing fit took him, and they rested a moment while Jenna held him, smothering the sound against her chest. He swiped red foam from his mouth, raggedly cursing his lack of breath. They moved on. At each adjoining passage Lakra took a turn, alternating right and left.

>*Jenna. I cannot breathe.*< He sank to his knees, his breath a tight-wheezed gasp, his mouth cloyed with the metallic taste of his blood. The beginnings of panic lurked at the edges of his awareness. He leaned forward, taking his weight on his arms, seeking to ease the constriction in his chest.

Jenna touched Lakra's arm. "I must help him. Please, hide us?"

Cael translated her words into mindspeak. Lakra eyed them in silence for a moment.

* I can detect no pursuers, but yes, I can hide us, * she

sent eventually. * I have scanned our passage, but none follow. It seems strange they do not try to retake you. *

With a brief frown, she moved from the passage into a side chamber that had several openings leading off from it. She disappeared into an opening to the left. Verra and Jenna pulled Cael to his feet and hauled him after her. They found themselves in a medium-sized room, once a bed-chamber by its furnishings. The air was musty both with age and the dry-rotting remnants of bedding that lined the sleeping alcoves around the walls. They lowered Cael to the floor, and he leaned his back against the wall with a low groan of pain.

>Gods, Jenna, I hurt!<

"I know," she breathed. She knelt in front of him and held his face in her hands, making him look at her. "I must mend the lung. I may have to move the broken rib to do that."

He nodded, his chest heaving with effort.

"It will hurt, Cael. A lot. I can't yet safely turn off either the pain centre or consciousness."

>Do what you must, chekuán.< He met her eyes in perfect trust, and he pulsed his confidence to her.

Jenna took his Keystone in her hand, turning it to catch as much of the dim light as she could. Its glowing depths surrounded her as she entered and floated over his essence. Using her training, she guided her awareness through his body, finding the damaged lung without difficulty. She assessed the position of bone fragments, noted the skewed angle of the rib that had made the puncture, and quickly withdrew.

"It is still attached. We can move it with pressure." Positioning Verra behind him, Jenna placed her hands against his lower rib cage on each side of his spine. "Push here when I say. Keep the pressure constant."

Verra spread her hands and nodded, her lips tight. Jenna knelt and embraced Cael around the ribs, locking her hands behind his back. She looked deep into his eyes, already feeling sick at what she must do. His steady golden gaze held only trust. "Now!"

Verra pushed as Jenna drew her arms together, squeezing inwards and down, maintaining the pressure until she felt the minute shifting she waited for. She gasped, struggling to control her reaction to his pain, the echo of it aching and burning, a dull knife in her own side. Cael's feral mind-cry seared her soul. His face was ashen as he coughed blood onto the floor beside him. He pulsed apology for his violent broadcast, and Jenna caught him as his eyes rolled, and he slumped sideways to the cool stone. The pain winked out.

Linking to lend him strength, she re-entered the Keystone, confronting many aberrations that pulsed hostile white heat at her. She identified the most pressing need, and began the process of pulsing it away through her own body. Within fifteen minutes, Cael ceased his laboured gasping; the bloody coughing stopped. His breathing improved to a steady wheeze and soon began to sound normal. His face regained its colour as his consciousness returned.

"Gods! What a gift you have." Cael grasped Jenna's hand, raised it to his mouth and kissed it. She felt a soft glow of pleasure as he pulsed his relief and gratitude to her.

"I have never seen the like of this," Verra breathed. "How does it feel, *chiaran?*"

Cael considered. "As cold water on burnt skin. As a wound eased by salve." He looked at Jenna, his gaze warm and sleepy. "And like the strength is being sucked from every muscle in my body." The corners of his mouth turned up a little as his eyes closed. *>Forgive me. I am weary,<* he sent to them all.

Jenna laid a reassuring hand on his shoulder. "The Healing magic uses the patient's own reserves to mend the body," she explained. "I can lend a little strength using the Linking magic, but much rest is needed." She brushed sweat-dark gold hair back from his brow as his face relaxed. "He's already asleep. I don't dare heal more of his injuries—he'll need days of rest if I do. We can't afford that sort of time if we are to escape from wherever we are." She looked at the delicate Althar woman. "Thank you. If not for your help, we'd all be in worse trouble."

The woman raised fine eyebrows, shrugging in eloquent mime. "She does not understand you. She only mindspeaks with Cael. He thinks I do not know." Verra flicked an uneasy glance between the two. "Jenna, this is Lakra."

Chapter Fourteen

The Torrent

"I do not believe it!" Jabeel's bellow of rage carried through the echoing stone corridors, causing many pairs of black eyes to turn in curiosity as to the cause of his anger. "How? How could they have escaped?"

"Sporting chance. Two minutes." Kavlek's grunted remark could have been interpreted as humour had he been more intelligent.

"It was never sporting!" Jabeel fumed. "Merely designed to look that way. The warding should have held them like rats in a trap." He slammed the door on the empty chamber. "Gather what you can and give the order to move out. The cursed Wayfinder will return outside the warding now that she has keyed this place, and she will not be alone."

"Where will we go?"

"Kordethal. See to it. Quickly!" Jabeel pulled the naj case from his pocket and rubbed waxy resin under his lip. He cursed in frustration. The warding had never failed before. Perhaps the fine-tuning he had attempted with the young Althar warder's talents was just a little *too* clever. He had been so confident, had come so close.

He snarled, loosing a shaft of Wielder's fire against the corridor wall, leaving a small, blackened crater smoking in the rock. The only place he was able to access his gifting since he had been neutralised lay deep in abandoned Althar settlements, where traces of ancient wild magic still lingered. That was an old score he intended to settle, and soon. The Hand would pay for their arbitrary decision: once the prophecy came to pass, he would have them. Ché Kevath would be destroyed and the land his for the taking. Even at his age, there was still time to enjoy power.

He rubbed more naj across his teeth and drew his lips over it. As the drug took effect, he went in search of Strick, his mood nicely elevated. Before he had gone very far, an abstract broadcast of pain reverberated in his mind, stopping him in shock.

The Empath! And not too far away, either. Jabeel knew that an involuntary reverberation of pain such as this had a limited range. Only an intentional message sent to a specific individual could travel unlimited distance. The Empath was still here—somewhere. The warding had not failed at all.

He discovered Strick arranging their fast departure. "Not so much hurry, my friend." Jabeel grinned with delight. "We have more time than I imagined. He is still here."

Strick gaped at him. "Impossible. The door was bolted on the outside . . . if they have not left through the Way . . ."

"Then someone let them out," Jabeel finished for him. "They are somewhere in the settlement. You would have heard him if not for your barrier. They cannot have gone far. The Empath is hurt beyond moving with any speed."

"If the Healer is with him . . ."

"You know nothing of the workings of magic," Jabeel snapped in impatience. "She will not heal him. It would render him incapable for days. No. They will keep moving, but they will be slow. Send a group of the most competent of this rabble after them."

"We stay?"

"No. We withdraw to Kordethal. The risk of discovery is too great. I believe Fate is still undecided on the outcome of this matter."

Jenna studied the fine-boned face of the Althar woman, acknowledging her delicate beauty with some reluctance. Why did this Lakra person keep appearing in Cael's life? Coincidence? A sharp elbow of jealousy jabbed her in the stomach.

They remained in the musty bedchamber. Jenna maintained the link, hoping to restore Cael's strength quickly. He still slept, wrapped in a faded tapestry to keep his naked torso from the cool stone. Verra sat, hunched and miserable, fighting her own private battle with their confinement. Lakra leaned against the wall in an alcove, her eyes closed.

"How far do you think we have come?" Jenna asked.

"Perhaps a mile, a little less. Ask Lakra. She understands very basic vocabulary." Verra's tension was growing. Jenna worried, knowing how close Verra had come to panic in the deep chambers of Sartz.

"Lakra? Where are we?" Jenna kept her voice low, aware their pursuers could be close. If they were pursued. She had heard nothing.

Lakra opened black eyes and yawned, her mouth pink as a cat's, an odd contrast to her milk-white skin. "Where?" she said, raising her brows. "Ré Shan."

"Gods! The Torrent? That is close to Kereál. Which end, Lakra?" Verra leaned forward in sudden eagerness.

Lakra's face showed confusion. Verra drew in the dusty debris of the chamber floor. The Torrent; its source; Lake Tuan. Lakra leaned over, indicating the mid-point of the torrent.

"Just under two miles from where it exits into the lake. Can he make it, Jenna?"

"Wait." Jenna watched Lakra as her finger traced the dusty line and flicked sharply to the left a small distance from the lake.

"Exit? Out?" Jenna asked, hoping she understood. Lakra nodded.

"A little over a mile—even better!" Verra brightened, seeing an end to her fear. "When Cael wakes he can send for help. Jabeel had better take cover. The Hand will send Wielders against him, surely!"

Jenna knew that, if necessary, the Hand could access a small army of Wielders, send them with Wayfinders, communicate via Empaths and supply many Healers and Linkers. All magic users followed a code of behaviour, and were pledged to the service of the land and its people.

Cael stirred. His fingers tightened reflexively on hers. She felt him slowly return to awareness, felt also the pain that greeted him.

"Cael? Are you in there?" Jenna squeezed his hand, waiting for his head to clear.

>Hm, in here. Somewhere.<

"We know where we are. It's an old mining settlement inside the Ré Shan Torrent. Are you all right?"

>I think so.< He opened his eyes with a sneeze and looked with curiosity at the musty tapestry that enfolded him.

"Best we could do, sorry." Jenna caught his pulse of gratitude and shared the pain-flare that the sneeze cost him.

"I hate to rush you, chiaran, but I need to get out of here!" Verra hugged her arms about her knees, rocking herself to and fro in agitation.

"Gods, Verra, of course—I will help . . ." He struggled

248

to sit up, fighting both the tapestry and his weakness.

"You will have to do it lying down, Cael. It's only been an hour. It's too soon." Jenna restrained him with a light hand. "Rest. You know the rules." He subsided.

Verra drew several deep breaths as he worked at her fear. "I thank you, *chiaran*. Gods, I hate stone." She dropped her head onto her knees and relaxed.

"Talk to Lakra. She doesn't understand much of what I say." Jenna chuckled as his eyes widened and his gaze flew to meet hers. "We know you can. You don't have as many secrets as you think."

"So it would appear," he said drily.

>*Lakra. It seems we are about even. I thank you for your help.*< Cael looked his thanks at her, and she lifted fine shoulders into an elegant shrug.

* Life-debt is not discharged yet, flatlander. You do not look good at all. *

>*I have been better.*< He flexed his body experimentally, realizing anew the damage he had sustained at Kavlek's hand. What began as a curse ended in a groan.

* Why does she not heal you entirely? *

Cael sent her an explanation of healing magic and its consequences.

* Ah. She is wise as well as beautiful. * Lakra smiled and glanced at Jenna with new respect.

>*Truth. I thank you again,*< he acknowledged. >*Excuse me for a short time. There are others I need to contact for help.*<

Lakra nodded her understanding. * I will be quiet. *

He contacted Gowan, relayed all he knew and left it in his mentor's hands to organise whatever he saw fit. He sent reassuring messages to both Telsen and Illiahn, knowing the anxiety they must feel.

* Cael. I must interrupt. There is mindspeak very close. Tell the others—they must be silent. *

>*I thank you. Verra, Jenna; we are pursued. Be silent, they are close. Gods! If they find us, I am helpless.*< He cursed silently. Three women to defend, and himself as weak as a baby. >*Lakra. How many?*<

She held up three, then four fingers. Increased it to five.

They waited in tense silence. The sound of booted feet reached their ears.

>*Some distance away yet. Perhaps two corridors?*<

Lakra nodded, yes.

>*You have hidden us well.*<

She gave a modest shrug. The footsteps began to recede. Cael flicked a questioning glance at Lakra. Wait, her answering expression warned. Anxious moments passed.

* They are out of mindspeak range, * she sent at last. * They will not hear us now. It will take them a very long time to search every chamber. *

"They have passed. They will be back, and closer next time." Cael looked at Jenna. "*Chekuán,* can you give me full-needs for a short time? I must be able to move." Not something he would ask in other circumstances; admitting he was not in control did not come easy to him.

He felt Jenna's fingers tighten on his as their clasped hands began to glow with the rose-gold aura of the full-needs link. She extended a hand to Verra. "Come join me." Verra shifted toward them and reached for Jenna's hand.

"Sheytan tells me strength can be borrowed as well as given. It doesn't hurt, Verra. Don't look so worried." A look of intense concentration covered her face. Her fine angular brows drew together, the ends sweeping up and out, a distant, flying bird. She pressed her lips together, and closed her eyes. The link flared more brightly.

"Gods!" Cael said with a quiet laugh. "I feel you, Verra."

Lakra watched with interest. * What is it they do? *

>*They restore me. With their own life force.*<

Lakra came closer. She offered a tentative hand to Verra, her face neutral. After a moment's hesitation, Verra grasped the slender white hand in her own.

Cael gasped as intense golden light filled the chamber, startled to feel Lakra in the link and astounded by the life force that flowed so strongly from her.

"Althar magic," Lakra explained. "Old. Strong here." She indicated the chamber. * Also my symbiot. *

Cael pulsed his gratitude to them all, feeling their strength course into his body. Within minutes he was sitting up, and before long, he was able to stand. Breaking the link, he limped around the chamber with difficulty. His injuries had stiffened as he rested. Intense pain flared in his pelvis, and he suspected injury to the bone. His ribs hurt with every breath, and burst into a new fire of pain if he moved incautiously. He ached all over, but he could move. Slowly.

Lakra touched his arm. * We move. I have a cache a little further from here. You collapsed before we could reach it. *

>*Cache?*<

* Your clothing. Weapons. Water. *

Cael relayed the information, and they exited the chamber with caution, knowing Lakra would alert them if she heard their pursuers. They trailed Lakra, stopping often for Cael to rest against the corridor wall as he dealt with pain. It was hard enough that his weakness was so exposed: he would not reveal how drained he was.

Once they hid, piled into a small recess inside a storage chamber, not daring to move, as the five Althar searched the network of passages behind them. Again they were passed by, unseen in their bolthole, pressed into each other in the confined space and barely able to breathe. Cael clamped his jaws. The pressure of the women's bodies caused him fresh suffering, but he endured without complaint. >*Intimate. Another time and place and I may have enjoyed that more.*< His wry comment brought smiles to them all as they extricated themselves with relief from the recess and continued on their way.

They reached Lakra's cache undetected. Cael put on his undershirt with difficulty, and allowed Jenna to help him into his shirt of fine wool, grateful for her assistance and the warmth of the clothing. He sat in a stone sleeping alcove, strapping the sheath of a well-balanced knife to each wrist, wincing as the leather bit into his raw skin. Ignoring the discomfort, he tightened the thongs and tested the movement of the blades. >*Nice.*< He nodded in approval.

* I know what you favour, * Lakra answered, handing him the waterskin. * We leave the settlement now, and continue along the Torrent. It will be harder to hide. *

>*How far?*< The water was brackish, but he was too thirsty to care, and took several long swallows before handing it back to her.

* Perhaps a mile, a little more. *

He nodded, his face grim. Gods! It would be torturous. He relayed the information. Jenna rested a light hand on his shoulder, and he felt her concern.

"How are you doing?" she asked.

>*Not good.*< He laid his hand over hers. >*If I cannot make it that far, you and Verra get yourselves out.*< There was no point lying to her. She already knew the extent of his injuries.

"I won't leave you, Cael, so don't ask me to." Her eyes

flashed blue fire at him, and her brows angled sharply. Her chin had a stubborn tilt to it that he had not noticed before.

>*Cael?*< A familiar voice spoke into his mind.

>*Gowan!*< Cael straightened in surprise, regretting the sudden movement as pain lanced through his side.

>*We are at the mouth of the Ré Shan. Where are you?*<

>*South end of the settlement, Gowan. We are about to enter the Torrent. The exit is close to a mile from here—a vent.*<

>*Have courage, Cael. The Hand gathers Wielders to send into Ré Shan against Jabeel. I am here with Quan and Chereth, and two others: Wielders from the Guild.*<

"Gowan comes with Wielders." Cael levered himself up from the alcove, gritted his teeth against the pain and motioned them from the chamber. "We cannot wait here to be discovered while the five still search for us." They followed Lakra down the corridor.

The hewn passages of the settlement soon gave way to a narrow pathway that ended at a wall of solid rock. Lakra met their puzzled stares with a smile. She pulled a small cube from her robe, displayed it to them between thumb and forefinger before pressing it firmly into the rock. As they had seen before in Sartz, the stone melted away from the morphed insert, leaving a wide opening and admitting a light mist of water vapour and the thunderous roar of the Torrent below them.

Cael turned to search Verra's face, his brows raised in question. "Is it well with you?" he asked. She paled as she stared through the opening and nodded once. He stepped through, and she followed him onto a wide shelf of rock that ran along the wall of the waterway.

Lakra spoke words and rubbed her hand against one side of the opening. The rock sealed, leaving the small cube protruding at the centre. She retrieved it and again took the lead. As she passed the others, Verra seized her arm. "Is it warded?"

Lakra frowned her incomprehension. Verra widened her eyes at her and made a frustrated sound. Crossing her wristbands over her head, she answered her own question. There was no response, no Way. Nothing.

Cael leaned his shoulder against the rock for a moment. He needed to rest, but could only take brief respite from the agonies he felt with every movement. Lakra waited for him, scanning the way ahead. The faded luminescence of the light-imbued rock extended only a short way past the settlement.

"Cael, can we help you?" Jenna asked, raising her voice over the roar of the water.

"There is nothing to be done." He grimaced as he resumed his careful progress, each step sending shocks of hurt through the bones of his pelvis, each breath raising fresh torment in his ribs. He saw his pain reflected in her eyes and pulsed his apology, wishing she need not share it.

Gods! The next part of the journey was to be lightless. Lakra's robed figure merged with the dark. * Hold onto my robe, flatlander, and have the others join with you. I do not wish to lose any of you. I grew up in Ré Shan and travelled this way many times as a child. The passage is not difficult, but it has been many years since I used it, and then not without light. * He took a handful of the soft wool of her robe, leaving one hand free to stay in contact with the wall. So linked, the four ventured into total blackness.

It seemed an eternity. The damp rock shelf narrowed in places, and Cael relayed Lakra's warnings of any potential difficulty. He slid his feet forward, maintaining contact with the stone, fearing to step into sudden nothingness. Small tumbles of rock had to be negotiated on hands and knees, and after each of these, the small procession halted as he strove to master his pain. He continued to support Verra, pulsing constant waves of calm, taking fear and tension from her. To Jenna, he sent encouragement, beginning to believe they might make it out.

* We are close. * Lakra paused, bringing them all to a halt. * There is a tunnel. We must crawl. I fear this will be difficult for you, flatlander. * The rock shelf narrowed and ended abruptly. A small, cave-like opening crouched in their path. Cael lowered his protesting body to hips and elbows and followed Lakra into the tunnel.

Oh, Gods. It was worse than he had thought. Kavlek's cudgel had severely damaged him. >*Wait, please . . .*< He rolled off his groin onto his uninjured side, taking a moment to master himself again. Sweat dripped from the hair over his brow, and he screwed his eyes shut against the sting, swiping his hair back from his face. When he began to move once more, it was a slow, inching crawl as he pulled himself along on his hip and one elbow. He increased his flow of support to Verra, and during a brief moment of rest, reached a shaking hand back, seeking contact with Jenna. >*Chekuán, I need your help again. Lakra?*< Lakra wriggled back to lie beside him and snaked a hand past him to Jenna, who activated the link. Light glowed around them, giving welcome respite from the darkness as he lay on his side, drawing strength from the women that flowed their life force into him. Tears shone wet on Jenna's cheeks as she looked past him to Lakra, her anxiety plain on her face.

* Flatlander. Tell your mate I will not leave you. *
>*Unnecessary. She knows. How much further?*<
* So close. Perhaps quarter of a mile. Hold on. *
May as well be half a world away. He lay still for another moment, feeling strength seep into his limbs, the women's

courage bolstering his resolve. He broke the link, and turned again to the relentless crawl through the tunnel, the monotony of pain now a familiar presence.

>*Cael.*< Gowan's sending pierced the protective layer Cael had wrapped around himself. >*I feel you. We are tracking you outside.*<

>*Lakra says we are close to the exit. Can you see the vent?*<

>*No, nothing. Who is Lakra?*<

>*Friend. Althar.*<

>*How do you fare?*<

>*Not well, Gowan.*< He shared his condition with his mentor. Showed the darkness and Verra on the edge of panic; Jenna sharing his every surge of pain; the Torrent that thundered beneath them.

A small gleam of light pierced the darkness before them as they exited the narrow shaft, and he heard Verra's glad exclamation over the noise of the water. They stood tall, revelling in the release from confinement and the return of light, however diminutive. Cael's legs gave way beneath him, and Jenna and Verra took his weight, his arms around their shoulders. They stumbled with renewed confidence toward the promise of exit offered by the thin, bright finger that pointed into the passage some thirty paces ahead.

* The access is gone. * Lakra peered toward the open vent, her face almost invisible in the gloom as she scanned the rock face.

>*What?*<

* The access. A ladder of rope and wood. It is gone. *

A slight movement drew Cael's attention to the five figures that waited in shadows below the vent.

"Shit!" Jenna reached for his arm that lay across her shoulders, fumbling the knife from his wrist sheath. The scene before him seemed to waver in a most disconcerting fashion, becoming dimmer than he thought it should be.

"No, *chekuán,* this is not for you to do." He tried to reclaim the knife, but found his arm too heavy to raise.

"The hell it's not!"

He staggered as she slipped from under his arm to stand beside Lakra, her stance an aggressive proclamation to those who waited. Her form shifted and weaved. He blinked hard and she stabilised.

>*Gowan! We may not exit. Althar await us.*< Cael sank to his knees, conserving what strength remained to him, and the hope he had nurtured died as he stared at the five who prevented their exit to safety. Pain and exhaustion threatened to claim him, and he knew he was close to collapse. Verra stood behind him, supporting him against her legs, her hands on his shoulders as she repaid his constant support of her fear. Thank the Gods she did, he reflected. He was unsure he could remain upright on his own.

"Jenna. They will *not* take him!" Verra's voice revealed her fierce determination.

"No." Jenna held the knife before her.

"Jenna . . ." He leaned heavily against Verra.

"Peace, Cael. Will you use the other?" Jenna indicated the remaining knife. He pulled it free from the sheath, knowing he was incapable of defence. Verra took it from him and stood at Jenna's side. He tried to rise but his legs betrayed him, and he staggered sideways, connecting hard with the rough rock wall. The ground rose up to meet him in a nauseating spin. His vision spiralled inward and winked out.

Jenna felt Cael's consciousness leave him, grateful for the sudden cessation of pain. Every instinct screamed at her to go to him, but she stood her ground. "Lakra?" she said, squeezing the words past the tightness in her throat. "Please, help Cael." Verra remained poised at Jenna's side as Lakra disappeared past her with a whisper of soft robes.

Moving slowly, wary of the blades the women held, the five Althar approached them. Jenna trembled with adrenalin and dread. She had never used a weapon in her life. Her fingers curled around the cool hilt of the knife. She balanced herself, took up her fighting stance. Verra readied herself with equal determination. Lakra spoke out from behind them, making herself heard over the rush of the torrent.

"Shemen li alakem, kuatha kethet li *tekana* kamala kor!" The five hesitated, darting glances at each other. The authority with which she had spoken obviously alarmed them. Jenna watched, waiting, as their expressions showed a mindspeak conference in progress. They appeared to disagree. One stood back, shaking his head, and another joined him with a gesture of deference to Lakra.

"Kuatha'na shemen, A'Thek," he said, not meeting Lakra's eyes.

Jenna risked a worried glance behind her at Cael. In that moment, one of the remaining three lunged at her. She spun. Without thinking, she dropped her shoulders and raised her leg to deliver a solid kick to his belly. Stepping forward, she followed through with an elbow to each side of his jaw. The final uppercut carried the full force of her desperate fear. He fell. Another was on her in an instant. She threw herself sideways out of his grasp. Her shirt tore; his fingers raked her side. A hand gripped the waistband of her breeches and held her fast. Dropping to the ground, she twisted, rolled, pinned the arm beneath her. Snatching the knife around, she held the point to the throat of the young Althar. His eyes were wide, his hand frozen in the act of reaching for the knife. A small runnel of blood welled and ran from his neck. Jenna pressed the blade even closer. He gasped, his breathing ragged, and reached reflexively for her wrist. She closed both hands around the knife hilt, holding the blade tight against his throat.

Lakra stepped quickly over the still form of the first attacker to where Verra struggled with the third Althar, and laid a hand on the neck of Verra's adversary. He stiffened, then like a puppet whose strings had been cut, crumpled into a heap. Verra lay panting for a moment, then retrieved the knife from where it had fallen and hauled herself to her feet.

"Keld!" Lakra glared at the young male beneath Jenna's knifepoint. "Adaka kel tu lamen ki gaharda t'avaren. Ki a'drei shemené adenei!" Jenna felt him flinch at her words.

"Shemené na, na! Karashe, A'Thek, karashe!" He swallowed, causing more blood to run from his neck. He loosened his grip on Jenna's wrist, withdrew his hand from her and held it open in tacit surrender.

"Karashe." Lakra's voice became curiously gentle. "Mercy." Her black eyes glittered as she reached down and held the side of the youth's neck in a firm pinch.

Jenna felt him go limp beneath her, although his eyes remained on hers for moments before they closed. She stared at the knife, at the blood that still ran from the small wound. The shaking began as she sat up. Lakra took the knife from Jenna's trembling hand and Verra pulled her to her feet, embracing her without words, shaking as badly herself.

"One dead," Lakra pronounced as she knelt over the body of the first to move against them. For the first time, Jenna saw the dark pool the Althar lay in, the wound at his neck beneath the jaw.

The uppercut. She had forgotten the knife in her hand, reacting to his attack the only way she knew how. Realisation hit her, and her vision fractured with tears as Lakra closed the young male's eyes.

"Jenna. It was us or them. You know that." Verra held her by the shoulders and shook her gently. "Cael would be back with Jabeel, and we would all be dead within the day." Jenna turned at the mention of him. He lay where he had fallen at the base of the rock wall. Giving the Althar's body a wide berth, she went to him.

Verra raised her face to the light from the vent. "Voices outside . . . Gowan! Quan!" she called, and kept calling until Gowan appeared at the opening. "By the Gods, Gowan, you truly are a very welcome sight!"

Jenna watched as Lakra retrieved the access ladder from where it lay, stashed behind boulders. The two abstainers had given her this last detail by way of atonement before they disappeared back along the passage to the settlement. Lakra had let them go, not meeting Verra's measuring look, and busied herself with arranging their exit. After several tries, Verra managed to throw the ladder high enough for Gowan to catch. He attached it to the thick iron hooks driven into the rock below the exit. Gowan and Quan descended, taking in the scene around them as Quan lit the passage with Wielder's fire.

Jenna sat beside Cael, quiet and withdrawn, blooms of dark red across her torn shirt. "Jenna?" Gowan knelt on one knee beside her and looked askance at the three Althar that lay still on the rock shelf, one in a darkening pool of blood. He frowned in apparent puzzlement as his eyes rested on Cael's senseless form. "This is *your* doing?" He indicated the dead Althar. Jenna nodded. He whistled softly between his teeth. "Are you hurt, child?"

She shook her head as fresh tears welled up and spilled down her face. "I didn't mean to kill him," she whispered.

He leaned closer to hear her over the noise of the Torrent. "You were defending yourself and Cael, Jenna." His voice was firm, his smile kind.

"I'm a *Healer,* Gowan. Even at the end, with my knife against his throat, I couldn't have killed the last one. Had he only known it, he could have turned the knife on me. He was stronger." Her voice shook, her throat tight with emotion. "If not for Lakra, he would have realised it before much longer." She made herself look at the body. "That one was an accident."

"A most fortunate one, as you will come to realise." Gowan patted her knee, glancing again at Cael. "How is he?"

Jenna wiped her nose on her shirt and swiped at her eyes. "He needs major healing. I couldn't do much, not while we needed to keep moving. That bastard Jabeel nearly killed him." She touched Cael's throat, felt the slow pulse there, smiled despite her tears. "He's still in there. He's a survivor." Taking his hand, she linked, lending him strength. "How will we get him out? He won't manage the ladder."

Gowan eyed the vent. It was at least ten metres above them. "I have two other Wielders besides Quan. They should be able to raise him."

She did not question him. Nothing surprised her anymore.

The Wielders did indeed raise him. Jenna watched, amazed, as six arcs of flickering blue energy met to weave a cradle beneath his hips and shoulders. As the Wielders raised their hands toward the vent, the cradle lifted Cael to the light where she and Gowan waited to guide his limp

261

body through the opening of the shaft.

Conscious once more and shaking with cold and shock, he sat resting his head on arms crossed over his knees. Lakra prepared to leave them. She and Quan were to seal the young male's body into a rock tomb, and would wait with Gowan until the other Althar recovered their senses. Gowan would question and release them, in hope of learning Jabeel's location.

Jenna shivered in the stiff breeze and pulled her torn shirt more closely around herself. Echoes of Cael's injuries ached through her body, and she wanted to sleep for days. "Whatever debt you owed is paid many times over, Lakra. I can't thank you enough for our lives." She waited as Cael translated and returned Lakra's reply.

"She says you owe her nothing. She acted as honour demanded, as did you. There are no regrets."

Jenna extended her hand to Lakra, who took it. "Ask her what she said to the rebels that caused two of them to stand off as they did. I'm curious."

Cael relayed, laughed once, cursed and held his ribs. Jenna winced at the stab in her own side. "She said 'harm the flatlanders and I will personally remove your manhood's ability to function.' "

Jenna lifted an eyebrow at him.

"She was deadly serious," he added.

"And did you?" Jenna looked into Lakra's ebony eyes. The pale rose lips curved into a slight smile, the delicate cleft chin lifted.

"It is temporary, she says, but will give them something to think about for a month or two."

Jenna chuckled in approval. "She is a good person. We're lucky to know her."

>*Truth.*<

Lakra nodded at Jenna as Cael relayed her words. Turning to him, she laid her hands over his, crouched before him and shared a long look. She leaned forward and kissed his forehead, then continued to the vent, backed down the ladder, and disappeared. Jenna swallowed, wondering what had passed between them. She rubbed her eyes and yawned. Jealousy was not an emotion she was used to. And it was certainly unpleasant.

"How will she return to Alth?" Verra asked as she opened the Way home.

Cael shook his head with a wry smile. "I asked. 'No more Althar secrets for flatlanders,' was all she would say. I suspect another magic we know nothing of."

Jenna helped him stand, feeling the pain it cost him. "Hang on just a little longer. I'll start the healing as soon as we get you to the den," she encouraged. As long as I can stay upright and awake long enough, she thought with weary cynicism.

>*Having my own personal Healer is proving to be very beneficial, chekuán.*< He pulsed his appreciation to her in a warm, affirming wave. Seeing his jaw tighten against the agony of movement, she slipped her shoulders beneath his arm and steered him toward the Way, hoping her waning strength would be enough to justify his faith in her.

Chapter Fifteen

The Four of the Prophecy

Jenna stumbled through the Way into the yard at the ranch. Cael leaned on her heavily although she knew he tried to spare her. Telsen released Verra from his embrace and hurried to assist them. Jenna saw his eyes flick to the blood on her shirt.

"Gods, Jenna . . . you are hurt."

"It's not my blood, Tel, but please, will you take him?" As Telsen relieved her of Cael's weight, she bent forward a moment, locked her elbows and leaned on her knees. The linking she had provided so often during their escape had drained her more than she realised. With a deep sigh, she straightened and followed them into the den.

Jolie knelt at the small hearth, feeding kindling into the newly lit fire. Cael had warned Illiahn they were coming and suggested she keep the children away. Jenna knew he did not want to frighten them with his appearance. "Jolie, we would be grateful for some hot tea," Jenna said. "We can handle the fire. Thank you for being so thoughtful." The girl nodded, wide-eyed, and ran to the house on her mission.

Cael sat at the edge of the bed, too stiff and sore to lie down. Jenna helped him remove his shirt and undershirt, unlaced the knife sheaths and eased them loose from the raw skin of his wrists. Each wave of pain sent answering shudders down her spine and left her with a sick feeling.

She hesitated, her fingers resting on the silver wristband she had never seen him without. "How does this come off?" she asked, seeking some release mechanism. The restraints in the chamber had forced the band to cut into his wrist, leaving a deep and bloody stripe at its edge.

"It does not." He flexed his fingers and tightened them into a fist. "No matter. It is only a scratch."

Telsen observed in tight-lipped silence as she assessed the damage. Jenna left him to watch with Verra, her awareness now deep in the Keystone and within Cael's body. She pulsed away hurts, and in her mind's eye, monitored the healing as the swellings began to recede; split skin melded and restored itself. Areas of dark bruising gradually lightened, changed from black to purple to blue, faded to yellow and finally disappeared altogether.

Jenna surfaced, weary beyond her experience. Not merely tired, her body protested even remaining upright. She had long since laid Cael back on the bed as the healing took its toll, and sleep claimed him. She rested her head on the firm warmth of his chest and closed her eyes for a few moments, feeling his breath stir her hair. It would be so easy to drift off to sleep. She started when Verra touched her shoulder and handed her a cup of sweet tea from the kettle that stayed hot by the fire.

"Is it finished?" Verra asked, concern on her face.

"Not yet. Soon." She accepted the tea gratefully, and when she was finished drinking, Verra massaged her shoulders while she again rested her head. After a few moments, Jenna smiled up at her. "Would you go tell Illiahn how things are? I know how she worries for him."

"Of course. I think I may stay and keep her company." Verra patted Jenna's shoulder and paused to give Telsen another hug on her way out of the den.

He closed the door behind her and crouched before the fire, feeding more wood into the flames. "Twice dead if not for you. I have seen the fighting style you taught him, but had never thought of you as dangerous. Verra told me of the fight in the Torrent." He glanced sideways at her, his expression bemused and a hint of a smile curving his mouth. "You surprise me again, Jenna: you demonstrated much courage." He brushed bark fragments from his hands and picked wood slivers from the rug, throwing them into the flames and causing crackling sparks. "I was afraid for him . . . for you all. I felt I had let him down, despite the circumstances that prevented me from reaching you." His dark eyes were troubled and his shoulders drooped. "We swore to protect each other. Not something I take lightly." Orange firelight reflected from his wristband. Jenna heard the conflict in his tone.

She shook her head with a tired smile, wanting to reassure this man who was becoming such a dear friend. "Tel. A wise man once prayed: God grant me the courage to change the things I cannot accept; the strength to accept those things that I cannot change; and the wisdom to know the difference. Or words like that, anyway. This is one of those things that you can't change. Sometimes, try as we might, we can simply do nothing." She tilted her head and leaned forward to catch his eye. "Stop beating yourself up. Your loyalty to him was never in question."

The fire crackled and spat. A stray ember landed at Telsen's feet, tainting the air with a hint of smoky pine. He stood, pushing his hands deep into his pockets, and nudged the smoking ember toward the hearth with his boot. "I know that," he said, the tension in his face abating. He shrugged. "I feel somewhat redundant, that is all. But I thank you for your comfort, Jenna, and for his life. I believe the Gods have a large hand in all of this. There is no woman better suited to him in all Camarrhan."

"That he has met yet," she qualified.

Telsen shook his head. "He need look no further. He knows that in his heart. Once his strong head accepts it also, there will be no more holding back. Are you sure you are ready?" He grinned at her and dropped into the large fireside chair.

She smiled back. "You're a very wise and kind friend, Tel. I hope you're right." She sighed and rested her gaze on Cael's sleeping face. "But for now, there's still more to heal. I didn't want to . . . expose this until Verra had gone." She removed Cael's boots and began to unlace his breeches with gentle hands. With great care, she eased the leather trews and blood-encrusted smallclothes from his body.

It was bad.

Telsen averted his eyes, his face pale with outrage, and cursed under his breath. Cael's groin was bruised, split and swollen. His hips and thighs bore extensive dark bruising, the leather having only partially protected him from the beating. As she again entered her awareness into his body, she discovered a fissure in his pelvis, a fine crack across the narrow width of the pubic bone. She pulled the thick blanket down to cover him, having assessed the extent of the injury. With a strained smile at Telsen, she let her awareness sink back into the stone, drift down through Cael's body and begin to heal again. The irony of being present in this most intimate of areas was not lost on her. Although they had not achieved intimacy, she was as familiar with his body as with her own, and concerned for his full restoration. After all, she had a vested interest in that.

Another hour and she was done. She wept a little, both her physical and emotional reserves depleted, and Telsen held her in silence. He released her as she quieted, and dragged the large chair to the bedside where she sank into it. Shaking out a blanket, he settled it around her and drew it up under her chin. Within minutes, she slept.

Jenna woke some hours later when Illiahn appeared at the door bearing a steaming basin and an armful of towels. "He would want to be clean," Illiahn explained as she set the basin beside the bed. "And you also need time to attend to yourself. I will see to him if you wish to go and bathe."

In truth, he was a mess. Although now whole, he still wore the evidence of his ordeal, and the air in the den was heavy with the odour of blood and sweat. Illiahn sat beside him, her eyes red from recent crying.

"I thank the Gods for you, Jenna. We have been together from the womb, he and I. I cannot imagine my life without him; no one knows me as he does, not even Brenn." She dropped a cloth into the basin. "Sharing him with you is hard for me. He has been alone for so long, and we are very close." She squeezed Jenna's hand, smiling in apology to take any sting from her words.

"We don't share anything yet, Illiahn, except the bond. We may never."

"Ah, but you do, Jenna. We have all seen the bond take its effect. You have his respect, his trust, even the beginning of his affections. He has desired you from the start. I do not think my brother would recognise 'the three' if they jumped out at him and introduced themselves."

Jenna could not keep the doubt from her voice. "I don't see anything but avoidance."

"Trust me in this, *chiara*. I know him well. Better than he knows himself, I suspect." Illiahn's amber eyes rested warm on her twin's face. She drew the blanket down to his hips and eased a towel beneath each side of him. Squeezing a cloth in the warm, scented water, she hesitated to touch him. With quick decision and without a word, she offered the washcloth to Jenna.

Touched by Illiahn's surrender of her claim, Jenna took another cloth. Together they cleaned him up, drawing each other deeper into relationship as the basin's water clouded with his blood.

"This is becoming a habit, brother." Telsen helped himself to a platter of food Illiahn had left on the table, as his words greeted Cael's return to consciousness. "Of course, having three of the most desirable women in the land fuss over you is probably worth all the trouble you seem to find yourself in."

Cael stretched experimentally, revelling in the release from pain and ignoring Telsen's amiable humour. His outstretched arm encountered solid, warm resistance; he turned his head to see Jenna lying beside him, clean and dressed, in a deep sleep.

"She stayed with you through the night, should you need her," Telsen explained, his mouth full of fruit and warmed bread. "She only left you long enough to bathe."

>*She was exhausted. She does not spare herself.*<

"Where you are concerned, brother, I fear not." Telsen grinned at him.

>*What will I do with her, Tel?*< The question was rhetorical, his tone bemused. He felt a curious new warmth for the woman beside him. Stray wisps of dark hair escaped her braid to lay, whisper-fine, against her cheek, and her lips were parted in a soft pout.

Telsen placed a mug of tea beside the bed and tossed him a sideways look. "You know my thoughts on the matter."

>*Truth.*< Cael studied her sleeping face. >*She is beautiful, is she not?*< He traced a light fingertip over her brow, down the high curve of her cheek where long lashes touched honeyed skin, and drew it across the slightly parted lips. So soft.

"She is." Telsen averted his eyes as the touch travelled down her neck and arced around the swell of her breast.

Cael frowned and withdrew his hand. He struggled to raise himself, but was quite unable to do so. Telsen pulled him up and bolstered him with pillows, and Cael scowled in frustration at the indignity of it. He reached for the mug of tea, almost dropping it as he realised the extent of his weakness, and cursed when Telsen leapt to catch the mug. "Again, I am reduced to infant status," he growled in irritation.

"No shame. Your personal Healer predicts several days for you to recover full strength. You should eat something." Telsen indicated the platter.

Cael grimaced. "I cannot. The healing unsettles my stomach."

Jenna rubbed at her eyes and raised herself on one elbow. "I haven't learnt how to avoid that yet, but Karessa tells me I will. I still have a few things to learn." Her sleepy smile rested on him, her deep indigo eyes alight as her gaze caressed his face. "I *can* brew a herbal that will help you, though."

"You should rest, *chekuán*." He laid a restraining hand on her arm.

"I will rest when I know you feel well." Jenna swung her legs off the bed and stood, tidying her braid with her fingers. "I'll tell Illiahn you're awake. She'll want to see you."

"Jenna," he said gently. "You need not spend yourself further for me."

Smiling, she tweaked his foot as she passed. "Your nature to deny your needs doesn't change my desire to meet them. I'll be back soon."

He did not protest again, knowing his discomfort also affected her, but pulsed her an enormous wave of warmth that embraced her in its depth. His eyes followed her form with appreciation as she left the den, and he was immensely grateful for the familiar stirring in his groin, proof that his healing was complete. Gods, he had feared for the future of his manhood many times during their torturous escape.

Telsen whistled between his teeth, a long descending note. "Take care, brother. Your resistance is slipping."

>*I think perhaps I have been a hard-headed fool, Tel.*< Cael rubbed his eyes tiredly, yawning despite having woken only minutes before.

Telsen raised his eyebrows. *You think?* his expression said.

"I know her more every day, and can find fault with nothing I discover. That she loves me with such depth astounds me . . . humbles me. The Gods know I have done nothing to inspire it." He turned troubled eyes on Telsen. "I have caused her strife, worry and hurt. Gods, Tel! Will it ever be any different? I suspect she would do better without the complications that seem to follow me."

"You argue with yourself alone, brother. The woman wants only you. If you want her too, your course of action is obvious."

Cael raised his eyes to the ceiling, avoiding Telsen's earnest gaze. He sighed, and continued honestly. No more hiding. "I want her. Sometimes I cannot be near her for fear it will rule me." He closed his eyes, covered them with one hand, shutting out reality with the light. "I seem to remember we had a similar conversation some months ago.

Nothing has changed. I am tired of fighting it, Tel, but afraid to surrender to it."

Afraid. There. It was said. Dragonfire threatened to consume him, and he was terrified of being overwhelmed.

"You fear you will be lost if you relinquish control? Gods, man, that is where relationship *begins!*" Telsen's dark eyes became intense. "When you free yourself to love completely, you find something different . . . something new. In your total acceptance, each of the other, you learn again to accept yourself. You are extended, brother, not diminished; controls become unnecessary, not relinquished." He stopped, apparently gathering his thoughts, and rubbed a hand over his jaw. Cael read his desire to be understood. Telsen continued. "You do not lose yourself, but discover another. You find peace with yourself, and the physical expression of all this transcends the mere meeting of need, and becomes a shared joy, something you will always seek together."

Cael stared at his bondbrother, stunned into silence by the passion with which he had spoken.

Telsen looked away and coloured. He was not given to long speeches.

"And that is how it is for you, brother?" Cael asked eventually.

"That is how it is."

Before he could make reply, Jenna returned with the promised herbal. She sat beside him and held the cup as he drank the sweetly fragrant brew, her hand resting on his arm, stroking his skin with her thumb.

>*Chekuán.*<

"Sorry." She removed her hand from him in an automatic response.

He took her fingers in his, replaced her hand and covered it with his own. >*We need to talk. About many things.*<

Her eyes were wide and dark, the pupils dilated with affection. Her lips curved into an uncertain smile.

Telsen left the den in discreet silence. He intercepted Illiahn and Verra who crossed the yard toward the den. His satisfied smile as he took their arms and turned them around told them that events were progressing well.

"Are they . . ." Illiahn stopped, reddening.

Telsen laughed. "No. He is yet incapable, *chiara*. He cannot hold a full cup, let alone a woman. They are but talking, and he allows her to touch him. It is a beginning."

Illiahn and Verra smiled in agreement, and the three walked arm-in-arm back to the house.

Later that morning the wind died. The sky clouded grey and turbulent, and distant thunder rolled in a dull boom from the south. Visible from the low windows of the den, the first rain began to fall, plopping softly onto the plants in the kitchen garden, setting broad green leaves nodding as heavy drops struck them.

Jenna watched the house anxiously, waiting for Verra to respond to Cael's call. She sat behind him on the bed, supporting him with her body as he lay against her. His eyes were closed, and he wore a fine luster of sweat on the pallor of his face.

A door banged open, and Verra flew from the house followed by Telsen. She hurried through the stone-walled garden to the den, dark curls tumbling around her shoulders as she cut across rows of winter vegetables, leaping them to avoid damage to the crop. She burst into the den with Telsen at her heels. He closed the door against the rain and brushed moisture from his hair with a hand.

"What is it? I . . ." Verra's words died as she looked at Cael.

Jenna struggled to keep her voice calm, but there was a quaver to her words. "I asked him to call you. I need Karessa. There's something very wrong here, and I can't find it."

"What happened?" Verra asked, her brow creasing into a frown. "He was looking so well." She sat on the end of the bed.

"He woke feeling sick. That's usual. I made an herbal to help him. That came back, as has any water he takes." Jenna stopped as his body spasmed, and she leaned him forward over the basin beside him, holding him as he heaved. "He's bringing up blood, and I don't know why. I can't leave him; he hasn't the strength to move."

"I will bring Karessa." Verra crossed her wristbands above her head and opened the Way to the Guild. With a worried glance at her charge, she crossed through.

Tense minutes passed. Telsen leaned a shoulder against the smooth wood of the window frame and drummed his fingers against the pane, staring out at the rain.

"Tel." Cael's voice was little more than a whisper.

Telsen turned. "Brother?"

"Not the scene you hoped for?"

"Not quite, but she *does* hold you." Telsen's crooked white grin was strained.

Jenna raised her eyebrows at Telsen. She lifted damp gold hair from Cael's forehead and peered round at his face, seeing his eyes half open. "Sounds as if you two have been talking about me." Incongruously, the thought pleased her.

>*A little, chekuán.*< He managed a faint smile.

The Way opened with its crystal song. Verra was back

274

with Karessa. "Well, handsome one," came Karessa's familiar greeting.

"Not so well, Healer," Cael murmured, amber eyes lighting at the sight of his old friend.

Karessa bustled to the bed, took his Keystone in her hand and fell silent as she searched the pattern within. "Is there any pain?"

"My gut is on fire. My bones ache. My head threatens to explode. Apart from that, no, not at all."

Karessa smiled, felt the clammy cool of his forehead and fingered the pulse at his throat. She turned to Jenna, her smile fading to concern. "I have seen this only twice before. You have recently healed him?"

Jenna nodded. "Yesterday."

"There was broken bone?"

"Ribs and pelvis," Jenna admitted, leaning him forward as his body spasmed again. "What did I do wrong?"

Karessa frowned at the blood darkening in the basin. "This is not your doing, Jenna. It is a reaction to the type of healing required to knit bone. He is sensitive to it. His energy flow is in chaos."

Jenna wiped his mouth and held him as he lay back against her.

"Can you prevent my stomach trying to take its leave of my body?" The pain in his eyes endorsed his lightly phrased request.

"I cannot. Only Galaen can reverse this condition. It will progress quickly, Cael. We need to act straight away." She sat beside him, waiting for the latest bout of heaving to stop. As he lay back, exhausted, she met his eyes. "I am going to turn off the pain," she said. "That will help you until we get you to the Hand."

"I would be grateful, Healer." His face looked drawn and tired.

Jenna stroked his cheek. "Take some more water." She brushed aside his protest. "It will ease you to have something to throw up besides your stomach lining." Every episode flamed inside her own stomach as she shared his discomfort.

Karessa nodded. "There is wisdom in that, Cael."

Jenna held a cup to his mouth and insisted he drink. Too weak and weary to protest further, he complied. And promptly lost it all.

Karessa again took the Keystone in her hand. "Relax, handsome one." Touching her fingers to his temple, she closed her eyes and fell silent for several moments.

"Jenna?" Fear filled his voice. "Jenna, I cannot feel you."

"Shh, it's all right. Karessa is taking your pain."

"No, Jenna . . . I cannot *feel* you . . . Jenna?" He fell quiet. His eyes glazed and drooped closed as he slumped against her. She wrapped her arms around him in a protective embrace, feeling his awareness slip away.

"He passed out, Karessa. Did you turn off consciousness as well?"

The old Healer's face set into lines of puzzlement. "No. Only pain." She raised his eyelids, felt again for the pulse at his throat and straightened in abrupt alarm. "Verra . . . take us to Ché Kevath, *quickly!*"

"What is it?" Sudden panic poked cold fingers into Jenna's stomach. "Karessa?"

Verra crossmatched the Landmark runes, then hesitated. "With respect, Healer. Ché Kevath? It is forbidden . . ." Conflicting needs showed on her face.

"You are all children of prophecy. It is permitted. *Now,* Verra!"

The Way shimmered open.

Telsen had waited in silence, a tense dark shadow, remaining at hand until needed. He lifted his bondbrother from Jenna and held him under the arms. Cael's head lolled against Telsen's shoulder. Verra held him beneath the knees, and together they lifted him. Before the blanket could slip from his body, Jenna wrapped it around his hips, preserving his remaining dignity.

Karessa laid a gentle hand on Jenna's arm. "Life is leaving him," she said quietly. Her faded blue eyes held an ancient sorrow.

"No! This is *not* Raef! The magic is *not* lost!" Jenna's voice shook. Dread threatened to overwhelm her. She caught Cael's hand as Telsen disappeared into the Way and threw herself into a reckless full-needs link, meeting Karessa's sorrowful gaze with denial.

Oh shit.

As the link took effect, she realised the extent of his need. Her life force stuttered, her knees buckled under her, but still she maintained the link. She felt the light abrasion of warm sand beneath her when she stumbled to her knees.

They laid Cael on the small white beach.

Jenna knelt beside him, calling his name, patting his cheek firmly, trying to draw him back, to help him hold on. Tactics learned in the emergency room.

He lay still and pale.

The Way winked out behind them.

"We are on sacred ground, child," Karessa whispered as she sank to her knees. "Ché Kevath. Centre of magic." She raised her head. "Galaen!" Her voice rang in rippling echoes from the exposed rock face that rose from the beach of the small lagoon.

Jenna gripped Cael's limp hand in silence, willing him to live. Rose-gold glowed brightly.

"Galaen!" Karessa called again and suddenly, she was there.

Luath stepped from the Way behind her, followed by Grinore and two other tall figures.

"The Hand," Karessa breathed in awe. "All five."

Galaen moved to Jenna's side. Grinore, Empath of the Hand, stepped over Cael to kneel opposite them. Galaen raised Jenna, tried to loosen her desperate grasp on Cael's hand. "You must leave him, child." Galaen spoke with gentle but firm command. "Let Kenethrel take your place. He is the keeper of Linker's magic. His power is greater than any you can command."

As she spoke, a chestnut-haired man appeared at Grinore's side. "Does he yet live?" he asked.

"He lives, but barely," Grinore confirmed. "His mind is beyond reach."

Kenethrel took up Cael's other hand and clasped it between both of his own. As the rose-gold aura flared around this new link, Jenna felt a sudden surge of power tremor through Cael's body and into her own. She gasped with relief and lifted her eyes to the source of the new energy. Kenethrel's smile was serene. "You see, Healer. It is well. Leave him before you exhaust yourself."

Jenna crawled away on hands and knees, spent from the effort of sustaining her dying mate. Verra went to her, and they clung to each other in silence, not daring to hope. Tears were a constant rain on Jenna's face, her throat a tight misery. Verra stroked strands of hair from Jenna's cheeks, making small sounds of comfort, her own eyes wet.

"I need to be with Tel for a moment," Verra said after a while. Jenna let her go. She had not registered Telsen's pain. He stood silent, his face a stark desert. He watched, arms hugged about his chest as the five keepers of magic surrounded Cael. Verra approached the dark sentinel, and he opened his arms to her, drew her in and held her, buried his face in her hair. His shoulders shook as Verra held him hard and long.

Silence fell.

The lap of water at the lagoon's edge quieted. Birdsong ceased.

Xirth, Wielder of the Hand, stood at Cael's head; Wayfinder and Healer on his left, Linker and Empath on his right. All were quiet and still, seeking the magic of the land, drawing power into themselves. Kenethrel remained in the link, kneeling beside Cael, flowing strength into him.

Xirth raised his hands. A streaming shimmer of moving air surrounded him, stirring his fine robes, lifting his silver hair. Fiery motes of blue light flickered from his fingers, then a streak of azure arced from each of his hands, travelling with electrified speed through each keeper, joining all five with a wavering filament of bright blue light.

Galaen took Cael's Keystone in one hand and touched the fingers of the other to his temple. Dark lashes swept her cheeks as the indigo eyes closed. Light blazed blue from the stone for an instant. Cael's body convulsed, and his spine arched from the sand. Nothing changed.

Kenethrel maintained the link.

Again, Galaen tried.

Blue light.

Convulse.

And again.

Galaen shook her head with a look of resignation. "He does not respond. I fear we are too late." Her voice held great melancholy.

Jenna's cry tore through the silence, wordless, primal. She threw herself across the sand, breaking the circle of blue light with her body, her voice a ragged wail. "Don't you *dare* leave me, don't you *dare!*"

Telsen reached to restrain her. Verra caught at her arm as she passed. The blue filament arced and spat, then included them in its circuit. Xirth began to lower his hands.

"No! Continue!" Galaen's attention was on Telsen. His wide silver wristband glowed with blue light, raising an answering flare from its runed twin on Cael's wrist. A fine filament of intense blue arced between them, ran to Jenna, joined Verra, forming their own circle of light.

Galaen gestured to Xirth. He dropped his hands.

Kenethrel released the link.

"Four in union," Galaen breathed.

The five keepers stepped away from the new circle as Jenna touched Cael's face. Ignoring the arcing blue light, knowing only that her heart was breaking, she smoothed the wayward gold hair from his brow for the last time and touched her lips to his. She imprinted the image of his face in her memory, noting every detail, each plane and curve. Her trembling fingers traced his tattoo, token of the dragon she had awoken but would never share. Pain too large to contain filled her soul until she felt she must burst from it, and the pressure inside her chest forced small choking sobs from her throat. Seeking again to feel the comfort of his essence surround her, she reached for his Keystone.

Azure light blazed as she touched the silver wire that encased the opal. Surprise pierced her grief as a steady flow of power coursed through the Keystone. She felt Verra, felt Telsen; felt them both as an intimate presence. Blotting her tears on her shoulder, she lifted her head, discerning the energy within the flickering blue filament that joined the four of them. She stared at Telsen in wonder. His brows drew together over his dark eyes and a grimace contorted his mouth; pulsing blue light poured from the silver band on his wrist to be swallowed up by Cael's band. His shirt rippled around his body as if caught in a whirlwind, and beside him, Verra's hair blew around her startled eyes, caught in the vortex of newly generated power.

Cael's Keystone glowed in Jenna's hand, and she felt her awareness propelled into its iridescent depths. Feeling the stillness of his essence, she screamed her anguish and desolation, screamed his name, her desperate fear finding a sudden release within the stone. The pattern flickered. His body arched again. Jenna felt a faint flutter in her mind, as a silken moth-wing surprises bare skin in the dark. Cael? Oh God, come back, come back! She pursued the flutter, but it eluded her, the moth disappearing back into the shadows. Moth. Surfacing, she raised wild eyes to Telsen. "Light, I need light in here."

He stared at her in dismay and swallowed. "How? I do not understand what is happening."

"He's lost, Tel. He's gone too far to come back alone. I know; it happened to me once." She clenched her fists in growing anxiety and cast her eyes over the faces that surrounded her. "Can no one help me?" Her voice broke, and fresh tears washed her vision.

"I will guide you if Xirth can create the light." Grinore stepped forward and Xirth followed. The blue filament accepted them as they hastened into its circuit. With brisk efficiency, Xirth wielded a soft incandescence of cobalt blue and handed it silently to Grinore. The Empath cupped the glowing ball in his hands. "I will join you, Jenna," he said, focussing his attention on the light.

Re-entering the Keystone, Jenna felt Grinore's presence

among the stillness of Cael's essence. She despaired, but soon the soft glow of Wielder's light that Grinore transmitted became brighter; the small ball shrank and intensified, becoming a tiny, blue-white beacon, illuminating the dimming pattern in the stone. Together, they called and waited.

A flutter. The pattern emitted a faint glimmer. There! Oh yes, yes! The surrounding essence warmed, the flickering dance of the motes within the stone began again to pulse in asynchronous waves, growing stronger as the beacon light dimmed in response.

>*He lives, child,*< Grinore confirmed.

Sobbing in hysterical relief, Jenna felt Cael's familiar whisper-soft brush on her mind and knew he was back.

Galaen joined her then, and when she had calmed, together they ordered the flickering motes of his pattern, realigning, strengthening, restoring order to the chaos they found there. Jenna watched as Galaen engaged the full power of the island, reversing the destructive cycle begun by the healing of bone. The pulsating waves again synchronised, stabilising into the dearly familiar pattern she knew so well.

When all was in order, they withdrew.

The blue light disappeared.

Telsen sat staring at his wristband, tracing the runed silver with a fingertip as Verra stood behind him, resting her hands on his shoulders. Confused apprehension filled her eyes.

"Four in union shall travail and prevail," Luath said.

"If the hearts of the one are true." Galaen completed the prophecy. "There is still hope for the land. The four still prevail." Her face was alive with relief.

"It appears they travail, at least," Xirth remarked drily as he dropped a hand to Telsen's shoulder. "We have a wild Wielder in our midst."

Jenna sat in dazed exhaustion, cradling Cael's head and shoulders in her lap, trying to understand what had occurred.

He lived. That was enough for now. Understanding could come later. "I miss you," she whispered, stroking his hair. "Please come back."

Chapter Sixteen

The Council

Cael lay in a private chamber at the infirmary, attended by a Linker until he should awaken. Jenna would suffer no one else to touch him other than Karessa, staying with him as long as her energy allowed, leaving him only when she had to sleep. She had earned the right to dictate events concerning him, and no one questioned her protectiveness. Trista hovered in the doorway of the chamber on occasion, staying to chat, but even she was not allowed near him. Karessa kept a close eye on the situation, but allowed Jenna to process her fears alone.

Telsen had remained at the Guild at the behest of the Wielder's mentor, and appeared now at the doorway, leaning halfway in the chamber as if anxious to be away. "Come. Verra is here; Illiahn has made your favourite supper, and you need a change of scenery."

She began to protest.

"Jenna. What use are you to him when he wakes if you have exhausted yourself? Come. There is a hot tub waiting for you." He raised his brows and quirked his mouth into a half-smile. "I promised Verra I would persuade you. Humour me?" He crossed to the bed recess where Jenna sat and held out his hand to her.

He was right, as usual. Jenna rested her gaze on Cael's sleeping face. He looked so vulnerable. "I don't want to leave him, Tel. I'm *afraid* to leave him."

"He is in good hands. Think of your own needs, Jenna. He is a man, and will not thank you for treating him as a child." His earnest expression touched her.

"Is that what I'm doing, Tel?" She frowned and chewed the inside of her lip in indecision.

"It could be taken that way." Karessa smiled as she entered the chamber. "Go take your ease, child. When he wakes, you will know it, but I will send for you anyway. Go!" She made shooing gestures as Jenna arose with misgiving.

Telsen grinned, and gave her a reassuring hug. "The children also wait to see you. Mi'Cael has made you something and is impatient to show you." He led her from the chamber, pausing to allow her a brief moment of hesitation as she glanced back at Cael.

Mi'Cael held a wooden bucket out to her. Jenna took it, mystified, and looked inside. Small holes studded the bottom of the pail.

"It is your rain shower," he said, his amber eyes round and serious. "In the summer when it is warmer, you can fill it with water and stand under it in the tub. It will be just like your home!"

Tiredness took over. Her eyes filled with tears as she caught the boy up in a close hug. "Mi'Cael, that is the nicest thing anyone ever did for me." She had told him various details of her world, the shower being only one.

He glowed with pride at his invention, showing her the rope he had rigged with Brenn's help to raise the bucket over the tub. He left her alone. A small wood burner heated the little room, and a water tank fed hot water into the tub as it heated on the burner. Buckets of cold water stood ready for the bather's comfort.

Jenna undressed and sank into the welcome warmth. Winter lavender floated in the water, and as always, she knew she had come home. She unbraided her hair, let it float free around her shoulders and rubbed lavender flowers through its length, sighing with pleasure. After a short soak, she towelled dry, wrapped her hair in a thick towel, pulled on her shift and her white wool dress.

Supper was wonderful. Illiahn and Brenn were kind, making general conversation and not pressing her for details of the happenings on Ché Kevath. The evening passed without contact from Karessa. Verra and Telsen slipped away. Jenna fretted. She wanted to be with Cael but did not desire to be seen as smothering him.

"Illiahn, I . . . want to sleep in the den, if I may."

Illiahn gave her a look of understanding. "Of course. Do you wish a fire?"

"No, thank you. I sleep warm." She left them and crossed the yard to Cael's den. Pushing the door closed behind her, she set down the oil lamp she had carried from the kitchen and lit the lamps on the table. She touched the pile of drawings that lay there and thumbed through them, recognising many faces in rough representation: Illiahn, Verra, Telsen, Mi'Cael. Uncanny likenesses captured in a few blunt lines and smudges of charcoal. Such a talent. She had not suspected this of him, and was awed at his ability.

Opening the large, loose-bound book, she turned the pages, finding detailed drawings of people she knew and those she did not. She saw the twins, Chad and Sorren, laughing at each other in mirror image. Verra, dark curls blowing around her face as she turned her eyes toward the artist. Brenn and Illiahn in close embrace. Telsen, his amused expression captured perfectly, his personality open on the page. There were finely rendered drawings of horses and the *"chekuán"* portrait she recognised. She reached the last few pages and stood amazed.

Her own face looked out at her. The first drawing was one of conflict as she looked back over her shoulder, brows describing angles of uncertainty. *Hmm.* She remembered those early days well. How he had perplexed her, avoided her, and how much it had hurt. She smiled at the memory. The next was a full-face portrait, her smile subdued, eyes warm, wisps of hair escaping her braid. How had he captured her affection for him so easily in this drawing? Something about the eyes, the smile. Did he really see her as this beautiful? Another, a scene of action and passion, depicting her in fighting mode, braid and feet flying. But not portrayed as anything but feminine and again, beautiful. And the last, in her Healer's dress, nine stones at her throat, hair cascading loose, her expression one of intimate warmth. She saw the depth of feeling that had guided his eye, his hand, and tears filled her eyes, fracturing the image.

Love. Was it possible? She dared to hope.

After a short while, she closed the book, at last knowing she had touched his soul. She stood before the table a moment longer and closed her eyes, feeling him as he slept still. An odd peace stole over her then, as a child who knows that no matter how dark and wild the storm outside, the lantern burns, the bed is warm and mother is home. Slipping into his bed, wearing only her fine wool shift, she drew thick blankets up around her neck against the cold. The faint scent of him lingered on the pillows, masculine and familiar, and she drew comfort from it as she drifted into sleep.

The Hand requested an emergency Council. A representative from each main town in Camarrhan gathered in the Council chamber at the centre of Illith. The gravity of the meeting was evident. Two Althar elders attended, as did three of the Hand, both quite unprecedented events.

Present in Cael's place for Kereál, Brenn shifted nervously in his chair, tapping his fingers on his thighs as he waited for the meeting to commence. While he often accompanied Cael to these meetings as his aide, he had never spoken in such a public venue. Cael had always handled village business at Council, but Brenn knew that this time he would be required to speak. Becoming aware of his anxious tapping, he clenched his fists and leaned forward on the heavy wooden chair. He rested his forearms on the wide slab of polished ebony that curved away from each side of the entranceway in a vast circle around the chamber. Skylights in the high ceiling captured the winter sun, which reflected on the polished wood and lit the stern faces of the Council members seated around it. Their attention focussed on the Althar elders seated at the centre of the arc, flanked on the left by Galaen, Grinore and Luath.

"I thank you all for attending this unusual and important gathering." Grinore's voice carried around the chamber, enhanced and amplified by the design of walls and ceiling. "We have gathered today to discuss matters of great import, both to Camarrhan and to Alth." He indicated the elders at his right.

"Arkell and Kohen are elders of the Circle of Alth. They are keepers of magic, as are we." His gesture took in Galaen and Luath. "Our goal is to restore good relations between our lands. Alth concedes that social change must be brought about within its borders in the long term. In the short term, however, Alth agrees its rebel youth must be disbanded, their leader discovered and detained. We have information that we hope will lead to the capture of Jabeel son of Kren son of Labicheth, who is responsible for many deaths over the past two cycles.

"You all know of the most recent attempt on the life of Cael son of Jarin of Kereál. He survives, as do the Healer and Wayfinder who access the cure for battle sickness. Jabeel sought also to remove them, so that he may continue his plan to breach Ché Kevath.

"Until now, we have been fighting shadows, unable to find where the renegades hide. Jabeel's own evil desires led him to disclose his location, believing he had the situation under control. He did not, and we have his last location as Ré Shan, deep within the Torrent that feeds Lake Tuan. Wielders sent after Jabeel found nothing. He and the rebels were gone." Grinore stopped speaking and gestured to Arkell. "Council will recognise Arkell of the Circle of Alth."

A low hum of comment greeted Arkell as he stood, his black eyes taking in the faces around him. Many wore looks of suspicion; others were neutral but guarded. His long hair gleamed blue-black beneath the skylight as he waited for quiet.

"Greetings, Camarrhan Council members. I am Arkell, Shaper of the Circle. It is my privilege to speak for Alth. My colleague here is Kohen, Warder of the Circle. Alth owes a great debt to Camarrhan, both for Kohen's life and for his magic, and we both have a personal interest in the three that Jabeel sought to destroy. We believe we can eventually discover Jabeel's new location, and will do so, but we have a certain request we would make of you." Arkell paused, scanning the faces around him, making eye contact with one or two.

"Our race does not procreate well. A delicate matter, but one you must know. Children are precious and few, and every year, more females are born infertile. Fertility is greatly honoured, and sometimes accompanied by a strong magic—that of A'Thek. We rely on our fertile females to provide us with children, and sadly, many couples must remain childless.

"My point is this: many of our youth, both male and female, run with Jabeel, seduced by new freedoms, promises of wealth and release from the cultural strictures of Alth. With them runs our hope of a new generation. If our newly maturing young people continue to leave us in such great numbers, our future is severely compromised. Alth's request to you is to leave our youth unharmed in return for the location of Jabeel. Our hope is that without his wealth and promises, they will eventually return to us as we seek to resolve our problems. Social change is slow, but we are determined and sincere. It will come, and it begins now.

"Councillors. Will you spare our young rebels? Alth deplores their actions against your Leaders and the raiding of your small holdings, but would beg for their lives and their part in the future of our race." Arkell turned, inclined his head to Grinore, and sat down.

The low buzz of conversation began again. Grinore stood, and gestured for quiet. "We would hear from any who would be heard."

A Leader to Brenn's left stood, resting large hands on the dark slab before him. "Health and strength, Empath."

Grinore acknowledged him.

"I speak for Twin Lakes, close to Kereál below the foothills. We have lost a Leader to the rebels. There is much anger in the town that Alth does not either control or discipline its young. Our outlying farms and small holdings suffer constant raids, and our women fear for their men as they seek to defend their livelihoods. As the elder says, change will be slow. How long are we to tolerate such situations?

"Removing Jabeel ends the threat to our Leaders, but the raids will remain as long as the rebels do. How does Alth propose to address the actions of their youth?"

Arkell stood to make reply. "Amnesty will be offered. Input into change will be sought and their needs acknowledged. Freedoms will be granted. It is our hope they will return to Alth of their own will. Any losses incurred by raids in the meantime will be recompensed by Alth."

Brenn's throat was dry, and his palms moist. Gods! Cael was far better than he at thinking on his feet—what was he to say to this new information? Drawing a calming breath, he stood and was recognised. "Health and strength, elder," he began. Cael always said it was all about confidence. All right then, he would show them confidence. He cleared his throat and went on with more volume. "I speak for Kereál in the place of our Councillor taken by Jabeel."

All eyes turned to him. He blinked at the sea of faces, hoping that he would make no political mis-step that Cael would have cause to regret later. Confidence.

"My brother has yet to awaken from healing, but I know he will bear Alth no grudge. His wish has always been for the resolution of tensions. No vengeance will be sought against Alth on his behalf. Kereál sympathises with Alth over its situation."

His mind turned to the sad implications of Arkell's revelations. "As a father, I am often reminded it is no easy job to raise children. I feel sorrow for the many of your people who remain childless and a great sympathy for the parents of those young who have chosen to reject them. Our own people know the youthful rebellion that accompanies the passage into adulthood. What parent among us can say otherwise?

"Arkell. You offer constructive proposals both for

291

change and recompense. Kereál stands with you." Heads nodded as conversation began. With only a slight wobble of the knees, Brenn sat, wiping sweaty palms on his breeches, glad his message had been well received. There were no further speakers.

"Council will recess for discussion. Resolution will be measured on the hour. You may either remain here, or return then." Grinore preceded Galaen, Luath and the elders from the chamber.

Brenn sighed, hoping Arkell's speech had been enough to win the support of all the Councillors. Resolution required at least twenty-five of the thirty Council seats to agree. Not all of them were parents. He looked for a discussion to join while he waited.

A messenger approached him. "Kereál?"

"Yes." Brenn followed as the messenger beckoned him.

"The elder wishes to speak with you."

They arrived at a private chamber where the Circle and the Hand were in discussion. Arkell stood as Brenn entered and offered his hand. "You are the Empath's brother?" he asked.

"Brother-in-law, yes."

Arkell showed no understanding.

"He is my wife's twin," Brenn amended.

Arkell nodded and gestured for Brenn to sit. "You spoke well. I wished to thank you for your support and understanding. How does your brother . . . in-law . . . fare? There is one who greatly desires news of him."

"He recovers. It is a slow process. He will remain at the Guild for some time. Who is it that asks, elder?"

Arkell smiled enigmatically. "A friend. How is the Healer?"

"She is well, but will not cease to fret for him until he awakens. They are bondmates."

292

"Ah. That explains much. She went to great lengths to protect him, so I hear."

"As did one of your own. Lakra."

A frown paid a brief visit to Arkell's face. "Lakra owed him a life-debt. That is now discharged. I was displeased at her methods, but respect the honour of her . . . commitment."

"We are grateful to her." Brenn refrained from further comment, sensing Arkell's discomfort.

"A message. Tell the Empath the symbiot will no longer be used as a weapon. We have traced Jabeel's access to the magic that makes this possible, and removed it. We believe this also removes the threat to the Healer and Wayfinder. Of course, should Jabeel be taken, *all* threat is removed." The black eyes dismissed Brenn as Arkell clapped a hand to his shoulder, and turned back to the discussion.

The Council chamber filled again on the hour. All waited expectantly for Grinore to begin. Brenn tapped impatient fingers on his folded arms. He regretted missing lunch and hoped the resolution would go smoothly and not necessitate further debate.

The proceedings began. To cast an affirmative vote, all a member need do was stand. To stay seated was negative; to be absent was to abstain. There were two empty seats.

The calling began. One after another, representatives stood in support of Arkell's proposal. Brenn stood for Kereál. The large man from Twin Lakes stood soon after with a brief grin at Brenn. "I have five sons," he said with a conspiratorial wink. "All of them difficult!"

Seven seats remained to be called. Illith and Keroin stood; Durran remained seated, as did Tredina and Koln. The last two, Carador and Riverton, eyed each other.

Brenn groaned. He knew there was no love lost between these two, and would not put it past them to vote in opposition to each other just for the spite of it. He shifted his stance and rubbed a hand over his jaw, unable to stifle the quiet curse that his agitation generated.

"Peace, man. Allow them their moment," Twin Lakes said at his left. The order of calling for the resolution was random, and the last to vote knew their importance.

Both members stood.

Brenn heaved a sigh of relief. Twenty-five. Enough to carry the resolution.

Jabeel's days were numbered.

Chapter Seventeen

Secrets

Summoned again. Cael rolled to the edge of the low couch in the homestead's living area, where Illiahn had insisted he remain under her watchful eye. He pushed himself upright and sat for a moment, waiting for the dizziness to pass, then groped beneath the couch for his boots. Finding them, he dragged them on and stood slowly, steadying himself against the wall with one hand. It had been six days since Ché Kevath, and he had been home for only two of those. His convalescence was slow, and he chafed against the enforced rest, missing the level of physical activity he was used to before his capture.

>*Verra? We are called to attend the Guild.*< He knew that would please her. Telsen remained at the Guild under Quan's tutelage. The "wild Wielder" discovered during events on Ché Kevath had been ambivalent about his newly detected gifting and unhappy about his separation from Verra.

"And where do you think you are going?" Illiahn stood in the kitchen doorway as he moved toward it, her hands on her hips and a determined look on her face.

"Peace, Illiahn. I am called." He smiled at his sister and raised his brows at her rounded belly. She had always treated him in a maternal fashion. "You will soon have another to worry about and less time to fuss over me." He kissed her cheek, pulsed her a wave of reassurance and moved her out of his way. "I am going to the den to change. I think I can manage such a trip."

Verra arrived as he crossed the yard. She flashed him a surprised smile and closed the Way. "You look better each day, *chiaran!* It is good to see you vertical again." She followed him into the den and waited while he stripped off his thick wool shirt, pulled on a fresh one and fastened the cuffs. "You are a wraith of your former self, Cael," Verra observed. "It has been a long way back this time, has it not?"

Cael grimaced, knowing he was pale and lean, hating the weakness that still plagued him. "Hmm. I think Tel would have no difficulty putting me on my backside at present. Give me another week, then let him try." He smiled wryly, forced to sit for a moment to ease the spinning in his head. Gods! Perhaps a week was an idle boast. He dragged his fingers through his hair, ordering it as best he could.

"You look presentable. Let us go discover what the latest fuss is about." Verra took his hand and hauled him to his feet.

"You are very keen to be away. Why would that be?" he teased. She gave him a hard poke in the ribs and ignored him, crossed her wristbands and opened the Way.

Jenna and Telsen met them at the Waypoint outside the formal entrance to the Guild. Telsen gave Verra his usual enthusiastic greeting, wrapping his arms around her and lifting her high off her feet, pressing his face into her hair and holding her close for moments before he set her down. Cael smiled at Jenna, feeling her physical response to him deep in his libido.

Gods, she was beautiful. Sunlight dusted her dark hair with bronze as she returned his smile, her head tilted in cautious welcome.

He drew a deep breath and let it go, stepped over the edge of resistance and put himself in the hands of the dragon. Holding his hands out to her, he raised his brows in invitation.

Her eyes widened, and for a heartbeat she did not move. She stepped toward him then without taking her eyes from him and placed her hands in his. Lacing his fingers through hers, he drew her arms around him, pulling her against his body in the bondmates' greeting. He touched his lips to her forehead, and she raised her mouth to him, her eyes full of questions. He kissed her gently, tasting her tongue on his for a moment. >*Mmm. Hello, chekuán. I am mindful of our audience.*< He made to release her, but she raised her hands to his face.

"I wouldn't care if the whole Guild was watching." Slipping her hands behind his neck, she drew his head down and kissed him again, keeping him longer this time. He felt the depth of passion in her as his body began to respond.

>*Gods, Jenna, stop! While I still can . . .*<

She released his mouth, wearing a light flush. "I don't want you to stop," she whispered. "I have wanted this for the longest time."

He touched his forehead to hers, rested it there a moment as he regained his composure. Telsen cleared his throat loudly. Jenna disengaged herself from him, pressing her hands to her pink cheeks.

>*Gods, Tel! I feel as if I am falling.*<

"You are, brother, after a fashion." They clasped each other's wrists in greeting, then Telsen pulled him into a bear hug. "It gets easier," he murmured, "and the landing is soft."

Cael took Jenna by the hand, and the four turned to

enter the Guild. "It seems the whole Guild *was* watching," he remarked, as white tunics and giggles scattered before them. Karessa stood with an arm around Trista's shoulders, beaming approval at them.

"Hello, handsome one. You will have to forgive the young ones. You and Jenna have become something of a legend."

Cael winked gravely at Trista and embraced the old Healer. "We are to meet in the discussion chamber with Quan. Are any of the Hand attending?"

"I believe Grinore would speak with you all. I am not required," Karessa replied.

His head swam, reminding him of his debility. "Forgive me, but I need to sit or I will fall." He smiled apology at Karessa, and Jenna pulled him toward the low stone wall at the edge of the steps.

"This is too soon, Cael. They should have given you more time," she said, sitting beside him.

>*Peace. I am well, just faint.*< He leaned his forearms on his knees, enjoying her woman-scent and the warmth of her breast against his arm as he waited for his head to clear. Turning to her, he studied her face. Concern furrowed her forehead and angled her brows, giving her the pensive quality that intrigued him. He wanted very badly to be alone with her.

"Now *you* stop," she said with a small laugh. "We have a meeting to get through!"

He made it to the discussion chamber, requiring another stop at the top of the stairs. Jenna had learned not to fuss over him. Male pride was the same in any world, it seemed, and he coped better with his weakness if she ignored it.

They sat together, and he held her hand beneath arms

folded over his chest. She stole a sideways look at him, not quite believing the change in his behaviour, but very happy about it.

Gowan sat with Grinore, Xirth and Quan, Telsen and Verra opposite them on Cael's right. Formal greetings already exchanged, they settled to business. Grinore broached the subject, resting calm grey-green eyes on Cael.

"We wish to discuss the events that took place on Ché Kevath on the day of your apparent death, son of Jarin."

Cael's fingers tightened on hers and a tremor ran through him. She stroked his hand with her thumb.

"The Hand seeks to understand what took place. Son of Corr, we have established that your unsuspected gifting lies in a recessive gene, usually inactive and undetectable. How it came to manifest itself with such power is a puzzle to us. We believe Ché Kevath itself aided the power of your wielding, but the initiation of it came somehow from you in combination with these other three. The bands you wear on your wrists." He gestured to Telsen, who held his wrist out to him.

Grinore examined the band. "Ah. Brotherhood runes. What was sworn?" he asked, running a hand through short, greying brown hair.

"Companionship, loyalty, honesty," Cael answered, exchanging an odd look with Telsen. "And each to defend the other to the cost of his own life."

"That last is usually discouraged in bonds of this nature," Grinore said with a frown. "Who wielded the bands?"

"A graduate of Quan's, previously of Kereál, now in Illith I believe. Gerain, son of . . . ?" Cael looked at Telsen in query.

"Jeth." Telsen supplied.

Quan nodded. "I know him. A great talent for wielding metal. The magic is strong in him. I know how he would have fashioned these." A wry smile touched his mouth. "And why. He was always one to fly in the face of conventional wisdom."

Xirth held Telsen's wrist, his fingers encircling the band. Soft blue light glowed from the silver. Cael's band remained unchanged. Xirth shook his head, raising dark eyes, still youthful, beneath his surprising shock of fine silver hair. "It is the protection clause you swore. I cannot affect the other band. Son of Corr, *you* are the catalyst for the magic. I do not know how this can be, but it is clear to me it was you who wielded your Hand on Ché Kevath. A Hand is rare. It requires a closeness of spirit, a communion of souls that unify for a common cause. It also requires one of each type of magic that the four of you share, between you. The bond of brotherhood; the Wayfinder's commitment; the bond of the dragon; each force combined with your individual giftings and was amplified by the sacred ground of Ché Kevath."

Xirth released Telsen's wrist and studied them all. "Never in our history has life been restored once lost. We would further investigate this phenomenon, and would take you all to Ché Kevath to do so. Son of Jarin, are you recovered?"

"I am well enough, Xirth." Cael met the Wielder's dark gaze.

Jenna privately disagreed, but said nothing.

Cael tightened his fingers on her hand. >*I thank you.*<

She smiled and dropped her forehead to his shoulder in acknowledgment. And saw Gowan's eyes on them.

>*Things have changed, Jenna,*< he sent.

She straightened in embarrassment.

>*Peace, child. We all knew you were the one. You are worthy of each other, and Fate has smiled on you both.*< His grey eyes met hers with the pride of a father as he pulsed an image of belonging, familial and warm.

Her cheeks heated. Were there no secrets from this man?

Grinore stood, pushing back his heavy chair with a scrape of wood on stone. "Luath comes. Prepare yourselves to leave."

Crystal rang as the Way appeared, and the Hand's copper-haired Wayfinder stepped into the chamber. Standing aside, Luath's cool blue eyes rested on the four. Inset silver discs glinted from his leather wristbands as he gestured to them in invitation. "Ché Kevath and the Hand awaits you, four of the prophecy."

Ché Kevath was beautiful. Jenna had not noticed her surroundings in the trauma of her first visit, and now the loveliness of the place entranced her. The island formed a hollow circle, allowing the sea entry through a narrow cleft in the rock to the seaward side. The cleft squeezed the surge of the ocean from it as it channelled through, entering with mannered calm into the small lagoon laying green and secretive at the island's heart.

On this, their third day on the island, Jenna sat at the lagoon's edge on warm sand as her smallclothes dried on her body in the pale sunlight. The winter did not touch the island, and while there was little heat in the sun, there was no cold or wind to be felt. The air was as warm as the sand, testifying to the magic of the place.

She had bathed at the foot of the small waterfall a small distance behind her, that cascaded into a rock basin forming a natural pool half the depth of a man. Proving that, half a man was visible. Cael stood under the fall, allowing the cool tumble to wash his hair and body clean. Jenna braided her damp hair into its usual thick cable, admiring the muscle movement of his lean form as he waded to the edge of the pool. Just before hauling himself out, he saw her watching and gestured for her to turn around. She smiled and turned, although long familiar with his body. Being a Healer was one thing. They were not yet lovers, and she respected his privacy.

The island's magic had fully restored him within days, and he was restless. Despite the peace of Ché Kevath, Jenna knew he missed the wide-open spaces of Kereál; the freedom to ride; to practise swordplay; to work off energy. He flopped to sit in the sand a few feet from her, pulling wet gold hair back from his face with both hands. Water dripped at the back of his neck, ran in occasional droplets between the long muscles on each side of his spine, and disappeared into his breeches. Low sunlight slanted across his face as he turned to look at her, rendering his eyes feral gold for an instant. So beautiful.

She had not seen much of him before today. The Hand had kept them all busy: questioning, probing their minds, emotions, giftings and abilities as they sought to understand the unusual access to power that accompanied the four's relationship. She had worked with both Galaen and Kenethrel today, learning to modify her own giftings for use in a Hand. The other three had worked with Luath, Grinore or Xirth.

She sighed. Talk about bad timing. Daily, she burned for him, but this was not the time or place to pursue developments between them. Grinore had warned them to abstain from sexual liaison, unaware of the situation that existed. Jenna smiled at the irony. The sanction applied to them all for the duration of their training, but Verra and Telsen had accepted it with good grace. Of course, the rest would probably do them good, she thought with a hint of jealous pique. She repented the notion as soon as it came.

>*Your thoughts, Healer?*< Cael leaned back on his elbows.

She grinned, allowing only a hint of wickedness to colour her response. "I was thinking how good you are to look at. And how beautiful this place is, despite the confinement of it." She leaned herself back, matching his angle, and scanned the tangle of vegetation that hung to the water's edge around the opposite side of the lagoon. All the shades of green she had ever seen, and some she had not, reflected in the calm surface of the water. Small white flowers adorned the higher canopy, carried over bush and branch by trailing tendrils of vine. Larger blooms spattered ample globs of red-orange and yellow across the lower layer of growth, like paint dripping from a titan brush. Tiny birds hovered around the flowers, probing for nectar with needle-like beaks, their brilliant wings strobe-lit with all the colours of Althar gems bright from the cutting. So similar to hummingbirds, and yet in the way of this parallel world, she knew they would be different in some small detail.

The only sounds were the waterfall and the larger birds that sent their occasional fluting song across the still lagoon. Behind her, an expanse of rock rose from the white sand, capped with low green growth and issuing the waterfall from a wide fissure halfway up its face. Steps carved into the rock zigzagged at the right of the fall, offering precarious access to the top of the small cliff, where she knew a plateau formed a natural arena. Xirth used the plateau to hone Telsen's command of Wielder's magic, evidenced by the scarred and pitted surface of the surrounding rock.

"Verra and Tel must be working hard today." Cael lay back, his hands behind his head to keep his wet hair from the sand. The four of them met here at the end of each day.

"Or perhaps we were let out of school early," Jenna said, digging her fingers through the warm top layer of sand to the damp cool beneath. "So what secrets have you managed to drag out of Grinore, O mighty Empath?" she teased.

"Ah now, I could tell you, but they would be secrets no more." He gave his distinctive two-syllable chuckle and flashed white teeth in a grin. "You no doubt have your own secrets from Kenethrel and Galaen. Have you felt the increase in power? The magic here seems to flow out of the ground." He pulsed his new strength to her.

She shivered, feeling suddenly afraid of the mind power he had just demonstrated. He was right. She had felt it herself, and had been able to tap into the island's magic with Kenethrel's leading, establishing a link far stronger than any she had managed before. She had also mastered the last facets of healing magic, and under Galaen's guidance, discovered secrets that would allow her to heal with Karessa's skill, but with greater power. Tomorrow they were to begin to work together as a Hand.

The sound of the Way sang behind them. Telsen emerged first, scowling and smelling like burnt toast.

"A little trouble with fire, brother?" Cael dodged, grinning, as Telsen threw a boot at him. Tugging off the other boot, the new Wielder headed for the waterfall, shedding singed clothes as he went.

Verra joined them, sympathetic eyes following Telsen to the water. "Oh, Tel." She sighed, and sat beside Jenna. "I know he is struggling with all this, but there is such power here—Luath has shown me so much these past few days."

Cael and Jenna exchanged looks. "Secrets?" they asked in unison.

"*Oh* yes." Verra tossed back dark curls and hugged her knees, ocean-green eyes glowing with satisfaction.

Telsen stood under the waterfall, arms folded over his chest, a rock-like figure of sullen resistance as the water cascaded over his head and shoulders.

"Our reluctant Wielder has not had a good day," Cael observed. "I think he needs a little brotherly counsel." He pushed himself up, brushing sand from his elbows and hands.

Jenna watched him hungrily as he pulled on his shirt, and she rolled over to enjoy the view from behind as he walked away from them. "Mmm."

"Your tongue is hanging out, Healer," Verra teased.

"I know." Jenna laughed. "At least he doesn't mind so much anymore."

"I think if you were both at home instead of here, there would be a lot of things he would not mind so much anymore." That was as direct as Verra had ever been, and she coloured a little at her own daring.

Jenna laughed again and gave her a playful shove. "Verra! You're getting to be so rude!" She watched Cael as he settled on a rounded boulder beside the bathing pool and spoke with Telsen, their masculine forms fading to shadowy silhouette as the light dwindled. With a sigh, she sat up, brushing sand from her smallclothes, and reached for her shirt.

As the sun slid out of sight behind the island's edge, long shadows rushed over them, broken only by a single thin shaft that stole through the cleft in the rock where the ocean leaked in. Some minutes later, the insistent evening chorus of birdsong had quieted when Cael rejoined them, trailed by a dripping Telsen who now wore a euphoric smile. Jenna exchanged a look with Verra and arched her brows at Cael. He shrugged.

>*Secrets!*< he sent, his expression not quite innocent. >*Should I not use them to help a friend?*<

Several days of frustration passed as the four began to function as a Hand. By the fourth day, they experienced the beginnings of success. Telsen held an inconsistent grasp on the magic, but with Xirth's guidance and Cael's continuing support, he was gaining the control he would need to wield their Hand. The Wielder's role was simple. He joined the others to the source of the land's magic, linking them together in such a way that their powers were amplified. Any member in the link was able to use their gifting drawing on the collective power of the group. On Ché Kevath, centre of magic, the available power was overwhelming.

Five figures stood on the plateau high above the beach, a thin line of blue light snaking between all to form a circle. Cael watched Telsen as he nodded to Xirth, who stepped out of the ring. The light wavered, spat sparks, but held. A rising stream of air rippled Telsen's shirt in a spiral motion around his body and flowed along the arcing light to stir the hair and clothing of the other three.

Cael grinned, noting Telsen's expression of fierce concentration, feeling the surge of latent power that connected them all. >*Relax, brother! It holds!*< he sent, resisting the urge to whoop in triumph. All morning they had tried and failed to hold the circle without Xirth. This first success was sweet.

Xirth nodded slowly. "You first, Empath."

Cael opened himself to the power, drew it in from each side of him and contained it, let it build until he dare not hold more. His shirt whipped in a wild spiral dance, hair flew around his eyes as he looked to Xirth, awaiting the command to release the magic.

Xirth raised his hand.

Cael released the energy.

Xirth staggered. A dull boom resounded through the arena; the rock beneath Xirth split into a fissure the width of a man's fist and ran several feet past him. A look of surprise crossed his face, but was soon mastered. "Well, son of Jarin! Nicely done. I see Grinore has advanced you quickly."

Cael caught Jenna's astonished eyes on him and pulsed a wave of peace to her. >*Chekuán? Your turn.*<

Galaen's indigo eyes were on Jenna, whose unbound hair blew around her face as the power flowed into her. She released the energy on Galaen's signal. No manifestation of sound followed, but the nine opals at her throat flared with azure light, as did every other Keystone present. Galaen smiled her pleasure at Jenna.

Cael knew that while she was part of their Hand, Jenna's healing power could also be used to injure or cause debility. He had been surprised to learn that all the giftings but one had such polarity when amplified by a Wielder's energy flow. A Linker became able to take strength rather than impart it; a Wielder became able to use his power to shield and defend his Hand while at the same time attacking with fire. As a Wayfinder, only Verra's gifting did not have an aggressive aspect.

Cael had long suspected another dimension to his gifting, but the potential for harm in the use of such mind-power left him ambivalent about it. As well for each of them that there would always be three others to moderate the behaviour of one, should such restraint prove necessary.

Gods, how entangled their lives had become.

One by one, the four's abilities were assessed and refined while they remained linked. They worked late into the afternoon, and were released just before dusk. Verra took them to the waterfall.

Galaen and Xirth watched them go. "They are strong. Even on the mainland they will be formidable." Galaen's gaze was speculative.

"The son of Corr does not relish his power. It does not sit easy on him."

"That is a good quality for a Wielder, Xirth. Power misused upsets the balance. It is no coincidence that the only magic-users ever neutralised were all Wielders."

"The temptation is great for those not committed to the service of the land," Xirth agreed, "but in this case his reluctance only limits him. The Empath assists him, have you seen?"

"Your Wielder is unaware he is being assisted. My great-niece's mate is as able as Grinore." Glossy chocolate-brown hair rippled as Galaen shook her head and laughed. "You did not manage to cover your surprise, my friend."

"Truth. I was concerned. The rock may have swallowed me had he not stayed his hand." Xirth chuckled, his dark eyes humour-bright. "Your Healer shows great potential also. Luath tells me the Wayfinder is already highly skilled, but he has imparted as much knowledge as it is safe for her to take from Ché Kevath."

"Our weapon is almost prepared, then?" Galaen raised her elegant brows at him.

"I believe so. A little more confidence for my Wielder, and the four are ready to unleash. Chiahn *will* be avenged, Galaen."

Sleeping Dragons

★ ★ ★ ★ ★

Several days later, Galaen pronounced the four ready. Alth had spoken that morning. A messenger from Sartz arrived at Twin Lakes, and their Empath relayed the message to Gowan at the Guild, and Grinore of the Hand.

In a process of elimination of old mines and settlements, Jabeel's location had been discovered. He had bolt-holed in Kordethal, an exhausted gem mine behind the falls at the source of the Ré Shan Torrent. Overlooked and all but forgotten due to its antiquity, Kordethal's existence had almost passed from memory, surfacing only during the search of old records and maps.

The four stood on the plateau as they received their final instructions. Xirth's silver hair stirred in the light ocean breeze. "Jabeel was a Wielder of great power before he was neutralised. That he wields still is testimony to that. We believe he remains deep within Althar settlements to access old magic. Once removed from it, he will again be powerless. In the meantime, be wary. Together you four are stronger than he, but he has used magic to take life. That is something you may not do. One without ethics or control is dangerous indeed, and I say again: be wary."

"The rebels are not to be harmed. Some injury may be inevitable if they resist you, but we have given Alth our guarantee of safe passage." Galaen's face was inscrutable. "This is an old score we settle here. In one action, we hope to resolve the past and secure the future." She opened her arms to Jenna, and they shared a warm embrace. "Your grandmother would have been so proud of you, child. You have her strength of spirit as well as her beauty. I would not lose you as well as her, but you have a destiny to fulfil. Go well."

She watched them as they left through the Way, the four whom prophecy proclaimed would prevail.

If the hearts of the one were true.

In truth, the "one" was having a hard time of it. The dragon reared daily for them both. Mellowed temporarily by Ché Kevath, Cael's tension was back to its pre-Lakra level, boiling over into flashes of irritation with their restrictions. How had he ever thought he could deny the bond indefinitely? He cursed in silence at the thought.

They had returned to the Guild that morning, and now gathered in Gowan's study to familiarize themselves with the layout of the mine. Cael sat leaning over the small table bearing the map of Kordethal, memorizing its maze-like structure of tunnels and shafts and noting likely places of concealment. Jenna stood behind him, her thumbs rubbing deep into the tight muscles at the base of his neck.

"If he is any deeper than here," Cael indicated a point on the map, "he has cornered himself. There are no exits past this shaft."

"He feels himself safe. Kordethal was all but forgotten. He knows this." Gowan offered them all a fragrant liqueur, pouring from a sapphire glass decanter into small, handleless cups. He pushed aside a pile of papers and an inkpot, and sat on the edge of his wide desk. Sunlight and oceanscent streamed into the study through the arched stone openings that served as windows, and the cry of a passing gull echoed around the chamber.

Cael leaned back in his chair, attempting to relax under Jenna's hands. He took a cup of the smooth, orange-scented liquid, reached back, trapped one of her hands in his and passed the cup to her over his shoulder.

>*Mmm. I thank you,*< he sent as she squeezed his

shoulder and moved to sit in the empty chair at his side. Gods! She smelled good. Unbraided today, her hair hung thick, glossy and fragrant to the small of her back. Her body moved invitingly beneath the cling of the fine wool dress she always wore when at the Guild.

Their time on Ché Kevath had left them all in peak physical condition. The magic that sustained the Hand had flowed through the four, manifesting in clear glowing skin, bright hair, an alertness of mind and a readiness to perform their function.

Cael found Jenna's new radiance magnetic. She turned and smiled as she saw his eyes on her. He shifted his gaze to the map again, sending her a low growl of frustration.

>*You are very easy on the eye today, chekuán. I wish we were anywhere else but here.*<

"Anywhere?" she whispered, leaning closer. Her breath tickled his ear, sending a shiver over his skin.

>*Certainly not Ré Shan, anyway.*< He flashed her a crooked smile and an image.

A faint stain crept into her cheeks. "Oh," she said. He felt her pulse rise.

"When you two are done?" Gowan addressed them both.

They held each other's eyes a moment longer, then turned back to the meeting, unrepentant. Telsen grinned at Cael, a past master of his friend's body language.

>*Do not say a word, Tel. Not a word. I can still put you on your backside, Wielder or no.*<

The grin widened, and Telsen raised his hands in mock surrender, his dark eyes dancing.

Verra nudged him with an elbow and scowled at Cael. "I hate it when you two do that. Let me in, or stop it."

"Stopped. Apologies, Verra," Cael said, disarming her with his most penitent expression. He hoped.

They were all ready for action. The time of preparation had left them all restless, anxious to exercise their new ability both individual and collective. The desire to see Jabeel meet justice was strong in them all, and each of them had reason to seek vengeance against him. Cael flicked a speculative glance at Jenna. She despised the man for what he had done to her grandmother, but Cael knew that the doubt Galaen had cast over her mother's paternity haunted her. What if Jabeel should claim to be Jenna's grandfather? What if he *is* her grandfather? He shuddered, not wishing to pursue that thought.

>*Gowan. I will be responsible for his safe delivery. The Althar also have nothing to fear from me.*<

>*And your Wielder?*< Gowan queried.

>*No. Only the Wayfinder holds a personal grudge against Althar, but we are four. One will not rule.*<

>*Jenna has cause to distrust Althar. You answer for her also?*<

>*I do.*< Cael pulsed him images of Jenna's dealings with Lakra.

Gowan's eyebrows rose in astonishment. >*Gods! There is much here that I did not know. This is Arkell's A'Thek?*<

>*Currently, yes. I was fortunate enough to incur her life-debt. Much aid was given.*<

>*As I understand. The debt was discharged when she aided your escape?*<

>*It was, but she remains a friend.*<

Gowan nodded. >*One more thing.*<

Cael waited.

Gowan ran his hand through his hair. >*Forgive me, but . . . are you . . . Have you and Jenna . . .*< Gowan looked away, trailing off into uncomfortable silence and radiating embarrassment.

Cael slumped into the chair. Blessed Gods, was there ever to be any privacy? >*Do you need to know this?*< he sent, unable to keep the irritation from his tone.

>*No, of course not. Your . . . status is your own business, but I would caution you. I see how things are between you, but succumbing to Dragonfire now will both distract you and drain your power, Cael. You* **must** *abstain until your mission is fulfilled. You will need all the power available to you to quell Jabeel.*< Gowan sighed. >*It seems I am always the bearer of bad tidings. Forgive me again.*<

The low conversation of the others faded into the background as Cael stared at his mentor. >*That is a harsh sanction. We were also restricted on Ché Kevath, and have had no chance to be alone.*< He gave a short laugh. >*At least I am experienced in dealing with such restriction. I cannot imagine how arduous it would be otherwise.*<

Gowan's mouth twitched. >*I think you can,*< he sent.

"And if *you* two are done?" Jenna's pointed comment ended the silent discussion.

Chapter Eighteen

Kismet

Cael shaded his eyes against the glare of snow, and scanned the rock behind the thin curtain of water. The mine was warded. Verra had brought them through the Way to the foot of a waterfall, one of two that fed the Ré Shan Torrent. Winter yet lingered, and the falls that would rage with such violence during the spring thaw now ran sluggishly beneath an overhanging lip of ice. He looked for the narrow shelf that would allow them access to the opening of the mine. The shelf was there. The steps were not. Time and many seasons of ice had cracked and sheared off slabs of rock that lay in a weathered tumble below the shelf.

Verra grinned at them. "My turn for secrets." She raised her wrists, crossed the bands and watched the Way portal open on the remnant of shelf that extended a foot or two to the left of the fall. She turned herself, watching the shimmering portal turn also, angling to provide a safe exit. Telsen and Jenna exclaimed in surprise. Another Way portal opened before them.

"The warding begins behind the water," she explained. "That is as close as I can take us. Just watch your step. There is no telling how safe that ledge is."

Cael gave her an appreciative look. "Interesting technique, Wayfinder." He looked upward at the Way portal and frowned. "The ledge looks a little insecure. Tel is the heaviest—if it bears his weight, we will all be safe." Telsen shrugged and moved toward the Way.

>*Nothing personal, brother, just practical. If you fall . . . I will make sure Verra is beneath you.*< Cael maintained a serious expression, and Telsen elbowed him as he passed, stepping into the portal with great dignity. Cael watched, fascinated, as his bondbrother appeared to exist on two planes at once.

"It is all done with mirrors," Telsen called from above, flashing his white grin and exiting the top portal. Testing the ledge, he sent a shower of small stones rattling down on them. "It seems strong, but perhaps one at a time?"

He edged his way along the shelf without difficulty until he stood behind the moving water, a blurred dark image behind the liquid curtain. Cael came through to join him at the mouth of the shaft followed by Jenna, and Verra closed the Ways behind her as she reached them. The mineshaft yawned before them. Out of the sun's warmth, their breath steamed in the chill air. Sharing a look of resolve, the four entered the wide tunnel.

Telsen wielded fire, throwing a puddle of intense blue flame ahead of them into the darkness. Althar light magic had long since expired here. They progressed through the shaft into the deepening cold, alert for danger. Wielder's fire lit their way, casting angular shadows on the rock wall as they passed. A faint, metallic odour hung in the damp air and settled into nose and throat, the smell translating into taste where it touched the tongue.

Cael held the ancient map of Kordethal in his mind, translating the maze-like puzzle into a sensible passage to where he believed Jabeel most likely to be. After many turns and switchbacks, the air began to feel warmer against his skin.

>*We are getting closer. There is heat ahead.*<

A distant grumble sounded: the groan of stone on stone.

>*An old heat wheel—so they have magic users here. Let us hope they have no Shapers.*< Shapers. Cael shuddered. The rarest of Althar magics, shaping allowed one so gifted to melt stone, using it as wet clay. Althar dead were entombed that way. Settlements, mines and the Guild had been fashioned by Shapers. As a child, he had seen a man disappear into the stone where he stood as a retribution for a crime against Alth.

The passage they followed angled steeply downward at the next turn. >*Tel, no more light. We do not want to give them warning.*<

As they rounded the next corner, the passage lightened; a dull glow became visible.

>*Stop. We are close.*< Cael's heart raced as adrenalin began to work in his body, heightening his awareness, preparing him for fight or flight in a reaction as old as time. He felt Verra faintly broadcasting fear; Jenna's apprehension; Telsen's stoic determination.

>*Verra?*<

She turned her face to him, her eyes expressing her need. He laid his hands on her shoulders as he lent her strength and comfort; took her fear of enclosed places. He watched her face relax. Thank you, she mouthed in gratitude.

>*Chekuán.*<

Jenna raised her eyes to his, made a sign with her hand. A round circle formed between thumb and forefinger. He frowned his incomprehension, and she kissed him instead.

Telsen gave him a tense nod, and the four continued silently toward the source of heat and distant voices. They clung to what shadows remained, close to the walls of the passage as they approached.

A bellow of laughter rang out. They stopped behind Cael's gesture.

>*Kavlek. I would know him anywhere. Tel, be ready. Wherever Kavlek is, Jabeel is not far away.*< He felt a sweat break out on his forehead, dampen the skin beneath his eyes. Gods! His memory of the tiny chamber in Ré Shan remained strong. He drew in a deep, shuddering breath.

Jenna leaned close and raised her lips to his ear. "We are four now, Cael. You're not alone this time." She rested against him, pressing her face against his shoulder.

They moved forward. Sounds of conversation floated from a passage to their left. Cael flattened himself against the rock as he recognised Jabeel's sardonic tone.

>*Gods! He freezes my blood. All of you, take care. He is an unscrupulous weasel. Be ready to link.*< He breathed deeply, calming himself, and opened his senses to the presence ahead of them.

Seven Althar. Jabeel. Beyond them, many more, but in this chamber, only seven. He sent out a mind probe. Gods! None of them had their barriers in place. He formulated an announcement, knowing his opportunity would be brief. Hopefully the Althar would see the sense in his offer of amnesty. Constructing a careful image, he prepared to pulse it before the Althar could engage their symbiot's shielding.

>*Tel. Begin the link.*<

Telsen signalled acknowledgment, his dark eyes meeting Cael's as he drew deeply on the source of magic.

Cael felt the power begin to grow as a flicker of azure ran from Telsen to him, joining them to the women, linking them in a circle of power. He threw his message to as many Althar as were unguarded and felt the backlash as barriers were raised in belated haste.

>*We go.*< They rounded the last corner, and stood in the entrance of a wide chamber.

Startled steel grey eyes bored into Cael. "So. The fair

317

one returns. And with the very people I desire to put an end to." Jabeel rose from his chair and backed toward his Althar allies. His gaze flicked to the thin blue filament that connected the four, and he gave a low chuckle. "A Hand, no less. How interesting. And only the four of you. So who is the lucky one with the double gifting?"

The four moved slowly into the square chamber and away from the entrance, keeping the stone wall at their backs. The azure flicker of their link played on the rough stone walls and highlighted the countenances of the occupants with a ghost-like glow.

Several Althar exchanged glances, flashed appeal to Cael, responding to his message of amnesty. He stood aside, let four of them pass as they exited the chamber, watching warily to be sure they intended no treachery. >*Jenna, watch the door.*< He turned back to face Jabeel and the remaining three Althar.

"How did you find me, my dear?" Jabeel asked, his face a picture of counterfeit interest. "Kordethal is an ancient stronghold. Even the Althar have forgotten it."

"Stronghold? It is a crumbling relic, Jabeel." Cael sensed Althar presence withdrawing from their vicinity, and dared to hope the odds were reducing in their favour as planned. He moved closer to Jabeel, the others backing him in close union. "Kavlek. Well met, my brutal friend."

"This is Kavlek?" Telsen's face darkened with threat. The large Althar shifted uncomfortably and avoided Cael's eyes. The blue filament spat and strengthened, echoing Telsen's emotional response.

"Peace, brother. It is this whoreson who wields Kavlek." Cael's cool gaze rested on Jabeel. "Is that not so, my *dear?*"

Jabeel smiled thinly at the heavy emphasis. "You are a quick study, fair one. Let me guess which one is your bondmate." A blaze of blue fire flew from his open hand, narrowly missing Jenna as she flinched away. "And who wields? Perhaps this one?" A blue bolt sped past Verra as she dropped to avoid it. The rock smoked behind them, filling the air with the burnt odour of spent magic. Cael knew Jabeel prevaricated, teased and played with them. His unease grew.

Telsen fronted the four, raising his hands as an opaque shield of cobalt blue light formed at his left arm.

"Ah. The brother. How nice. I commend you, fair one. All appear dedicated to you." He moved to stand between the Althar that remained to him.

>*Tel. One of them is a Shaper.*< Cael knew it in an instant, warned by Jabeel's confidence. His sending also reached the women as they stood behind their Wielder.

Jabeel flung up his arms and unleashed a bolt of energy to strike the rock above them. Stone cracked and fell, and Cael cursed as a heavy slab sheared off and struck his shoulder, sharp-edged, opening skin and muscle and searing him with sudden pain. "Coward's tactics, Jabeel. Are you not a man?"

"Only tactics, fair one. Counter as you see fit."

>*It is not Kavlek.*< Cael probed the two remaining Althar, finding only their barriers. He caught a minuscule shifting beneath one and felt his skin crawl as with a thousand fleas. >*The tall one. Quickly!*<

Telsen loosed blue fire at the tall Althar, knocking him from his feet where he lay stunned. The rock rippled beneath them. Verra cried out as she sank to her ankles into the suddenly liquified floor. Telsen spun in horror and she grabbed at him, sinking to her knees in the rock. She clung to his arm in panic. He held her up, braced his legs in a wide stance and swivelled back to face Jabeel.

"No concentration, Wielder," Jabeel gloated. He flung his arms forward and loosed a bolt from each hand.

Telsen deflected them, and shards of rock cut into flesh as the bolts hit the wall. He hauled Verra from the treacherous floor, landing her beside him on solid rock. "That was unwise, you son of a snake." His expression spelt danger.

"Ah. So that one is yours?" Jabeel's eyes gleamed with speculation as he regarded Jenna with new interest. He raised his eyes to the rock ceiling. "Oh my dear boy. You cannot protect your women, can you?" Jabeel's next bolts whined overhead and blasted them all with sharp rock fragments, drawing blood wherever they found flesh, and splitting Cael's cheek and lip as he sought to protect Jenna and Verra from the worst of the debris. Telsen roared with defiance as he endeavoured to deflect Jabeel's bolts with the cobalt shield, and the spitting blue arc that joined them flared brilliant azure in response to the power he drew.

"Just let me touch him—we'll see how strong he is after I remove parts of him." Jenna's muttered words spat boiling acid as she pressed forward against Cael, and he felt her indignation at Jabeel's dismissal of her gender. He planted himself firmly, not wanting her to risk herself in her anger, and felt her answering affront at his resistance.

>*Jenna, stop. He seeks to antagonise us. If he divides us, he will defeat us. Do not allow it.*< He felt her subside, seething with reluctance, and pulsed his understanding and support.

The tall Shaper still lay dazed, and Telsen threw deft blue fire against the remaining Althar, cuffing them from their feet and binding them in cords of power, even as he continued to blaze assault at Jabeel. Jabeel parried and dodged with agility, but could not avoid Telsen's every shot. His shirt front smouldered in patches, and wisps of pale smoke curled from his coat. Cael felt the man's fatigue. Thin lips drew in a parody of a smile as Jabeel came up against the wall at his back. Pressing himself against the rock, he threw a glance at the tall Althar who now stirred beside him. "Strick! Release me from this farce," he spat.

Gods. >*Tel. The Shaper!*< There was no hesitation from Telsen. Cael felt the flow reverse, course into him and stir his hair and clothing. At the same moment as the rock behind Jabeel began to ripple, Cael loosed the energy of the link in a blast of mind-power at Strick. The Althar's breath whooshed out as if he had been struck in the belly, and he doubled over where he lay, winded and retching. And distracted from the mischief he had been about to wreak. Handing the power back to Telsen, Cael saw the rock wall solidify once more. Jabeel tore himself from his coat, that hung from its shoulders, trapped in the now solid stone.

"So we must settle this here and now, fair one?" he said with a hint of a sneer. "How tedious."

"You are lucky I did not wait for you to be *within* the wall." Cael felt gratified at the sudden lack of colour in Jabeel's face. "You will not escape, and you will not defeat us. What will you do?"

Jabeel sighed and dropped his hands. He said nothing, but emanated deceit and cunning, and Cael knew the man was not to be underestimated. >*Let us remove his support system. Stand ready, Tel. He is not done yet, no matter how it looks.*< Swiping blood from his mouth, he turned his attention to the Althar and spoke to them in their own tongue: a speech prepared with Arkell's help. He imbued his words with the power of command so recently learned from Grinore. Thank the Gods for secrets.

"This is not your battle. Our quarrel is with one of our own. Alth awaits your return with forgiveness and promises of reform, and this one is not worthy of your loyalty. Leave us while you may." His voice held stern authority, allowing no room for challenge.

"Adrek, Strick—stay. I have need of you." Jabeel's plea went disregarded as the two fled from the chamber, released from Telsen's bonds of fire. "Kavlek?" he appealed.

The last Althar stood beside Jabeel, shadows of uncertainty playing over his broad face. "*Karashe*, Empath. Mercy," he said at last, dropping his head in deference: real or otherwise Cael could not say.

"Go." Cael's eyes were hard as he remembered the agonies inflicted on him at this Althar's hand.

Telsen growled and grasped Kavlek's shoulder, spinning him around as he passed.

>*No, Tel. I promised Gowan.*<

"I did not promise." Brown eyes locked on alien black for an instant. Blue fire erupted in Kavlek's groin. He dropped like a stone, choking with pain, both hands reaching between his thighs.

Telsen was distracted. Cael was also off-guard.

"Cael, look out!" Jenna's words synchronised with Verra's warning cry, and Cael jerked his head around in time to see Jabeel raise his hands again.

Jabeel loosed a vicious streak of power, and Telsen swung his arm up against the bolt. Too late. It glanced from the edge of the shield and shot past him. Smoke hazed the chamber, and the light of the Wielder's fire hung in brief suspension, as fog traps the light from a lantern. Cael knew in a slow-motion moment of sick horror that he was directly in its path.

Something slammed into him from behind. His knees buckled beneath him, and as he was forced out of the bolt's trajectory, his ears resounded with Jenna's fierce cry.

Rolling to regain his feet, he saw her chest catch the azure fire. Her body lifted and slammed into the rock behind her. Her indigo eyes flew wide open, her expression one of surprise as she crumpled to the ground. Cael staggered, and his head snapped back in echo of the impact.

Her eyes lost focus. Closed.

Cael dropped to his knees beside her as the pain ebbed from his body along with her consciousness, and Verra flew toward her with a cry of alarm. Telsen stood defensively between them and Jabeel. As the blue filament flickered and wavered, Cael steadied himself with great, heaving breaths and drew on the power. Every last remnant of magic he could draw from the fading link. The blue arc spat, sparked, disappeared.

Their Hand was broken, but their Wielder still stood.

Jabeel threw blue fire.

Telsen deflected it, sent answering fire. Jabeel's bolts were stronger, each one sending Telsen staggering under its force as he parried.

Jabeel smiled, his confidence returning. "Wielder . . . you are but a boy! Surrender while you can." He stood smirking before them, power sparking between his hands, his flagging energy restored at the prospect of victory.

Boy.

Cael stood tall at Telsen's back.

>*I want him, Tel. He is a dead man.*<

"Come now, fair one. You must know you are beaten."

Cael's eyes flashed amber fire. A terrible rage consumed him. He pushed Telsen aside and flinched as Wielder's fire scorched past his chest, disregarding the smell of burnt flesh in his anger. The physical pain was nothing compared to the anguish in his soul, and his wrath overloaded the safety levels of his conditioning, boiled over the boundaries imposed on him by culture and training, leaving only a primitive and long-suffering fury. The image of blank indigo eyes filled his vision as he summoned the stored power of their link.

A roar of pain escaped him with the release of the energy.

Jabeel flew against the rock wall behind him, arms flung wide and pinned against his control. The rock sundered to each side of him, and split in a resounding crack as fissures spread beneath his outspread hands. His expression of surprise became calculating, his voice oily and provocative.

"You see, my dear. You are enjoying this . . . go on, take your pleasure."

Cael's brow ached with a fierce frown. His muscles twitched against the remnants of restraint that he still managed to preserve. He maintained the mind-power that held Jabeel, knowing the man's destiny was in his hands. "You sicken me. You were never worthy of my concern." His voice was low and full of disgust.

"Nevertheless, you must do something, my dear." Grey eyes held his as the battle of wills continued. "You know she will not survive if you do not help her." Jabeel's gaze slid past Cael. "Life already leaves her, fair one. What will you do?"

Reason left him. Cael launched himself at his tormentor, grasped the narrow throat and squeezed as hard as his grip allowed. He held Jabeel against the rock wall, noting with detachment how dark the man's face was becoming. Fear flickered in Jabeel's eyes as he choked, unable to draw breath past the iron grip on his windpipe.

Telsen stood beside them and laid a restraining hand on Cael's arm. "This is not for you to do, brother."

Cael maintained the pressure, watching the grey eyes as

they dimmed, noting the odd way the pupils began to dilate and how the light seemed to ebb, as at the end of a day.

"Cael. You must release him. Cael!" Telsen shook him. "It is over, brother. Release him!"

Cael blinked, hearing the consternation in his bondbrother's voice. He focussed on Telsen's anxious face as if seeing him for the first time. His hand ached. Staring at his fist, he realised what he had almost done. He let go. Jabeel slid unconscious from his grip. Cael's stomach spasmed. Bile burned in his throat and he choked it back, appalled at his loss of control. Gods, never had he thought himself capable of such a monstrous act. He backed away, rubbing his hands on his breeches, trying to remove the taint of filth as the beginnings of self-doubt gnawed at his conscience.

"Cael." Verra's quiet call drew him back to himself. He stumbled to where Jenna lay in ominous stillness. A thin trail of bright scarlet trickled from her mouth, and Cael's hand shook as he wiped it away with a gentle thumb. He raised her head and felt the warm weep of blood in her hair.

Blinking against his misting vision, he lifted her with great care and cradled her in his arms, supporting her head against his shoulder. Her heart still beat beneath the acrid scorched wool of her shirt. She still breathed. Without a word he turned and strode back the way they had come.

Dim pools of blue light still glowed in the passages, freeing Cael's mind from the necessity of navigation. Verra walked beside him, running every few steps to keep pace with his long strides. Telsen caught up with them, Jabeel's limp form over his shoulder, the man's wrists bound behind his back with filaments of Wielder's power.

"Cael—does she live? Gods man, speak to me . . ."

"Leave him, Tel," Verra said, her voice tight. "We will know soon enough."

Cael's jaw ached but he kept it tight-clenched. His eyes did not move from the way ahead, his pace did not slow. An immense chunk of cold ached beneath his ribs, choked off emotion, allowing only the thought required to exit the warding of the mine.

Within minutes, they stood on the platform behind the falls. Verra opened the Way on the ledge where the warding ended and stood back in silence. Cael edged toward the shimmer. He kept his back against the wet rock face and slid his feet sideways, maintaining contact with the ledge, unable to see past his burden where he stepped. Reaching the Way, he slipped through without looking back.

The four were returning. The Hand had received Cael's call and stood waiting on the plateau. His tone had been stark, his message succinct. >*We have Jabeel, but Jenna is hurt. Wait for us in the arena.*<

The Way sang open. No one appeared. Galaen exchanged looks with Grinore.

"He does not communicate," Grinore said. "We must wait."

Moments later, bloodied and wet, Cael sidestepped from the Way with Jenna limp in his arms. He laid her down, knelt beside her and rested her head carefully on his arm. Help her, his eyes pleaded as Galaen approached them. She read his pain and fear, wishing she could ease him. Turning, she sought Grinore.

Grinore's sending preceded her request. >*I have him, Galaen.*< She thanked him with a grateful glance and sank to her knees beside Jenna. Kenethrel took Jenna's hand and began a link. Galaen assessed the injury and sank her awareness into one of Jenna's Keystones.

Xirth moved to the Way as Telsen exited, bearing Jabeel. Telsen dropped Jabeel at Xirth's feet in silence, and joined Cael at Jenna's side, his shirt already rippling around him as he drew power into himself. Xirth nodded at him in approval and wielded a fine blue filament around Jabeel, binding him to the rock where he lay, his breath a harsh rasp through his damaged throat.

Verra closed the Way behind her and hurried toward the huddled group. She placed herself between the brothers and dropped a comforting hand to Cael's shoulder. Scorched and bleeding, the three drew power from the thin blue streak that ran through them, brightening as the spiral of air around their Wielder grew stronger.

>*Galaen?*< Cael's sending was a tight question, and she knew what he asked.

"She lives, Cael, but much power is needed. I cannot do this alone." Galaen gestured to Kenethrel and moved to intercept the blue arc, including herself in their link, drawing on the magic that flowed through them all. Kenethrel joined them. Galaen's eyes widened at the strength of the flow, then flew around the circle to find the source and rested on Cael where he knelt at her left. He lifted his head and intercepted her regard, meeting her eyes steadily. Shaking her head in astonishment, she began the healing.

After an hour, Jenna slept, her body mended. Galaen surveyed the three with a pensive expression. All were hurt, scorched by Wielder's fire or bleeding where exploding rock had pierced their skin with shards and splinters. Cael had shared some images of the battle at her request, but now remained strangely silent. His chest bore a wide, raw burn, a shoulder wound still oozed blood into his shirt, and his cheek and lip were split and swollen. Telsen's broad chest and shoulders evidenced several wide swathes of scorching, and tiny stone fragments peppered the fair skin of Verra's face and neck. Galaen had offered them healing; Cael had declined. He raised Jenna, lifting her again in his arms, and asked Verra for the Way.

Galaen's heart went out to him, to them all, but still she maintained the distance required of her. A member of the Hand could not show favour, could not involve herself with family. All had been foresworn, many years ago. Now, her life was the land and the keeping of its magic. The workings of Fate were not to be disturbed, no matter what transpired, no matter who became embroiled. It had always been so, but her heart ached for Jenna and her mate, as it had for Chiahn. "Son of Jarin. Where do you go?" Galaen asked.

He did not turn. His voice was distant. "Away from here, Galaen. I am done with this. You have what you wanted. Leave us alone."

She watched as they left. "He blames me." Her tone was regretful.

"No, Galaen," Grinore said. "He knows you followed prophecy. He is weary. They all are. Give him time, and allow him his life back for a while."

"Fate is not done with him, Grinore." Galaen smoothed back long dark hair and sighed as she gazed down at the still lagoon. "One of his power will never truly call his life his own. The strength of his gifting equals yours and is furthered by the love shared between the four of them. I felt it in their link. I did not understand this before. Their power will one day exceed our own."

She frowned at Jabeel, still caged in blue light. "Xirth, remove that creature, will you? It offends me. The confinement in Illith will hold him, if Luath would be so kind."

Sleeping Dragons

★ ★ ★ ★ ★

Cael sat in the infirmary outside the chamber where Jenna lay. Healers had washed her clean, clothed her in soft linen and left her to sleep off the healing, attended by a young Linker. He watched as Karessa removed the last fragments of stone from Verra's face.

Telsen also lay sleeping. Karessa had healed the burns that seared his chest and arms, her face tight as she muttered with disapproval at how the four of them had been used.

Trista probed the ragged wound in Cael's shoulder, feeling for stone splinters to be removed before Karessa would heal him. Leaning his head back against the wall, he closed his eyes, managing the pain of the examination. The girl moved to his other side, picked up a basin of water and began to sluice stone dust and shirt fibres from the burnt flesh where Jabeel's bolt had scored his chest.

>*Trista.*<

She jumped, startled by his sending.

>*You have gentle hands. You will make a fine Healer.*< He opened his eyes and gave her a weary smile.

She blushed with pleasure at the compliment.

Karessa finished with Verra and turned her attention to him. "Thank you, Trista. Come, sit." She beckoned him over to her and sat him down before her. "I hope this is the last time we have to do this," she said, fixing him with a resigned look.

>*Unlikely. When will Jenna wake?*<

"I am unsure. From what you have told me of the healing, it could be a day or two."

Cael raised his eyes to her, unable to keep the torment from his face, trusting her with his raw emotion. >*I could not protect her, and he almost killed her. Gods! I thought she*

329

was gone. < Emotional shock echoed in his sending, and he dropped his head into his hands with a quiet curse. >*The bolt that hit her was meant for me. She took it. Deliberately.* <

Karessa patted his knee in a maternal fashion even as her tone conveyed a Healer's concern. "Cael, she is your mate; she could do nothing less." She raised his chin in a gentle hand, and he saw her understanding. "You are hurt and weary. It has been an eventful day. Do not try to analyse any of it until you have rested." She reached for the Keystone at his throat, and he felt her begin the healing process.

When he awoke from the first hour of his healing sleep, Cael stayed with Jenna, doggedly refusing to leave. Karessa had a pallet laid on the floor of the chamber, and he collapsed on it with gratitude and slept like a dead man for hours beneath the blankets she threw over him.

The next day found him restored, but again, he resisted any suggestion of leaving her. He remained resolute, and Karessa had food brought to him and sent him away only to wash. He would stay until Jenna awoke, whatever Karessa thought or said about it. He slept on the chamber floor for another night, waking with the water-colour wash of dawn. He felt Jenna's wakefulness.

"Cael." Her voice was a parched whisper.

The Linker left them alone. Cael sat beside her, reaching for water as he felt her thirst. "Welcome back," he said, in echo of their first meeting.

She smiled, and he knew she remembered.

He raised her, helped her to drink.

She had no memory of the bolt of Wielder's magic that had struck her, and for that, he was glad. Lifting her hand to him, she touched the faint new scars on his shoulder and chest. "You've been hurt so much, and so often," she whispered, and he felt her regret for his pain. Her drowsy indigo eyes held a tender concern, gentling his heart open, and he knew all his reserve was gone.

"Rest, my Lady," he murmured. He leaned over and kissed her forehead lightly. Her hand rested on his thigh, and he was pleased for it to remain. He stayed until her eyelids drooped closed again, and he felt her awareness slip back into restoring sleep. Tucking her arm back beneath the covers, he stroked her cheek once, and slipped quietly from the chamber.

Chapter Nineteen

Dragonfire

At last, spring arrived. The land came alive under the coaxing of the vernal sun and shook itself like a dog rousing from a winter sleep. Renewal of life and green began in response to the ancient rhythm of the seasons.

The ranch hummed with activity. Brenn's best mares were stabled, due to foal and requiring his careful attention. This batch of Kereál's finest animals would bring a top price at the late-summer horse markets.

Jenna pulled on thick gloves and joined Illiahn and Jolie in the kitchen garden. They were planting the first of the kitchen crops that would provide fresh summer vegetables in a few months, and Myst followed behind them with a water can, sprinkling each new plant as it was firmed in. Her small face was serious with concentration as she tilted the heavy can with the assistance of Raen. Muddy water ran in small rivulets over their winter boots and settled into murky puddles before the earth drank it in. Illiahn straightened. Jenna threw her an anxious glance as Illiahn stretched her back and yawned.

"Let me do all the bending over and kneeling bits, Illiahn. It must be uncomfortable for you."

"A little," Illiahn conceded, patting her roundness. She carried twins again, and Jenna observed how quickly she tired.

"If you won't rest completely, at least choose only the light tasks. Growing two babies is hard work enough."

Illiahn turned fond amber eyes on Jenna. "Yes, Healer," she teased. "You are done with your own work today?"

"I am, unless there's an emergency somewhere. The wife of one of the tavern keepers is due to deliver anytime, so I won't rule that out." Jenna took over the planting with Jolie as Illiahn rested on a low bench beside the garden wall.

"Kereál is proud to call you a daughter, Jenna. We have needed a Healer of your skill since Karessa was called to the Guild. I have heard it said in the village that your gifting exceeds even hers."

"I have Galaen to thank for that," Jenna said with a wry smile, aware that she was committed to service as a result. The four could be recruited at any time, at any new need. They had all become local heroes, unwilling as they were.

It had only been two weeks since she had returned home from the Guild, carried through the Way in Cael's arms as he continued in his new, protective behaviour toward her. In an ironic reversal of roles, he had cared for her, meeting each need almost before she became aware of it.

She recovered quickly, and had begun to assist Kereál's Healer. After several days, the village Healer had acceded her position to Jenna. Chagrined, Jenna had refused, but the woman had been insistent, and genuinely happy to have one of such power to serve Kereál. A holder of the nine was always in demand, and a real blessing to the community she served.

"Is Cael in the village again?" Jenna sighed. She had not seen him since breakfast. He often absented himself these days, being an integral part of the village's affairs in his role as a Leader. Arbitration of minor disputes, administration of local law and the general workings of the township ate most of his time. She knew he had responsibilities, but missed him terribly. It even appeared to her that he just might be avoiding her again. "I'm *sure* he used to be here more often."

Illiahn smiled. "Telsen is complaining of that also," she said. "But I think he misses a sword-mate as much as he misses Cael's company." She leaned against the wall, basking in the gentle warmth of the spring sun. "He is not in the village today, but was called to attend Gowan. He did not seem too displeased, so I do not think it is bad news."

Jenna frowned. "Possibly to do with Jabeel's judgement day. We're all required to be witnesses."

Illiahn gave her an odd look, like a bird eyeing a juicy worm. Seeming to reach a decision, her tone became brisk. "Time for some tea, I think. Jolie, will you take the girls inside and help them clean up?"

Jenna smiled as Myst and Raen skipped after Jolie on their way back to the house. "They're beautiful children, Illiahn." Almost four years old, they were lively and intelligent, secure in their small experience of their world.

"I thank you, *chiara*. Now then. You were not raised in our culture. It appears that there is much you should know that your mother would have taught you herself had *she* known. Forgive me, but I am going to speak plainly."

Jenna raised her brows in a comical *oh really?* "How unlike you." She brushed a tendril of dark hair from her face with the back of an earthy glove, and squinted in the sunlight at Illiahn. Grasshopper before the master, she thought, having some idea of the topic.

Illiahn stretched her legs before her, circling her ankles as Jenna had advised her to do. As always, she came straight to the point. "The bed in the den is built for two, Jenna. I think you should be in it tonight."

Jenna's mouth fell open, closed again. "Illiahn—that's

none of your business." Her eyes were wide with indignation.

"You think not? If I had not received the same advice some years ago, Brenn may never have asked me. I put myself in his bed because he did not." She tilted her head at Jenna, appearing completely at ease with the conversation.

"Didn't he want you there?" Jenna felt heat rise in her cheeks. Verra would have kittens if she heard this. Kittens *and* puppies.

"Of course, but he was too much of a gentleman to ask me." Illiahn directed a very pointed look at Jenna.

Confused, Jenna rubbed her face, leaving a dark streak of loamy earth across her cheek. "Why didn't he ask you to handfast?"

Illiahn looked puzzled. "Because we had made no commitment to each other."

"Handfasting is *not* a commitment?"

"The handfasting is but a confirmation, a public declaration. The real commitment is honoured in the bedroom."

"So sex comes first, is that what you're saying?"

Illiahn sighed patiently. "No, Jenna. Commitment comes first. Then sex. It is the woman's prerogative to instigate that. A man of integrity will not ask. Do you understand now?"

"And everyone here knows this?" Jenna was mystified.

"It is just the way of things. There are exceptions, as with anything. An Empath may choose to whom he offers his bond, but will not press the issue. It is the woman's choice to accept or decline his offer. It is rarely declined," she said with a small smile. "Most women desire to be a bondmate, with all its . . . benefits."

"I'm more confused than when we started this little chat. I assume you're about to offer me more sage advice?" Jenna frowned, feeling the strangeness of the cross-cultural issues they explored.

"I will if you allow me to, *chiara*." Illiahn hesitated, her eyes holding apology. "Cael waits for you to approach him, but is solicitous of your health. He is concerned you are doing too much too soon, and as a consequence, he removes himself daily so you will not observe his need for you. He . . . does not want to pressure you into a response he fears you are not ready to give." She sat up straight, then leaned forward as far as her pregnancy would allow. "You are fully recovered?"

"Yes, I think so."

"You want him still?"

"I have never stopped wanting him."

"Then show him, Jenna. He has sent that he will be home later tonight. He will share a meal with Gowan. They are not done talking." She stood and flexed her back. "Light the fire in the den and wait for him. He is beyond resisting you—he merely waits for you to make the first move."

The rest of the day passed in nervous apprehension for Jenna. She trusted Illiahn's advice, but feared Cael's reaction. He had kept her at arm's length for so long she had become used to it. Supper came and went. She could only pick at food, not meeting Illiahn's eyes as she helped to clear the kitchen, and escaped to the bath as soon as she could.

The small bathtub steamed as she drew hot water from the tank above the wood burner, and added cold from the buckets. She threw in a handful of fragrant dried lavender, swirling the blue fragments through the water. She undressed and sank into the tub, submerging herself, feeling her hair swirl around her skin. Too nervous to linger, she lathered a soapy herbal gel through her hair, appreciating the fresh green scent as it mingled with the lavender. She rinsed, left the tub and towelled dry, pulled on her shift and dress, and made a clandestine exit through the kitchen garden to the den.

The soft glow of firelight and oil lamps soon betrayed her presence as she drew a wide comb through her hair, drying its scented length before the fire.

Gowan set his cup down, staring into the leaping orange flames of the fire in his study. >*I prefer it to Wielder's fire. It is somehow more passionate, more primal.*<

Cael agreed, enjoying the colour and smoky scent of the wood fire in the vented recess built for the purpose. They shared a deep red wine after talking into the early evening. Business had been discussed, Jabeel's impending appearance before the Council, among other concerns.

Cael rolled a last mouthful of wine around his tongue, enjoying the full fruit flavour and dry, peppery aftertaste. >*I must be away, Gowan.*< He set his empty glass on his old mentor's desk and rose, stretching to his full height, his fingers inches away from the ceiling. >*I thank you for your frank counsel and your friendship. You were always the one I would seek when in need.*<

Gowan inclined his head. >*Your gifting outdoes mine, Cael. There is nothing more I could ever teach you, but as mentor, I am always here when you have need.*< He rose to see Cael out. >*Give my kind regards to Jenna. I am sure she will come to you in her own time.*<

Cael grimaced, pulled his fingers through his hair and rubbed his neck. >*I do not understand why she delays still, but I am almost at the end of waiting. Gods, I am a lit fuse.*< And I hope the discovery of that does not frighten her off, he thought wryly. *>There is one more thing I need to do here before I return, though. I hope the craftsman will not mind the late hour.<* Gowan smiled in understanding as Cael left the study, heading deeper into the Empath's keep.

Jenna heard the sound of voices in the yard as Illiahn hailed Verra from the front steps. Her heartbeat quickened in apprehension.

Oh shit. Was this such a good idea?

Too late. Footsteps approached the door. The handle turned, and the door opened with a faint protest of iron hinges.

Jenna turned to see Cael in the doorway, his face alive with shadows cast by the flames of the fire. He stood frozen a moment when he saw her, then stepped inside, removed his cloak and tossed it across the table. There was sudden tension in every line of his body. A feral light flared in his eyes. He remained still, his jaw tight, his expression unreadable. A small shiver of fear suggested itself through her gut. *Kia kaha*—Be strong.

The intensity of his gaze demanded her response. She approached him with slow steps, her eyes locked on his. Reaching behind him, she pushed the door closed and he stepped aside as she secured the latch. She turned back to him, laid both palms on his chest and kissed him gently.

Still he made no move toward her, but his amber eyes betrayed his need. His desire was a live animal in the room, a tangible presence that crackled with tension. She was surprised there were no sparks. Tremors of anticipation and apprehension conflicted in her body and grew into arousal with the speed of electricity. Holding her shift by its hem, she slid it up past her thighs, past bare hips, revealing herself inch by inch until the fine garment whispered over her head. She dropped it to the floor, shaking a cascade of scented hair from her shoulders. Daring him to resist her, she stood naked before him, aware of her own beauty. Now misinterpret *that,* Cael.

"Jenna . . ." His breath caught as she slipped her arms around his waist and drew herself against his body, reaching up to press her mouth to his in a kiss both tender and demanding. His arms came about her then, holding her hard to him, his kiss fervid and hot. The animal crouched.

She realised again the size of him as his arousal became evident. With the wisdom of womankind, she knew this was not the time for romance. His growing urgency emanated from him in violent waves, and the shivery encounter with fear returned to prickle at her spine. So this was the dragon? Her own arousal was fierce. She felt the heat of his flesh through the linen shirt, his hands warm and firm on her back and in her hair, and she wanted him, needed him to overwhelm her with his body.

She fumbled with the ties of his breeches, loosening the cords with trembling fingers as he kicked off his boots, pulled his shirt over his head and dropped it to the floor. Within heartbeats he was naked, and she was tumbling backward onto his bed, his body covering hers and his scent all around her. She mouthed his neck and tasted salt on his skin, ran greedy hands over his back and pulled him to her.

He groaned, a low animal sound, and buried his face in her neck, tasting the soft curve of her throat as his body sought hers. She slid fully beneath him and opened herself to his seeking, raising her hips to embrace him within her body, feeling his delight as he discovered her, the distinction between their physical sensations blurring until she could not tell where she ended and he began. She moaned as he moved, and he froze, held back, rolled himself onto one elbow.

"Have I hurt you?" he panted, golden hair falling over desire-dark eyes.

With a wanton smile, she shook her head, her chest heaving. "*Oh* no." Drawing him back to her, she held him close and caressed him with avid hands, kissed him with hungry lips, moved invitingly beneath him. "You're delicious," she breathed, "don't stop."

>*Gods, I don't think I can.*< His breath was hot on her neck as his soft gasps played with her ear.

They moved together then, fast and hard, sweat-slick flesh connecting in a firm and exultant rhythm, until the rising wave of his impending orgasm picked her up and rushed her toward her own climax. The sharing was intense. As their bodies spasmed in orgasm, she felt the bursting flood of him inside her and he shared the body-shaking exhilaration and rhythmic pulse of her own release. He cried aloud, as lost as she was in the meeting of long-denied need, each feeling the extremes of the other's pleasure and near drowning with the newness and intensity of it. Satiation leaded Jenna's limbs while she lay gasping beneath him. Cael's chest lay hot over her breasts, and sweat puddled between their joined flesh. He dropped his face and kissed her neck, taking his weight on his elbows and stroking her hair from her damp forehead. She circled her hips and pressed them against him, eliciting another groan of pleasure.

"Gods, *chekuán.*" He cupped her cheek in his hand and kissed her mouth. "You have turned me inside out!" Resting his head on her shoulder, he caught his breath.

Jenna ran her fingers through his thick hair with one hand and stroked the other over the long muscles of his back. She kissed his temple. "I think the dragon and I are going to be very good friends," she said with a throaty chuckle.

★ ★ ★ ★ ★

They stirred a short time later, still entangled, drowsy and warm. The fire had burnt down to embers, but the single oil lamp still burned, casting desert-deep shadows across the dunes of Cael's muscled body. She reached a tentative hand to brush the familiar golden tangle from his eyes, and he caught it, drawing her fingers to his chest. Her eyes widened as she felt an odd stickiness beneath her fingertips. Raising herself on one elbow, she was startled to see not the sleeping dragon, but a freshly tattooed dragon rampant.

He met her eyes with his steady golden gaze. "I cannot fight it, Jenna." He spoke with quiet calm. "I do not know what I can offer you, but I know I cannot fight it anymore." He smoothed her hair, searched her face. "My life was never truly my own. Nothing has changed. I cannot promise you security, although I will defend you with my life." She shivered, and he pulled the blankets around her. "I . . . cannot deny that the effects of the bond have drawn me, but I believe we could grow to great love. Who can say." He paused, and his hand tightened on hers. >*It remains that I cannot be without you, chekuán. You are a part of my body, my soul. Please stay with me.*<

Tears ran from Jenna's closed eyes as she felt the simple truth of his confession, understanding from his new calm that he had at last processed and conceded to the implications of their unintentional bonding. She turned and kissed him then, sealing her acceptance of his offered self. Desire rose again as his lips sought her breast, strong hands pulled her closer to him and began to caress her thighs, the curve of her back, the swell of buttocks and secret places. Jenna trembled under his touch, hungry for more of him. "I thought you were an innocent, my love," she whispered, her body arching with surprised pleasure as he found her most sensitive places.

>*Innocent yes, but not ignorant* . . .< He mouthed her throat.

She gave herself over to him.

They made love three more times that night, each time more slowly, learning each other, giving and taking pleasure by turn, each exploring the other's body. Shyness was abandoned and pretence discarded until, spent, they slept in a dishevelled nest of blankets until dawn.

As she awoke to his steady breathing and felt the warm solidity of his body against hers, she felt a transcending joy. His inexperience had not mattered at all. Along with his evident knowledge of the process, he had felt her every reaction to him, knowing immediately what pleased her. When she had shown him what more was possible, he had responded with raw passion, returning whatever she gave him as he applied himself in turn to her pleasure. She stretched in languorous rapture, thinking of his words the night before. Turning her head, she studied his sleep-peaceful face. Beautiful man.

"You won't have to die for *me*, Cael," she whispered, tracing the firm line of his gold-stubbled jaw with her fingertip. "I wouldn't *want* to live without you."

Illiahn paused at the window of her bedroom as her brother, clad only in his breeches despite the morning's cold, emerged from the den and crossed to the yard pump.

Working the handle with a creak of metal, he thrust his head under the clear stream, gasping at the cold as he doused himself, then turned his head to drink in long, thirsty swallows. He straightened, shaking water from his hair and raking it back from his face with his fingers. Drop-

lets darkened the leather of his breeches and glistened gold
on his skin in the pale morning sun. With the Empath's
ability to feel another's eyes on him, he raised his gaze to
the window, grinned and blew her a kiss. She smiled back,
both at his light mood and the newly extended tattoo. She
feigned an expression of shock, pointing with exaggerated
interest at his chest. He laughed aloud then, and her heart
rejoiced to hear it after so long. She turned away from the
window, knowing her counsel of the previous day had been
timely. Certainly the dark cloud had lifted from Cael's dis-
position. Time alone would tell if the bond could overcome
all their differences.

The new lovers walked hand in hand to the kitchen door,
and shared a quick embrace before going in. Jenna's experience of the last few days had shown her that a longer embrace meant missing breakfast, and today already promised
to be a difficult one. They both needed to still the
dragonfire for this day, at least.

Cael ducked his head and kissed her neck. >*Mmm. Perhaps we would not miss much of the meeting if we were to be
only slightly late?*< His amber eyes danced with wicked invitation, and she laughed, more than a little tempted. She
kissed him, realising too late that he was serious.

Some time later, she lay atop him, catching her breath as
she rested her head against his heaving chest. His heart beat
loud in her ear, slowing its pace from sprint to jog. She
lifted her head as he shook beneath her with silent laughter.
Sliding from his body, she eyed him curiously. "Okay, come
on," she said, smiling and taking his face in her hands.
"What's so funny?"

>*Just a thought, Jenna. Forgive me, but I had never thought*

to be . . . ridden so often.< He laughed again and wrapped his arms around her, pulling her close. >*That is not a complaint, merely an observation. You are delectable, however you decide to assault me.*<

With a satiated grin, she realized she had been quite aggressive. "Well, my love, if you will keep a girl waiting so long, you must live with the consequences." She kissed him, stroked his face fondly and rolled from the new-mussed bed before he could instigate a further embrace. "Speaking of consequences, we are now very late." She tossed him a towel and poured water from the ewer on the washstand into the basin. A cold scrub. Ah well, it was worth it.

They dressed again, and Cael called Verra. To his surprise, she and Telsen arrived in minutes. As Jenna re-braided her hair, Cael investigated the cloth-wrapped bundle that Verra handed him.

"Breakfast." She grinned. "I knew this morning would be no different, Council or not."

With a wry smile, Cael pulsed his thanks and bit into a wedge of fragrant warm bread as he strapped knife sheaths to his wrists.

"Expecting trouble?" Telsen asked, lounging in the sun-filled doorway.

"Just habit, Tel," he said, his tone light. "But I do not mean her to take harm ever again. Whatever it takes."

Telsen watched him thoughtfully as Verra handed bread and fruit to Jenna. "You need not always be on your guard, brother. To do so would be to live your life jumping at shadows."

Cael held his gaze a moment, tightening the straps of the sheaths. "*Whatever* it takes, brother. I will not be without her." He grinned then, and winked at Jenna.

344

Jenna took a dried peach slice and a wedge of buttered bread from Verra's offerings. "Verra, you are a kind and considerate friend. Thank you." She ate quickly while she threw a long cape of Linker's green over her Healer's dress, feeling a small pang of guilty embarrassment at their indiscretion.

Verra grimaced at the sun's position when they left the den. "We may yet arrive before the judgement begins," she said, as the Way sang open before them.

Cael closed the door behind him and held the remains of the bread wedge in his teeth as he fastened his cuffs around the knives. He slipped an arm around Jenna and squeezed her close, finishing the bread in a couple of bites. *>Breakfast I can live without, but you, on the other hand, I fear I cannot.<*

"So the dragon finally rules?" Jenna said, laughing and returning his embrace. He had become a different person since the end of his denial: relaxed, humourous and attentive.

"Not the dragon, *chekuán*." He kissed her. "I am *your* willing slave."

Verra rolled her eyes, holding the Way open with a grinning Telsen beside her. "Should I have brought lunch as well?" she said.

They hurried through the Way without further delay, smiling their apology.

The Council chamber filled as the public gallery overflowed to the streets outside. It seemed that all of Illith desired to see Jabeel on the mercy stone. The four sat together, close to the centre of the arc formed by the immense ebony slab that served as a bench before the seated Council members.

Xirth, Grinore, Galaen and Arkell sat at the centre of the arc, an austere group, waiting to call the meeting to order. Fortunately for the tardy four, the chaos caused by the public cramming had delayed procedures. The loud buzz of speculative conversation filled the chamber, punctuated by the odd burst of nervous laughter.

Grinore stood, a commanding figure in a flowing golden robe, scrutinising the people amassed before him. The room quieted in anticipation. Grinore began.

"Councillors and people of Camarrhan and Alth." Grinore turned to acknowledge Arkell. "You all know the matter before us today. Before we begin, Alth would address you." He seated himself and Arkell rose, his bearing one of great authority.

All eyes were on the dark-eyed man as he spread his hands on the polished ebony before him.

"People of Camarrhan, Councillors and elders." Arkell turned to honour the three members of the Hand. "I speak for Alth. We share your relief at the capture of Jabeel, and would congratulate the four of the prophecy who accomplished it." A smatter of applause started, swelled and grew until all in the chamber stood applauding. Arkell waited. The public gallery whistled loudly and seethed with movement as all tried to gain a clear view of the four, who looked at each other in embarrassed discomfort.

Arkell continued. "It is well to applaud them. Personal sacrifice in the service of one's land is to be greatly honoured. It is also so in Alth." He paused, then addressed the four directly. "Alth owes you a debt of honour. At the risk of your own lives you spared all of our race that you encountered, even the one who caused you such grievous harm, Empath." He inclined his head toward Cael, who acknowledged him in surprise. Arkell turned his black eyes to

346

Telsen. "That one will recover, Wielder, and we thank you for not damaging him permanently." He smiled, and a ripple of laughter ran around the chamber. Of the many stories that now circulated around Camarrhan, the tale of Telsen's retribution was a favourite.

He turned his attention to Verra and Jenna. "Camarrhan grows strong women. There are two of our youth who can testify to that to their shame, and one who will testify no more because he underestimated both your ability and your resolve." He bowed slightly in their direction and again addressed the chamber. "Those who assisted Jabeel most directly will be disciplined. Amnesty has been offered to those who would return and change is guaranteed. Many return to us daily, and our hopes for the future generations of our race still live." He paused again as murmurs of approval rose from the gathering. He turned to Grinore. "Alth rests."

Grinore stood again, waiting for quiet as Arkell sat down. He gestured toward the back of the chamber. The heavy doors swung inward.

Jabeel entered, a circle of blue light around his shoulders and chest, another around his thighs, each maintained by a Wielder who walked at each side of him.

Silence fell. Tense faces followed Jabeel's progress toward Grinore. He reached a wide circle of red stone set into the floor, the words "Justice and Mercy" inscribed at its perimeter. Standing in the centre of the circle, Jabeel spread his arms as far as the Wielders' confinement would allow.

"Here I am Grinore. What will you do with me?" His tone was unrepentant.

"Be silent. You stand on the mercy stone. Turn and face your accusers, for all Camarrhan waits to judge you."

The slim figure turned with sardonic slowness, as Jabeel raised cold grey eyes to the Council. "Judge away," he said.

For the next hour, Jabeel's activities were recounted to the Council. The deaths of the Leaders were detailed as his greatest crimes, and caused much angry rumbling from the gallery. Witnesses were called to testify, the four included. Council listened, enthralled, to the story of Cael's encounter with the death-shaft, subsequent events in Ré Shan and the final battle in Kordethal. Jabeel stood in mute defiance throughout, and when all was said, took up a bored stance and affected a yawn.

"You have an opportunity now to speak on your own behalf, Jabeel. You do not help yourself by such a display," Grinore said with disapproval.

"Would you rather I danced for you, Grinore? It seems at least four others were willing to do so." A cold smile twisted Jabeel's thin lips and he threw a look over his shoulder at Cael. "I see you are all restored. A happy ending, just like every good children's story." He turned back to the Council. "You are all children. All of you! Believing the stories handed to you by those who seek to keep you that way. There are other worlds out there, worlds all around us that offer advance, enterprise, freedom from labour!"

Grinore stood, concerned at the outburst. Galaen shook her head. "No. Let him speak."

Jabeel's lip curled. "The mother herself. Why do you not allow these children the freedom to choose advancement, Galaen? Why must this land function in such a primitive way? There are better, easier ways of living, but you will allow none of it. Why?" His gaze swept the Council. He stabbed a finger at the members of the Hand. "Because they control the magic. Tucked away on Ché Kevath, tampering with your lives, manipulating events to suit themselves because that is how they remain in control. I sought to free

Camarrhan from its dark ages." He paused for effect, looking from face to face around him. "We do not need magic! How many of you can access it? Two handfuls in a hundred, that is all. How democratic is that? A genetic co-incidence decides your fate: gifted or ungifted, privileged or not. The use of technology is not the evil your controllers would have you believe, but a different kind of magic. One that is available to all!"

Doubt and confusion showed on many faces as Jabeel finished speaking. He turned to bestow an ungracious smile on Galaen.

Galaen stood. "What he has failed to mention, Councillors, is that his aversion to magic only began when his own gifting was removed from him, and *that* only when it was used to cause great harm in the lives of others." Her voice rang with disdain. "The only way Jabeel may now experience the power he so craves is to remove magic from the land. He seeks to serve his own selfish aims, not you, the land, or your future." She surveyed the room. "The Hand seeks only to protect Camarrhan, to keep the balance and harmony of the land and its magic. Without magic, there would be no balance. The land would suffer, gradually decay, and the people with it. Look at yourselves! You are strong, proud, contented. And it is because the land and its magic sustains us all, not just the gifted."

A murmur of dissent began. The sense of confusion in the chamber intensified.

"Jabeel's actions were the cause, however indirect, of the loss of healing magic from the land. You all know how that affected us. Injury; sickness; birth. None could be assisted, and many died or could not be fully restored, remaining disabled or disfigured. Is this what you wish for your children? I do not wish it for any of you."

Jabeel folded his arms and stared at the back of the chamber in stony silence.

"If the prisoner has nothing further to say, we should begin. The Hand is not on trial here. All issues that cause you concern will be discussed fully at a later date."

Heads nodded in agreement, the tension caused by the impromptu debate lessening somewhat.

The vote began.

Jabeel's guilt was not in question, being evident to all from testimony and on his own confession. All who stood voted for his death.

At the end of the calling, only Kereál remained. Twenty-nine Councillors stood waiting.

"Kereál abstains, but would not leave the Council," Cael said, remaining seated.

Grinore eyed him curiously, but said nothing. Twenty-nine was more than enough to pass the death sentence. He stood, and Jabeel turned to face him.

"Jabeel, son of Kren, son of Labicheth. This Council has passed the death sentence upon you. Evil such as yours cannot be permitted to abide in the land. You remain unrepentant, and therefore you will be eliminated along with your evil. For crimes against Camarrhan, its people and the Hand, you are to be entombed."

Jabeel blanched. Cael felt the bravado slip from the man as he absorbed the meaning of Grinore's pronouncement. No single hand would take Jabeel's life—he would die slowly, in thirst and misery. Unless mercy was offered.

Cael stood. "Kereál would speak, Grinore."

He was recognised.

Cael directed a serious gaze at Jabeel, who averted his eyes. "In my anger I almost took your life myself and would have felt pleasure in it. Yet I considered myself the better man. I know now that violence hides within us all. A strong enough motivation will lead us to betray all we think we honour." He reached for Jenna's hand and clasped it tight. "You were weak and allowed evil to claim you. Perhaps you only lacked a friend wise enough to divert you from your course." He glanced sideways at Telsen with a pulse of gratitude. "Whatever the circumstances of your fall, I would offer you absolution. No man should face his death without a single soul to stand beside him." He turned to face the elders of the Council. "This man has no family to stand for him. Kereál would offer mercy." >*He is not your grandfather, Jenna. There is nothing of him in you; I would feel it.*<

"Then why stand?" she whispered.

>*Because he is alone. He has always been alone. You and I have known what that is, but for us, Fate did not allow it to last for a lifetime.*<

Grinore's slow nod was echoed by Galaen and Xirth. Xirth stood, his robes stirring slightly as he drew power and fed it into the mercy stone. The Wielders flanking Jabeel withdrew their lariats of confining energy.

The stone circle beneath Jabeel's feet began to glow with a blood-red intensity. His chest heaved and his eyes widened as the circle rose into a column, bearing him several metres above the floor.

"Mercy is offered. One stands with the condemned. The stone shall decide." Xirth wielded. The stone absorbed his azure energy, turning the red glow to plum.

A light hum filled the air as the column began to rotate, turning Jabeel so he was visible to all at every angle. The hum intensified to a high-pitched shriek, causing all present to cover their ears. A thin shaft of purple light shot from the edge of the mercy stone, then another, and another. The column stopped rotating.

Jabeel stood surrounded by three shafts of light that connected the stone column to the ceiling of the chamber.

"The stone has spoken. Mercy will be given if three stand with the condemned." Xirth lowered his hand. The column returned Jabeel smoothly to the floor. The light beams withdrew into the stone.

Cael still stood alone.

Jenna gazed around the chamber. Holding her chin high, she rose to stand with him. Her eyes were unreadable indigo depths, but he sensed her total support of him and her quiet pride in his demonstration of clemency.

Telsen folded his arms over his chest. Both he and Verra remained seated. There was no movement from the public gallery or the Council.

Tense moments passed.

Jabeel waited, trembling. The dreadful sentence still stood.

A collective gasp ensued from the chamber as Xirth slowly rose from his seat.

"Wielder's magic is seductive," he began. "The potential for power is great. I condone nothing, son of Kren, but stand with these to grant you mercy. Your consciousness shall be taken from you before you are entombed. The sentence is to be carried out tomorrow."

Jabeel closed his eyes for brief moments, regaining his composure. He faced Cael. "What do you hope to gain, son of Jarin? Personal absolution? Favour?"

Cael felt only pity. "Do you still not understand? Life is not about gain. Peace, man! I merely do not desire that you should die in suffering."

"That is all?" Jabeel's expression was incredulous.

"That is all," Cael confirmed.

Puzzled grey eyes held Cael's steady gaze as the Wielders

restored Jabeel's bonds. He turned and they escorted him from the chamber. As they reached the door, he stopped. Turning back to the Council, Jabeel again sought Cael.

"Why?" His expression pleaded for understanding.

Cael considered the forlorn figure before him. "Because I would harm only myself by seeking your pain, but can give much by refusing to do so. Do you begin to understand? Life is about choices, Jabeel, and making the right ones. I choose not to seek vengeance, but to offer you peace."

Jabeel held Cael's eyes for a long moment. "I thank you, my dear." His eyebrows lifted in his usual sardonic fashion. With a slight bow, he turned and left the chamber.

The door swung closed, blocking him from view.

Council dispersed slowly. The interchange between Galaen and Jabeel had sparked much discussion. The four stood amongst a small crowd, all anxious to speak with them, one or another. Cael was in particular demand and by the look of him, was beginning to feel harassed by the close attention. Verra intercepted his warning look, one she had come to know over their years together. She needed no sending.

Empathic overload could be a cruel torment for those so gifted; his barriers could not limit the clamouring barrage of emotion and thought indefinitely. Verra had often rescued him from large social gatherings. She excused herself from the women with whom she had been conversing, grateful for the chance to get away, and slipped an arm around Telsen's hips. "Excuse me, Wielder."

He turned from his admirers and flashed her his wide grin. "Wayfinder."

"He is reaching saturation point with all this, Tel. He wants an escape," she murmured, her face close to his ear.

She tilted her head in Cael's direction.

Cael's face was strained, his mouth tight behind his polite smile. Jenna held his arm, behaving as the perfect foil, answering questions when he would not, smiling and commenting when he could not, his limit reached some time ago.

Verra opened the Way behind him. As the sound of crystal rang, heads turned her way. She smiled and shrugged. "I am sorry, but we must go. The Healer has an imminent birth to attend."

Cael sent her a grateful glance. >*Very inventive, Verra.*<

They said quick farewells and made their escape to the peace and sanity of Kereál.

Chapter Twenty

Beginnings

Jabeel's sentence was carried out as pronounced. Thanks to the provision of mercy by the three who had stood for him, his consciousness was taken from him. Galaen did not deign to speak to him, but she watched his grey eyes until they dimmed and closed. His senseless form was laid in a small, vented chamber and sealed deep within the stone catacombs of Illith.

When all was done, a contented peace lay over Camarrhan. The days lengthened as spring progressed. The sun gained heat again and coaxed the land to produce its lush green covering once more. Stick-legged foals strutted and kicked in high spirits beside patient mares in the enclosure around the ranch. Brenn rested his elbows on the fence railing, his face alight with pleasure as he watched their antics.

"A fine crop." Cael leaned beside him, eyeing the foals. "So which would you recommend?"

"Tel favours black. What of Verra?"

Cael pointed to a sorrel filly. "Tel has his black; Verra rides her chestnut. Why not the pair of sorrels? They are exquisite."

Brenn's mouth curved into an oddly secretive smile. "I had reserved those for another couple." He glanced sideways at Cael, who raised an eyebrow, unsure of Brenn's implication. "Why not match the pair they already own? The black filly and the chestnut colt. What do you think?"

"I think you are a genius, brother. His and hers. A perfect gift." Cael grinned his agreement.

"A very generous gift," Brenn amended.

"Perhaps. But there are advantages. The colt remains local and available for stud, you have made a sale, and I have solved a gift problem."

Brenn indicated a dark bay filly, more active than the others, longer of limb and of more delicate structure. Sunlight burnished the animal's coat to a rich chocolate.

"That one is a *chekuán*. See how she teases, bites and runs? I have not been able to get close to that one. She will take time."

The corners of Cael's mouth twitched. *Chekuán.* He chuckled. Stepping onto the lower railing, he swung his legs up and over the fence. Leaning back against the sun-warmed wood, he crossed his ankles and arms and waited.

"What are you doing, man?" Brenn asked, his tone puzzled.

>*A chekuán, brother, as you so rightly put it, takes time. I am waiting.*< He extended a careful tendril of mind-power, caressing the animal's consciousness, calming and affirming the skittish baby with sensory images of comfort.

The filly tossed her mane, stamped and snorted. She stood still, trembling, eyes wide and ears alert. She turned as if in indecision, her hooves pawing at the soft ground, then began to approach Cael with dainty steps. She stopped in front of him.

He did not move. >*Come, small one, there is no harm here.*<

The filly extended her neck, long-lashed eyes wide and wild, the delicate nostrils dilating as the soft muzzle touched his shirt. She sniffed and blew, pushed her muzzle into his ribs and shook her head with a gentle snort.

Cael reached slowly toward the animal and laid a hand on the sleek neck. She flinched, but stood firm as he rubbed the satiny hide, moved his hand to scratch the base of the twitching ears.

"Gods!" Brenn's voice broke the spell and the filly shivered away to run in a spirited circuit of the paddock, tail held high as a banner. His expression was almost comical. "What did you *do?*"

Cael gave him a self-deprecating smile. "Secrets, brother. I could not resist showing off. Forgive me." He felt Jenna's approach and showed no surprise as her arms came about his neck from behind.

She stood on the lower fence rail and rested her head against his. "What a beautiful baby," she said, indicating the wayward filly.

"She is a *chekuán*. Perhaps you two would suit each other." Cael held her arms, enjoying her closeness.

"Enough of horses for now." She wrinkled her nose. "You two both reek of them. Illiahn has asked me to make sure you are both ready in time. She said to use a stick if necessary."

Brenn grinned at Cael. "My wife knows us well. I do not wish to add to her stress this day." He left them, making for the house.

Cael climbed back over the fence and dropped to his feet beside Jenna. >*You smell somewhat better than I do,*< he sent, pressing his face into her glossy chocolate-brown hair and inhaling deeply. >*Mmm. White flowers.*<

She wriggled out of his embrace, laughing and fanning his horse-reek from her nose. "I have a mission, my love, and no matter how desirable I find you, you won't distract me from it this time! The tub is full. Take a turn after

357

Brenn and keep your sister happy." She reached up, kissed him and smiled. He tugged the end of her braid and turned away from her, heading to do as he was bidden. "I'd hate to have to take a stick to such a lovely butt," she called after him.

He flashed her a dark look over his shoulder as he entered the cool of the house.

The last day of spring was, by long tradition, the day new couples declared their commitment to each other in public handfasting. The ranch hosted it this year in honour of Verra and Telsen. Rows of horses stood tethered to the rail beside the barn for those who would not stay long. The home paddock held others, and carriages and carts of all sizes lined the fence.

The Way sang open many times as the gifted appeared, some from the Guild, others from villages all around Camarrhan. The homestead's verandah boasted lines of light wooden tables, borrowed from friends in the town. Later, these tables would groan with the weight of food brought by all that attended. Jenna hung the last of the beribboned flower garlands on the verandah posts, lifted her skirts clear of her ankles and hurried down the steps, searching for Cael in the crowd. She spotted him with a knot of young men from the village, and smiled as she recognised Sorren and his twin brother among the group.

The yard buzzed with conversation as Jenna wove her way through the gathering. Families and friends of those who would handfast today waited expectantly for the formalities to begin. Skirts of varied colour and design swished around sandal-wrapped ankles as the women moved around the yard. The Kereál contingent was easily recognised. Jenna's French braid had become the preferred style, as at the Guild, but they had made it their own. Some wore double braids, and many decorated the weaving with bright-jeweled pins and combs. "Kereál knotting" was spreading fast.

Verra stood with the other brides to the left of the balcony, making polite conversation. Tied back and bound with green silk, her unruly curls hung in dark spirals to the middle of her back. Her dress, likewise of green, was of a simple, flowing cut that clung to hip-curve and flattered the gentle swell of her breasts, the colour turning her ocean-eyes to a vivid emerald. For once, her wrists were bare. She had shed her responsibility to Cael for this week, leaving him in the hands of a substitute from the Guild. She rubbed her exposed wrists and beckoned to Jenna as she passed. Diverting her course toward the brides, Jenna waved at Cael, who had watched her approach. He lifted his head in understanding. >*Waiting for you is what I do best, chekuán. I am a very patient man.*< His wink belied his words.

Reaching the brides, Jenna smoothed a maverick curl back from Verra's anxious face. "What?" she asked, searching the wide green eyes.

Verra grasped Jenna's hand. "There is still time, *chiara*. Illiahn would lend you her handfasting cloth . . ."

"No!" Jenna cut her off. Taking both Verra's hands in her own, she softened her tone. "Please, leave it. It isn't going to happen. This is *your* day." She gazed with affection at her friend's earnest face. Verra had become as close as a sister and Jenna had no wish to hurt her. And besides, *Cael hasn't spoken of it*, she thought, glancing toward him and catching his eye. Verra followed Jenna's gaze, pushed out her bottom lip and frowned. Cael raised his brows at Verra's petulant expression, and Jenna could not help a smile.

"Have you asked him?" Verra persisted, twining a long dark curl around her forefinger.

"No, and I won't, so be still. There has been change enough in his life without me pushing for more."

"Some men require a push, *chiara*. Cael is one of them." Verra's eyes held no guile, and Jenna hugged her on impulse.

"There will be no pushing," she said gently, releasing her friend and stepping away. "It's not that important to me." *Shit. What am I saying? I want him forever.* "Now, relax and enjoy the day." With a fond smile, she left Verra to await the ceremony.

Cael turned from the group of men as she reached him. "It is well?" he asked, his gaze resting on Verra.

"Hmm? Oh yes, she's fine. She still thinks we should join them."

He frowned and met her eyes in sudden concern. "And what do you think?"

"I think, my love, that we have moved quite fast enough for this month. Don't look so worried—I already have what I want." She pushed gold hair back from his eyes as had become her habit, and was rewarded by the flash of his quick grin and his low, two-syllable chuckle. Her eyes sought Telsen among the huddle of men, young and not so young, who waited on the right side of the balcony.

He fretted in black leather breeches and boots, and a dark-blue linen shirt beneath a sleeveless vest, also of black leather. The device of the Wielder was stitched in azure thread at the breast of his shirt, visible beneath the open vest. His close-cut hair shone dark as a wet otter, his brown eyes anxious as he waited.

"Tel looks good enough to eat." Her tone was mischievous, and she smiled at Cael's raised eyebrow. "Almost

360

as good as you." She tilted her head, appraising Cael's tall form. He was clad in a similar fashion, but in tan leather. His flowing shirt was of soft, cream-coloured linen, the dragon rampant device of the Empath worked in gilded thread over his heart. His tawny eyes and hair completed the picture of a young lion, and on an impulse, she wanted to show him. "Share?" she asked.

He shared her impressions, looked startled, then pleased as she explained the beautiful but dangerous creature he had seen. >*You flatter me, chekuán.*< He squeezed her hand as a hush grew over the yard.

It fell to the oldest of Kereál's Leaders to officiate at the handfasting, and he stood now at the top of the front steps, a large figure, smiling broadly and clad, as were all the men, in the formal attire suitable for the occasion. After a brief welcoming speech, he called on the grooms to come forward.

"Men of Kereál, you stand before us this day as a testament to all who stand with you that you desire to take your chosen to wife. A man of honour does not give his commitment lightly, neither will he retract it once given." He turned to the women. "Women of Kereál. Your chosen stand before you. A woman of honour will stand at the side of her chosen, to become one with him, pledge herself to him and hear his pledge in return. Do not keep him waiting," he added with a grin.

The women approached the line of men, skirts rustling, some with shyly downcast eyes, some proud and confident. All stood before their man, each holding a long strip of embroidered cloth.

Jenna leaned into Cael as Verra's flushed face turned up to Telsen, meeting his eyes with a long, tender look. "We are *all* represented on that cloth," she whispered. "We worked on it for days."

As the pledges were exchanged, Cael tugged Jenna in front of him, wrapped his arms around her and rested his chin on her shoulder. Verra bound Telsen's hand to hers with the cloth strip in a symbolic joining of their lives. The men pulled their women into an embrace, and sealed the ceremony with a kiss. Telsen released Verra last, causing a ripple of laughter as he grinned and pulled her back for another kiss. They surfaced to applause, and each couple stood hand in hand as the Leader spoke the final words.

"Two have become one. You are each extended into the other. Seek each other's happiness; be loyal; be loving; be patient and strong. Honour your commitment made this year, and the pledges you have taken. You leave this place as husbands and wives." He beamed in benediction as the newly wed couples dispersed into the crowd, seeking out their family groups.

Jenna opened her arms to Verra and hugged her hard. "Congratulations," she breathed, kissing the still-pink cheek. "That was wicked of Tel, but quite inspired, I thought."

Cael and Telsen shared a bear hug with much enthusiastic back-clapping, and then somehow the four of them were all laughing and embracing in a tangle of arms, a quorum of warmth and closeness that none around them dared to intrude upon.

The evening was cool. Smoke curled from the homestead's two chimneys as the last evidence of the handfasting was cleared away by workers employed from the village. The festivities had lasted until after dark. Food and drink had been shared and lively music had inspired dancing, but the falling dark convinced all but the hardiest revelers to seek their homes and their own fires.

Verra and Telsen had departed. They were to spend a week without responsibility to any but themselves. Cael had insisted on it in the face of loud protest from them both. Jenna missed them already.

Cael yawned and stretched, and she felt him relax beneath her. Her hand lay warm inside his shirt, stroking his chest. She shifted against him as he moved, then settled again, feeling the glow of firelight on her face as she gazed into the low flames. They lay together on one of the low couches in the living area beside the kitchen, having just put the still-excited twins to bed in the nursery.

Jenna had bathed Mi'Cael. Well, supervised, really. He was too big now to be bathed, as he was quick to point out. Just six years old and already showing every promise of growing into a beautiful man like his uncle. Mi'Cael sat by the fire wrapped in a thick towel as his blond hair dried. He was working on a carving of a tiny horse, his face serious with concentration as the tip of his tongue protruded between his teeth.

Jenna's gaze turned to Illiahn, seated across from them in a deep easy chair. Her golden hair fell across her face and lay around the pale-fuzzed head of the infant at her breast. Small contented feeding sounds arose from the child, and Illiahn stroked the round, moving cheek, her face serene. Brenn could be heard above them in the nursery as he lay the other baby in his crib, replete and drowsy from his turn at his mother's breast. The new twins, as yet unnamed, had arrived three weeks ago and thrived already. A boy and a girl. Both blonde.

Mi'Cael stood and approached Jenna, holding out the small wooden horse. "It is a *chekuán*," he announced with pride, holding his towel up around his chest. Illiahn held out a clean woollen tunic to him, and he dropped the towel and tugged the garment on over his head.

"It's beautiful, Mi'Cael. You have a good eye." Jenna handed back the carving.

"No, it is for you," the boy said, with a conspiratorial glance at Cael.

Cael nodded at him, his expression warm and encouraging, and turned his golden gaze on Jenna. "It is a handfasting gift, Jenna. For next spring, if you will have me. The bay filly is yours."

She said nothing, but closed her fingers over the small horse and swallowed hard against the sudden lump in her throat, aware of three pairs of amber eyes on her.

"I will have you, Cael," she said, her voice husky with emotion. "Of course I will have you."

Mi'Cael's enthusiastic response burst into her mind as she buried her face in Cael's chest, and she felt the low rumble of his pleased laugh as he drew his arms tight around her. A strange feeling flowered somewhere under her ribs. Melting against his masculine warmth, she identified the emotion with a sense of wonder. It was complete and unrestrained fulfillment.

Illiahn's glad smile turned to her son, who leaned on her chair and stroked his new sister's downy head with a gentle finger. Her face was suffused with love for her children, but held a faint sadness as her eyes rested on Mi'Cael's tunic.

On the breast, above the heart, was stitched in static repose a small, sleeping dragon.

About the Author

Cat Collins lives on the west coast of the Coromandel Peninsula in New Zealand with her husband (a Peter-Pan by nature); the youngest of her three sons (a budding Rambo); and two spoiled cats. She is a cook, fitness instructor and hopeless romantic. A member of the Online Writing Workshop for Science Fiction and Fantasy (formerly the Del Rey Digital Workshop) for three years, she attributes any writing skills she has acquired to the workshop and its members. *Sleeping Dragons* is Cat's first book, but the sequel is complete, and so is a third novel set in the same fantasy world.